THE
TRIALS
OF THE
WARMLAND

Ex Libris

THE FERAL WORLD

TRIALS
OF THE
WARMLAND

GADDY BERGMANN

Flying Pen Press Fiction

Flying Pen Press

www.FlyingPenPress.com

Trials of the Warmland, a novel of The Feral World series, shelve in Fiction
Flying Pen Press Fiction
First Edition, first printing, continuous printing on demand
First date of publication February 2008
Author: Gaddy Bergmann, www.GaddyBergmann.com
Editor: David A. Rozansky. Publisher@FlyingPenPress.com
Cover Designer and Cover Art: Laura Givens, ArtDirector@FlyingPenPress.com.

ISBN: 978-0-9795889-4-5

Flying Pen Press Fiction is an imprint of
Flying Pen Press LLC
18601 Green Valley Ranch Blvd., Suite 112 No. 4
Denver CO 80249
www.FlyingPenPress.com

All Flying Pen Press titles, imprints, and distributed lines are available at special quantity discounts for bulk purchases for sales promotion, premiums, fund raising, educational or institutional use.

Trials of the Warmland text copyright ©2008 Gaddy Bergmann
Trials of the Warmland compilation copyright ©2008 Flying Pen Press LLC
Cover copyright ©2008 Flying Pen Press LLC
All rights reserved. No part of this book may be reproduced in any form or by any means without the express written consent of the Publisher, excepting brief quotes used in reviews. For permission to reproduce any part or the whole of this book, contact the publisher.

Flying Pen Press Fiction, Flying Pen Press, and the flying pen nub logo are trademarks of Flying Pen Press LLC. The Feral World is a trademark of Cyan Productions LLC for its series of novels.

This is a work of fiction. Names, characters, places, and incidents are the products of the author's imagination or are used fictitiously. Any resemblance to actual events, locales, or persons, living or dead, is entirely coincidental.

Library of Congress Control Number: 2008922411

Publisher's Cataloging-In-Publication Data
(Prepared by The Donohue Group, Inc.)

Bergmann, Gaddy.
 Trials of the warmland / Gaddy Bergmann. — 1st ed.
  p. : map ; cm. — (The feral world ; 2)
 ISBN: 978-0-9795889-4-5

1. Regression (Civilization)—Fiction. 2. Wilderness survival—Fiction. 3. Social conflict—Fiction. 4. Science fiction. I. Title.

PS3602.E746 T75 2008
813/.6   2008922411

Manufactured in the United States of America and in the United Kingdom
Printing by Lightning Source Inc. and Lightning Source UK Limited

Map of the Warmland

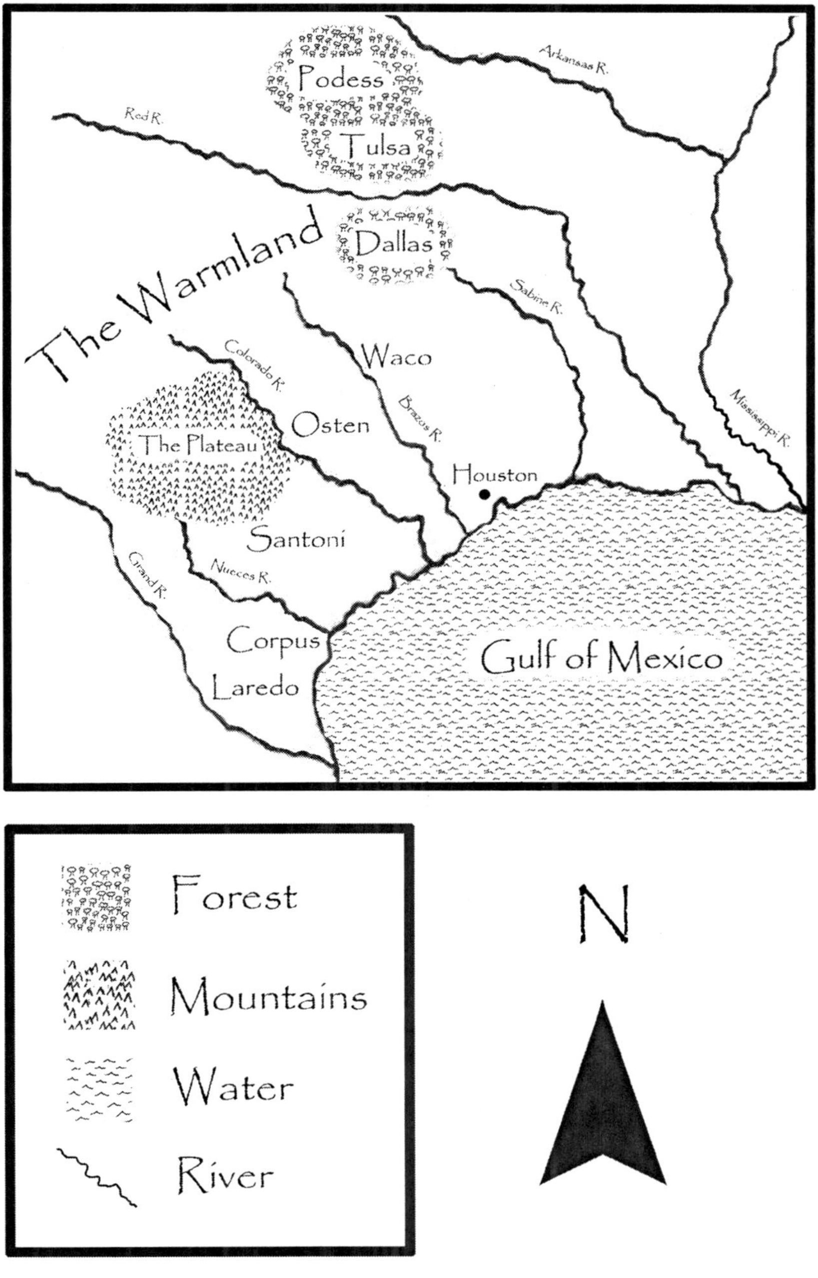

Other titles
in *The Feral World* series
by Gaddy Bergmann

from Flying Pen Press Fiction

Migration of the Kamishi
Riders of the Mapinguari, September 2008

Available wherever great books are sold.

"There is no progress, only change."

Dedication and Acknowledgments

This book is dedicated to Harold Tyus, whose knowledge of aquatic ecology is inspiring, and whose passion for conservation is contagious.

It is also dedicated to Philip J. Motta, for showing me so much about the marine environment and its inhabitants.

Finally, I am thankful to Nathan Goldstein, Jake Olsen, Mike Thompson, and Mike Uchida for their encouragement, support, and unblinking evaluation of my work.

Synopsis of *Migration of the Kamishi*

> *...Soon the Ravashi men were rampaging through the camp and killing everyone they came across. Mercilessly, they slaughtered every defenseless woman and child they encountered outright. The vulnerable and confused Kamishi men scrambled for their weapons. Soon, they were ready to do battle. In the chaotic sea of struggling bodies, some of the men went off singly to strike back at the Ravashi. Others gathered around Trent, who with his shield and dagger in one hand, and his spear in the other, led his men into combat. The Kamishi stabbed and impaled their attackers, but as soon as they did, a fresh Ravashi warrior would kill them in turn. Farlo fought bravely, his skill and strength serving him well. Rippling with tensed muscles, he struck at his enemies, who came at him from all directions. He managed to take out nine Ravashi before he himself was stabbed in the back and fell over, dead. Blake fought well, too. He skewered Ravashi right and left, deftly deflecting their blows with his shield. Out of the corners of his eyes he could see his friends Terak and Pellu, Joel and Manosh doing their best to thwart the Ravashi hoard...*

On Sunday, April 13, 2036 CE, the asteroid Apophis collided with the Earth. Despite humanity's best efforts, billions of people died and civilization soon collapsed worldwide. Cities were reduced to Rubbletowns, the world fell into a long, cold, dark winter, and death descended on the planet. When the dust finally settled and the Earth warmed again, people grew accustomed to the idea that their old world and old lives were gone forever. Eventually, they even embraced it. They came to refer to the impact of the asteroid as the Great Crash, the ordeal they had survived as Rakamahn, and the world that had emerged transformed as the New Days.

Three thousand years later, North America had returned to a wild state, and people lived in a way that had been almost forgotten. They no longer farmed crops or animals en masse, but rather lived off the land as hunter-gatherers. They no longer had nations or organized governments, but lived in nomadic tribes instead. Having long ago abandoned 21st Century technology, they had no telecommunications, motorized vehicles, clinical medicine, electrical devices, nuclear power, or computer information systems. Instead, they relied on man-made tools, simple hunting and crafting techniques, and their wits to survive.

For guidance in this vast, untamed land, people turned to their teachers, oral traditions, rituals, and religion. Most people were Bebelishi, and followed the teachings of an ancient book called the Bebel. This book contained the old texts of the Jews and Christians, but after the Great Crash, it also contained three more books — the Book of Causes by Jonathan, the Book of Means by Belgrath, and the Book of Conduct by Ecolta. Learning from their books and their traditions, the Bebelishi lived simple lives, maintained balance in their world, and strove to resist the temptations of greed that had led their ancestors astray.

In the northern Great Plains, just east of the Black Hills and the Badlands, lay the territory of Kamis. Its residents, the Kamishi, were peaceful, nomadic people, who hunted the animals with which they shared the plains: bison, deer, pronghorn, horse, and llama.

All of that ended one autumn morning when the Ravashi came and slaughtered all of the Kamishi. All of them, that is, except for a young man named Blake, his best friend Manosh, and Blake's two dogs, Saamu and Rita, who managed to escape. Seizing the opportunity, the refugees took their sacred book, the Bebel, and fled from Kamis. They headed south toward the Warmland, a place of fabled comfort and abundance. Blake and Manosh soon realized their journey would not be easy, but being resourceful, they forged onward. They evaded a stampeding herd of bison, and then survived a confrontation with the Marishi tribe, but they were always haunted by the evils they had witnessed at the hands of the Ravashi.

The travelers wandered across the plains and passed through woodland. As skilled hunters and warriors, they faced wild cats and hungry bears, always heading south toward their destination, the Warmland. One night, the weather turned bitterly cold, forcing the travelers to seek shelter in a Rubbletown — an old ruined metropolis that had become a kind of small mountain range unto itself. Once there, they witnessed a small gang of men chasing a lone woman across the hills of debris. Blake and Manosh scared off the thugs with the help of

Saamu and Rita, and then located the woman. Although she was wary at first, the woman eventually warmed up to the men and their dogs, introduced herself as Lana, and allowed the travelers to stay with her as guests for the night.

The next day, Lana showed her guests around the Rubbletown and, having grown up in this strange place, she knew just where to take them. She showed them stores full of supplies, parks alive with plants and animals, strange hunting grounds, and even the old library where she read the still intact books almost everyday. Blake and Manosh liked Lana so much that they invited her to join them. Lana gladly agreed, and soon the tiny tribe — the last of the Kamishi — was off for the Warmland again, now bigger by one.

One day, the group came across a giant crater in the middle of the prairie. When they realized that this was one of the places where Apophis had impacted the Earth, they became fearful that the spirit of the terrible asteroid might still dwell there, even 3,000 years after the Great Crash. Their curiosity got the better of them, though, and they decided to walk through the crater after all. Reaching its center, they were surprised to discover a dense grove of trees. However, when two giant, hairy beasts began to emerge, the Kamishi became terrified. Although Lana thought she knew what these creatures might have been, even she could not ignore the overwhelming fear they inspired. Concluding that the monster Apophis was still alive, the travelers ran away as fast as they could.

Blake and Manosh showed Lana the ways of the plains, where they were out in the open and exposed. They taught her valuable new skills, from hunting big game to weathering fierce storms, and Lana was keen to learn all she could. Huddling for warmth against the cold and the snow, Blake and Lana found themselves powerfully drawn to each other. Although a happy development for them, it also sparked jealously in the heart of Manosh.

In time, the Kamishi reached another forest, where they found plenty of food. When a big cat attacked them, they banded together to ward it off. Then they devoted a day to observing the Sabat — their day of rest. Like many Bebelishi, Blake, Manosh, and Lana were fascinated by the Great Crash, and read Bebel passages to each other from the books of Isaiah and Ecclesiastes, and from the Book of Means by Belgrath.

When the travelers unwittingly trespassed into the territory of Podess, they were brutally attacked. Saamu was killed in battle with a spear to the chest, and the others were kidnapped and incarcerated in an insect-infested Rubbletown dungeon. Working together, they eventually escaped by setting fire to the place and overpowering the guards. Terrified of being recaptured, the Kamishi ran away into the night.

Now the small tribe of the Kamishi find themselves wandering through a forest once more, but this one is warm, moist, and humid. They are nearing their goal. They are on the verge of entering the strange, new world of the Warmland…

> *The Kamishi faced much uncertainty, for they were going to a place unlike any they had ever known before. However, they had each other and this brought them comfort. Bitter cold, dangerous animals, and even other human beings had tried to destroy them, but none had succeeded. Blake, Manosh, Lana, and Rita had faced them all and survived. Now, they knew that by relying on one another, they could overcome any obstacle in their path. They may have been the only Kamishi remaining, but they were determined not to be the last.*

Chapter 1

Blake, Manosh, Lana, and Rita walked together through the shady forest. The air was warm and the sky was clear, but here beneath the trees, only a few beams of sunshine passed through the dense, green canopy. Quaking leaves filtered the light, and the earth shimmered like the trembling surface of a pond. Glowing columns leaned here and there as countless radiant particles hung suspended in the air. The forest was thick with the scent of growth, and it seemed as though everything had something else clinging to it. On the ground, tan-colored shelf fungi grew on rich, soft fallen logs, while lush vines and woody lianas covered the standing trees. Small animals chirped and chattered, but remained unseen in the thick foliage.

Blake was at the head of the troop. Calm but alert, he surveyed his surroundings as he went along. His wolfish dog, Rita, followed along faithfully behind him, while Manosh brought up the rear. Lana was in the middle; the men had insisted that she occupy this position for her own safety, and she had consented. The people all had light brown skin, dark brown hair, and warm brown eyes, but the two men were considerably taller than Lana. Blake and Manosh each wore a simple coat and pants made of animal hides; Blake's was made from pronghorn, and Manosh's from mule deer. Lana wore a long, black cloak. It was thin and frayed, but it served its purpose. Rita was a large and powerful dog, but her build was lean and her movements graceful. Her thick fur was mostly brown, with black along the back and patches of white on the face, chest, paws, and tail. Rita's eyes were a beautiful, crystal shade of blue.

The Kamishi were resourceful people, and they needed only a few supplies to help them survive. Each of them carried simple spears, bows, arrows, or knives as weapons. Manosh's leather bag contained wooden bowls, dishes, and utensils. Lana had some special tools, including fire sticks — matches — from the Ruins of an old convenience store. Blake used his bag to carry both copies of their sacred text, the Bebel. He also toted books from the ancient library they had found in the Rubbletown. As the eldest member of the tiny tribe, it was his responsibility to keep the books safe.

Although well rested, the Kamishi were hungry. In the late afternoon, their hunger became too much to bear. Having eaten only fruit for some time, they had developed a craving for meat. So, they decided to use Rita as a coursing hound. Their intent was to find rabbit, grouse, pheasant, or anything else the dog could catch.

Eventually, they came across a small flock of wild chickens. The males sported plumage vivid in blue, green, and gold, and the large, elaborate combs on their heads were a rich red. The females, although more drab, were pleasantly colored in a woody brown, with white flecks or spots rimmed in black, and they had attractive ruffs of bouncy, shiny feathers around their necks.

When Blake and the others noticed the birds, they fell silent and crept slowly closer. A sentry chicken detected the Kamishi's presence and gave out a sharp call. The other chickens scattered, but Rita furiously rushed right into the mass of fleeing prey. The dog closed in on a relatively sluggish hen as it lifted off the ground, swiping at the bird with a forepaw. The hen collided with the ground, clucking and flapping. Rita trapped her between her jaws, sank her teeth into her flesh, and vigorously shook her back and forth. Then she shifted her senseless prey within her mouth and delivered the finishing bite.

Blake, Manosh, and Lana eagerly stepped forward.

"That was some performance!" exclaimed Lana. "I had no idea she was that good."

"Oh, yes," said Blake. "She's very good." Blake patted his dog on the flank and gently took the chicken from her mouth. Rita had become accustomed to letting her master take prey right out of her mouth. As a puppy, she would scarcely tolerate it. Now, her obedience and respect for Blake was far stronger than her selfish tendencies. Besides, it usually worked out better for her this way. Blake, like a kind father, would cook the meat for her or, as in this case, pluck the feathers out of the bird and make it easier to eat and digest.

Blake, Manosh, and Lana joined hands and closed their eyes. Then Blake spoke. "We thank You, Creator, for granting us this food, and we thank the spirit of the bird for giving its life to nourish us. May the spirit of this bird forgive us for killing her, and may she know that we hunt so that we may live. Let her depart in peace, and let her find safety in the next world. Telpah."

"Telpah," echoed Lana and Manosh. With that, they stood up and continued their trek through the forest.

Later that night they gathered some wood, built a fire, and waited for dinner to cook. Blake and Lana basked in the fire's light and warmth. They sat on a log, content and pleased with the way things were going. Manosh, however, kept his distance from the others and sat with his chin in his hands without muttering a word.

Lana looked at Blake, and with her eyes asked him what was wrong with Manosh.

Blake rolled his eyes and shook his head as if to say, *I'll tell you later.* Then he said, "I can hardly wait to try that chicken."

"Oh, you're going to like it," said Lana. "In fact, it should be ready now."

Blake removed the roasted chicken from the flames and examined it. "It's definitely ready, all right. Who wants a leg?"

"I do," said Manosh, tersely. Blake tore off a drumstick and handed it to Manosh, who snatched it away without even thanking him. A scowl flashed across Blake's face, but then he turned to Lana. "Lana, do you want the other leg?"

"Sure," she said. Blake gave her the other drumstick. "Thank you." She bit into it, chewed, and savored it in her mouth before swallowing. "It's good!"

"I thought so," said Blake. For Rita, he removed a wing and a breast and held it out for her. Gently, she took it in her mouth and walked off a short distance. She set it down, sniffed it, and licked it. Then she began biting off chunks and bolting them down. Blake cut out a thigh for himself. Then he impaled the rest of the chicken on the pole once more and set it aside.

"Hey, Manosh," called Lana, "how is your shoulder?" Manosh took off his coat and exposed his healing puma-inflicted wound. Where there had once been a giant gash, there was now a large, jagged, but almost linear scar. There was still scabbed blood in its core, but the edges were sealing themselves nicely and the corners were slowly coming closer together. "It looks like it's doing all right."

I think it's healing. It doesn't hurt anymore, really, but it's still hard to move my shoulder without irritating the wound."

"Mm-hmm, and your neck?"

"Fine. I had forgotten all about it."

"That's good."

"Thank you for asking." When he finished his meal, Manosh quietly slipped into the shadows and went to sleep. Blake and Lana were not tired, so they stayed close to the fire for warmth, sitting next to each other on a fallen log and talking, while Rita lay with her head between her paws nearby. They watched the orange flames and gray smoke rise from the glowing wood, which snapped and popped from time to time.

"Are you two getting along?" asked Lana.

"No, not really. How did you know?"

"Well, the fact that you haven't spoken to each other for the past two days, or barely even looked at each other, I'd say is a pretty good sign that something is wrong, wouldn't you?"

"Mmm. I suppose it is."

"So what's wrong?"

"Oh," said Blake, waving his hand. "He's just jealous."

"Jealous? Of what?"

"Us. Don't tell him I told you, but he said that he was tired of the way I always steal the girls away from him."

"Really?" asked Lana.

"Then he said that he likes you, but he's not going to do anything about it because he wouldn't be able to come between you and me."

Lana smiled a wry smile and gave Blake a nudge. "Well, he's right, you know." Blake smiled as well.

"I'm beginning to see that," he said. Blake and Lana stared into each other's eyes for a moment. Blake leaned toward Lana and waited. When she leaned forward in return, he began tenderly kissing her lips. The couple tilted their heads and turned to face one another. Blake brought his hand behind Lana's head, stroking the back of her neck and running his fingers through her hair. She wrapped her arms around his shoulders and rubbed them slowly. They became more passionate, their movements more vigorous. Blake caressed Lana's soft cheeks and held her head gently between his hands. Then he took hold of her slender waist, while she explored his lavish hair. She touched his lean, robust chest, her lips intertwined with his.

They moved from the fallen log to the earth and faced one another by the fire, still kissing and embracing. Blake's lips left Lana's and drifted toward her jaw and neck. He kissed the angle of her jaw, first softly and then more forcefully with his mouth open as Lana tipped her head back in blissful surrender. She clutched Blake's body as he rose and smothered her, cradling her in his arms. Blake's lips moved down Lana's graceful neck to her collarbones, inhaling her alluring scent. She gave out a soft, gratified moan and exhaled deeply next to Blake's ear, gently nibbling it. Their passion continued for a moment. Then Blake sat back to look at Lana, and the two of them stared into one another's eyes again. Lana leaned into Blake, who held onto her and rested against the log. They lay there together this way and watched the fire once more. Lana held onto Blake's hands and took a deep breath. She was at peace.

Chapter 2

The next morning, Blake and his friends resumed traveling. Still in the woods, they noticed that the trees were becoming smaller and sparser. *We'll be leaving the forest soon,* thought Blake, *probably sometime today.*

They had been walking for about an hour when suddenly, five men popped out into the open from their hiding places. They stood ready in front of the Kamishi, brandishing long spears and wooden shields. The spears were decorated with feathers just behind their points. The shields were almost as tall as the men whom they protected, and they bore the large, intimidating faces of animals in blue, red, green, black, and white. There was a jaguar, snake, bull, and bear, and the face of a lion graced the shield of the man in the middle. All of these men dressed in jaguar-skin loincloths and toted leather canteens over their shoulders. The central figure stood tall with his spear at his side, while the men flanking him casually pointed their spears at the travelers. The man in the center appeared to be the leader, for he was significantly older than his comrades, and had a more dignified and respectable appearance.

These men greatly alarmed Rita. She barked loudly and rapidly at them as she bared her long, white fangs, and the hairs all over her body stood on end, especially along her back, making her appear ever bigger and more menacing than she already was. But she did not attack.

Oh no, Blake thought, his breath and his heart quickening, *This is it. They are well armed and outnumber us. I can't believe we came this far only to die like a bunch of turkeys!*

"I am Tegg," said the proud man in the Common Tongue of the Bebelishi, "Chief of Tulsa." He had to raise his voice to be heard over the dog's barking, but he maintained his composure. "These are my tribesmen, Plott, Frenn, Dendin, and Raoul," the Chief said, gesturing to each man as they nodded in turn. "We are Bebelishi."

Thank the Creator! They are Bebelishi! thought Blake.

"Silence the dog," said Tegg. Blake kneeled beside Rita. In soothing tones, he told her to be quiet as he stroked her head and chest. She promptly fell silent, but anxiously licked her lips as she calmed down. "Who are you?"

Blake stepped forward. "My name is Blake," he said with a shallow bow, also speaking in the Common Tongue. "I am leader of the Kamishi. These are my friends Manosh and Lana. We are also Bebelishi." Tegg peered at them quizzically.

"I have not heard of your people before."

"That is understandable. We come from the northern Great Plains."

"That is so far from here! What brings you to Tulsa?"

"Our tribe was attacked by the Ravashi and we are the only survivors. Kamis is no more. We are migrating."

"Ho, ho!" chuckled Tegg. "Migrating! Well, I can see why you would choose to leave the harsh life of the northern Great Plains, but you may not settle down here. We have no room for you here."

"We do not intend to make Tulsa our new home. Rather, we hope that we may safely travel through your territory and find a place to live beyond it." *I had better not mention the Warmland. The legend is so widespread, who knows how many people want to live there? The less competition, the better.*

"Ah, you seek the Warmland then."

"Yes," said Blake, hiding his disappointment.

"I don't blame you. It is a fine region. I have been there myself."

"You mean you didn't stay?" *I shouldn't sound so excited about it! What if these people beat us to it!*

"No. I have friends there, but my home is here. Perhaps there will be a place for you there." Blake gave an imperceptible sigh of relief. *Maybe people aren't very likely to migrate there after all. Our chances might be better than I thought!* Tegg approached Blake and extended his hand in a friendly gesture. Blake took it and the two men bowed slightly to one another. "Welcome to Tulsa, Blake." Then Tegg faced the others, "I welcome you, as well, Manosh and Lana." Manosh shook Tegg's hand and bowed as well. Lana gave a gracious, nymphlike nod and bent her knees as she offered her hand, and Tegg held it briefly. "It is good to meet you," he said graciously. "Come, walk with us. We will offer you safe passage through Tulsa, and we will escort you part of the way."

"That is wonderful!" exclaimed Blake, enthusiastically. "Thank you, Tegg."

"You are welcome," he said. "We only ask that you do not hunt on our land."

"That is a fair request, and we are happy to comply."

"Good. Come, then." The two groups merged into a larger one and walked together through the woods, amicable and relaxed. "We were patrolling this area when we spotted you earlier this morning."

"Oh?" said Blake.

"We decided to watch you from a distance for a while because we'd never seen anyone dressed like you. We have good relations with some neighboring tribes, hostile ones with others. Because we didn't recognize you as belonging to any tribe we knew, we decided that perhaps you were either traders or representatives from some new tribe looking to do some trading. That surely would be worthy of a peaceful meeting."

"That's right," said Blake, "and thank you for keeping an open mind. We've already had a few dangerous encounters with other, more belligerent tribes, so we're glad to see you're more willing to talk than do battle." Tegg smiled courteously. "But we represent only ourselves. We're not traders, either, so I'm afraid there's no transaction to be had here."

"That's all right," replied Tegg. "We don't mind letting some passersby through. Perhaps we'll meet again in the future, after all. Wouldn't it be horrible to make a new enemy rather than a new friend?"

"It sure would," said Blake.

"So, we're glad to escort you through Tulsa, even if we don't trade. Come; let us show you around. We can walk south with you for a while, but then we must return to our village."

"Of course," said Blake. "Thank you for your hospitality. After what we've been through, you really have no idea how much we appreciate this."

Chapter 3

Tegg led the assembly through increasingly thinning forest country. The trees gradually became shorter and more widely spaced until they gave way to the wide-open expanses of grassland with which the Kamishi were so familiar. Finally, the group emerged from the forest and walked out onto the plain. There, Blake, Manosh, and Lana were amazed at what they saw — an enormous herd of creatures that they had never seen before. They reminded them of bison, but their shoulder humps were smaller, and their fur was much shorter and lighter in color — a sort of tawny gold. Their horns, however, were much longer and thicker than those of bison. They jutted straight out from the sides of the head and made right angles to bring the points forward. Both sexes were powerfully built, but the bulls were even more massive than the cows, and their muscles rippled like fickle mountain ranges beneath their short pelts. The bulls could also be distinguished by their larger horns, which spanned twice the width of the body from one point to the other. These beasts lived in a giant herd of more than a thousand animals, and casually grazed or walked along with their heads low. When the humans appeared, one of the giant bulls on the outside of the herd raised his head and snorted. Suspiciously, it watched them as they passed through the field.

"Wow!" said Blake. "Those are magnificent! What are they?"

"They are called texins," said Tegg. "They are wary of us because we often hunt them. For now, we will just walk by and avoid them, but don't get too close. They won't hesitate to gore you if you do." Blake flashed his eyebrows up and cocked his head in dismay. "We're not the only animal that hunts them, though. Wolves and lions hunt them as well."

"Oh, no," said Manosh. "Not lions. I've had it with lions."

"It sounds like you've had some bad run-ins with them," said Tegg.

"We have," Blake admitted. "A stampede actually."

"Mmm. Very dangerous. But don't worry. We won't provoke a stampede here as long as we're quiet." The grouped walked on, keeping their distance from the menacing texins. Tegg remained vigilant, but turned his attention to Blake. "So, you and your friends are headed for the Warmland, eh?"

"Yes. Do you know when we can expect to reach it?"

"Soon," said Tegg. "Where will you go once you get there?"

Blake paused sheepishly. "I don't really know."

"You don't know very much about it, do you?"

"No, I'm afraid not," said Blake. "What we do know, we have only heard from the Legend. But you used to live there, didn't you, Tegg?"

"I was never a permanent resident, but I used to make trade trips down there for the tribe when I was younger and more adventuresome."

"What can you tell us about it?" asked Blake.

"What would you like to know?"

"Well, I'd like to know about its borders, the lay of the land, and what there is to eat there."

"All good questions," said Tegg. "Let me begin by saying that the Warmland certainly deserves its name. The climate is even warmer than here, and more humid as well. People squabble about the Warmland's borders, but I think a fair description is to say that, once you have emerged from the forest, left the plain, and have passed the swamps, you have reached it. Once there, you will notice that the terrain is varied. There are parts that have strange trees called palms with broad, rubbery leaves. Other parts are grassy. The soil is rich, dark, and fertile, and it shows in the number and health of the plants that grow there. There are bogs, swamps, and lagoons within its borders, as well as stretches of sand. There are also many rivers and lakes, and a long coastline where you can see the Gulf of Mexico."

"What's that?" Blake asked.

"It's like a small sea that connects to the ocean. As for food, there are deer, rabbits, and other animals I'm sure you're used to down there. There also many, many fruits. You can turn to the Gulf for food, as well."

"What can you eat from the Gulf?" asked Blake again.

"Well, there are fish, of course, and there are plants called kelp. There are many other hard-bodied animals you can catch, too, like crabs."

"What are crabs?"

"You know what crayfish look like, right?"

"Sure."

"Well, they are kind of like crayfish, only rounder."

Blake nodded. "If we leave tomorrow morning," he said, "then how much longer will it take us to reach a good, habitable area where we can settle?"

"Well, you'll probably leave the forest soon. Then you'll have to pass through the swamp. Only after that will you reach the Warmland. As for where you can settle, you could always try to find an unclaimed area and make that your home."

"I was considering doing that…"

"I would advise against that, though," said Tegg, "because then a tribe could come in and uproot you. No, I think you should try to get a resident tribe to accept you."

"We're prepared to do that," Blake replied. "So who should we go to?"

"There are several tribes, but the tribe that I know best and deal with the most is the Corpushi. They live far south of here, deep in the Warmland, on the shores of the Gulf of Mexico. Their Chief is Zaaru, and I know him well. He is a good man and a friend of mine, but if I were you, I would approach him cautiously. He is loyal once he knows you, but he is distrustful of strangers. When you meet him, tell him that I send my good wishes, that I directed you to him, and that I approve of you. Perhaps that will help persuade him to take you in."

"We'll do that, Tegg," said Blake. "Thank you."

The two tribes continued to walk together for hours. They talked and learned from each other for most of the way, often not far from huge herds of the ubiquitous texins. The Kamishi told the Tulsashi about the northern Great Plains and the Rubbletown, and the Tulsashi told the Kamishi more about their woods and the Warmland to the south. At last, they came to a large watering hole, where many of the wild cattle were drinking. Most of these beasts immediately stopped what they were doing — water dribbling from their mouths — to look at the people. Some particularly skittish individuals even bolted a few paces away from the shore before they realized that the people did not presently represent a threat.

"Well, Blake," began Tegg, "this is as far as we will take you and your friends. The rest is up to you. We wish you good luck in your journey. I hope that we can meet again."

"So do I," replied Blake as he shook hands with his host one more time. Manosh and Lana thanked Tegg and his tribesmen as well and said their goodbyes. Then the Tulsashi turned around and headed north toward their village, while the Kamishi continued traveling south.

Chapter 4

The Kamishi encountered another giant herd of texin cattle a few days later. The texins grazed peacefully with their heads down in the tall grass, but their thick, sharp horns were so long that they were visible above the vegetation. Some of the texins looked up warily now and then, but they seemed to know that the humans were not hungry, and casually continued to swish their tails and feed.

The Kamishi walked on for some time under the pleasant late-morning sky. The fields were wide and green. Long grasses bearing chubby spikes at their tips swayed in the breeze. Here and there, a scrawny, thinly foliated tree could be seen sticking up out of the ground.

A short distance away, the grass trembled nervously. Only twitching at first, it then began to shake more vigorously. Like a contagious, fleeting ailment, the grass would quake in series, one clump ceasing to move as another began. Closer and closer these quivering blades came, and that is when Lana became aware that they were not alone.

"Did you hear something?" she asked.

"I thought I did," said Manosh.

"Well, I did. The grass." She turned to face the direction from which she heard the sound, but there was no movement.

"It's probably just the wind," said Blake.

"Maybe," Lana said, "but it was different."

"I don't know," said Blake. "Let's just —"

"Shhh," said Lana, holding her hand out. "Quiet. Don't move. Just listen." They stood there for an endless moment, motionless and completely silent, but nothing happened.

"Come on, Lana," whined Blake.

"Shhh!"

"There's nothing —" Just then, the grass stirred again.

"Did you see that? There's something out there. Did you see it?"

"I saw some movement," said Manosh. "Let's head for that tree ... and have your dagger ready."

"Okay," agreed Blake, who had seen the disturbance as well.

They walked toward the nearest, scraggly tree at a leisurely pace, glancing back only occasionally to monitor the progress of whatever was following them. The grass rustled once more. Then, piercing the plain, a lioness leaped out into full view.

"Run!" cried Blake. Then he, Lana, and Manosh dashed toward the tree as fast as they could. Rita ran with them, for she was aware of the threat, too. The dog was faster, though, and stayed slightly ahead. The people's blurry feet whispered with each pounding step; their eyes were wild with terror.

The lioness immediately pursued, her eyes focused stoically on her quarry, her legs fluidly propelling her forward. Her mouth was open only slightly as she breathed deeply. She was the ideal balance between tension and tranquility, fury and composure. Several times faster than the humans, she quickly closed the gap between herself and her prey, despite their head start.

The people could only continue sprinting toward the precious tree. It would not be long now.

Just then, another lioness sprang out from hiding in front of them. Lana screamed.

"Turn!" hollered Manosh. "Turn this way and run!" As a unit, they veered to the right and made a mad dash for a more distant tree. Then another lioness appeared and flanked them. She lunged forth and extended her massive forepaw toward Manosh, causing him to stumble and fall. He called out reflexively.

"Manosh!" cried Blake, turning to look at his friend and stopping dead in his tracks.

"Run!" Manosh shouted, clumsily getting back onto his feet. "Never mind about me, just go!" The lioness groped around Manosh's legs, throwing him repeatedly off balance. With each nudge from her muscular paws, Manosh felt as though she would knock his legs right off his body. He managed to dodge quickly enough to move forward. Blake was reluctant to obey his friend's orders, but when he saw that Manosh was running again, he resumed running as well.

Rita was the farthest ahead, followed by Blake, and then Lana. Manosh remained in the back of the fleeing group. All of them sprinted like never before.

"Keep moving, Lana," huffed Blake, and then looked back to see the three lionesses approaching rapidly. "You've got to make it to that tree. If they knock you down, kick them, punch them, yell, bite, anything! Just keep going!" Lana nodded.

The lionesses were right behind Manosh. The closest one, only a few short feet away, lunged forth and with her outstretched paw, tripped Manosh again. He came crashing down into the earth, his chin digging into the soil amidst the roots of the grass, his top and bottom teeth smashing into one another and sending gritty flakes everywhere. Manosh fell with such force that he rolled twice and landed with a jolt on his belly.

Suddenly, he heard a subdued, demonic growling behind his head and felt the hot, humid breath of his pursuer on the back of his neck and ears as she crouched and snorted over him. Manosh swiftly rolled himself over and stared directly into the face of the lioness. Her eyes were fixed on him. Her expression of alert anticipation was gone and replaced by one of cool, determined rage. Manosh tried to scream but he could not, for he was too terrified to utter even one sound. Desperately, he batted at her forelimbs, but she did not even flinch. Manosh heard her moist mouth open as her tongue writhed and her lips curled back to reveal her long, shining fangs.

The lioness bit down on Manosh's neck and he felt the four sharp points of pain. Deeper and deeper the lioness clenched her jaws, trapping Manosh's windpipe between her teeth. He gasped and convulsed, but he could not breathe. The lioness squeezed and sank her fangs deep into his throat, her powerful jaw muscles bulging as they contracted and collapsed Manosh's trachea with a soft crunching sound. She held her grip while he thrashed about wildly.

Manosh tried to heave but he could not even get his chest to rise due to the blockage. His eyes were wide, his mouth agape. His back was arched and his fingers were spread far apart. Gradually, his resistance waned and he became more sluggish. Then, staring blankly forward, Manosh completely ceased all movement.

Blake and Lana ran on, with Rita well ahead of them. Lana looked over her shoulder and screamed.

"Blake! They're coming!" she cried. Blake turned around to see two lionesses bounding through the grass a short distance behind, their tails swishing excitedly. One of the lionesses was slightly closer than the other. Her ears were pressed flat against her head as she coursed through the plain several times faster than the humans. Softly she grunted and puffed, her huge paws rustling with each graceful, heavy step.

"We're almost there, Lana! We're almost there!" Within seconds, they were under the almost bare branches of a small tree. Lana looked up at a sturdy limb that hung overhead, but her heart sank as she realized that she could not reach it.

"It's too high! I can't make it!"

"No, it's not. Come on, I'll help you," said Blake. "When I say 'jump,' then jump." Blake looked back at the rapidly growing lioness, and then put his hands firmly around Lana's waist. "Jump!" he shouted. Lana pushed off the ground while Blake whisked her up, lifting her high enough to grab the branch. Lana took hold of the branch, her knuckles white, and tried to pull herself up while Blake pushed up on her buttocks.

"I can't do it, Blake!" she said, straining.

"You can! Just pull!" Blake put his hands under the soles of Lana's feet and shoved her skyward. Lana rose and swung her arms over the branch, tucking it firmly into her armpits. Then she hoisted herself up while Blake still pushed below until he could no longer reach her feet.

Closer and closer the lioness came until she could almost touch her prey. Thirty feet, twenty feet, ten feet. With a long stride, she prepared to deliver her deadly blow to Blake. Blake looked up at the branch, crouched slightly, and with all of his power, he jumped. His fingers skimmed the rough branch, but he failed to secure a firm grip. He looked back as the lioness leaped toward him. Once more, he jumped and fell short of the branch. Lana seized his wrist with her right hand, and he took hold of hers. Struggling, she tried to pull him upward, but to no avail.

"Climb, Blake!" cried Lana.

"You'll fall!"

"No I won't!" she said. "Now do it!"

Reluctant to compromise Lana's safety, in his whirring mind Blake decided to go ahead and chance it. "Okay, now don't move!" he groaned, "and hold on!" With both hands, he ascended her arm as though it were a rope.

Lana stifled a cry of pain. She thought Blake would tear her skin right off. The lioness swatted at one of Blake's legs. With her broad, rugged paw, she delivered a mighty blow to his calf, which sent him swinging. Blake rocked back and forth as he hung tightly onto Lana's arm, which felt as though it was on the verge of popping out of its socket, but he managed to hold on and continue climbing. He climbed hand over hand until he came within reach of the branch. Then he quickly took hold of it, lifted himself up, swung his leg over, and anchored himself firmly to the tree.

Blake sat down precariously next to Lana. The two of them looked down at the two lionesses, who in turn looked up at them. Then one of them stood up against the tree, extended her claws, and pressed her broad paws against the bark. Then she wrapped her limbs around the narrow trunk and began to ascend.

"Oh, no!" cried Lana. "What are we going to do?"

"Climb," said Blake. He and Lana looked up and found that, despite the tree's small stature, there were still a few branches overhead that might be able to support them. So, they climbed.

So did the lioness. Although weighing some three hundred pounds, she was remarkably nimble and agile. Propelling herself with all four limbs and using her tail for balance, she steadily made her way up the trunk. Soon, she neared the branch where Blake and Lana had been sitting, but by now they were even higher up. The lioness continued climbing.

"I don't like this," said Lana as she looked down at the determined lioness. "She's still coming."

"I know," said Blake, directly below Lana. "Just keep going. She can't keep this up forever." Blake was determined to put Lana and himself beyond the reach of the lioness. He knew that this predator was more than twice the size of a typical human being. Even if she were the best climber in her entire pride, her weight would limit how high she could actually climb. However, Blake did not know if the tree trunk's higher reaches or higher branches were thick enough to support a human being, while still thin enough to fail a lion. It was a gamble he had to take, though; there was no other choice. For Lana's sake, he pretended to be confident that his idea would work.

Blake and Lana climbed higher and higher, but the lioness continued to climb after them as her compatriot looked on and circled below.

"Keep going, Lana," said Blake encouragingly as he looked up at Lana. "Not much more." Eventually, however, Lana reached a point where she could go no further.

"That's it, Blake. The branches are getting too thin up here. I can't hold on to them without breaking them, and I'm lighter than you, so if they won't hold me, then they won't hold you, either."

"All right," Blake said. "We should be fine up here." Blake and Lana were some twenty feet above the ground, but when they looked down they saw the lioness continuing to come closer.

"We're not fine!" exclaimed Lana as she began to panic. "She's still coming!"

"Relax," said Blake in a deliberately calm tone of voice. "We're still higher up than she is."

The lioness, however, approached Blake. Straining only a little bit to pull herself up even further, she cocked her head to one side and partially opened her mouth in preparation to attack. Then she lunged forward and snapped at Blake's lower foot — his right one — but Blake quickly moved it out of the way and gave the lioness only a mouthful of air.

The lioness, unwavering in her resolve to secure a meal, gripped the trunk's bark with her claws and readied herself for another strike.

"Be careful, Blake!" screamed Lana. She was becoming hysterical.

Blake said nothing. He was well aware that there would be no escape from the lioness's vice-like bite. If she were to succeed in latching onto him, then with one or two jerks she would be able to dislodge him from his perch and send him falling. Hitting the ground with his head, neck, or shoulders first, he would probably die upon impact and become one of the easiest kills the lioness had ever made. Alternatively, he might hit the ground feet first, receiving excruciating pain and becoming immobile. In that case, the lioness or her sister would be able to walk right up to him and simply snap his neck like a twig.

The lioness snapped at Blake's foot again, and again he dodged the attack. This time, however, Blake was prepared for a counterattack. In one fluid motion, he swung his foot away from the big cat's mouth, and then swung it back around and slammed his heel into her head, directly between the eyes. The lioness flinched, but it would take more than a simple stomp from a human to disable the seasoned predator. Blake was prepared, and he stomped on the lioness's head again in the same spot. The mighty lioness roared her displeasure, but she did not budge.

All right, thought Blake. *How about this one then?*

Instead of stomping on the lioness's forehead, Blake decided to kick the side of her head instead. Winding up only a little, Blake then delivered a powerful blow to the big cat's left temple with the ball of his foot. Blake felt his foot connect with the lioness's body and he felt her course fur bristle against the soul of his moccasin. Her head lurched to the right, but she quickly recovered and prepared to strike again.

Blake seized this opportunity to try again. He slammed his right foot into the side of the big cat's head once more, and this time he felt his big toe gouge her left eye. Although not permanently injured, the lioness was startled enough to lose her grip on the tree trunk and she began to slip.

Now's my chance!

Summoning all the strength he could muster in his awkward, clinging position, Blake delivered one more kick, this time to the lioness's neck. She emitted a high-pitched growl and slid further down the trunk until she could no longer maintain her position. This forced the lioness to cling to the tree trunk in a facedown position in order to avoid a certain plummet and a chance at injury or even death. Abandoning her prey, the lioness scurried down the trunk and bounded onto the ground. She shook her head in agitation at the blows she had received, and then joined her sister in looking up at the people in the tree.

The two lionesses lingered for a few minutes, but they soon gave up when they realized that their prey was too high up and that the tree was too thin to climb. Standing next to each other, the cats peered out across the savanna. Their keen eyes scanned for movement while their agile ears rotated on their heads to listen.

"Are you all right, Lana?"

"I … I think so, and you?"

"Fine, fine," said Blake. "Can you see Manosh from up here? And where's Rita?"

"I can't see either one," replied Lana. The two of them looked around for Manosh and the dog, but to no avail.

Blake noticed that Lana was rubbing her right arm gingerly. "How is your arm?" he asked.

Lana rubbed her shoulder, then moved down to her forearm and gently caressed it. "It's okay, I suppose. My shoulder is kind of sore, though."

"Mmmm," said Blake with a nod. "How about your skin? I thought it was going to come off there for a second."

"So did I," Lana said, "but it's fine." She took Blake's hand in hers. "I'm glad you're all right."

"Me too, Lana. Thank you for saving me."

"Thank you, too," she said. Blake kissed her, and they touched their foreheads together and hugged.

The two lionesses below found what they sought, and faced the same direction with their ears pointed attentively forward. Then they trotted off together. Blake and Lana, high up in their perch, watched them as they went out into the plain and approached the third lioness, who had already begun to rip open their meal. When her companions arrived, she snarled at them but permitted them to approach and nudge her affectionately. She stood up with the kill locked safely between her jaws. Then the three of them slinked away, dragging the corpse of Manosh with them. Blake gasped.

"That's Manosh!" he cried, pointing. "Lana, they got Manosh! I can't believe they got Manosh." Lana stroked his shoulder silently. "No, it can't be. He got away. You saw him, right? He got up after he fell and ran away. That can't be Manosh. Maybe it's something else. Maybe it's a texin calf. They sort of look like us from far away. Maybe that's what it is." The two of them carefully scrutinized the dead body as the lionesses left with it, but it was all too obvious what it was. "No," moaned Blake, "no, no, no…"

"I'm sorry, Blake," Lana said. Blake buried himself in her arms as she stroked him softly. "There was nothing anyone could've done. Not you, nor I, nor Rita. They were just too strong." Blake nodded and looked up once more.

"I know. It's just that … it's just…" He could not finish his sentence.

"I know, Blake," said Lana, "I know." She touched him lightly on the shoulder. He looked at her with grave eyes, and carefully negotiating the narrow branch, she crept toward him and hugged him. Blake powerfully returned the hug. The two of them remained in the tree for another ten minutes just to be certain that there was no danger. When they felt it was safe enough, they came down to the ground again. Blake's eyes felt tired, and his chest felt heavy, but he forced himself to stay alert. As he turned himself around, he looked off into the distance and whistled for Rita. There was no response.

"I hope she's all right," said Blake.

"I'm sure she is," said Lana nervously.

"You didn't see … you know … you didn't see them get her, too? Did you?"

"No," she said soothingly, "no I didn't. I'm sure she's fine." Blake whistled again, but no Rita.

"Where *is* she?" Blake said, putting a hand to his forehead. Lana looked about and put her hands on her hips. "Damn it!" Just then, Rita came running through the tall grass. "There you are!" Blake kneeled and greeted her, petting her and examining her for injuries. Despite her generally excited appearance, she seemed fine. Blake stood up and faced Lana, a stoic look on his face.

Lana looked at him quizzically. *How can he be so calm?* she thought.

Blake took her hand, which was trembling. "It's okay," he said.

Lana gave Blake a terse nod. They looked into one another's eyes. They could see that something was horribly wrong, but neither one realized that they were feeling the same way. Blake and Lana suppressed their terror and confusion as though these emotions were dangerous themselves, and they dared not lose their composure until they felt safe. Neither Blake nor Lana was fully capable of comprehending what had just happened. Not yet. They still had too much fear, and that was the danger that had to pass. It was best to let the matter sink down, away from view — at least for the time being. Despite the calm that was so casually restoring itself on the plain, the violent disturbances with Blake and Lana were still transpiring.

Then, without a word, they neared one another and embraced. They held each other for a while, clutching each other tightly. They said nothing. They did not have to. After that unnerving experience, all they wanted was to touch. Then they stood apart and looked at one another again. Blake clapped his hands for Rita to follow, and they walked onward.

Chapter 5

The following night, Blake and Lana lay together beside the fire. They had just finished their meal of roasted rabbit. Rita was asleep with her head between her paws while Lana leaned on Blake's shoulder. Blake had his arm wrapped around Lana, his head resting against hers. He absentmindedly caressed her arm and the back of her hand as they watched the soothing fire, entranced by its lively dancing.

"What are you thinking?" asked Lana. Blake sighed.

"Everyone I've ever loved is dead." *Everyone except you.* Lana wrapped her arms around Blake's body and sighed as well. Comforting him, she turned toward him, nestled her cheek against his chest, and held him tightly.

"I know, Blake," she said, "and I'm sorry. I don't know if this will make you feel any better, but I know exactly how you feel. Everyone I've ever loved is dead, too." *Except for you.* "My whole family is dead, and has been dead for two years. You and I are in the same situation, Blake. We have both lost everyone who is dear to us, and we are both hundreds of miles away from home."

"Well, that doesn't make me feel much better," said Blake, "but it does help." Lana smiled. "Being ripped away from everything you know and love, it feels so scary."

"And lonely."

"And lonely, too, yes. Can I tell you something, Lana?"

"What?"

"I'm glad we have each other." Lana raised her head and grinned.

"So am I, Blake."

"I mean, it gets scary out here. A few nights ago, I woke up in the middle of the night. I opened my eyes, and I looked up. Everything was so still and quiet. There was no moon out, and I could see every star in the sky. It was beautiful, but at the same time, I was afraid. There we were: just you and me ... and Manosh, and the dogs — just the five of us. Who knew what kinds of dangers were out there? Warriors, predators. All sorts of things. We're so vulnerable right now,

Lana. It's a very frightening thought." Lana nodded and hummed her understanding. "But I'll tell you this. With you here with me, I don't feel lonely. Not even a little bit. I don't know what I'd do if you weren't with me now."

"Me neither, Blake. Ever since you found me, I've been so happy. I haven't been happy for two years. Now that we're together, I don't feel lonely at all. In fact, I've never felt this way before." Blake paused, and looked deep into Lana's big, gleaming, brown eyes.

"I love you, Lana."

Lana beamed and hugged him tightly. "I love you, too, Blake."

"I've never felt this way about anyone before, either."

"I don't believe you," said Lana. Blake was shocked. His eyes widened and his mouth dropped. He was not expecting to hear those words.

"Why not?" asked Blake, hurt. "Do you think I'm lying?"

"No, I don't —"

"Because I'm not. I wouldn't lie to you."

"I know you wouldn't. I just think you've been through a lot and you've forgotten."

"Forgotten what?"

"Lauren, your girlfriend back in Kamis."

"I haven't forgotten about her."

"Didn't you love her too?"

"Yes, but that was different."

"How was it different?"

"Well, it was just different that's all. I loved her in the sense that I cared about her and I wanted her to be happy. We'd known each other ever since we were kids. We grew up as friends, and then when we got older, we were drawn to each other and spent more time together. It was only natural that we would love each other." Blake paused. Then he touched Lana on the shoulder. "I've only known you for a few weeks, Lana, but I feel that we have become very close in that time."

"We have."

"I can already see that the love I have for you is stronger than the love I had for Lauren."

"What if Lauren had ... no, I'm sorry. I'll stop."

"What is it?"

"No, I shouldn't ask," said Lana. Blake took her by the hand.

"Ask me. I want you to feel free to ask me anything you like. It won't do you or me any good to carry around some sort of burden. Now, what is it?"

"Well, if Lauren had survived the Ravashi attack," began Lana, "and if she had come with you and Manosh on your journey, would you still want to be with me?"

"Yes," said Blake, "I would choose you over her. I love you more than anyone, Lana. I don't want anyone else. Just you, and that's the truth."

"Blake," she said, "that's the most wonderful thing anyone has ever said to me. I never thought the day would come that a man would tell me what you just told me." Lana looked at Blake with appreciation and admiration as tears began to form. They hugged each other tightly, powerfully for a moment, engrossed in each other's presence. Then Blake peered deep into her eyes. He ran the back of his hand down the side of her face, fully absorbing her lovely visage. Lana cocked her head and smiled. Then they brought their faces together and kissed passionately, embracing one another as they explored each other's luscious lips and supple skin. Blake clutched Lana by the shoulders and held her close to his body. His lips left hers and he began to kiss the corner where her jaw met her neck. Lana tilted her head back and sighed as Blake gently mouthed her there, engrossed in the seductive feeling of her yielding firmness and her captivating scent. He tugged on her ear, and then moved down her neck to her collarbones, tenderly kissing her, mouthing her. Slowly, he began to disrobe her, to which she silently consented. First, sliding her cloak off of her shoulders, he then removed the black garment in one, fluid motion and let it fall to the ground. Lana was now only in her loincloth.

Lana felt Blake's powerful chest and shoulders beneath his mantle. She fondled the mantle avidly, eager to remove it yet both savoring the sensation of it on Blake and the anticipation of seeing his naked body. She soon decided to remove it, and with Blake's accommodating movements, she did so, leaving him in only his loincloth as well. Lana caressed his solid abdomen and ran her fingers up toward his nipples, which she encircled with her adept fingers, chilling him with exhilarating relaxation. She then brought her hands around to his broad back and rubbed him hungrily.

Blake seized Lana and pulled her toward himself. Gingerly, he touched her elegant breasts and placed his hands around them. He could feel their resilience and their softness. He stroked them with the tips of his fingers and palms of his hands, much to Lana's elation. Then he brought himself closer and kissed her flush on the lips while his chest rubbed against hers. The two of them were becoming intertwined, and a thrill surged through them. They ran their fingers through each other's hair and excitedly kneaded one another.

Lana squeezed Blake's arms, and then vigorously moved down toward his waist and legs. She let her hands delicately hover over the insides of his thighs. Blake now became completely devoured by passion. He cradled Lana's head in his hands, but then brought his hands down to her thin waist and shapely hips. He squeezed her insatiably, and then began to fondle her thighs as well. Lana breathed her longing for Blake. Then, unable to contain their desire any longer, Blake and Lana removed each other's clothing until they were completely naked.

Lana looked at Blake's face. His strong chin and jaw line, his stark features, his dark hair and skin. She gazed into his brown eyes and saw how consumed he was by passion. Yet she could also see his kindness and his admiration and love for her. She glanced at his mouth, and despite its serious impression, she noticed that the corners were slightly upturned, revealing his happiness. She could not resist him.

Blake gently lay Lana down on her back and came over her. He was spellbound by Lana's beauty, her long hair falling around her head, her sparkling eyes inviting him in the dim light, and her faint smile irresistible. He glided over her sacred body, enthralled by her presence. They touched and intertwined; a symphony of hands and embraces. They longed to join together. They were ready to begin, to unite. Then, on that splendid, twinkling night, they consummated their love for each other.

Chapter 6

When Blake awoke the next morning he lazily reoriented himself. He felt something hugging him, so he rolled over slightly and opened his eyes. He realized that he could not easily roll over, so he turned his head instead and found Lana at his side, her arms around him, still sleeping.

And then he remembered.

A broad grin appeared on his face. He watched the sleeping woman for a moment. She was even lovely when she slept. Her mouth was expressionless, but sealed, giving it a refined appearance. Her eyes were shut, and her body was limp and relaxed. She looked so peaceful. Blake caressed her cheek. She stirred and leaned into him, burying her face into his shoulder. Blake smiled in amusement. Then he bent down and kissed her lightly on the forehead.

Lana's eyes fluttered open. She reflexively surveyed her surroundings and then looked up at Blake. She smiled as well.

"Good morning," said Blake.

"Morning," said Lana, still waking up.

"Come on, get up. We've got to get going."

"Okay, okay," she said reluctantly. She sat up and stretched in an exaggerated fashion, groaning all the while. "We should get something to eat first."

"In a moment," said Blake as he stood up. He looked around at the early morning plain, golden in color as it made its transition from darkness to light. It was his favorite view ever since he could remember. "It's hard to believe we're almost there."

"I know, but be patient. We're not out of danger yet."

Blake suddenly remembered Manosh. He felt a heavy presence in his chest, which then managed to diffuse to the rest of him. Blake sighed and imperceptibly shook his head. He could not get rid of that feeling. It was not like hunger or fear. It was deeper. He set that feeling aside and decided to ignore it and defer it for another time. Then he was able to look at the world through clear eyes once more.

After breakfast, Blake and Lana continued to head for the Warmland, with Rita tagging sluggishly along. They walked through the prairie for a while, but then the landscape shifted abruptly. They found themselves leaving the broad, flat plain with its green and yellow grass, and entering the swamp. The ground here was black with thick, rich mud. The surface was pockmarked with pools of shiny, black water, some shallow, some deep, some small, some large. Separating the pools were low ridges of moist, newt-skinned mud. Tall, impoverished trees drooped over the whole of the swamp. They covered it like a deranged, obsessed guardian, only letting in thin shafts of light between the grimy branches and skimpy leaves.

"This is revolting," said Blake as his feet sank into the soil past his ankles.

"Actually," said Lana, "I kind of like it. It feels good." She took a big step forward and the earth beneath her planted foot splashed. As her other foot became buried in the mud, the swamp uttered a hollow "bwomp" sound. "See? It's not that bad." She took another step and this time her leg sank in past her knees. Lana let out a soprano guffaw of surprise.

"Yech," said Blake. "I can't believe this."

"Oh, stop complaining and come over here and have some fun!" Lana forged recklessly onward, sometimes standing in just a few inches of murky water, sometimes nearly up to her waist in thick mud. She stood up and looked back at Blake, who was steadily trudging along. "Come on! Hurry up!" she giggled.

"Look at you. Your legs are filthy. They're covered in mud!"

"I know! Isn't it great? But don't worry. It'll come off in the water. Now come on."

Blake approached Lana, slowly working his way through the stubborn sludge. Deeper and deeper he sank, and slower and slower he went. The two of them had to lift their legs high and take short, slow strides to make progress through the thick mud. The swamp continually sucked at their feet and dislodged their moccasins, forcing Blake and Lana to carry their footwear by hand.

Rita was having difficulty negotiating the terrain as well. With her relatively narrow paws, she was sinking, too. However, because she walked on four limbs instead of two, and was lighter than her human companions, she was able to move more easily and quickly. Fortunately for Rita, she did not sink past her chest, and that helped support her weight. When Rita emerged from the muck, Lana could not help but laugh at the unknowing dog, whose fur was blackened and spiked with the mud. Blake first scowled at Lana, for he did not see anything amusing in this predicament. After looking at Rita's comically decorated coat and hearing Lana's contagious laughter, even he could not help but feel light-hearted and began to laugh as well. Rita looked up at them in droopy bewilderment. Unable to understand why they were looking at her and making their distinctive, curious noise, she looked forward and continued through the sludge.

They trudged onward, slowly but steadily, sloshing their way through the mud. Their legs were extremely tired, and their thighs ached. It was exhausting just trying to walk in the swamp, where the earth gave way beneath their feet with each step and required much more energy than normal. Not only was it tiring, but aggravating as well. They walked on in silence as they looked at the ground and listened to the tedious sloshing of their footfalls. The swamp became progressively deeper and deeper, until they were constantly waist-deep in black sludge. Suddenly, Lana stepped into a particularly weak point in the swamp and quickly sank up to her chin. She screamed as she held her head up to avoid inhaling any of the gurgling, murky water. Blake spun around and raced in slow motion to her side.

"Don't get too close!" gasped Lana. He was approaching her cautiously when he started to feel himself slipping into the sinkhole as well. Fumbling, he shifted his weight backward and fell onto his buttocks with a lazy splash. Lana was still sinking, the mud rising past her chin and seeping upwards toward her mouth. "Help!" Blake got up and, leaning forward, he extended his hand out to Lana. Her gooey, mud-covered hand emerged from the ooze, shining and black, with the fingers spread apart.

Lana continued to sink. Her ears were partly submerged and the mud was crawling into the corners of her mouth. She boldly held her head up to breathe, but the mud leaked in and caused her to cough, so she held her breath instead. Blake clasped her by the wrist and she by his. He began to lean back and pull. Lana budged a little. Blake watched her arm and head rise from the muck, but he failed to move her any further. The harder he pulled, the more he slipped and sputtered. Still clutching her wrist tightly, he fell over and his hand sank into the mud. Blake promptly got up again and resumed his futile pulling and straining, but he only became more and more dislodged. Slowly, Lana began to sink once more.

"Push, Lana! Push!" cried Blake desperately.

"I'm trying, but it's no use!" Just then, Lana felt a tug and she began to move. She watched as Blake himself was moving backward. "Hey! It's working, it's working!" In her frenzied mind, she puzzled over how Blake had managed to get a foothold. Then she saw what was happening: Rita had Blake's mantle between her jaws and was pulling steadily on it, stepping back with powerful, carefully-placed steps. Fiercely, she held onto the coat, her nose crinkled and her lips curled. Slowly, Rita and Blake made progress, until they dragged Lana out of the sinkhole like a giant hooked fish that was too tired to fight any longer. As soon as she felt firmer mud beneath her knees, she crawled forward under her own power to escape that deadly pit.

Lana, covered in slime, glistened as she lay in the mud and gasped for breath with her hand on her chest. Her hair was drenched and slicked back, thick cakes of mud near the tips.

"We made it," heaved Blake.

Lana sighed. "Thank you," she said.

"We should be thanking Rita." Rita, who was also lying in the mud, cocked her ears and raised her head. Blake gave her a warm hug and a pat on the side, and Rita wagged her tail. Blake, charmed by Rita's endearing body language, rubbed her on the head. Rita licked Blake's face affectionately and then walked over to Lana and licked her face, too. Lana giggled and pet the dog's wet fur soothingly. "Well, come on," said Blake after a few minutes of rest. "Let's keep moving."

"Okay."

"This time, be more careful."

"I will," Lana said, rising. Then they continued their sluggish journey through the swamp.

Chapter 7

Later that afternoon, Blake, Lana, and Rita emerged from the swamp, which gradually gave way to sandy soil and shrubby plant life. Thankfully, they stepped out onto the firmament and welcomed the sound of weeds rustling as they brushed past their legs. They had not even realized how much they had missed that sound. Their entire bodies were covered with mud, which caused the sand to stick to the soles of their bare feet. The mud was drying and crusting, but slowly because of the great humidity in the air. Blake surveyed his surroundings. Pine trees, palms, and shrubs filled this flat land, and the sky was a pale blue.

"So where do we go now?" asked Lana.

"I'm not sure. We need to go a little farther. Just a little more."

"How much more?"

"Not much. We need to do some scouting, some exploring. We need to find out more about the food available, the refuges. We're not done yet."

"But we're close, right, Blake? We've almost found a place for ourselves, haven't we?"

"Almost, but we can't stop yet. Come on. I don't want to waste any time."

"All right," said Lana. They walked farther out over the sandy soil.

"Oh, I can hardly wait until we find a new home!"

"Patience, Lana. It could be a while. I just hope we don't run into any trouble first."

"I know, I know, but tell me the truth. Aren't you the least bit excited?"

"Am I excited? I'm more than excited. I've been dreaming of coming to the Warmland for years. Ever since I heard of it, I've wanted to go. And after what happened in Kamis, I saw it as the only place I *could* go. Now, after how far we've come, after all that's happened ... I can hardly wait. But I'm not ready to rejoice yet, and I'm not going to gloat over what we've accomplished so far. It'd be foolish to celebrate when we haven't even finished what we set out to do in the first place — find a new home. After we've done that, *then* we can look back in satisfaction and be happy with what we've done."

"It's never too soon to be happy, Blake. Be happy that we've made it this far."

"What about Manosh? He didn't make it…" Blake frowned oddly despite himself. He alternately looked down at the ground and away at the tops of the trees.

Lana touched him on the arm. "I know. I wish he could've been here, too, but we'll never forget him, Blake. And we're here now. Manosh would want us to be happy. You know that, don't you?"

Blake stiffened. "We still have farther to go. You coming?"

Lana sighed and faintly shook her head. "Right beside you."

They hiked onward through the mosaic of pale, dry sand and dark, moist mulch, curiously examining their environment as they went along. Things here were rather different from what Blake and Lana were accustomed to. It was more humid and warmer than either the northern Great Plains or the Rubbletown. Pine trees abounded here. They stood straight and tall, while long strands of gray-green moss hung leisurely from their branches. The understory was overgrown with dwarf palm trees. They covered the forest floor, rendering the ground scarcely visible. The saw-like edges of these plants were sharp enough to tear skin, so the travelers dared not pass through them, preferring to stick to the well worn path before them instead.

The canopy of this forest was incomplete, and daylight managed to peek through the patches between the pines. Nevertheless, the shade available was a welcome relief from the glaring sun. Wherever the travelers looked, the ubiquitous green and brown of the plants surrounded them. The pleasant stillness and quiet of these woods, interrupted only by the occasional buzzing of a mischievous insect or a distant signing bird, were reassuringly peaceful and welcome.

"This place is amazing, Blake," said Lana, "I can't believe how many of these plants there are."

"I know. I've never seen anything like it." They walked on at a brisk pace, occasionally clambering over a fallen log, treading on a piece of bark, or crinkling a pile of needles underfoot. Rita trotted right along with them, sometimes ahead, sometimes behind, but never far away.

Chapter 8

The travelers trekked for hours through the open woodland. At Blake's behest they pressed onward. They took short breaks only infrequently and continued marching late into the afternoon. When the sun hung low in the sky and prepared to descend below the horizon, they were still walking.

"Blake, when are we going to stop for the night?" asked Lana.

"Soon," replied Blake.

Lana felt as though she were already half asleep. The sound of her own footsteps was mesmerizing, and she seemed aware of little else. She was oblivious to the small woodland birds that hurriedly called back and forth to each other before nightfall. "How's Rita holding up?" Lana asked.

Blake looked back at his dog, who was keeping pace right behind him. Her tongue was lolling out, and her steps were not as quick as usual, but otherwise she seemed no worse for wear. "She's fine," he said at last.

"For now," said Lana.

"We can't bed down for the night until we find a good spot."

"Oh, they're all the same," Lana muttered.

"No they're not! We can't just stop anywhere, Lana. We have to choose a campsite that's safe. You know, I'm surprised at you. You're usually so quick to pick up on things, and you've learned so much since we left the Rubbletown. Why aren't you curious now?"

"Fatigue has a way of beating the curiosity out of me," said Lana, acerbically.

"Well … I suppose." The pair walked on quietly for a few paces.

"Sorry, Blake. I didn't mean to snap at you. I'm just tired, that's all."

"I know," said Blake softly. "Me too. Soon. Soon."

The group persevered. Eventually, Blake detected an odd odor and sniffed pensively at the air. "Can you smell that, Lana? What is it?"

"It's fire, but whatever's burning, I've never smelled it before. What do you think it is?"

"It smells kind of tangy and pungent — almost spicy. It's probably one of these pine trees."

"Well, it's kind of nice, even if it is a bit strong. Wait, look over there!" said Lana, pointing ahead into the distance. "There's smoke coming from over there. Do you think it's natural or artificial?"

"Hmmm ... Well, it doesn't seem very big," said Blake. "It's probably someone's campfire. Why don't we go over and have a look?"

"Are you sure we should? What if they aren't friendly?"

"But what if we find something worthwhile?"

"I don't know..." said Lana.

"Come on, let's go check it out."

Lana paused to consider the proposal. "How would we get there? The spikes on these shrubby palm trees look pretty sharp. I don't want to go running through that stuff, and I'm pretty sure it would be bad for Rita, too."

"True, but I don't think we'll even have to leave this path. Whoever made it must come through here often; it looks pretty well maintained. I think the fire is more or less straight ahead of us. Let's just follow the path and see what happens."

"Well..." Lana said hesitantly. "All right."

Blake grinned approvingly, and the group continued marching along the path. The endless woodland, with its tall pine trees and thick shrubs, grew darker with the approach of dusk. A pillar of smoke rose up in the distance, and Blake, Lana and Rita gravitated toward it like moths. As they drew closer, the pungent odor became stronger and the smoke more visible.

At last, the group traced the smoke to a fire in the center of a clearing, and realized that this was indeed a small campsite. Of average size and brilliance, the fire was strong enough to cook by or glean some warmth from, but it was clearly for mundane and not festive purposes. It allowed people to follow it from a distance, as they had done, but it was small enough to manage and pose little risk to the surrounding woods.

Arranged in a loose circle around the campfire, six tan colored tents made of deer hide stood facing the center. A few items could be seen on the ground, such as a spear, a drum, a few hand tools, and some eating utensils. Blake and Lana exchanged glances. Lana, who was still unaccustomed to visiting foreign territories, watched Blake closely. Blake, however, was experienced at dealing with strangers, and knew what to do. He signaled Lana to wait, then cupped his hand to his mouth and shouted. "Hello!" he cried in the formal Bebelishi language, and his voice carried through the stillness of the woods. "We greet you in peace!"

Suddenly, a startled head popped up from behind the nearest tent and spun around to look at the visitors. The man to whom it belonged was rather young, about Blake's age. His eyes were wide and his brows were raised. He was clearly in the middle of eating a turkey drumstick, for he held the food to his mouth in one hand with his teeth clenched on the meat, mid-bite, and grease could be seen faintly glistening around his lips. The young man immediately dropped his food, and in a rushed manner, hastened to finish chewing and swallowing. He quickly snatched up a spear from somewhere out of Blake and Lana's view, and abruptly faced the travelers.

"Who the hell are you?" the man shouted agitatedly in the Common Tongue.

"We mean no harm!" replied Blake. "We are merely weary travelers, my woman and I, with our dog." Rita sniffed uneasily at the strangers but made no move against them.

Blake's reply seemed to satisfy the man, who became more at ease and took several cautious steps forward. He shouted a few words in an unfamiliar language, and two other young men emerged from the bushes to join him. As a group, the threesome approached the travelers.

"We are Dallashi. I am Brillum," said the young man. He gestured to his companions. "These are my friends, Beldek and Thomas. Who are you?"

"We are Kamishi. I am Blake, and this is my woman, Lana. We come from the northern Great Plains.

"You have come a long way, then. What brings you to Dallas?"

"We escaped from our enemies, the Ravashi, and are now searching for a new home." Rita stood by quietly, alert but calm.

"I see," said Brillum thoughtfully. "Well, that is a difficult position. I'm sorry you had to flee your homeland. Where are your tribesmen?"

"We have none," said Blake. "I'm afraid we are the last of our tribe. Actually, there was one more, my friend, Manosh, but a lion took him about a week ago. We also had another dog with us, Saamu, Rita's mate, but he died as well defending us against the Podeshi."

"Oh, my. Those are sad things to endure. Again, I offer my condolences."

"Thank you," said Blake.

Brillum paused for a moment. Then he began moving back toward the center of the campground. "Please, let us return to the safety of our hearth," he said. Beldek and Thomas did as he asked, and Blake and Lana courteously followed suit. Soon, everyone was seated by the fire.

"Thank you for your hospitality," said Blake. Brillum smiled faintly and gave a terse nod, but Blake still felt a bit nervous. Although Brillum was friendly and polite, his formal demeanor was distracting. Blake knew how to conduct himself in the proper manner, but he hoped to establish a rapport with these strangers and ease the obvious tension in the air. He decided to make some conversation. "Lana and I were just talking about how different and interesting Dallas is."

"Oh?" said Brillum.

"We're more used to wide-open plains with small, dense stands of trees. This place seems to be something in between, like an open forest."

"That's a good way to put it. We call it the 'flatwoods' for that reason. The trees you see are longleaf pine."

"What are the smaller palm-like plants?" asked Lana.

"We call them 'saw palmettos,' after their sharp edges. Perhaps you've noticed that part."

"We have," nodded Blake. He raised a bare leg and revealed the long, thin scab along his calf. "I tried to walk through them, but I quickly learned not to!"

"A good lesson to learn," replied Brillum. "May I offer you some food?"

Blake smiled. "Why, yes. Thank you again."

Brillum tore off two pieces of roast turkey and offered them to his guests. They accepted graciously and began to eat.

"This is delicious!" Lana exclaimed.

"I'm glad you like it." After a pause, Brillum spoke again. "You have come so far from the northern Great Plains. May I ask how you found yourselves here?"

"There's a legend that tells of a great land in the South..."

"What legend?" asked Brillum quickly.

"One that tells of a place called the Warmland that lays far to the south where the land meets the sea, where winter does not reach, where water is plentiful, and where life abounds. Although dearly guarded by the tribes who inhabit it, the Warmland is said to be a place of peace and prosperity. It is blessed with great fertility and abundant animals, and many different kinds of hoof beasts — even larger than any in the North — roam there in great numbers. It is said that the Warmland is a place of beauty and comfort, and that anyone living there would be sure to enjoy a good life. I first heard this tale when I was just a boy, and I have been infatuated with the Warmland ever since."

"I see," said Brillum. "Well, what you have said is virtually the same account as I've heard before…"

"Is it true then?" asked Lana. "Is there a Warmland like that?"

"Well, the Warmland does have those things, but…"

"But what?" asked Blake impatiently.

"Well, it's true that the Warmland is a pleasant place to live, and that it's comfortable and beautiful, but that's not all it is."

"No?" asked Blake, dreading to hear what else Brillum might say.

"For example, winters are mild and warm, but cold can still find the Warmland, and it does become chilly from time to time. Winter is also the dry season, and it can become harder to find water then. Besides, the summers can be ruthless. The Warmland is moist, and its air is thick and humid. On the other hand, the breeze is sweet and tender, and the spring and autumn are beautiful times of year."

"Oh," said Blake, visibly puzzled.

"You see, the Warmland is a place of contradictions. Its climate may be favorable to us humans, but it is favorable to other creatures as well. That is why insects torment Warmlanders, and why such large, dangerous creatures inhabit it as well."

"Insects?" asked Lana timidly.

"There are large swarms of biting flies, mosquitoes, and small insects almost too tiny to be seen, known as no-see-ums, that inhabit the Warmland. They harass people with painful bites and sap them of their blood, but they also carry horrible diseases, like yellow fever and malaria, which they can transmit to anyone they bite."

"Oh no," mumbled Blake. Blake was beginning to doubt the tales he had heard for so long.

"You mentioned hoof beasts," said Brillum. "Well, they may provide much meat, but they are aggressive and dangerous, and difficult to catch, too."

"Oh my," said Blake, "that sounds awful." Blake wondered whether coming here was a good idea after all. He had traveled over a thousand miles, and he had brought his best friend, his new girlfriend, and his two dogs with him. He had thought that he was leading everyone to a new home, but now Saamu was dead, and the recent loss of Manosh was still painful. Blake shuddered at the thought of Rita getting hurt, and he could not even bear to think about anything bad happening to Lana. A knot formed in Blake's belly.

"But the climate is good, right?" asked Blake.

"Not always. In the summer, the Warmland is horribly hot and prone to fires that consume acres of woodland or grassland. Horrible winds and storms can pop up, and there are strong rains in the wet season. The weather does change, though; autumn is the season of the hurricanes."

"Hurricanes?" asked Blake.

"They are powerful storms, strong enough to uproot trees, flatten fields, toss animals about, and destroy villages. During the hurricane season, people keep a watchful eye and are quick to seek cover when they see signs that a large hurricane is coming."

What have I done? Have I brought them here to die? I have been selfish. It would be bad enough if I had to pay for my rashness, but at least that would still be only me. Now Lana and Rita might have to suffer for my bad judgment. What have I done?

"Such is the Warmland," said Brillum. "In truth, any place has its contradictions. Any place has beauty and ugliness, pleasure and pain. Such is the way of it. It keeps everything in balance."

It's still too soon to give up, thought Blake to himself. *It couldn't be that bad. In any case, we can't turn back now. We've come so far. There must be something we can do.*

"I suppose you're right," said Blake. "Nevertheless, we have come all this way in search of the Warmland."

"Well," interjected Beldek with a cock of his head, "you're not the only ones."

Just as I feared! thought Blake.

"The legend has attracted many pilgrims from the North in search of a better life. You are not the first, and you will not be the last."

"How many?" asked Blake.

"Many thousands," answered Beldek. "Each year sees more Newcomers."

"How can this be?" asked Lana, astonished. "How can the Land support that many people?"

"The land is rich and fertile," said Thomas, "and the sea is harvested as well. It is not much of a strain on the Warmland to support that many people. Well, at least it is not much of a strain for the Warmland herself. Her residents, however, are a different story altogether…"

"What do you mean?" asked Blake, squinting.

"The people do not tolerate so many Newcomers," said Thomas. "They do not allow people to stay."

"Ah," replied Blake, "as I suspected."

"Indeed," said Brillum, "but some people get through just the same. Not in the thousands, of course, but perhaps several hundred have managed to set up territories in the Warmland and now live as Warmlanders."

"Tell me, Brillum," began Lana. "Where is the Warmland? How close are we to reaching it?"

"You already have," said Brillum. Blake and Lana looked at each other excitedly.

"Then we've arrived!" exclaimed Blake.

"But will you stay?" said Brillum. "That's the question."

Blake and Lana's spirits sank once more as they became aware of the possibility that they would have to turn back. Blake thought to himself. *If we can't stay here, then where will we go? Perhaps we could go back to Tulsa and ask to stay with Tegg and his people. Maybe they would take us in ... wouldn't they?* Just then, Blake had an idea.

"We were advised to seek someone out when we reached the Warmland," he said.

"Who gave you this advice?"

"Tegg of the Tulsashi."

"Oh, Tegg!" said Brillum. "Everyone knows Tegg. He is a good man and a good leader. Who did he advise you to look for?"

"He said we should speak to Zaaru of the Corpushi," said Blake. Brillum and the others laughed out loud. "Is there something funny about that?"

"Only the fact that Zaaru is more distrustful of strangers than anyone else in the Warmland! In fact, all the Corpushi are wary of strangers. Good luck talking to him!" Blake and Lana exchanged glances quickly and saw discouragement in each other's eyes.

"Perhaps we have a chance anyway," said Lana. "I'm sure we could speak with him and show him how valuable a contribution to his tribe we would make."

"There's always a chance," said Brillum, "but it won't be easy. Do you realize how much farther you must go?"

"No," said Blake soberly.

"The distance itself is not that great; it's more the terrain you must be concerned with."

"This land seems quite flat to me."

"It is. I'm not talking about slopes or elevation. I'm talking about the area and its inhabitants."

"Perhaps we misunderstood wise Tegg," said Blake. "He said we should seek out the tribe that lives where the land meets the Gulf of Mexico. Is the Gulf not close to here?"

"No," said Beldek, "it is far. To reach Corpus you must go still farther south to the coast. Surely that is what Tegg was referring to. That is where the Gulf is, and that is where you will find Zaaru and his people, the Corpushi."

"You have about five hundred miles left to go," said Brillum. "I only pray that you stay safe. The way to Corpus is dangerous. For one thing, the heat in the daytime can be deadly, although it is not quite so bad this time of year. Still, maybe you should only travel during the cooler times of the day."

"Oh," said Blake, thoughtfully.

"Also, the tribes have had about all they can stand with Newcomers," continued Brillum, "so they do not take kindly to them. And you will have to pass through many swamps. Be careful in these areas. The waters are full of parasites, insects, snakes, and gators…"

"Gators?" asked Lana.

"They are a giant reptile with sharp teeth and powerful jaws," replied Brillum. "They have been known to take people every now and then, so be careful."

"We will," Lana said quietly.

"That's not all," said Beldek. "The fields have their dangers, too. You already know to be wary of lions…"

"We know that only too well," said Blake.

"Well, even the hoof beasts are dangerous here," said Beldek. "Beware of the elephants."

"What are those?" asked Blake.

"They're huge gray animals that live in the savannas. Elephants are as tall as two men, and they have giant ears and a long trunk."

"What's a trunk?" asked Lana.

"It's their nose," replied Beldek. "They also have tusks, which are two enormous teeth that stick out the front of their mouths. They are usually wary of humans, but beware; they can be unpredictable."

Blake and Lana's heads were spinning with images of the monsters they would have to face.

"Perhaps the worst things," said Brillum, "are the Astronauts."

"What sort of animals are they?" asked Lana.

"They are humans … but they're not like us."

"Are they not Bebelishi?" asked Blake.

"That's right, they're not Bebelishi, but there's more. They live near the Gulf of Mexico in an area known as Houston. Most of the time they're not there, but when they come, they can be trouble."

"What kind of trouble? Who are they?" asked Blake nervously.

"Legend has it," said Brillum, "that during the Great Crash, only a fraction of the people survived into the New Days, but that a small group left the Earth in a giant ship and escaped…"

"Ah, yes," said Lana. "We know this legend. It says that those people fled to the Moon and started a new civilization there, which is why we see lights in the dark part of the crescent Moon today."

"Exactly," said Brillum. "We refer to those people and their descendants as the Astronauts, and we believe they're not confined to the Moon."

"Oh?" said Lana.

"We believe that they watch the Earth, not only from their home, but while flying around in aircraft. They also return to Earth from time to time. Since the Crash, the Astronauts have been coming to Houston. They've even turned it into a big city of Management."

Blake and Lana were shocked.

"A city of Managers?" said Blake. "That's incredible. There are none!"

"There is one that we know of," said Brillum, "and that is Houston."

Blake became excited. "Then there's a chance we'll meet the Astronauts! Oh, Lana, this is wonderful. I have wanted to meet the Moon People since I was a kid!"

"It's not so wonderful," said Brillum. "Stay away from the Astronauts; they're not what you think."

"What do you mean?" asked Blake.

"They're people, but not like us. For one thing, their skin is much lighter, and they're also very thin. Their clothing is different, too. They wear these strange, shiny suits; big masks over their faces; and sometimes even big, round helmets."

"And they have powerful tools and weapons," said Beldek.

"Weapons?" repeated Blake. "What kinds of weapons?"

"None of us know how they work. The Astronauts just hold these little devices in their hands, and when they squeeze them, they make light."

"So?" asked Blake. "Light is not a weapon."

"It is in the hands of the Astronauts," Beldek said. "If this light touches you, you can't move. You might pass out. You might even die."

"That's right," said Thomas, "and that's not all. They also have metallic sticks. If they touch you with them, then your whole body gets stiff ... and painful, too. No, my friends, stay away from the Astronauts."

"But why would they do these things? Are they war-like?" asked Blake.

"Not really, but they are evil. They are heartless and cruel, and they hate everyone and everything that is not their own kind."

"Why do you think that?" asked Lana.

"Because," replied Thomas, "from time to time, they abduct someone."

"Abduct?" she asked.

"They fly in at night, very quiet and secret-like. Then they sneak into a camp or a village and just steal you away." Blake's and Lana's eyes grew wide with fear, but Thomas continued. "Then they stick you in their ship and fly you back to Houston, or even all the way back to the Moon. What they do with you after that is anyone's guess. If you're lucky, they might return you to your village, but sometimes, people who've been abducted are never seen again."

"Oh my," said Lana. "That's horrible."

"Can nothing be done to stop them?" asked Blake.

"No, nothing, and the Creator knows we've tried. The Astronauts can stop anyone who gets in their way. They temporarily paralyze you with their lights or their sticks, and if that doesn't work, they just kill you. They might leave you alone or they might abduct you, too, and we don't know why."

"What happens to the paralyzed victim?" asked Blake.

"They usually return to normal after the Astronauts leave. Just ask him," said Brillum, gesturing to Beldek. Blake looked at Beldek, inviting an explanation.

"I tried to attack an Astronaut once," began Beldek. "He shot some sort of bright green light at me and I couldn't move at all. I could still see everything, and think, and breathe normally, but I just couldn't move until they flew away in their ship. It was terrifying. That's why everyone fears them so much."

"How often do they come?" asked Blake.

"Fortunately, not very often," Beldek replied. "They've left us alone for the past few years, but during that time, they've taken people from other villages. We never know when they're going to come, and we feel helpless against them when they do."

"When people are returned," said Thomas, "they feel tired. Exhausted."

"But how do you know all of these things?" Lana asked.

"Because … I was abducted myself."

"You were?" asked Blake. "Can you talk about it?"

"It was a long time ago," said Thomas. "I was just a boy then. That was the same time they shot Beldek with their weapon."

"What did they do to you?" asked Lana.

"To be honest, I can't really remember. All I remember is a strange green light and some hands grabbing me from my bed. They paralyzed me and took me somewhere, but I don't know where they took me. That's all I can remember. The next thing I knew, I was lying on the ground just outside the village. I felt so tired and groggy, I could barely move."

"That's awful," said Lana.

"That's when we found him and brought him back home," said Brillum.

"It took me a few days," Thomas said, "but I recovered, thanks to my family and friends here."

"Thank the Creator that you are well now," said Lana.

"Yes, and I'm grateful that I can't remember too much of the ordeal, either. But I was lucky; sometimes people are taken away and never come back."

"So, you see," said Brillum, "that is why you must steer clear of Houston. Unless you want to risk letting the Astronauts get you, I suggest you avoid them."

"That's good advice," said Lana in a hushed tone. "Thank you."

"We'll be wary of all these dangers," said Blake, "but we must find Corpus and speak with Zaaru."

"Very well," said Brillum, "but all of that can wait. Right now, it's getting dark and you have no place to go. Why don't you camp with us tonight and rest up for your journey tomorrow?"

Blake and Lana exchanged approving glances.

"Thank you," said Blake graciously, "but are you sure it's all right?"

"Of course," replied Brillum. "After all, we might end up as neighbors someday, so we might as well start getting to know each other tonight. Come. Please stay."

"Well, in that case," Blake said, "we'd love to. Lana and I are actually quite tired. Again, we appreciate your hospitality."

The group spent the rest of the evening sitting around the bonfire, chatting and getting to know each other. Brillum and his friends shared their food, serving Blake and Lana turkey and water, and giving Rita some tasty scraps. Soon, the atmosphere became much more casual, and laughter even found its way into the group.

Lana and Blake shared the tale of their migration from the North in detail. They told the Dallashi about Kamis — Blake's old home — and about the Ravashi's surprise attack that killed everyone except Blake, Manosh, Saamu, and Rita. They told them about the Rubbletown where Lana used to live, and about how Blake and Manosh had found her and inducted her as a full member into the remnant — but still proud — Kamishi tribe.

Blake and Lana also told the Dallashi of their journey through the Great Plains. They recounted their discovery of an impact crater made by a fragment of the asteroid Apophis, and spoke of their horror at finding giant creatures living at its center. Blake believed that these were spirits from that terrible celestial body, but Lana was not so sure. Nevertheless, because the Dallashi men had firsthand experience with extraterrestrial threats, this particular tale frightened them. They knew that Apophis had brought the devastating effects of Rakamahn — that time after the Great Crash when the Earth had been transformed forever. Although Brillum and the others did not quite know what to make of Blake and Lana's story, they had no difficulty in believing that spirits from the asteroid could still haunt the Earth, even after some three thousand years, and still wreak havoc on the planet once again if they could.

Blake and Lana told their hosts about the Podeshi tribe to the north, who had killed Blake's dog, Saamu, with a spear to the chest. They told them about the filthy underground dungeon overrun with insects in which the Podeshi had imprisoned them, and from which they had narrowly escaped in the middle of the night. Brillum, Beldek, and Thomas were captivated by the story and were eager to hear more. They were fascinated by how Lana and Blake had evaded the lions, but saddened to hear once again of how Manosh had died.

The Dallashi laughed when they heard how Tegg and his men had taken the Kamishi by surprise, and they nodded knowingly when Lana and Blake told them about the dangerous swamp nearby. When the travelers' tale finally came to a close, the hour was late, and the fire was dying. The night was calm and still, and even the insects had fallen silent. Everyone looked forward to getting some rest, and soon they were all asleep.

Chapter 9

In the morning, the company cleaned up the area around the bonfire. Blake and Lana tidied up and cleaned utensils while the young Dallashi warriors packed up their supplies and prepared to return to their village. Soon, everyone was ready to leave.

"For the time being, we are traveling in the same direction," said Brillum. "Let us walk together for a while, and we can show you around."

This place fascinated Lana and Blake, for it was entirely new to them. These were the scrublands. The group passed diminutive shrubs and majestic oak trees. Every once in a while they came across stands of saw palmetto and lone palm trees. Gentle grasses grew everywhere in the sandy soil.

Soon, they reached a clearing in the woods that teemed with big game. Brillum held up his hand for everyone — his tribesmen and the Kamishi alike — to remain hidden and quiet. The group concealed themselves in the shrubbery and stealthily came as close to the animals as they could without risking detection. Still crouching, they looked on.

A mixed herd of texins and horses grazed out in the open. Deer and goats browsed among the bushes, while pigs rummaged around in the soil below. Off in the distance, Blake noticed another kind of hoofed beast that he did not recognize. Tall and lanky with a short coat of light brown fur, they each had one large, conspicuous hump in the middle of their backs.

"What are those?" whispered Blake.

"Camels," replied Brillum.

"I've never seen them before."

"They're common enough around here."

"Amazing," said Blake. "They look like huge llamas."

"What are llamas?"

"There are llamas back in Kamis and all over the northern Plains," said Blake. "They have thick wool and can tolerate very cold weather, but they're not much bigger than a deer."

"Doesn't sound much like a camel to me," said Brillum.

"No, but their faces — they both have those big, split lips and that broad, fuzzy nose."

"Maybe they're cousins."

"Maybe so," said Blake, "how strange."

Walking amongst the texins and horses was a group of giant wingless, flightless birds. They had long legs, a long neck, and a mop of brown, shaggy-looking feathers hanging from their bodies. Keeping their tiny heads just above ground level, they fed on leaves, fruits, and insects as they slowly walked along. Lana pointed at them excitedly to get Blake's attention without making too much noise.

"What are those?" she asked, tapping Brillum on the shoulder.

"Those are emu," he said. "They're the biggest birds around."

"They're birds?"

"Of course. Look at the beak. They're usually gentle enough, but don't get them angry or they'll kick your guts out."

"Why would they become angry?" asked Lana.

"We hunt them from time to time. They make a fine meal, but sometimes, instead of trying to run away, they turn around and charge you, so it can be difficult. To be honest, I've never gotten this close to them without spooking them before."

"I've never seen anything like this," Lana whispered excitedly as she stared wide-eyed at the field before her.

The emu interrupted their ceaseless grazing, raised their heads to a height only slightly higher than their domed backs, and looked in the direction of the bushes. All of the humans instantly fell silent and froze to avoid detection. With their keen orange eyes, the birds scanned their environment for the slightest movement. The texins and horses, ever aware of their avian neighbors' activities, also stopped grazing. Relying on their hearing and smell, their ears swiveled and their nostrils twitched, but none of these disparate animals detected anything out of the ordinary. When they were satisfied that they were in no danger, the herds resumed their feeding. The emu returned to their sociable activity of ambling together and plucking plants and bugs from the earth. Brillum and the others decided to leave these creatures to their own affairs. Cautiously, they crept back into the scrub, found the path once more, and continued with their trip heading south.

As the sun climbed higher into the sky, the temperature rose and the humid air became ever stuffier. However, as long as the travelers stayed in the shade of the woods, they remained relatively cool.

Blake took a swig of water from his canteen and wiped the sweat from his brow. "Hot, isn't it?"

"Kind of," said Brillum. "The wet season is hotter."

Blake groaned. He turned to Lana. "How are you doing?"

"I'm having a great time!" she said enthusiastically. "How about you?"

"Oh yes, lots of fun," said Blake sarcastically.

"Oh, don't be such spoilsport."

"What? But I'm just…"

Suddenly, there was a rustling in the brush ahead, just off the path. Brillum, his eyes narrowed, motioned with his arm for the company to stop, and they immediately complied. They looked toward the disturbance and watched the shrubbery jiggle randomly and subtly. With another gesture, Brillum directed his troop to follow him.

A head popped up out of the bush. It was a black bear standing on its hind legs and looking around. It sniffed the air and took in the many strange smells. Then, dropping back to all fours again, it loped of into the woods and out of sight.

"A black bear," said Lana.

"You must have those where you're from, too," said Brillum.

"They were actually quite common. I used to see them walking around in the parks and foraging among the Rubble. I even knew where a few of them hibernated for the winter."

"Really?" Brillum asked. "Did you ever go into one of their dens while it was sleeping?"

"Only by mistake. I ran away because it puffed and charged at me. It didn't really chase me, though. I guess it was just bluffing. It must have been more interested in getting back to sleep than eating me."

"I would be," joked Brillum.

The troop continued its march. At one point, they startled a pair of coyotes standing by the path. Although curious at first, the seasoned coyotes soon ran off, unwilling to allow humans to get too close to them. At last, the travelers came to a fork in the road.

"This is where we part company. My men and I must go this way," said Brillum, pointing to the fork on the right. "Our village is not far from here, to the west. You go that way."

"Thank you for all you've done, and for bringing us this far," said Blake. "Could you tell us where we should go from here?"

"The directions are simple enough," said Brillum, sketching a map of the Warmland in the sand. "Corpus is south of here, like so." Brillum scratched a line through his drawing. "Take this path; it's more direct. You will have to ford several rivers, but at least your trip will be shorter that way, and you will be able to avoid Houston. Keep going until you reach a big Rubbletown. That is Corpus."

"A Rubbletown?" asked Blake. "The Corpushi are not Managers, are they?"

"No, not at all," said Brillum with a smile. "They hunt the hoofed beasts of the southern Great Plains, but they are a sea-going people, too. They occupy the Rubbletown of Corpus as a home for themselves and other creatures, too. Corpus lies about two hundred miles from here."

"Very well, Brillum. Thank you," Blake said, and they shook hands. Blake and Lana exchanged parting words with Beldek and Thomas as well. Then they packed their belongings and, with Rita at their heels, walked the sandy path through the flatwoods once more. They were grinning; they were not home yet, but at least they had finally reached the Warmland.

Chapter 10

When morning came, the sun roused the Kamishi from their slumber. As usual, their campsite was minimal. Winter was nearly here, but the nights felt downright pleasant to Blake's and Lana's northern blood. With no sign of rain, there was little need for shelter, so the couple simply slept out in the open. They lay together, covered up by the same deerskin blanket, while Rita stretched out on her flank nearby. Their leather tote bags of supplies leaned against the base of a tree a short distance away. A small, blackened circle was the only sign that they had lit a fire the night before.

When Blake awoke, there was a refreshing chill in the air. He sat up, stretched, and noticed that Rita was gone. *She must be off wandering again.* Then he looked down at Lana, who was still asleep beside him. *I hate to wake her up.* Blake carefully extricated himself from the blanket, but Lana woke up anyway. Soon, they gathered their belongings and prepared to leave.

When they had finished, Lana glanced at the sun as it hovered above the trees, so warm, radiant, and generous. Blake came to her side, wrapped his arm around her shoulder, and kissed her softly on the cheek. Lana closed her eyes and smiled. She turned to Blake, looked at him tenderly, and kissed his lips. They held one another for a moment, then reluctantly withdrew, their hands lingering on each other's arms. At last, they bent down to collect their things and Blake called for Rita. When the dog appeared, Blake gave her several friendly pats. Then the group was on their way once more.

The flatwoods gave way to rolling hills. Patches of tough, wiry grass were plentiful here. These quaint little plants were a pleasant, yellowish-green in color, and they grew in short, many-bladed clumps. There were fewer saw palmettos here but still plenty of pine trees. Moss hung from their branches in abundance, giving the woods a crowded but serene appearance. The air was thick and stuffy, even in the shade of the trees, but at least it was cooler than being directly under the sun itself.

The travelers walked on all morning, stopping every now and then to nibble on some nuts or berries they found along the way. They rested for a while at midday but did not have lunch, simply because there was not enough to eat. Still hungry, they resumed traveling.

"It's so hot," gasped Blake as he wiped his brow. Lana nodded and hummed her agreement. The couple walked along at an even pace, while Rita trotted ahead of them.

"It's only the middle of the afternoon," said Lana. "Maybe we should heed Brillum's advice and just rest for now."

They soon located a relatively thick pine tree and set their belongings down beside it. Rita lay down on her side, panting, her eyes half-shut. Lana reached into her bag and brought out a drinking flask. Only a small amount of water remained inside, but she shared it with her mate and the dog. Then Lana lay down flat on her back and stretched audibly.

Blake lay down beside her. "Ah, that feels good," he said with a sigh.

The woods were silent except for the whisper of the breeze that blew through the trees and gently rocked their branches. The light scattered as it came down through the moss and the pine needles, throwing sparkling glints of gold here and there. Tranquil colors permeated this place — the cool green of the ubiquitous plants, the warm brown of the earth below. Gently sloping hills lay ahead, carpeted with grass and bathed in the glaring yellow light of the midday sun. Blake and Lana watched the hills as they rested, quietly planning which way they would go.

Just then, the Kamishi heard a twig snap behind them. Rita quickly rotated her ears and turned her head in the direction of the sound, but Blake and Lana only looked at each other. The sound was soon followed by leaves rustling and more twigs snapping on the forest floor. Blake watched Rita's nose twitch as she sniffed. Then he and Lana turned to see the source of commotion for themselves.

A large wild boar came into view, busily foraging among the trees. It had thick, black fur and a conspicuous ridge of hair running down its back. It swept its head back and forth and shoved its long snout into the leaf litter as its rooted around for nuts, tubers, and even small animals to eat. With prominent tusks jutting from the sides of its mouth, this large, rotund, and powerful-looking beast was intimidating.

Blake remained silent and motionless as he observed the animal, but Lana could not tell whether he considered it a threat or not.

"What is it?" she whispered.
"It's a pig," he replied.
"Is it dangerous?"
"Maybe."

Blake rose to his feet as slowly and quietly as he could, but the boar detected him and instantly fled into the brush. Blake took off after it, and Rita immediately followed, leaving Lana still sitting alone on the ground. By the time she stood up, the woods were quiet again. A couple of swinging boughs on a bush were the only sign that anything had just happened.

Lana began tracking the others. She crouched as she looked around and listened, pushing back branches and twigs with her hands to clear a path. She went as fast as she could, but she did not rush; that could lead to careless, dangerous mistakes. She walked this way and that, looking for some kind of sign in the soil, the litter, or the plants that someone or something had recently passed through. She found a few clues here and there, but nothing certain.

Lana heard a shrill, ear-piercing squeal coming from some distance away in the thick foliage. Then she heard it again when she turned to face it. She ran amid the trees and vines, jumping and ducking every now and then to avoid them. At last, she arrived at a clearing in the woods.

There, she saw Rita doing battle with the boar.

The pig confronted Rita, brandishing its fearsome tusks and refusing to back down. The upper pair was more curved and the lower pair was longer, but both were razor sharp. The boar kept its mouth slightly open. This exposed the lower tusks enabled them to lash out at any time. Whenever Rita came close to the pig, it viciously swiped at her and swung its head violently from side to side.

Rita managed to avoid these blows. She bobbed, weaved, and barked, apparently enjoying the fight as though it were some kind of game. She ran around the pig, darting in and out, with just one goal in mind — to bite the back of the pig's neck. If she could just grab hold of it and hang on, she would be able to control her prey and gain a measure of safety from those cruel tusks. Paradoxically, in order to be safe from them she had to get past them, which was exceedingly dangerous and difficult.

Lana noticed Blake out of the corner of her eye. He stood off to one side of the clearing and watched the battle between his dog and the boar. His knife was drawn at the ready in his hands, but he did not advance yet.

Rita went in for another attack. She growled and lunged at the boar's neck once again. The boar squealed in fright.

This was the sound Lana had heard. A chill ran up her spine.

The boar grunted angrily and charged. It slammed into Rita, knocked her off her feet, and barreled under her as she rolled over its back. The boar made an about-face and charged again, but Rita stepped aside and evaded the attack.

Now she was on the offensive again. She leaped forward over the pig's head and clamped down on the nape of its neck. This time, it was the pig's turn to retreat. Rita held on. The clash between them slowed as Rita shifted from snapping at her foe to grappling with it. She brought her flank next to the boar's left side. Then through shear brute strength, she held the boar steady.

The boar tried to wriggle free and slash with its tusks, but it could no longer outmaneuver the dog. The boar stopped struggling.

Blake seized this chance to strike. He moved in closer, slightly behind and to the right of the boar, opposite Rita. He picked up the boar by one of the back legs until the hindquarters were clear of the ground. Then he stabbed his knife directly behind the boar's shoulder blade and drove it deep into the middle of the chest. The pig screamed in agony and thrashed about. Blake removed the knife and struck again, this time at the throat. This technique was the fastest and most humane way to kill an animal — or a human — that Blake knew.

Blood flowed freely now from both wounds. The pig continued to struggle for a moment more, but as it lost its energy, its cries and movements subsided. It collapsed on the ground. A moment later, it was dead.

When Lana saw that it was safe, she came forward. Blake attended to his dog. He looked Rita over for injuries and was glad to find none.

"Is she all right?" asked Lana.

"She's fine," said Blake. "This used to be easier back when both Saamu and Rita were on the pig and Manosh and I could work on killing it together, but I think we did pretty well today."

Blake and Lana stared at the carcass of the large boar.

"Is it dead?" she asked.

"Yes, it went down fast. I aimed for its heart, and it looks like I hit it. Anyway, we'll have food for several days now. Come." Blake took Lana by the hand. Together they kneeled beside the dead pig, bowed their heads, and prayed. When they were done, they rose to their feet once more.

"Will you help me butcher this, Lana?" asked Blake.

"Of course. Let's get started."

Together, they quickly carved the pig for its meat, bones, and hide. Then they built a fire and set to grilling and smoking all of the edible parts. Lana worked on cleaning and drying the pelt for materials, while Blake worked on preparing all the food. However, he also removed the tusks for himself as souvenirs and mementos of his achievement. Rita, as a reward for her efforts, got an entire hind leg all to herself, which she immediately, zealously began to consume. The Kamishi would now be well supplied for weeks. They would have plenty of cooked meat to eat and plenty of dried meat for later. The kill provided an abundance of fabric for making garments, and they now had more bones, teeth, and ivory than they could use.

Chapter 11

Blake, Lana, and Rita spent several days at their campsite on the edge of the woods. They stayed until they finished all of their grilled meat, saving their cache of dried meat for their journey. They felt full and content.

They sat relaxing by the fire one evening. Rita was avidly gnawing on a shank bone.

"We should leave tomorrow," said Blake.

"Why?" asked Lana. "Why can't we stay here?"

"We have," said Blake.

"No, I mean for longer."

"How long?"

"I don't know," said Lana. "Maybe we could settle here."

"Here?" asked Blake, taken aback. "Are you crazy?"

"Why not? It's beautiful here."

"So what? Where's the water? We haven't seen a pond or river in weeks. Besides, don't you remember what Tegg told us? It's not safe to settle down just the two of us. Some tribe might come through and wipe us out if we did. We have to follow Tegg's advice; we have to find Corpus."

"That's hundreds of miles away!"

"That doesn't matter. We have to keep going."

"We've reached the Warmland, Blake. We've made it. Why do we have to keep going?"

"Because..." said Blake, avoiding eye contact. He clenched and unclenched his fists, took a deep breath, and exhaled noticeably through his nostrils. "It's for Manosh."

Lana pursed her lips and said nothing.

"Don't you see, Lana? He would never have left Kamis if it weren't for me. I'm the one who told him to come to the Warmland in the first place. If it hadn't been for me ... he might still be alive." Blake stared at the ground.

Lana inched closer to him. "No, Blake," she said. Blake looked up at her. "It's not your fault."

"Yes it is," he mumbled.

"No, it isn't. What happened to Manosh was a tragedy, but it was nobody's fault."

"I should've done something. I should've…"

"No!" exclaimed Lana. "They were lions, Blake! And they would've killed you, me, and Rita, too, if they had the chance. We're lucky to be sitting here at all."

Blake tossed a woodchip into the fire.

"You did what you had to do. In fact, you did what you did to save *my* life, Blake. If you hadn't been there for me, then you would be sitting here talking with Manosh about how *I* died instead."

"I guess I'm just bad luck," said Blake.

"What?"

"Well, I talked you into coming here, too, didn't I? If it hadn't been for me, you wouldn't have been attacked by lions, either."

"Are you kidding?" asked Lana, raising her voice and squinting in annoyance.

"No."

"This is ridiculous," Lana said as she rolled her eyes and looked away. She threw her hands up and let them fall to her thighs with a slap. "You feel guilty for bringing me here?"

"Yes," said Blake.

"Well, don't! Don't you see? You and Manosh saved me." Lana had become impatient with Blake, but her tone softened again. "I was living in that Rubbletown all alone for two years when you two came along. I was *happy* when you asked me to join you, and after all we've been through, I'm *still* happy to be with you."

Blake reached out and took hold of Lana's hand. Tenderly, she held his hand in return.

"I bet Manosh was happy to go with you, too," she said.

"I don't know," said Blake. "He didn't really want to go. He wanted to stay behind."

"Well, from what you've told me, he probably wasn't thinking straight. You probably helped him do the right thing."

"How?"

"Didn't you tell me that your entire village was destroyed?" asked Lana. "Everyone except for you, Manosh, and the dogs was killed, right?" Blake nodded. "Then why would Manosh want to stay?"

"He wanted revenge. He wanted to stay behind and kill as many Ravashi warriors as he could before they killed him. We did take our revenge on a few soldiers, but then we took the dogs and ran away."

"You did the right thing, Blake."

"I did?"

"Of course," said Lana affectionately. "Manosh was angry, and so were you. Anyone would be. But you had the good sense to leave that tragic place behind and keep going."

Blake looked down again. "If it hadn't been for me, Saamu would not have been killed by the Podeshi, either."

"That's right, Blake, because he would've been killed by the Ravashi instead! Don't you see? If it weren't for you, Manosh and Saamu would've died in Kamis, and I'd still be stuck in that Rubbletown. You have nothing to feel bad about. You've done nothing but try to help us. Things are going to go wrong, Blake, but that's not your fault. You want to live, and you've given the rest of us a new chance at life, too. You haven't done anything wrong. Not to Manosh, not to Saamu, and not to me. You have no reason to feel guilty, Blake. You should only feel proud of what you've done and what you're trying to do." Lana looked directly into Blake's eyes. "I know I do."

"Thank you," said Blake, "but I failed Manosh."

"You did everything you could."

"It wasn't enough."

"Then forgive yourself," said Lana.

"Someday I will, but only if I succeed in finding us a new home. I have to get us to Corpus, Lana. I failed Manosh, but I can't fail you. Do you understand?"

"I do, and I know you're doing all you can so we make it."

"Then you can see why trying to settle here is not good enough. This place can't support us, Lana. We can't build a life here. There's no future here for us. We have to keep going until we find a new tribe. If we don't, we're finished. I believe the Corpushi could be the tribe we need to help us start again."

"What if they're not?" asked Lana.

"Then just by going there, we will see new things and meet new people. We will learn what we need to learn about the Warmland to survive here."

"We already know the Tulsashi and the Dallashi," said Lana.

"But Tegg said that his people would not accept us, and we don't know whether Brillum's people would, either. Zaaru and the Corpushi are our best hope right now, so we have to find them."

"The way there is dangerous," said Lana.

"That's true," said Blake, "but it would be more dangerous to stay here, not knowing what else is out there."

Lana looked at Blake, smirked, and shook her head. "You're a stubborn man, Blake, but you're smart, and you have courage, too." She paused to think. "All right, you've convinced me. We'll leave tomorrow morning."

"I'm glad to hear that. You'll see. We're doing the right thing."

"I know," said Lana. "I believe you."

Chapter 12

The Kamishi continued along the edge of the wood, where the shady trees met the grass-covered hills. When they found another path, they followed it. It was not clear who or what had made it, but whatever its origin, it was useful. They walked on together in silence.

Shadows grew longer as the afternoon light turned from brass to gold. A pleasant breeze swept along the forest's edge, cooling the travelers and lifting their spirits.

As dusk approached, an enormous flock of starlings rose into the evening sky. Flying above the tree line, the small dark birds congregated by the millions in search of food. They formed a cloud that expanded and contracted, forming strange bands, orbs, and crescents as they flitted about. The sounds of their beating wings and shrill calls carried through the air.

The Kamishi decided to stop for the night. Blake found a suitable spot at the foot of a large tree overlooking the grassy hills.

"How about here, Lana?" asked Blake.

"Seems fine to me," she said. She plopped down by the tree, leaned against it, and closed her eyes. Blake sat down beside her and propped his arm on one knee. He leaned in close to her.

"Are you tired?" he asked.

"Yeah," she said.

"How tired?"

"Really tired," she said. "I couldn't possibly stay awake for another minute."

"Not even one more minute?" asked Blake, a wry grin on his face.

Lana smiled but did not open her eyes. "No, not even one more minute."

"Not even half a minute?" he asked, whispering directly in her ear.

"No," creaked Lana, stifling a laugh, "not even half a minute."

"Are you sure?" Blake brushed his lips against Lana's cheek and kissed her lightly. Then he moved in front of her and rubbed his nose against hers.

"Well," said Lana. Her splendidly deep, dark eyes opened and looked directly into Blake's. "Actually … I'm not really that sure after all."

Blake caressed Lana's upper arms and kissed her full lips. She felt warmth course through her body and a tingle run up her spine.

"So how long do you think you can stay awake then?" asked Blake between kisses.

"We'll see, all right, Blake?"

Blake hummed contentedly. "Mmm … I love it when you say my name."

"You say my name now," pleaded Lana.

"Lana," said Blake softly.

"Say it again."

"Lana … Lana," he breathed.

"Oh, Blake," she sighed as passion welled up inside her. Lana moved away from the tree and lay down on the grass with Blake hovering over her. He parted his lips and pressed them against hers. Lana delighted in feeling the moisture of his mouth, and the warmth of his breath. She slipped her tongue between his lips and met with his. Their mouths caressed one another as they moved slowly, powerfully from side to side.

Blake supported himself on his knees and one muscular arm, and ran his palm over Lana's cheek. He was fascinated by how smooth and soft it felt. He ran his fingers through her long, black hair, and brought his hand around behind her head. Then he rested her neck in the crook of his arm and brought his other arm underneath her back. He embraced her and gave her lips one more kiss before moving down her face to her neck, tugging on her as she moaned softly. Enthralled with Lana's body, he firmly kissed the angle of her jaw, tugged on her bronze skin, and delighted in the sounds that escaped from her lips. Then he did the same thing to her other side, igniting Lana like a flame.

Now it was Lana's turn to explore Blake's body. She exerted some pressure to roll him onto his back and got on top of him. Blake and Lana looked into each other's eyes, and all reservation left them; they wanted each other. Quickly but adeptly, Lana removed Blake's clothing and began kissing and rubbing him all over his chest and belly. Then, as if in one smooth motion, she disrobed.

Blake's eyes took in the glorious sight of Lana's full breasts. He reached up, briefly cupped them, and slid his palms over their surface. Lana closed her eyes and moaned. She arched her back and tilted her head to let her long hair hang down like a cape. Then Blake pulled her toward him and embraced her naked body against his. He rubbed his hands all over her back, clutching her all the while.

"Oh, Blake," she cried. "Blake, I want you now." They kissed each other wildly, and Blake rolled Lana onto her back once more. Still holding each other tightly, they pressed their cheeks together and then their foreheads, not daring to separate for even a moment. As their passion grew, they could no longer control themselves. At last, they gave in to their desire, and made love.

Chapter 13

The following morning, Rita eagerly woke up Lana and Blake with her wet nose and tongue. The dog had had a restful night, and now, eager to find food and start traveling again, she was busy at trying to rouse her masters.

"All right, Rita, all right," giggled Lana. "We're up, we're up. Just give us a minute." Lana sat up and stretched. She leaned over to Blake, kissed him on the cheek, and hugged him. "Wake up, Blake. Time to get up."

Blake slowly came back to life. His eyes were still shut, but he smiled broadly when he felt Lana beside him. He hugged her back and kissed her lips.

"Ah," he said. "Good morning."

"Morning," said Lana. "Did you sleep well?"

"Very. Say, how late is it, anyway?"

"Oh, the sun's only just come up." They stretched for a while. It took Blake and Lana a few minutes to shake off their grogginess, but they soon became active again.

"What can we eat around here?" asked Lana.

"We've still got lots of dried pig meat."

"I don't want to go through that stuff too fast. We need to make it last."

"That's true," said Blake. "Well, there don't seem to be many berries left on the bushes, but I'm sure we can find something."

"Like what?"

"Oh, I don't know. We'll see, I guess." Blake turned to his dog. "Come on, Girl. Come on!" he said enthusiastically. Knowing that a hunt was afoot, Rita began bounding back and forth excitedly. "We'll be back soon, Lana. Would you see if you can find a few things, too?"

"Sure," said Lana. Blake gave her a quick kiss and left, taking Rita with him. Lana looked around for a fruiting plant. She wandered away from the campsite and found a bush with a few berries still on it. She picked every last one of them and deposited them in her small wicker basket, but this was not very much. She looked around the bases of trees and collected some nuts, but this was still not enough. At last, she decided to look for underground tubers. She ducked down beneath a few choice shrubs and scraped away the soil with her knife. There, she found several potato-like structures growing a few inches beneath the surface. She cut them out and soon filled her basket with these starchy plants. Then she headed back to camp.

Meanwhile, Blake and Rita searched for prey. They heard rustling in the leaves, and Rita sprang toward the sound. A small animal darted back and forth, and Rita did her best to catch it by sticking her muzzle under the leaf litter and snapping at it every now and again. The creature darted under a bush. Rita shoved her head in after it, but it escaped out the other side. Rita noticed this, so she circled the bush and continued her pursuit.

Blake stayed a short distance behind and tried to determine what kind of animal they were dealing with. The creature was agile and quick, so he concluded it was some kind of small mammal. Blake jogged after his dog and her prey as they moved off into the distance. He knew that he could not keep up with them, but he wanted at least to keep track of them.

The animal moved in a zigzag pattern, successfully avoiding the powerful jaws of the dog. It bolted in another direction, but Rita anticipated the move and snapped it up. When she lifted her head, Blake saw that she held a sizable squirming rodent between her teeth.

"Good job, Rita!" exclaimed Blake as he caught up with her. The dog held her head high and her wagging tail low as she looked up at her master. She was proud of her catch, but she knew that it could still escape unless she or Blake disabled or killed it.

Blake studied the animal as it struggled in vain to escape Rita's firm grip. It was large for a rodent, with thick brown fur and a long, round tail. It had small ears, numerous whiskers, and big, orange-colored incisor teeth. It was clearly a rodent, but Blake had no idea what kind.

"Finish it, Rita," he said. The dog was happy to comply, and she vigorously shook her head back and forth. This maneuver often killed her prey, but today it only stunned it. The disoriented rodent fell limp in Rita's mouth.

Rita let the animal drop to the ground, and Blake picked it up to examine it. It was still alive, but hyperventilating and apparently terribly frightened. Blake wanted to be as humane as possible, so he grabbed the rodent by its long, rope-like tail, walked toward a large tree, and quickly thrashed its head against the bole, instantly breaking the neck. With a few brief twitches, the animal died quickly.

"Good job, Rita. Good girl," said Blake, patting the dog's head. Rita lowered her ears and tail, and closed her eyes. She appreciated the praise, but she knew that she would soon be getting a meal as well.

Blake sat down on the ground and inspected the rodent. He was certain that he had never seen this particular type before, although it did remind him of the muskrats and beavers he used to see back in Kamis. The feet in particular caught his eye. All four were clawed, but the hind feet sported prominent webbing. *Ah ha! With these webbed feet, this thing must be aquatic. It's odd finding an aquatic animal out here in the woods like this, though. Unless ... we must be near water!*

"Come on, Rita!" cried Blake, and he and his dog enthusiastically ran back to their campsite to find Lana. When they arrived, Blake held his prize high for Lana to see.

"Oh my!" she said. "What is that?"

"Rita found it near some bushes. I don't know what it is, but it looks good. We'll make a nice meal out of it. Here, Lana, look at this," said Blake as he sat down next to her. "Look at its feet. They've got webbing on them."

"Kind of like a frog."

"Exactly. We caught it on dry land, but it must be a good swimmer. We can't be far from water now."

"Oh, good," said Lana. "I was hoping to find someplace where we could refill our canteens."

"We probably will soon, and we should stay there for a while; get some water, make some tools, find some more food. Speaking of food, what did you find?"

"Look over here," said Lana, pointing to her sizable pile of berries, nuts, and tubers. "I didn't have to go very far to find them, either. They'll go well with ... well, whatever that thing is."

Blake's face assumed an inquisitive expression. "Do you still have any of those fire sticks we found back in that Rubbletown?"

"Sure, I still have a few packages."

"Good. Go find some branches to make a spit. I'll get the meat ready."

"Okay," said Lana, and off she went.

Blake took a small stone knife from his cloak and made a slit up the rodent's belly. Then he carefully cut away the hide and set it aside to be cleaned and dried later. He used his knife to separate and remove the innards from the body. Then he poured a small amount of water from his canteen over them and washed away the blood and soil.

Lana returned with some logs, and then she and Blake set up a spit to roast their catch. Rita watched from a short distance away. The dog waited as patiently as she could, but her fidgeting hindquarters, salivating mouth, and frequent lip-licking betrayed her anticipation. Blake used some nearby wood to dig out a shallow fire pit. Then he lowered the logs into place and arranged them into a pyramid for burning.

"Go ahead, Lana. Try and light it," he said.

Lana reached into her bag and brought out an old matchbook from the small collection she kept there. Manosh had discovered these relics from the Old Days in an ancient, buried store several weeks earlier; now it seemed like years had passed since then. Lana removed a single match and scratched it across the book's rough surface. After several tries, the fire stick lit up. Lana slowly brought it toward the fire pit and set it down atop the wooden pyramid. The fire quickly grew and it soon burned steadily.

Blake sharpened the longest stick Lana had brought, impaled the dead animal lengthwise, and left it close to the end of the stick. He placed the contraption on the supporting posts and suspended it over the growing fire. Then he coiled the animal's entrails around the bare part of the stick and tied the ends together to secure them in place. Now the meat was ready for broiling.

"Would you mind watching the food while I go look for some materials to make tools with?"

"Sure, go ahead," said Lana.

"Okay, I'll be right back." Blake got up and disappeared among the bushes.

Lana watched him as we wandered off, admiring him from behind: his tall stature, his noble posture, and his subtly powerful build. She smiled to herself as she thought about how lucky she was to have him. For a fleeting moment, the thought occurred to her that Blake could use this opportunity to run off and leave her behind. She briefly felt anxious, but then she immediately felt ashamed for even considering such a thing. She knew he would return at least for Rita. Moreover, Lana knew that he loved her and would not leave her behind, either.

I must have trouble with trusting people, thought Lana.

For a moment, Lana puzzled over why that might be. Ever since her family had died and the attacks from the gang in the Rubbletown had begun, her faith in humanity and her belief in love had been shaken to the core. Lana's ability to trust anyone had been completely eroded. However, when she befriended Blake, Manosh, and the dogs, she felt tenderness return to her heart. Lana felt alive once more, and for that she was grateful.

Now, their friend Manosh and their dog Saamu were dead, leaving Blake and Rita as Lana's only remaining family. Still, that spark of life had returned, and it burned deep inside Lana once more; she had someone she could trust again. Blake and Rita were her world now, and she trusted them with her life. Lana wrapped her arms around her knees and leaned back, smiling to herself. She watched the fire dance and jump, and occasionally she reached for the spit and rotated the meat so that it would cook evenly.

Blake was having difficulty finding enough stones for tool-making. The few he did find were small or brittle. There were also artificial rocks left over from the Old Days, known as Cement, but these were brittle, too. Blake decided to make his new projectile weapons entirely out of sharpened wood, rather than attaching spearheads or arrowheads of hewn stone to them. So, he cut some fresh, suitably sized sticks off a few trees and headed back to camp.

When he stepped through the bushes, he saw Lana attending to the food. It warmed his heart to see her there, and he was in awe at how such a mundane moment as this could seem so profound to him. Here was his woman, his mate. Though not his wife yet, he knew that she was his, and he hers. Seeing her at his hearth like this, he felt a new kind of contentment unlike any he had known before.

Lana saw him out of the corner of her eye. "What are you smiling about?" she asked.

"You," he said as he bent over and kissed her on the lips, "I'm smiling because you're here."

Lana beamed. "You're sweet," she said as Blake sat down. "Did you find what you were looking for?"

"Unfortunately, no. There are practically no good stones here at all." He took out a handful of the stones he collected. "See the darker ones? We can use those, but the rest — the lighter colored ones — are not as good. I thought I'd bring them along anyway just in case we needed them later. For now, we can carve our new spears out of wood. I found these branches here; they should do fine. We might have to sharpen or replace them more often than stone tips, but we'll be all right." Lana nodded her understanding. Blake sat down next to her, and together they watched over their food.

When the meat was ready, Blake gave Rita all the entrails, and she quickly devoured them. However, he split the rest of the rodent down the middle, gave half of it to Lana, and kept half for himself. Then the two of them sat down and ate their breakfast at a leisurely pace. Rita finished her share long before they finished theirs. Then she took up a position directly in front of the people and patiently waited for any more meat they might throw her way. As it turned out, the rodent provided more food than either Blake or Lana could finish, so they tossed their leftovers to Rita. Again, she bolted down her portion hungrily, and soon the meal was done.

The Kamishi spent the rest of the day at the same site, grateful for the chance to rest for a while. Blake taught Lana how to make spears from the sticks he had cut down — they were still green inside — and he showed her how to sharpen their tips by whittling away at them with a knife. Then it was time to straighten the shafts. Blake was missing some of the tools he normally used for this task, and he apologized to Lana.

"You have to use heat," he explained. "Normally I would use a heated stone or an arrow wrench, which is a bone with a hole in it, to straighten my arrows. Unfortunately, I haven't had anything like that since Kamis, so we'll have to do the next best thing. We have to lay these arrows down on a flat surface and rub their curved parts with another piece of wood. When they get hot, we can straighten them out. It's really not the best way, but it will have to do for now."

Blake got to work and slowly straightened out one stick after another. Lana joined in and soon they had a bundle of sharpened, straightened sticks. But they were not arrows yet.

"We still have at least one more thing to do: we have to tie them up together and leave them out to dry."

"For how long?" asked Lana.

"Oh, it depends. They dry faster when it's hot out, but they dry more slowly when it's humid. Here, I'd give them at least a full day. Then when they're dry, it's best to put fletching on them."

"What's fletching?"

"Feathers, usually. You attach about three of them to the back of the arrow to help it fly straight." Blake sighed. "Unfortunately, we don't have any feathers either, so we'll just have to make do without. I'm really sorry, Lana. I'm not teaching you the right way to make arrows."

"It's all right, Blake," said Lana. "I understand. I know we don't have the best materials right now, but I get the idea, and I'll know what to do later when we do." She smiled and Blake relaxed.

"We have to let them dry, and not too fast, either, or else they might warp. Let's just bundle them and put them in a nice, warm, dry spot. Then we can come back tomorrow morning and see if they're ready, all right?" The two of them bound the sticks up and put them in a secluded space, away from direct sunlight, and left them alone.

Blake and Lana found a place in the shade where they could rest and make themselves comfortable, while Rita lay down beside them. As they reclined, they discussed their travel plans.

"We're running out of water, Blake. When are we going to get some more?"

"Soon, I think. That aquatic rodent we caught couldn't be far from water. I bet we'll come across some soon."

"I hope you're right. Our canteens are low."

"I know, but don't worry. Even if we do run out, there's plenty of vines around here, and we can squeeze water from them."

"Really? I didn't know that."

"Of course. It just takes a little work, that's all. Anyway, we probably won't need to. We should find some water tomorrow."

"I just hope it's clean water," said Lana. "We could get awfully sick from dirty water."

"We could filter it through our clothing to get rid of the grit and dirt and then just boil it. Of course, we don't have any dishes to boil it in, but we could make some. Don't worry. We'll be fine."

Blake's calm confidence and expertise helped ease Lana's mind. He had fears and vulnerabilities, too, but his attitude to adversity gave him strength. Blake was not cocky. He admitted his limitations, either to others or inwardly to himself, and this inspired trust in him. There was no pretense of heroism, only optimism and dedication. Lana was still concerned about the group's welfare, but her belief that they would be all right was growing.

Chapter 14

The group traveled through the woods for several days until one morning, they realized that the trees were getting sparser and the bushes denser. The earth was more exposed to sunshine here, and grasses and flowers could be found in abundance. The sand was white, fine, and as dry as could be, but the air remained humid. Summer had come and gone, and winter had already arrived in the North. But here in the Warmland, the weather was as pleasant as a northern autumn day.

Blake and Lana trekked through the bush together, while Rita alternated between staying close to them and venturing off to explore on her own, although she never strayed far. Blake and Lana soon noticed the diversity of plant life. There were several kinds of pine and oak trees, a variety of shrubs, and many flowers growing right at ground level.

"I think we may have an easier time finding something to eat around here," said Lana. Blake nodded in agreement. That afternoon, they stopped to rest at a nice, shady spot under an ancient oak tree. Blake and Lana found some large seeds and nuts, which they devoured hungrily and washed down with water. After a nap, they were on the road again.

That evening they walked along a well worn path, but it was not at all clear who or what had worn it down or used it recently. They came across a large patch of palm trees, which grew taller than saw palmettos and had fan-like fronds. Low-lying, thorny bushes surrounded the palm trees. The branches of these bushes were thin but sturdy, and their bark was gray and brown. Their leaves were dark green and waxy. Lana and Blake stopped to inspect these plants. They took note of their appearance and texture, and looked them over for fruits, but found none. Rita sniffed around the wide, fibrous bases of the trees. She did not find anything to eat, either, but she did discover a wide variety of fascinating scents from other animals that had been there before her.

Suddenly, there was a scuffling deep within the underbrush. Something was rummaging around, loudly snapping twigs and dry leaves as it moved. This startled Blake, Lana, and Rita, all of whom snapped to attention and looked in the direction of the sound. Blake protectively swept Lana backward and stepped in front of her, although he had no idea what to expect himself. Rita's ears stood erect and her nose twitched as she tried to learn as much as she could about the disturbance without being able to see it.

The noise grew louder as whatever made it crashed through the underbrush toward the Kamishi. Judging by its sound, the path it followed was nearly straight, although it seemed to weave slightly from side to side. Blake froze and clutched his spear tightly. His eyes grew wide and he held his breath. His heart pounded forcefully within his chest in anticipation of the monster he was about to face.

To his surprise, a small rotund animal erupted from the bushes and zipped past him to the left. Then a second, identical animal ran past him on the right. Blake and the others swiveled in place to watch these strange creatures as one of them continued to chase the other.

Their color was a dark yellowish-gray, and they had sparse, course hairs all over their bodies. Each had small, black eyes; a long head with a sharp snout; and large, pointed ears. Their most distinctive feature, however, was their coat of armor, made from small, tightly woven nodules. A large, round shield covered the forequarters, another covered the hindquarters, and nine narrow, interlocking, rigid rings surrounded the mid-section in between. Additional rings encircled the long, thick tail. The broad feet, with their splayed toes and prominent claws, also bore scaly armor. There was even a protective cap on the head; only the ears seemed unprotected.

Rita was fascinated by these two crazed animals, but they remained in the open for only a moment before diving back into the brush once again. Then they were gone. It took Blake and Lana a moment to overcome their shock.

"What were those?" asked Lana.

"I have no idea," replied Blake. "I'm just glad they're small." Then the travelers continued their hike through the woods.

છે ભ

The next day, the path that Blake, Lana, and Rita had been following became less and less clear, and they soon found themselves walking between shrubs once more. Eventually, they emerged from the woods and roamed over hills covered in tall, chartreuse grass. The day grew hotter as the sun rose higher in the sky. A vigorous breeze blew, but it, too, was hot. Exhausted, depleted, and thirsty, the travelers found some shade and rested. Their canteens were empty, so Blake turned to the only source of moisture available — vines. He located a creeper on a tree and cut it into several long segments. Lana watched him with great interest. She had never learned any special techniques for obtaining water in her old Rubbletown because there had never been the need, but she was eager to learn from Blake now. Blake sliced the vine segments open and patiently squeezed them with his powerful hands. In this way, he slowly drained enough water out of them to fill one wooden bowl. Blake handed the bowl to Lana and let her drink first. Then he poured some of the clear liquid into a second bowl for Rita, who lapped it up greedily. Finally, he finished what remained of the juice himself. It was warm and tasted somewhat sour and starchy, but it was good. Then, weary from the midday heat, the Kamishi slept for about two hours. The weather was bearable when they awoke later that afternoon, and they set off once more.

That evening the air cooled off. That was a welcome change for the travelers. Blake and Lana walked hand in hand and closer together for warmth. When the sun began to set, they sat down atop a hill, and Rita lay down right next to them. They watched the sun sink into the horizon as a breeze brushed past them. Blake put his arm around Lana, who leaned into him and rubbed against him. They watched the light gradually fade and the colors of the sky change from blue to violet. The scant clouds that lingered in the west glowed with the reflected rays of the sun, and their brilliant gold hue turned to a vivid pink. Then, they went gray as the sun began to disappear.

"How far do you think we went today?" asked Blake.

"Oh, I don't know," said Lana. "Hard to say. We must have come more than thirty miles since this morning."

"Wow," said Blake. "Now I know I'm tired."

"Me too. I can't wait to go to sleep, but there's no real cover anywhere around here."

"I guess this place is as good as any then."

"I suppose," said Lana. The two of them lay down on the cool, soft sand and cuddled together.

Then Blake turned to his mate. "Lana?"

"Yes?" she said.

"I want to tell you something."

"All right."

"I love you," Blake said.

Lana smiled broadly. "I know you do. I love you, too," she replied.

"Yeah, but…"

Lana giggled. "What is it with you tonight?"

"I want to tell you something."

"I know," she giggled again. "Now what is it?"

"Well, it's just that…" Blake hugged Lana tightly and kissed her as he held her in his arms. "I'm glad you're a part of my life."

"Oh, Blake," she said, fawning over him. "I'm glad you're a part of mine, too."

"Really?"

"If it weren't for you, I'd still be back in that Rubbletown all by myself, lonely and afraid. Ever since I met you, I've seen so many wonderful things and met so many interesting people. There's not a day goes by that I'm not thankful you found me."

"For now…"

"What do you mean?"

"Well, I'm just worried. I mean, here we are. We've come all this way, and for what? What if we don't find a home here? Even worse, what if something happens to us? What if we're killed?"

"Blake, we both knew that we were taking a chance when we left our homes to come down here, but it was a chance worth taking. Even if we don't find what we came here for, it was worth it just to do what we've done!"

"I think so, too, but…"

"What?"

"If something happened to you, I just couldn't forgive myself."

"What? But everything is going just fine."

"Well, look at what happened to Manosh."

"Oh, I see," said Lana. "Now I see what's going through your mind. You feel responsible for Manosh's death, don't you?"

"In a way. He would never have come down here if it weren't for me. He would still be alive if it weren't for me."

"Blake, the two of you were fugitives. You were the last of your tribe, and you had to stick together."

"I know, but if I hadn't insisted that we migrate to the Warmland, he might still be alive."

"He might, or he might not. If you two had stayed in the northern Great Plains, the Ravashi might have found you and killed you, too."

"Perhaps…"

"You gave him so much, Blake. You gave him friendship, and you gave him something to look forward to. No Blake, blame the lions for what happened to Manosh, if you want, but don't blame yourself."

"What if you die, too? Then that would be two people who died in a land far away from their home because of me."

"We don't have a new home yet, Blake, but we will soon. Don't worry. Everything is going to be just fine." Lana stroked Blake's shoulder soothingly and kissed him on the forehead. Blake was calm and quiet, for his fears were assuaged.

"I'm glad you're safe," he finally said.

"So am I!" said Lana with a chuckle. They hugged one another tightly and then Blake spoke once more.

"Lana, I want you to know that I've never loved anyone the way I love you. Never have I met anyone as gentle or as loving as you are. I've always wanted to meet a woman just like you. You are smart and caring, and you are so beautiful. I want to spend the rest of my life with you."

"Oh, Blake. I want nothing more than to spend the rest of my life with you, too."

"Then, Lana let me ask you this: Will you marry me?"

Lana's eyes widened, and Blake could see them sparkling in the pale twilight. Her jaw dropped and she covered her mouth with her hands as tears welled up in her eyes. Blake heard a small squeak come from her. Then she hugged Blake tightly and refused to let go.

Blake embraced her and, smiling faintly said, "Does that mean you will?"

"Yes!" she cried. "Yes, I will! Oh, Blake!" Then she gave him a long, spirited kiss on the lips.

"I love you, too, Lana. I love you so much. I don't know how I ever made it without you in my life." His eyes were now watering as well, and he felt a catch in his throat. "You are the woman I've always wanted to be with. I wish I could tell you how much I love you."

"There's no need," said Lana, her voice cracking as well, "because I love you just as much." They maintained their embrace, and then rolled onto their backs and watched the wispy clouds above floating by.

"So when do you want to get married?"

"As soon as possible," Lana said, grinning broadly.

"When do you think that will be?"

"Well, naturally we will need a tribal official to perform the ceremony, and witnesses. Since neither of us knows anyone around here, at least not yet, I guess I'm not sure when that will be. I'm sure once we find a new home, then we'll find someone who'll marry us. Don't you think so?"

"That sounds fine to me."

"Oh, this is so exciting, isn't it?"

"More than I can say."

They stared at the darkening heavens as the stars began to emerge, one after another until the sky was filled with them. They talked about what they had seen and about their concerns with what was yet to come. Then, after a while, when they could stave off their weariness no longer, they kissed one another good night, curled up together, and fell fast asleep.

Chapter 15

One day, Blake, Lana, and Rita come across the Ruins of a town from the Old Days, where ancient structures still recognizable as houses protruded from the soil. The wood had vanished long ago, but some of the brick, concrete, plastic, and even metal had survived. The Kamishi, eager for something useful, scoured the place, but they did not find much. What little remained of these houses was open and bare, giving access to the elements and accelerating the return of material to the Earth. Nevertheless, Blake and Lana found several knives that were rusty but fairly sharp, as well as some white plastic bowls, still smooth and in good condition. They also found shiny trinkets, metallic jewelry, and colorful gems in an assortment of sizes.

"These could come in handy for trading," said Lana, squirreling the goods away in her leather satchel.

The two of them searched long and hard for fire sticks, but found none, and neither they nor Rita could find any food. Lana and Blake considered staying here overnight to take shelter under a low, sturdy shack. But in the end, they wanted to find Corpus more than they needed to rest, and decided to continue on their journey.

The Kamishi passed through endless sandy fields. They walked amid numerous, tall palm trees, which were home to a wide variety of colorful birds. Their giant, noisy flocks filled the sky as they flew from roost to roost in search of fruit.

One evening the group reached a broad river and paused to gain their bearings. Luscious plants covered the banks, and the rich odor of the water and its denizens filled the air. Fish rose to the surface every once in a while, but it was impossible to see beneath the murky surface.

Insects swarmed here. They buzzed directly over the water, cavorted in clouds above the ground, and raced about among the trees. A multitude of mosquitoes and sand flies thrived here, eager to torment any animal that happened along. A large population of dragonflies followed the biting insects to make a meal of them in turn. Numerous female insects tickled the surface of the water with the tips of their abdomens, laying their precious eggs. It was at this time that the fish took advantage of their proximity to devour them.

The travelers were utterly miserable, as swarms of gnats and mosquitoes tormented them. They constantly hit themselves in a vain attempt to rid themselves of the blood-sucking hoard. Poor Rita held her head low as she flicked her ears spasmodically whenever an insect attacked her. The mosquitoes were unbearable. They crowded around the traveler's faces, and like tiny suicidal warriors, they would enter their ears, nose, mouth, and eyes, only to be instantly squashed by a frenzied hand or finger. Each time a mosquito buzzed in Blake's ear, he went mad with irritation and slapped at it furiously, occasionally even hurting himself.

"Stop doing that, Blake!" said Lana. "You're making me nervous."

"I can't stand this anymore!" cried Blake. "They keep pestering me in my ears with their infernal buzzing. It's driving me crazy!"

"I know. It is torture, but we can't just keep smacking ourselves like this. What are we going to do?"

"Well, it's getting late…"

"We can't stop here," Lana said. "These insects are horrible."

"All right," said Blake. "Then let's find a way across this river. There must be some kind of bridge or fallen logs somewhere we can use to cross."

"This river is too wide. We'll never be able to cross using driftwood, and I don't see any bridges anywhere. There's no time to make a raft, either. We'll just have to swim across."

Blake mulled over this idea. "Well, dusk is not far off, but it is pretty warm out tonight." He paused. "All right, let's do it."

"Okay," said Lana. The two of them began walking along the shore, looking for easy access to the water, still slapping themselves against the mosquitoes. They finally found a suitable spot and prepared to cross. Lana, however, stopped what she was doing to stare at something far away in the distance.

"What is it, Lana?" asked Blake. "What do you see?"

"Look over there," she said softly, pointing at an object hovering in the sky. "Do you see that?"

Blake followed Lana's finger to something approaching from the southeast. "Yeah," he said, "but I don't know what it is." The object was about a quarter of a mile away, but it was coming steadily closer.

It flew silently, still remaining high above the trees, but gradually descending as it neared the travelers. The object was circular in form and looked like a giant upside-down bowl. It was also quite large, about twenty feet in diameter. It rotated as it hung suspended in the air, and it emitted a bright, whitish glow from its flat, bottom surface.

"It looks pretty big, doesn't it?" asked Lana. "How big would you say it is?"

"Oh, it's bigger than a typical family tent," replied Blake. "I'd say it's as big as a specialty event tent."

"It seems like it's coming this way," said Blake.

"Yeah," said Lana pensively. "In fact ... I think it's coming straight toward us."

"I've never seen anything like it. What is it, Lana?"

"I'm afraid I know," replied Lana softly.

"Afraid? Why should you be afraid?"

"Because I think it's an Astronaut."

"Oh no," said Blake. The impact of this realization fell on him like a boulder.

The large flying machine was getting closer. It hovered some sixty feet above the ground and made its way over the grassy field, closing the distance between itself and the travelers. A low, thrumming noise accompanied the machine as it glided smoothly through the air, casting a circular shadow on the ground. Blake, Lana, and Rita could see it more clearly now. On its flat, bottom side were four, circular lights that glowed a bright orange and emitted their energy a short distance beyond the surface of the vehicle. The topside of the machine had a more complex structure. It was dome-like and consisted of numerous panels arranged around its circumference. Large, reflective, black windows formed a complete circle halfway up the dome.

Blake and Lana watched in horror as the ship came nearer. Rita, ever protective of her human companions, stood in front of them and barked at the coming ship. Slowly, the ship drew closer. It circled around the people and the frantic dog, and reduced its altitude to thirty feet, twenty feet, ten feet, and then just five feet above the ground. Lana saw one of the panels in the front of the ship open up. Then she saw a small, pole-like object protrude with a sharp device visible at its tip. The pole then began to move and Lana realized that the machine was aiming at Rita.

"No, Rita, no!" cried Blake, fearing for his dog's life. But the dog would not be silent, and the machine would not be deterred. It locked onto its target and fired a small dart directly into Rita's flank. Rita yelped momentarily, but then continued barking. Her renewed aggression was short-lived however, as she became increasingly dizzy and weary. Then she lost her footing and fell to the ground.

Blake and Lana were horrorstricken. They wanted to run and hide, but they couldn't even bring themselves to move, let alone run away. Besides, trying to escape was probably useless anyway. This machine could fly through the air and shoot projectiles, so it was almost certain to capture anyone who fled from it. Unable to think, Blake and Lana simply cowered and clung to one another in fear. The low, throbbing hum of the machine was almost deafening now. A strong, warm breeze emanated from the vehicle's undercarriage and wafted over Blake and Lana, blowing their hair about their face and shoulders. They could smell the air that came from the machine: a sort of hot, sterile odor that was completely alien to them.

The machine's gun pointed at Lana.

This is it, thought Lana to herself. *Goodbye Blake. I love you.* She felt a brief, sharp pain in her side. When she looked, she saw that the same kind of small dart that had struck Rita was now embedded in her own skin. *Goodbye.*

Blake and Lana stared fearfully into each other's eyes, but they could not speak. Blake held Lana's head in his hands. He wished there was something he could do, but all he could do was hold her.

Lana found that she could no longer keep her head up or her eyes open. She fell unconscious, and Blake caught her as she became limp in his arms. He held her tightly, but she did not move at all.

Suddenly, Blake felt a sharp pain in his side. He looked down and found that he, too, had been hit with a dart from the flying machine. Beginning to feel weak himself, he hastened to lay Lana down while he still had the strength. Then he collapsed on the ground next to her.

Chapter 16

Lana opened her eyes and awoke. She looked around and found herself in a large, well-lit cell. The walls and ceiling were all made of metal, and a bright light in the ceiling shined down on her. One of the walls, however, was not metal, but made of a thick, completely transparent material. Lana realized that she was lying on a bed of some kind. It, too, was metallic, but she was seated on a soft, comfortable mat atop the metal bed. A thin blanket covered her.

Suddenly, Lana remembered what had happened. She sat up with a start, threw off her blanket, and hugged herself defensively, looking around the room through frightened eyes. She thought about Blake and Rita; as far as she knew, both were dead. *What did they do with Blake? What did they do with Rita? Did they bury them? What did they do with them?*

Then Lana remembered that she had been certain she would die, and yet here she was, still alive. *Maybe Blake and Rita are still alive, too. Or maybe I'm dead after all. Maybe I died and went to the Afterlife. This is not how I imagined it, though. It doesn't seem heavenly at all, but then, maybe this isn't Heaven. Maybe I'm still alive. Could I be ... a prisoner of the Astronauts? Could I be inside Houston?*

Lana's room was quiet and peaceful, and she soon realized that she was in no danger, or at least, no immediate danger. *Our things? Where are our things?* Lana noticed that the leather satchels she and Blake had been carrying, and their tools and weapons, were all gone. *They must have taken them away. They must have taken our things.*

Lana noticed that her old black cloak was gone and that she had on a new outfit instead. It was a gown, entirely white and made of soft, woven fabric, with no sleeves and a hem line just above the ankles. Lana also felt very clean. She inspected her body and came to appreciate just how clean she really was. Her skin felt smooth, her hair felt soft, and both carried a faint fragrance. Lana brought her hands and her hair to her nose and sniffed them gently, noting the strange, soapy smell. *Somebody must have washed me while I was out.*

Lana examined the area around her and decided that she was in no ordinary room. This place was neither a permanent residence nor a quarters for guests, but rather more of an enclosure. Lana saw a small stool-like elevation with a hole in it in the corner and, based on her experience in the Rubbletown, surmised that this was the toilet. A large container of water stood just a few feet away. Lana put her bare feet down on the white, shiny floor. It was cool to the touch. She noticed a pair of slippers beside her bed. Slipping her feet into them, she found they fit perfectly and decided to wear them. She stood up, walked to the container of water, brought a handful to her lips, and took a drink. The water was cool and delicious, so Lana helped herself to several more handfuls until she was satisfied. Then she wiped her mouth on her gown, turned to the window at the front of her enclosure, and peered out.

It was comparatively dark on the other side of the window, so visibility was poor, but Lana could see enough. The chamber in which she sat was at least three feet higher than the one on the other side of the glass. Never before had she seen anything quite like that outer room. It was many times larger than hers was, and it was perfectly clean and filled with a multitude of bright, shiny things. She noticed that some of these things had small lights on them. Others bore glowing panels or displayed luminous letters. Some were clearly tools and utensils, although Lana had no idea what they were for. Other things appeared to be transportation devices with small wheels at their bases. There were numerous containers of various sizes, apparently intended to hold fluids or to measure them out.

Where am I? What is this place? I must be a prisoner inside Houston. Yes, that must be it. I can hardly believe how clean and orderly everything is. This must be what the Old Days were like. Yes, this must be how the Managers used to live. I had no idea it would look like this.

Just then, a door on the far side of the room opened up, and someone walked through. Lana watched intently as the strange figure strode through the doorway and touched a button on the wall. Numerous ceiling lights came on. Lana could now see the entire space and all of its machinery. She was amazed that the illumination in the room went from twilight to daylight in a fraction of a second. The being made its way to Lana's enclosure. At first, Lana thought it was an odd-looking person, even though its height was slightly greater than that of the average man. But now, fully illuminated under the ceiling lights, it was clear that this figure was not even human.

Over its entire body, the being was covered in a kind of smooth, elastic, cream-colored, form-fitting skin. The material shone under the glow of the artificial light, making it seem more like a sort of tightly fitting bodysuit than skin. Upon scrutiny, Lana realized that this covering was completely devoid of pores, hairs, feathers, scales, sweat, and slime.

The being had two arms and two legs, but they were not the limbs of a human. The arms were long and slender, and the shoulders rather narrow. The hands each had one thin thumb and only two thin fingers, which appeared to be their natural state rather than a deformity. The legs were lanky, too, but they did not move the way a human's legs moved. They were more like the legs of a bird, for the feet bore three long, forward-facing toes and one long, opposing toe in the back. The ankle was held well off the ground, and the knee was so high that it was less noticeable than the ankle. Thus, like in birds, this being's legs gave the illusion of having backward-bending knees relative to humans.

The body of the being was stout, stocky, and rigid. The neck, on the other hand, was relatively long and supple. Perched atop this graceful neck, the head was the strangest feature of all. Although somewhat small and round, it contained two large, forward-facing eyes. These were the only facial features the being possessed, however. There was no nose, no mouth, no eyebrows, and no ears of any kind.

This creature thoroughly puzzled Lana. She had never such a minimal being before. It was as though it were not alive. Lana looked down toward the region around the base of the creature's legs. It had no tail or buttocks of any kind, nor did it have any body cavities to suggest genitalia or a means of excreting wastes. Perhaps this was to be expected, since without a mouth, it had no clear way of ingesting nourishment. It was as though the creature was alive all by itself, independent of food, drink, or mates for its continued existence.

If it never eats or drinks, then perhaps it will never die. I guess a being like that would have no need for reproduction, since it would never need to replace itself. Maybe it's immortal. If so, then how was it created? Are there others like it around? And how long has it been alive? Maybe it isn't even alive at all. I wonder ... I didn't think they would be like this, but ... could that be an Astronaut?

The being appeared intimidating and alien, but Lana was intensely curious about it. She watched as it approached her enclosure, thoroughly fascinated. Its speedy gait was oddly deliberate and distinctly birdlike. Once it stood before Lana's window, the light of her enclosure fell on its body and illuminated its minimal face with the two big eyes and nothing more.

Lana made eye contact with the being and maintained it for what seemed like an eternity. The being showed no sign of life, no warmth, and no emotion. It was neither kind nor aggressive, neither patient nor angry. It simply watched Lana.

Eventually, it broke eye contact with her, not out of shyness or acquiescence but out of a need to look at other things. It looked her over from head to toe, taking in every detail. Then it looked about her room, checking to see that everything was as it was meant to be.

Lana instinctively took a few steps back, horrified by the cold silence of this entity. Just then, the strange-looking being raised an arm, and Lana retreated to her bed. The creature pointed one of its fingers and pressed a button on the wall. Lana suddenly heard a sound, and a panel on one of the walls inside her enclosure opened up. A tray slid out with a napkin, a cup of fruit juice, and a dish of hot beef strips with steamed vegetables. The aroma was delicious, and Lana's mouth began to water.

She suddenly felt hungry. Cautiously, she walked toward the tray and picked it up. Then she sat down on her bed and began to eat her meal. It tasted even better than it smelled, and Lana found herself hungrily devouring the food, quickly shoveling it into her mouth with her hand. The being on the other side of the glass watched her all the while. Lana greatly resented this, but she was too hungry to worry about the bad manners of a captor she couldn't even identify.

Once she finished off the meat and vegetables, she wiped her mouth and hands on her napkin. Then she raised her cup, quaffed its sweet juice, and wiped her mouth and hands on her napkin once more. Lana stood up and walked toward the open panel on the wall to replace the tray, which quickly withdrew into the wall with a soft hissing sound. When the panel closed again, the wall appeared exactly as it did before — nearly featureless. Lana sat back down on her bed and returned the stare of the creature on the other side of the glass.

After a few minutes, the being appeared satisfied with the observations it had made, so it pivoted abruptly and began heading for the exit. Upon reaching the door, it pushed a button and turned out the lights. Then it opened the door and disappeared.

Lana leaned on the glass as she watched the creature go. Once it was gone, she slumped against the glass and let herself slide to the floor. Lana stared blankly forward for a while, then tears began to form in her eyes.

I'm all alone. Again. Blake and Rita are dead, and I'm all alone. I hope they got a proper burial ceremony. I'll never see Blake again.

Lana began to miss Blake terribly. Her sorrow hung like a weight within her chest, and she felt as though even breathing were difficult. Her limbs felt heavy and tears streamed down her face. She wished Blake could be there to hug her, to kiss her. She wanted to feel the warmth of his body. She wanted to see him smile, to hear him laugh. She wanted to hear his baritone voice, but she was certain that she would never see him again. Lying on the floor, Lana buried her face in her hands and wept.

What are they going to do with me? How long will they keep me here? I wonder if they'll ever set me free at all. She lay there on her side weeping softly, her knees pulled up toward her chest, her hands covering her face. When she finished crying, she sat back up, sniffled, and dabbed at her moist eyes and cheeks with her gown. Then she got back into bed, pulled the covers over herself, and went to sleep.

Chapter 17

When Lana awoke, she was once again disoriented and confused as to where she was. When she remembered what had happened, she did not feel very much like getting out of her bed. She had no idea how much time had transpired since she was last awake. It could have been a few minutes, it could have been hours. Somehow, based on how groggy she felt, she was inclined to believe that at least a few hours had passed, but there was no way of knowing what time of day it was. There were no windows to the outer world, and there was no way of knowing the position of the sun, or what the weather was like outside. All she knew was that she was in her enclosure, and that she remained unharmed, at least physically. When she remembered that Blake was gone, she realized that she would not get out of the ordeal altogether unharmed after all.

Lana stared at the ceiling for a while and then at the wall. At length, she stared at the toilet and decided to use it. Reluctantly, she got out of bed, went to the big window, and looked outside to make sure no one was watching. The room was dark and empty, and there was no sign of life at all. The space seemed strange to her, now that she knew what it looked like when it was illuminated. Confident of her privacy, Lana used the toilet and washed up. She drank some of the water from the large container nearby and dried herself off on her gown. Then she sat down at the window and stared out into the darkness.

Minutes passed, then hours. Occasionally, Lana got up to stretch or walk about, but she always came right back to the window to stare out into the dark, unoccupied room again. She kept her eyes on the doorway through which the creature had walked before. *It's only a question of time before he comes in here again. When he does, I'll be watching.* However, Lana was not certain what she was watching for. She wondered if she would notice some weakness in the creature, or some defect in her confinement apparatus. Lana hoped to find such weaknesses, exploit them, and escape. But she doubted that she would. Everything seemed so perfect, so neatly measured out and taken into consideration that she doubted if she would ever find a way to escape. *I'll probably just have to sit here and wait for whatever is going to happen.*

Eventually, the doorway opened again and someone stepped through and turned on the light once more. Lana immediately perked up and watched intently. This time there were two figures. One figure appeared to be the same one she had seen before — that same, vaguely birdlike, nondescript being who had visited last time. The other was a man, rather tall and thin, but unlike any man Lana had ever seen. For one thing, his skin was much lighter than she was accustomed to seeing. His short, dark brown hair was straight and shiny, and neatly combed to one side. His head, however, was the only part of him that was actually visible.

The man wore some kind of all-white suit, although there were several insignias, panels, and buttons of various colors on it. The suit concealed the man's entire body below his head; a high collar covered his neck, and white gloves and white boots covered his hands and feet. A black belt was cinched around his waist, and various tools and implements hung from it.

The man looked serious as he approached Lana's enclosure, while the other creature followed closely behind. Soon they stood before Lana — merely a few feet away. Lana could scarcely believe it when she saw that the man's eyes were blue. She instinctively stepped back out of fear, despite the thick barrier of glass between them. The man and his companion stood watching Lana for several minutes. This made her extremely uncomfortable. She became angry and scowled at them, but they continued to stare it her just the same. Finally, Lana had had enough.

"What do you want from me?" she cried instinctively. The sound of her own scream startled her in the small confines of her enclosure, but the two figures outside had not heard anything at all. The man raised his hand and pressed a button on the wall next to Lana's enclosure. Lana suddenly heard a sound, as though some- one had just opened a hole in the wall and allowed her to hear what was happening outside.

"Could you repeat that please?" the man said slowly. He used the Common Tongue, but he spoke with a thick, alien accent. His voice was low and resonant, and its tone was grim.

Lana was puzzled by her chamber's sudden ability to let in sound. It also seemed odd to hear this very strange-looking person speaking the Bebelishi language. Nevertheless, she responded.

"What do you want from me?" repeated Lana in the Common Tongue, this time more timidly.

"We simply want to study you." The man said it as though simply studying her was a very benign thing, when Lana was already in great distress.

"Let me go," demanded Lana.

"Not yet," said the man. "Not before we have finished our studies."

Lana shuddered at the thought of this strange man and his strange assistant studying her as though she were not a person worthy of respect. She had already been harmed and treated like an object, and she was afraid that it would only get worse. Moreover, she was angry. However, Lana decided that it would be a strategic mistake to throw a temper tantrum at this time, so she contained her anger and merely stared back at the two visitors with contempt in her eyes.

"What time is it?" she asked. She was thoroughly annoyed at not knowing what was happening outdoors.

"It is about eight o'clock in the morning," said the man.

"How long was I out?"

"Your first period of unconsciousness was about six hours. Your second period of unconsciousness was about eight hours."

"How do you know my language? You couldn't be Bebelishi."

"I have studied your kind extensively," the man replied, "but there is always more to learn, which is why you are here today. May I ask you a few questions?"

"All right," said Lana. "Go ahead."

"What is your name?"

"Lana. What's yours?"

The man looked at her quizzically. "One should never become attached to one's subjects," he said.

"Never mind that," said Lana. "This is an introduction. What's your name?"

"I am Dr. Henry Lindberg. What is your age?"

"Nineteen."

"Thank you," said Dr. Lindberg. "Have you ever given birth to any children?"

"No, not yet," said Lana. "Are you about through with your questions?"

"Yes, that is all for now. Thank you for your cooperation. Is there anything you need before we leave?"

Lana thought for a moment. "I need to know something."

"Very well. What do you need to know."

"Who is that?" Lana pointed at the pale, smooth, shiny entity standing next to Dr. Lindberg.

"Oh, this? This is my assistant, Verax."

"What is he?"

"A robot."

"What's a robot?" asked Lana.

Dr. Lindberg chuckled smugly to himself. "A robot is an artificial being."

Lana gasped softly. "Artificial? You mean you made him?"

"Well, I did not build him all by myself, but yes, I made him."

Lana was taken aback. "Why didn't you give him a mouth or someplace he can pee and poop out of?"

"A robot does not really need food or drink like you or I do. And it does not need to … eliminate waste, either. Its body is powered by electricity."

"What's that?"

Dr. Lindberg huffed as his patience wore thin. "It is energy. Actually, this entire laboratory runs on electricity."

"Oh," said Lana with a frown. Then she half whispered as though she were afraid someone else would hear. "So, this whole place is alive then?"

"No, and neither is Verax."

"You mean he's dead?"

"No, he is simply not alive."

"But he can move around…"

"That does not matter. He is not even really a 'he' anyway, even though we call him that. Verax is a machine like all these other machines," said Dr. Lindberg with a sweeping motion of his arm.

Lana looked on as she pondered what Dr. Lindberg had just said. Despite his strange accent, his words seemed clear enough. It was the things he talked about that made no sense. Lana would have to think about these new ideas further. For now, though, she had run out of questions.

"Is there anything else?" asked Dr. Lindberg.

Lana came out of her trance and looked into her captor's eyes again. "Yes," she said. "I want to go for a walk."

"A walk?"

"Yes, a walk. I feel so cramped in here. I need some exercise. Could I go outside please?"

Dr. Lindberg furrowed his eyebrows and fell silent. It was as though he were imagining all the possible ramifications of either granting or denying Lana's request. At last, he made his decision.

"Very well, we can let you out, but only for a short time," he said. Lana brightened immediately. "But I will warn you now," said Dr. Lindberg, "if you give us any trouble, we will not hesitate to knock you out again. Do you understand?" Lana nodded. With that, Dr. Lindberg reached down to his belt and removed two devices. He turned to his robot and handed it one of the devices, keeping the other for himself. "Keep your gun on stun, Verax," said Dr. Lindberg. "If the woman makes any hostile movements, or if I give you the command, your orders are to shoot her under stun mode only. Is that clear?"

"Yes, sir," said Verax dryly, "that is clear."

"Good," said Dr. Lindberg. Then he turned back to Lana. "All right, Lana. We are going to let you out now, but you must obey us. If you do not, we will stun you again." Lana nodded once more. "Very well, then." Dr. Lindberg pressed a series of buttons on a wall panel and entered a code into the computer. There was a dull popping noise, and the window at the front of Lana's chamber rose and disappeared into the ceiling above.

Lana watched as the thick, heavy glass was lifted up, mystified at how it could do so if no one was pushing on it. She concluded that this was yet another trick that these Managers had mastered, and decided to ignore it for now. Then she turned her attention to the laboratory outside. Gingerly, she sat down on the floor of her chamber and let her lower legs dangle. Her feet nearly touched the floor of the main laboratory and her toes skimmed it. Hopping down, Lana felt the cold hardness of the floor, which was somehow not nearly as pleasant as that of her own chamber. However, it was not altogether uncomfortable either, so she took a step out and looked around. Lana swiveled to face her own chamber; it was curious to look at it from this perspective. She felt bigger all of a sudden, and stronger, too.

Lana suddenly realized that her chamber was not the only one of its kind in the room, but rather only the first in a long row of identical chambers along the back wall of the laboratory. There were about twenty of them, and Lana was shocked when she saw the animals living in those other enclosures.

The one right next to hers contained a puma. The puma was pacing nervously, but it interrupted its usual routine to look Lana directly in the eye. This startled her, and she reflexively took a step back before realizing that this creature was imprisoned just as she had been. The puma resumed its frantic pacing.

Lana carefully walked over to the next cell in the series. This one contained a giant lioness lying on her side, sleeping soundly. Lana moved on to the next enclosure to find a large black bear. The poor bear, unable to truly pace like the puma, was swinging the anterior part of its body from side to side as it faced the glass. Lana glanced back at Dr. Lindberg with a concerned look about her.

"Where are all these animals from?" she asked.

"They were collected from this general region," replied Dr. Lindberg.

"What are you going to do with them?" she asked, horrified.

"We study them."

Lana shook her head in disbelief. She turned her attention to the fourth cell, where she saw six small animals of some unknown type. Their fur was grayish-brown and of medium length. They had a fairly short tail, and a pink, somewhat human-like face. They also had tiny hands, which they used for picking things up or sifting through each other's hair. Most of them, however, huddled together and looked about nervously with wide, clever eyes.

"What are these?" asked Lana.

"They are called macaques," said Dr. Lindberg. "They are a kind of monkey. They are primates ... just as we are primates."

"How long have they been here?"

"About a week. We do not intend to keep them for much longer."

Lana continued to make her way down the line. The next chamber housed a coyote, who watched his visitors intently. Lana walked over to the next enclosure and was surprised to find Rita standing in it.

"Rita!" she cried. "You're all right!" The dog wagged her tail frantically while her tongue lolled out of her mouth and her ears pressed flat against her head. Rita barked excitedly inside, although the noise she made was completely inaudible to those in the laboratory. Lana pretended to stroke and pet the dog through the glass, making happy, high-pitched sounds all the while. "Hello, Rita! Hello!" she cried. "I'm so glad you're all right." Inspired by this development now, Lana turned her attention to the next chamber in the row. To her amazement, this one contained Blake.

Blake was standing up, his hands and face pressed against the window. Lana gave out a shriek of surprise and joy that alarmed both Dr. Lindberg and Verax. They promptly put their hands on their guns, but they did not fire. Just as they expected, Lana rushed harmlessly toward Blake's enclosure. The couple tried to touch one another through the glass. They knew it was futile, but performing the gesture seemed important. They tried to kiss each other's lips, but they only felt the cold, hard material between them. Still, they were overjoyed to see one another again. Blake was shouting something inside his chamber, but Lana could not hear a word he was saying. Lana looked back at Dr. Lindberg.

"Make it so I can hear him the way you did before!" she said.

"Very well," said Dr. Lindberg. Approaching the enclosure, he pressed a small white button on a panel next to the glass. Lana heard the curious sound she had heard before, and then miraculously, she heard Blake's voice.

"Lana!" he cried. "Lana, are you all right?" Blake was now sobbing in earnest, calling to his mate while his voice broke and his breath jumped. Tears flowed from his eyes as Lana pressed her hand against his.

"Yes!" cried Lana, herself beginning to sob. "Yes, I'm fine. I thought you were dead, Blake."

"No, I'm fine. I'm just fine. Where are we?"

"We're inside Houston, Blake. The Astronauts are holding us captive so they can study us. They say they don't want to hurt us, though."

"Who are those two behind you?" asked Blake.

"That man is Dr. Lindberg," said Lana, pointing. "That other creature is called Verax, but I don't know who or what he is. I'm just glad I found you, Blake."

"Me too, Lana. You're sure you're okay?" Blake asked again.

Lana couldn't help but laugh this time. "I'm fine. Don't worry."

"Have you seen Rita?"

"She's right over there," said Lana, pointing.

"Where?" Blake asked.

"She's in this room right next to yours," said Lana. "It's just like the one you're in — just like the one I've been in until now. They have a whole bunch of them. You can't see them from where you're standing, but they're all in a row along this wall. They have cats and bears and monkeys. They're keeping all of us as specimens for study."

"Why? What ... what's going on?"

"I don't know, Blake. Don't worry about that right now, my love. Are you sure you're all right?"

"Yes, I feel fine."

"Thank the Creator," said Lana.

"Why?" interrupted Dr. Lindberg. "You should be thanking me instead. I'm the one who brought you here safely."

Lana and Blake exchanged glances. They had no intention of thanking someone who was keeping them captive for no good reason.

"Come, Lana," said Dr. Lindberg. "I think you have gotten enough exercise for now. It's time to return to your chamber."

Lana began to feel her stomach turn. "No, no wait!" she exclaimed.

"I warned you," said Dr. Lindberg. "You must not give us any trouble."

"I won't. Just listen. Please, let me be in there with him."

Dr. Lindberg was not surprised at this request, for he had anticipated it. In truth, he thought it was a good idea. Just as it was healthiest for the macaques to be housed together, so too should the humans. After a moment's hesitation, Dr. Lindberg agreed.

"Very well. I will ask your mate if he agrees to this. What is the man's name? Blake?"

"That's right," said Lana. "His name is Blake."

Dr. Lindberg directed his attention to Blake. "You in there! Blake! This woman has requested to be housed together with you. Do you agree to this request?"

"Yes!" exclaimed Blake. "Of course! Please, let her in."

"Very well. I am about to open the enclosure to allow her to enter your chamber. Please stand back and do not attempt to escape. If you do, either my assistant or I will fire upon you, causing you to become unconscious once again. Do you understand?"

"Yes, I understand," said Blake.

"Good. Now please stand back." Blake gladly complied and stood with his back against the far wall. Dr. Lindberg pressed a series of buttons on the panel next to the window. Just as before, the window rose up into the ceiling. Instantly, Lana leaped into the chamber and ran to Blake.

The two lovers had never been so relieved to see one another. They hugged tightly and kissed each other long and hard. As Dr. Lindberg lowered the glass into place again, Blake and Lana continued to cling to one another. Once the chamber was locked and secured, Dr. Lindberg and Verax put away their weapons. Then Dr. Lindberg pushed another button, and a second bed emerged for Lana from the chamber wall.

"We will leave you now," said Dr. Lindberg. "We will return again later in the day to check on you." Blake and Lana held each other tightly as they stared at their captors.

"What about my dog, Rita?" asked Blake.

"She is safe," said Dr. Lindberg.

"I understand that," said Blake, "but she'll get lonely all by herself. Can't you put all three of us together in a bigger room?"

"No, I'm afraid not, but we'll make sure she's well cared for, and we'll allow you to visit her later. For now, you must stay in your present accommodations." Dr. Lindberg turned around and headed for the exit. Verax followed him out and turned off the laboratory lights as he left. All was dark and quiet as it was before, and Blake and Lana turned to each other once again.

"I'm so glad you're here," said Blake.

"Me, too. I can't tell you how happy I am that we can at least be together."

"You don't have to. I already know." Lana smiled warmly and kissed Blake once more.

The two of them spent the next hour comforting one another, talking about what they had experienced, and about what they thought and felt. They spent time stroking, caressing, and massaging one another. At last, they removed their pads and sheets from their metallic beds and set them down on the floor. Blake lay down beside Lana and draped his arm over her waist, while Lana pressed her back to Blake's belly in a spooning position. The reunited lovers held each other like this for a while, relieved to be together again. At last, they fell asleep.

Chapter 18

Several hours later, Lana shook Blake into waking.

"What is it?" he asked, his eyes and voice straining.

"It's morning."

"How can you tell? Haven't we been inside this whole time?"

"They turn the lights on and off in here, I think to make us feel like it's day or night. I just woke up myself."

"Oh," said Blake. "Anyway, it doesn't really matter. I guess we're stuck in here until Dr. Lindberg or that Verax come back. What is Verax, anyway?"

"Dr. Lindberg told me it's a robot," said Lana. "It's an artificial being that gets its energy from something called 'electricity' instead of food or water. But that's all I know."

Blake exhaled through puffed lips and shook his head. Then he suddenly remembered his beloved dog. "Do you suppose Rita's all right?" he asked desperately.

"I think so," Lana said frankly. "I only saw her for a moment yesterday, but she seemed healthy. Lonely and frightened, but healthy."

"Good. I hope we get to see her soon."

"Me too," agreed Lana.

Just then, the massive doors to the laboratory swung open and Dr. Lindberg and Verax marched in. They did not even acknowledge Lana or Blake, whose cage was near the end of the menagerie. Instead, they began their daily inspection where Lana had previously been held. The scientist and his assistant walked toward the first cell in the series and soon fell out of sight.

"Lana," whispered Blake.

"What?" whispered Lana.

"Do you think they can hear us?"

"I'm sure they could if they wanted to, they can do so many other things I don't understand. But I think they're looking at the other animals, so they're probably not paying any attention to us right now."

"What are they doing?"

"Dr. Lindberg told me that he keeps all these creatures — including us — for some kind of study. I don't know what he's studying, exactly, but maybe that's what he's doing right now. Maybe he's examining each of the animals to see how they're doing."

"How long will that take?"

"I don't know," confessed Lana. "A while, I guess."

"Good," said Blake.

"Why?"

"Listen, I think we should try to escape when they come over here."

"What?" cried Lana.

"Shhh!" hissed Blake harshly, emitting a sound that was nearly as loud as Lana's exclamation. "Not so loud! We want to keep this quiet, all right?"

"All right, all right, Blake, but you don't know what you're saying. We don't know what we're up against."

"We can't stay here!"

"I know, but we can't just clobber them on their heads and run away. I don't even know if Verax can be clobbered at all. We have to think."

"All right. Well, maybe not today, and maybe not tomorrow, but eventually we have to get out of here."

"Agreed," said Lana.

"Good. Now, here's the plan. For today, our objective is to get Dr. Lindberg and Verax on our side. Get them to like us, to trust us. That way, they will let us see Rita. And they might even let us walk around this place and see what it's like. The more we know, the easier it will be to escape."

"Don't you think they know that, Blake? Dr. Lindberg is going to be suspicious of everything we do. He's going to expect us to escape."

"But he won't know how or when. We can use that to our advantage."

"All right. So what do we do today?" asked Lana.

"We talk to him and try to get some information. If we can, let's convince him to let us out of here for a while."

"He's probably going to assign Verax to watch over us."

"That's fine," said Blake, "as long as we can stretch our legs and look around."

"That does sound good," said Lana.

"Yeah. I'll go crazy unless I get out of here soon. If the other animals feel anything like I do, they're probably already insane.

We're just cooped up in this tiny little room. There's nothing to see or do anywhere. All we can do is sit around all day and stare into the darkness. I feel so cramped and restless, I can hardly stand it."

"I know," said Lana, giving Blake a hug. "I know. I feel the same way, but let's be patient. We'll find a way out." They sat there holding each other in silence. After a while, Dr. Lindberg and Verax stepped in front of their cage. Dr. Lindberg pushed a button on the wall, and spoke.

"Good morning," he said. "How are you feeling?"

Blake and Lana both muttered that they felt fine.

"Good. Glad to hear it." Dr. Lindberg scrutinized them carefully, making notes on a tablet all the while. Blake and Lana stared in disbelief as they watched the scientist make his observations. His gaze met theirs several times, but he said nothing, giving them only a terse, puckered smile while he made his notes. For several minutes he stood before them, carefully eyeing their bodies to assess their condition. He also observed their body language to assess their mood, but he never spoke to them, other than his initial, flat greeting. After a while, when he concluded his examination, Dr. Lindberg shifted his weight and turned to move on to the next cage. "Thank you! See you later."

"Wait!" exclaimed Blake, rising quickly to his feet. Verax kept a watchful eye on the tall, powerful male human in the enclosure, even if he was behind an impenetrable barrier. "Don't go yet! I wanted to talk to you."

"Oh?" said Dr. Lindberg with a tilt of his head. "What about?"

"Well, um ... that is ... I was wondering..."

"We were wondering," said Lana, "if it might be possible to step outside for some fresh air."

"Hmmm," said the scientist, "well, we usually only do that with specimens that have been with us for a long time, and that are going to continue being with us." Lana bristled at the scientist's reference to her and her mate as *specimens*. "You two have only been here for a few days, but then, we don't usually keep humans, so I'm not entirely sure how long it takes for a human to become, er..."

"Stir crazy?" asked Blake sardonically.

"Yes, that's it," said Dr. Lindberg, oblivious to Lana and Blake's irritation. "Stir crazy."

"I'm sure you can imagine how quickly a person can become stir crazy in a place like this. You are, after all, human ... aren't you?"

"Who me? Oh yes, of course!" said Dr. Lindberg with a chuckle. "Despite the fact that you and I look so different, we are still both human. Your kind and mine have not been apart for all that long. You know, actually, I happen to be an expert in this particular field." Dr. Lindberg was always ready to give a lecture on his research. Now, his usual phlegmatic demeanor gave way to a more animated one as he prepared to engage these fresh, new minds, despite the fact that he considered them simple. "My people, the Lunari — or Astronauts, as you refer to us — live on the moon."

Blake and Lana watched Dr. Lindberg closely. It was not that they were particularly interested in "human interstellar population genetics." Rather, they were amused by how enthusiastic this generally cold and austere man had suddenly become. More importantly, they knew that they were building a rapport with him, which might help them attain freedom in the near future. Patiently, they listened.

"True," he continued, "some of us live down here on the Earth Research Center part of the time, like I do. For the most part, though, we stay on the moon. Our ancestors left the Earth for Luna just prior to a horrible asteroid collision..."

"The Great Crash," said Lana. "We know."

"Ah yes," said Dr. Lindberg. "I had forgotten that your kind also keeps track of history through written and oral folklore."

"The Bebel," she said, "and tradition."

"Anyway," said Dr. Lindberg, "the apocalypse — the Great Crash — was only about 3,000 years ago, and your kind and my kind have not mixed since then. That's really not a very long time in terms of the natural world. The Lunari and the Earthlings are still both very much human."

"Well then," said Blake, "you must understand what it would feel like to be in a cage such as this."

"More or less," admitted the scientist. "Of course, I've never actually been in such a predicament myself, so I can't know for sure how it feels. But yes, I can imagine."

"Not very pleasant then, is it, Dr. Lindberg?" asked Lana.

"No, no it's not."

"Then why do you do it?" asked Blake.

"Do what?" asked Dr. Lindberg.

"Why do you put Earthling people in cages if you can imagine what it would feel like?" Blake said.

"Well, because…" Dr. Lindberg paused, contemplating his answer. "Because we must learn. We must study and we must learn."

"You just told me you can imagine what it would feel like to be one of us," said Blake.

"But we need answers. We must study your race to understand you better."

"Why must you understand us better?" asked Lana.

"So that we can know what the Earth is like now, better understand our own origins, and plan for the future."

"Then why don't you study your own people?" Blake asked.

"We do. We do that, too, but we must also study the Earth population of *Homo sapiens* to better understand the species as a whole."

"Do you keep your own kind in cages?" asked Lana.

"No, of course not," scoffed Dr. Lindberg. "That would be…" He caught himself.

"That would be what?" said Lana. "Cruel?" Dr. Lindberg stared at her blankly. "Why don't you just talk to us?"

"That would be too dangerous."

"Too dangerous? How so?" Lana asked.

"We've watched you," said Dr. Lindberg. "We've seen the kind of violence you're capable of. It's much safer this way."

"Maybe so," said Lana, puzzled by the realization that Dr. Lindberg was just as frightened of her kind, as her kind was of his. "But don't you think we could work something out?"

"Perhaps…" Dr. Lindberg's voice trailed off. "Perhaps we could." Suddenly, Dr. Lindberg steeled himself, as if a tiny voice inside his head had just reprimanded him. "That is out of the question! Now that's enough of this nonsense. I must continue with my research. Verax will come by later today to escort you to an area outside where you can get some exercise. Come, Verax." Dr. Lindberg marched on to the next enclosure in the series, followed closely by his robotic companion.

Blake and Lana exchanged glances, and then smiled and hugged one another. They knew that they had just made a small victory, despite having tested the limits of their captor's tolerance. Now they could look forward to going outside, getting some fresh air, and learning more about their prison. Content with their meager accomplishment, Blake and Lana reclined together and stared out the window of the enclosure into the dull, sterile gray of the laboratory beyond.

Chapter 19

Later that afternoon, Lana and Blake were napping soundly, collapsed one atop the other like two puppies in a litter. Lana was once more the first to awaken, and sensing her stirring, Blake awoke shortly thereafter. To their surprise, Verax was watching them silently from the other side of the glass.

"What is it?" barked Blake.

"I am waiting to escort you to the exercise area," replied the robot. Upon hearing this, Blake and Lana quickly stood up and straightened their sleep-crumpled clothing.

"We're ready!" said Lana. "We are definitely ready."

"Very well, then," said Verax. "Please prepare to be let out."

"All right," said Blake. "What do we need to do?"

"After I open the front glass, you are to step down and stand still so that I can confine you in chains."

"Chains!" exclaimed Blake. "We don't need to be confined in chains!"

"Blake, please," said Lana. "Let's do as they say."

"Don't they trust us? We're not just going to run away, you know!"

"I know that, but they don't know that. Please, Blake, just be compliant for once, all right? Do it for me. Please."

"Well," said Blake, "all right. I'll do it for you." Blake turned to Verax. "All right, Verax. We're ready."

"Good," Verax said, and entered a code into the panel on the wall. With a low, humming sound, the front glass slowly receded into the ceiling. Blake and Lana, still intimidated by such feats of magic, unconsciously stepped back. Soon, the panel was fully open. "All right, you may step down now."

Blake and Lana complied by their captor's wishes, and hopped down to the cold, hard floor below. They noticed that Verax had been holding several metal restraints in one hand all along.

"Spread your legs and keep your arms at your sides," said the robot.

Blake and Lana complied once again as they attempted to retain their dignity in vain. Verax took out two pairs of leg-restraining chains and locked them onto their ankles. The chains stretched between their feet and rested on the floor, for they were long enough to allow easy walking but short enough to prevent the long strides necessary for running. Verax placed handcuffs on Blake's and Lana's wrists and snapped them smartly shut.

Blake scowled at seeing Lana bound. She noticed this and gave her mate a reassuring glance. They both knew that, although their movement was restricted, they were, after all, being allowed access to another area, which made the inconvenience of the restraints well worthwhile.

"All right," said Verax. "We are ready to proceed. Please follow me." The robot pivoted and began heading for the laboratory door with Lana and Blake close behind. The loud clanging of their chains was already beginning to get on their nerves. It wasn't that the sound itself was so noisome. It was simply that it served to remind them that they were still prisoners, and despite the ostensibly noble aims of their captors, they were still afraid that they would not live to see freedom ever again. Blake forced the grim thought that he and his mate might eventually die in this dreary place out of his mind, and replaced it with the hope that they might soon be free once more.

They walked to the lab door, which Verax pushed open. Blake and Lana followed him out, and a sense of awe overcame them when they realized that they were about to encounter the outer world for the first time since their capture. As they stepped into the hallway, they felt a sort of quiet fear creep into their hearts. The crude darkness of the lab was a stark contrast to the bleak brightness of this corridor in which they now found themselves. Bright, fluorescent lights shone down upon them from the ceiling, which was itself, like the walls and the floor, glaringly white.

Verax was unimpressed by all this brightness and continued to walk down the corridor at exactly the right pace for the humans, who shuffled along behind him. They walked on like this for some time as Verax led Blake and Lana around several turns and bends. They passed four doors that looked exactly like the one for the lab where Blake and Lana were being housed. Each time, Blake asked whether the door they had just seen was the one that led back to their own laboratory, but Verax always patiently stated that they led to other labs. The trio walked on for what seemed like hours to the humans.

"Is there no one else here?" asked Blake. "No other people like Dr. Lindberg? No other robots like you?"

"There are a few, but not many," said Verax, "and they are stationed elsewhere in the facility at this time. So, the probability of seeing them right now is very low."

Blake was amazed at how regular and uniform everything looked. For all he knew, they had been walking in circles all this time and Verax had no intention of taking them outside at all. Still, he did have the distinct impression of directional, rather than circular travel. It was simply too difficult to gauge direction because of the lack of landmarks. The walls had very few markings on them, save for the occasional doorway, instrument panel, or placard. Blake tried his best to read the signs as he passed them, but it was very difficult. The characters resembled the letters he had learned in Kamis, but they were arranged differently. As often as not, if he did manage to sound out the words, they made little or no sense.

"Lana," whispered Blake. "Have you been able to make out any of these signs on the walls?"

"Some," whispered Lana. "They seem to be about safety precautions and emergency procedures."

"Why would they say that, though? This place seems so peaceful and quiet. About the only danger I can see is getting bored to death. What kinds of dangers did those signs describe?"

"Well, it seems there are a number of things that can go wrong here. Certain substances, I'm not sure which, can explode, or leak, or get out of control and do a lot of damage."

"Really? I had no idea. I just thought we were in some kind of artificial cave. Didn't you?"

"I suspected there was more to it. Based on what I read about the Managers back in the Rubbletown, I knew they often had places like this where they made and stored things, and I knew there were risks involved. I wouldn't worry though, Blake. Everything seems to be under control."

The trio eventually took a right-angle turn and came to a dead end. That is, it would have been a dead end, had there not been a massive door at the end of the hall.

"This is the exit," said Verax flatly. "We will go out through here."

Lana and Blake looked at each other. Both excitement and anxiety were plainly visible on their faces. Verax approached the door, entered a code into the wall panel, and swung the door open. Afternoon sunlight flooded the hallway and overwhelmed the dreary glare of fluorescent lamps. Lana and Blake squinted for a moment and held their arms up to shield their eyes, but soon lowered them as they grew accustomed to the light. Now they knew the time of day again, and they found that reference to reality invaluable. Despite their stoicism, they couldn't help but smile as the sunlight brought much needed warmth to their hearts.

Blake and Lana peered out at the real world through the doorway. They saw the welcoming grass on the ground and the blue sky with its sparse clouds floating in the distance. It seemed as though years had passed since they had seen such a sight, even though they had been captured only a few days ago. Verax stood to one side and allowed the humans access to the door. Then all three stepped through, and Verax shut the door behind them.

The area where they now found themselves was a sort of courtyard just outside the building that housed them. Known as the Sun Run, it was where animals were brought for observation and exercise. A metallic fence separated the Sun Run from the much larger Outer Field, which stretched all the way out to the Research Center's border. Lana and Blake could see the border in the distance and were disappointed to learn that the Field was off limits. For now, though, the Run was generous enough.

As they stepped out, Blake and Lana felt the joyous tickle of gritty sand and grass on their bare feet. The two of them took in their surroundings: the sunshine, the vegetation, the other animals, and the enclosing fence. A few rabbits and a small herd of deer foraged peacefully near some bushes, but when they saw Verax, they immediately bounded to the farthest corners of the Run. Blake noticed that, although many of them came near the fence, none actually touched it, and he wondered why. However, he set that question aside and explored the Run with Lana instead. Although they both appreciated this opportunity for recreation, they did not forget that their mission was ultimately to gather as much information as possible about the Research Center so that they could escape.

"You are free to explore the Sun Run for the next hour," said Verax. "I will wait for you here, near the door." Verax assumed an at-ease posture beside the door, and continued to survey the Run.

"Well, you heard him," said Lana with a grin. "Let's explore!" Blake smiled back at her weakly. Although his spirits had been raised, he knew he was still a prisoner. In a way, getting this small taste of freedom only further steeled his resolve to escape, and he felt the bittersweet taste of determination deep within himself. Yet, whenever Lana smiled, she always managed to make him feel happy once more.

"All right," he said. "Let's explore." Blake was in his escort mode. He always felt protective of Lana, and it was always his pleasure to walk along her side as a sort of bodyguard. Considering their present predicament, he felt especially protective of her now. It was not that he thought her fragile, for he knew that she was perfectly capable of fending for herself. Yet, somehow he knew that she received an extra benefit from his attention, and he knew that he certainly benefited from her company, as well. So, together, they strolled about the grounds. For a few moments they walked hand in hand, but then soon abandoned it because the encumbering chains they wore kept getting in the way. Nevertheless, they continued to walk side by side as they studied the grass and shrubs, and even surreptitiously inspected the walls and fence. "We can talk, but we'll have to make it seem like we're just idly chatting away. That way Verax won't suspect anything."

"Agreed," said Lana. "What are you thinking?"

"These animals look healthy enough. I wonder why none of them are trying to get past this fence. I don't see any barbs or sharp spines on it anywhere. You'd think that if they couldn't leap over it, then they'd at least try to climb over or crawl under it."

"Maybe they already know something about the fence that we don't," said Lana.

"Like what?" asked Blake.

"Oh, I don't know. Maybe they already tried to escape before but were punished or something."

"Punished?"

"Yeah. Maybe Verax or Lindberg shot at them. Or maybe…" Lana's voice trailed off.

"Maybe what?" asked Blake.

"Maybe this fence is booby-trapped," said Lana. She and Blake covertly scanned the fence and the area around it for snares, trapdoors, and guy wires, but found none. "I don't see anything."

"What if the fence itself is a trap?"

"What do you mean?" Lana asked.

"Well," Blake began, "if these Astronauts have magic that can make windows move by themselves and torches burn without fire, then maybe their fences have special powers, too. Let me try something." Pretending to examine a wildflower, Blake picked up a handful of moist soil with grass in it and threw it at the fence. There was a brief zap, a small spark, and the mass of dirt fell apart.

Blake's and Lana's eyes widened in amazement, but Lana noticed that Verax was monitoring them with his unblinking gaze. She crouched beside Blake, feigning a similar interest in the earth.

"Careful, Blake," she whispered. "I think Verax is watching."

"It's all right," said Blake. "I think we just found out what we needed to know: this fence can hurt you if you touch it."

"These animals seem to know that already."

"They probably found that out the hard way then," said Blake. "We're dealing with powerful magic here, Lana."

"Or energy," she said thoughtfully.

"What?"

"Remember how I said that Verax gets his energy from electricity? Well, Dr. Lindberg told me that his whole laboratory runs on it. That must be what powers this fence, too."

"In that case, maybe the Sun Run isn't a good place to escape from after all," said Blake.

"I guess not. What about the wall of the building itself?"

"Let's have a look," said Blake.

Casually, the two rose up and walked over to where a shrub was growing next to the actual Research Center building. Feigning interest in the shrub, they inspected the material of the wall, but found no surprises. The wall was a bright cream-white color, apparently painted with some sort of protective coating. Blake gave it a light tap, which produced a soft ringing sound. Then he quickly placed his hand on the wall to absorb the vibrations before they could attract Verax's attention.

"Must be made from some sort of metal," said Blake. "Strong one, too." The entire wall consisted of repeating panels of this material, with long but neat seams visible wherever they met. Other than a few control panels with mysterious buttons, switches, and ports, the wall was virtually featureless.

"Do you think we could pry these panels apart?" asked Lana.

"Maybe, but I wouldn't dare try now. Not with Verax here. We could practice back in the cell, though."

The couple moved on and walked around the periphery of the Run. They walked past the actual gate that led to the Outer Field, slowing their pace as they took a moment to study it. The gate appeared extremely sturdy. Its hinges were thick and tough, as was the latch, and there were several locks on the jamb, all of which were firmly secured. Not wanting to appear suspicious, the couple resumed walking again. They watched the deer and the rabbits, and they examined the shrubs. Everything seemed normal and healthy, except for the fear in the eyes of the animals. However, there were no obvious flaws in the design of the Run, and no apparent means of escape.

"I think we're stuck here," said Lana.

"At least for now," said Blake. After they had come full circle, they approached Verax once more. The robot let them back into the building and escorted them to their chamber. After they had entered the lab, Blake and Lana saw Rita standing in her own enclosure, looking on anxiously. "May we go to her?" asked Blake.

"Yes," replied Verax. Eagerly, the couple ran toward the dog, who at first stood at attention with her entire body erect to confront what seemed like enemies.

"Look at how brave she is, Lana!" cried Blake. "She must not know it's us." When they pressed their hands against the glass, Rita realized that these two humans were her own. She whined and begged and scratched at the glass. "We'll see you soon, Rita! I wish I could make you understand that, Girl. We'll see you soon."

Verax guided Blake and Lana into their own cell. He took off their chains and sealed the enclosure. Then he turned around and left the lab, leaving the humans to sit idly on their bench once more.

Blake and Lana spent the rest of the afternoon lounging around, talking every now and then, and napping quite often. Eventually, their own internal clocks told them that it was time for bed, so they snuggled together on the bench and covered up with the thin blanket provided. The fluorescent lamps continued to glow, but Blake and Lana drifted off to sleep for the night.

Chapter 20

Blake and Lana settled into a routine at the Earth Research Center, and spent most of their time enduring long periods of inactivity and boredom. Each morning, the electric lights turned on and Verax came in to check on the humans. With a push of a button, he ordered a machine to give them breakfast through an opening in the wall, and left. After their meal, Blake and Lana lay about in their cell until midday, when Verax brought them lunch. Then they napped and lay about some more until Verax escorted them to Rita's cell. He allowed them to put a leash onto Rita, and then took all three of them to the Sun Run. After letting them stay outdoors for a while, Verax brought his charges back inside, returning the dog to her cell and the humans to theirs. Then, Blake and Lana waited for dinner, and stayed awake until the lights shut off at night. Every day proceeded in this same, mind-numbing way. One day melded into the next, and Blake and Lana felt completely disoriented and lifeless.

Their time in the Sun Run seemed pleasant, but even that quickly became tedious and tiresome. Blake and Lana looked forward to seeing Rita, but they were disappointed that their time with her was so short, and that they always had to part with her. They pleaded with Dr. Lindberg to let Rita stay with them, but the scientist refused to back down on his position that the dog be housed separately. He felt strongly that animals should always be kept in single-species enclosures, and made it clear that no exceptions would be made. The couple acquiesced and contented themselves with seeing their dog only once a day, afraid that if they continued to object, they would lose what few privileges they had.

Trapped in a room together, Blake and Lana often found themselves having sex. At first, this was fun and exciting. Given the ongoing trauma of their captivity, they gladly consoled each other and made love several times a day. However, as time went on, their lovemaking became less and less frequent until it eventually ceased altogether. One reason for this was the dreariness of their enclosure, which seemed to drain the zest for life right from them. Another was that their intercourse was overdone, and like any overdone activity, it became uninteresting. The main reason, however, was that they had come to suspect they were being watched.

One day, in the middle of their union, Lana and Blake noticed a small, black-and-white, rectangular box suspended in a corner of the ceiling outside their cell. They watched it pivot in place until a small, shiny, circular opening on one end turned to face them. It was as though this machine had an eye, and as though this eye was now trained on them and watching them closely. A feeling of shyness, embarrassment, and worst of all, shame, overcame them. Their passion quickly subsided and they parted. That was the last time they made love at the Earth Research Center.

ಲ ಆ

Lana and Blake sat idly in their cell one morning. Breakfast was behind them, lunchtime would not come for several hours, and they had run out of things to do. Blake lay on his bed staring at the ceiling. Lana sat on the floor with her back against the wall and stared through the glass at nothing.

"Do you think there are other robots like Verax?" she asked Blake.

"I don't know. I suppose," replied Blake, dully.

An empty minute passed.

"Do you think there are other people here like Dr. Lindberg?" asked Lana.

"I don't know. I suppose."

Another minute passed.

"Do you think there are other flying machines here like the one that captured us?"

"I don't know. I suppose."

More silence.

"How big do you think this place is?"

"I don't know!" Blake suddenly shouted. He sat straight up in bed and glared at Lana. Blake roared at her. "I don't know, all right? How many times do I have to tell you? I don't know! I don't know!"

"Well, I'm sorry!" Lana yelled defensively. Her voice began to crack. "I was just trying to make conversation! I just wanted to talk to you! I just..." Lana could talk no more and caved in on herself. She tucked her legs to her chest, her back still against the wall, and lowered her head into the space where her arms wrapped around her knees. Then she wept.

Blake watched her, disgusted with himself, and horrified at what he saw. The only other time he had ever seen Lana like this was when he had first met her back in the Rubbletown. He, Manosh, and the dogs had frightened off that gang of men, and had entered her cave-like dwelling to offer their help. There, they had found her terrified, anguish-stricken, and huddled in a corner, but still defiant and ready to defend herself. That image of the feeble, wretched, innocent person in the Rubbletown had been seared into Blake's memory forever; it was the same person as the beautiful woman he had fallen in love with. All Blake had wanted for Lana was happiness, but now his stomach turned when he realized that he was responsible for making her miserable again.

"No, no, no," said Blake in hushed tones as he got up from his bed. He kneeled down beside Lana and moved to embrace her. "Lana, I didn't..."

Lana shrugged him off forcefully and leaned against her own bed, her face buried in the mat. She showed Blake her back and continued to sob.

"Lana, I'm sorry," said Blake, fumbling for the words. "I didn't mean it. It's just...this place. It's so..."

Lana voicelessly shooed him away with one hand and he backed away from her. Then she crawled into bed, faced the wall, and pulled the covers up over herself.

Blake rose to his feet and softly pounded a fist against the wall. He wanted to yell in frustration, but refrained from doing so — with great effort — to avoid upsetting Lana any further. *I'm sorry. I'm sorry. I'm sorry. I'm just so goddamn bored out of my head, I lost my patience. It's not your fault. You didn't do anything wrong. I'm just going crazy in here.* Blake looked through the glass at the lab on the other side. He glanced back at Lana. She was still sobbing beneath her blanket, so he went back to staring at the lab.

A few painfully long minutes later, the front door to the lab opened and four figures walked in. Blake recognized two of the figures as Dr. Lindberg and Verax. The third figure was another robot, almost identical to Verax, except its shiny, plastic body was slightly darker, making it almost tan instead of creamy white. The fourth figure was a Lunari woman. She was just as pale as Dr. Lindberg, and her eyes were just as blue. Her hair, like Dr. Lindberg's, was dark brown and shiny, but it was longer, hanging down almost to her shoulders, and a bit wavier, too. And like her associate, she wore an all-white suit that covered her whole body except her head, and that bore various small, colorful insignias and decorations.

Blake watched the two scientists and their robotic assistants approach him and come to a stop right in front of his cell. Neither the Lunari nor the robots said anything. Rather, Dr. Lindberg and the woman simply appraised Blake — as well as Lana behind him — and jotted a few notes down on their clipboards. Blake felt his heart race within his chest, but did not let his alarm show. Instead, he flicked his head over his shoulder in Lana's direction and issued a warning.

"Lana," he hissed. "Lana. Dr. Lindberg and Verax are here, and there's somebody else with them."

Lana sat up and looked out the front glass. Her eyes were red, puffy, and moist from crying, but she composed herself and swung her legs over the edge of her bed. She planted her feet on the floor, narrowed her gaze, and scrutinized the Lunari visitors.

Dr. Lindberg and the other woman noticed Lana's state, and wrote furiously on their notepads for a while. When Dr. Lindberg finished writing, he pushed a button on the wall next to Blake and Lana's cell and opened a communication channel.

"Hello, Blake. Lana. I'd like to introduce you to someone. This is my colleague, Dr. Petra Dunkel, and her assistant, Yeda."

Dr. Dunkel blankly nodded her head in acknowledgment. Blake and Lana said nothing.

Dr. Lindberg continued. "They're going to help us with a procedure today. We're going to let you out of your cell and take you to another room, where we're going to try something new, all right?" Again, Blake and Lana stared at the scientists and said nothing. Dr. Lindberg fumbled for a moment. "Um, right. Well, let's get started then."

Dr. Lindberg pushed another button, and the glass front wall to Blake and Lana's cell retreated upward and disappeared into the ceiling. Blake and Lana hesitantly came forward and lighted on the floor next to the Lunari.

"There," said Dr. Lindberg flatly. "Now, Blake, you're going to come with Verax and me into that room over there." Dr. Lindberg pointed to a doorway on one side of the lab. Blake could see bright light coming through the door, and white walls in the room on the other side. "Lana is going to go with Dr. Dunkel and Yeda into an identical room, except it's over there." He pointed to another doorway on the opposite wall.

"Wait," said Blake. "You can't separate us."

"It's all right," said Dr. Lindberg. "It's only for a little while."

"I don't care. We're not going."

Dr. Lindberg became stern. "I'm afraid you have no choice in the matter, Blake. Now come along and don't cause trouble."

"No. You can't make us."

"We *can* make you, but believe me, you don't want us to. Now come along."

"No."

Dr. Lindberg turned to his robot. "Verax. Escort this subject to the testing room."

With that, Verax's powerful, three-fingered hand clamped down on Blake's upper arm and began to pull on him. Blake felt a sudden revulsion to this feeling. He scowled defiantly and tried to jerk his arm away, but the robot's grip remained firm. Blake jerked again, but it was no use, and the robot continued to hold onto him.

A surge of anger overtook Blake. He lashed out at Verax and slammed the flesh of his fist into Verax's compact body. The robot lurched from the blow but regained its balance and tightened its grip. Blake kicked at Verax's birdlike legs, but Verax simply sidestepped the attack. Blake made one final attempt at pulling away, but the robot seized Blake's other arm in its free hand.

This angered Blake even further, and he began to struggle more vigorously. The other assistant, Yeda, came to Verax's aid and took hold of Blake by the ankles. Now the two robots held Blake clear off the ground like a human hammock, but he continued to resist.

Suddenly, a wild jolt of pain coursed through Blake's body. He felt as though all of his muscles had tensed at the same time. This sensation lasted for a few seconds, but then it stopped almost as suddenly as it had begun. Blake felt his body become limp and soft against his will. As soon as he felt himself regain control, however, he tried to tear himself free of the robots. Then another flash of pain overpowered him, and this one lasted longer than the first. Blake's jaw clenched. His eyes slammed shut and his throat tightened. His arms and legs burned with strain, and his skin felt hot, prickly, and itchy.

The pain stopped again. This time, Blake was sure he could not move and stopped resisting. Verax and Yeda released their hold on him, and he fell to the hard floor with an odd thud.

Blake saw a strange, bright blue light out of the corner of his eye. He rolled his eyes and craned his neck until he located the source — a small, black device in Dr. Lindberg's hand. Two small, metal prongs protruded from one end of it, and a flickering, blue-purple light formed a jagged, fluctuating line between the prongs. Blake could hear a faint, buzzing sound coming from the device.

Electricity.

Disoriented, eyes half-open, Blake wearily looked around for Lana. At last he found her looking back at him. She stood by, partially blocked by Dr. Dunkel, but with fresh tears in her eyes.

No. I must stop. I will not make her cry. Ever.

Blake clumsily rolled over onto his belly. He lifted himself onto his hands and knees, and slowly rose to his feet. He felt dizzy, weak, and tired, but remained standing. Blake opened his mouth to speak, but strange, slurred words came out instead.

"Okay," breathed Blake. "We'll go. But only … for a little while."

"Of course," said Dr. Lindberg, a thin smile on his lips.

Verax once again wrapped his hard, plastic fingers around Blake's arm. Blake looked at the white, mechanical hand. This time, that was all he did. Dr. Lindberg walked toward the door on the far wall and Verax followed, taking Blake along with him. Blake offered no protest. He did, however, look over his shoulder for Lana, and found that her fate was the same as his. Dr. Dunkel led the way to the other testing room with Yeda right behind her, guiding Lana by the arm. Lana was compliant, but like Blake, looked over her shoulder.

Lana and Blake made eye contact and continued to watch each other for as long as they could. Each saw the other move farther and farther away until, at last, the Lunari drove them into their respective rooms and shut the doors behind them.

Chapter 21

Blake stepped into the testing room and raised an eyebrow. The entire room was white, and bright lights shown down from their recessed positions in the ceiling. The floor was smooth, with a dull shine. The walls had a matte finish, but were completely devoid of signs, images, or panels of any kind. There was only one piece of furniture to be seen — a single reclining chair in the middle of the room. Dr. Lindberg and Verax coaxed Blake toward it.

"Sit down here, Blake," said Dr. Lindberg.

Blake feared getting more electrical shocks, but he was nevertheless reluctant to comply. "Why?" he asked.

"We are going to conduct a new procedure today, and we need you to be seated for it."

"What kind of procedure?"

"If I told you that," said Dr. Lindberg, "then it could alter the outcome of the procedure."

"But I need to know what you're going to do."

"Now, Blake. You don't want me to have to shock you again, do you?"

Blake glared at Dr. Lindberg, but then acquiesced. Without a word, he sat down in the chair.

The chair itself was not uncomfortable. Like the rest of the room, it was completely white. Blake noticed that the upholstery was a leathery material, but chided himself for not being able to determine what sort of animal it had come from.

"Now then," said Dr. Lindberg, "just put your arms up here on the armrests and lean back."

Blake did as he was told, and Dr. Lindberg let the back of the chair tilt rearward until Blake was nearly supine.

Blake was beginning to feel more at ease, when he noticed that Dr. Lindberg had a blue plastic box in his lap. The scientist released the lid and swung it wide open. Then he removed a thin, plastic bag; a long, rubbery tube; and several small, narrow packets. He unfolded the plastic bag, connected the rubber tube to it, and suspended the device from a hook behind the chair. Then he grabbed one of the packets and began to unwrap it.

Blake watched with great curiosity as Dr. Lindberg removed a clear, plastic cylinder from the wrapper, but he became anxious when he noticed the long, metal needle at one end.

"What … what is that?" asked Blake.

"A syringe," said Dr. Lindberg.

"What are you going to do with it?"

Dr. Lindberg turned to Verax. "Strap him in."

The robot immediately complied, and before Blake could do anything about it, his wrists, ankles, chest, and hips were all belted to the chair. He struggled, but only for a moment.

"Just sit still!" snapped Dr. Lindberg. The scientist tied another rubber tube to Blake's upper arm and allowed the veins in the crook of his elbow to engorge with blood. He wiped a small, moist pad over the exposed area. The pad emitted a strong odor, and Blake frowned when he smelled it. His moistened skin felt cool, but it soon dried and felt normal again.

Then Dr. Lindberg inserted the needle end of his syringe into one of Blake's veins. Blake felt a sharp, stabbing pain; his eyes widened, but he kept silent, for Kamishi men always endured pain with dignity. Dr. Lindberg held the syringe in one hand and slowly pulled on its expanding back end with the other.

Blake refused to look away and studied the syringe. To his horror, he watched it fill with dark, rich blood — his blood.

"What are you doing?" asked Blake nervously. "Is that my blood? Are you taking my blood? What are you going to do with my blood?"

"Yes, it's your blood. We're just going to examine it, measure a few things in it."

Blake frowned. *Blood is precious. Blood is sacred. You can't just take it like that. Not without good reason.* Blake remained sour as he watched Dr. Lindberg draw the blood, but he noticed that his pain was subsiding and that his anxiety was fading.

"You know," said Blake, "this is not so different from some Bebelishi rituals. I've never had them done myself, but I know those who have. Blood letting, scarring, stuff like that. It's not so different."

Dr. Lindberg absently hummed in accord.

Blake watched the scientist work until the syringe could hold no more blood. Dr. Lindberg withdrew the syringe, removed the needle, and discarded it into a small, plastic box. Then he capped the syringe and carefully placed it into another container for safekeeping. With blood collection complete, Dr. Lindberg first loosened the rubber tubing on Blake's upper arm and then removed it altogether.

"Verax, put the monitors on him."

"Yes, sir," said Verax. The robot proceeded to fasten several small devices to Blake. He slipped an elastic band onto Blake's wrists and ankles. Blake noticed that the bands felt soft and fuzzy, except for a single metal button embedded within the fabric. On his wrists, this button was near the base of his palm. On his ankles, it was on the inside of his leg, just above the instep. Verax also placed a larger elastic band around Blake's head. The band was similarly soft and fuzzy, but Blake could feel three buttons pressing against the skin of his forehead.

"All right, Blake, that's it," said Dr. Lindberg. "We're going to leave you now. We'll be back later." Then the scientist and his assistant left, and closed and locked the door behind them, leaving Blake all alone in the room.

Blake sat there quietly. He looked down at the restraints and the bands on his limbs. He looked all around him at the white, featureless walls and the bright, pale lights. Nothing moved unless he moved. Nothing made a sound unless he made a sound. Everything was perfectly still. At first, this was soothing to him, but as the minutes wore on, Blake became bored. He began to fidget and squirm, drumming his fingers on the armrests and rocking his feet back and forth.

Blake endured this agonizing silence for a long time, although he could not be sure for exactly how long. Then, when he thought he was about to go out of his mind with boredom, the lights suddenly went out and everything became pitch black. Blake could see absolutely nothing. There was no light at all, not even a sliver beneath the door or a warm glow from the lamps overhead. Everything was completely and utterly dark. Blake's eyes tried to adjust, but it was no use. Blake stared blankly into the perfect blackness and sighed.

Just then, a light came on. Blake squinted at the brightness of it while his eyes readjusted, but he could already tell that this light was relatively soft and rather green in color. He looked around when his vision returned to normal, but he could scarcely believe what he saw. He was in the middle of a verdant field. Tall, green grass and countless red and yellow flowers surrounded him. There was a stand of tall, lush trees on a low hill only a few hundred feet away to the right. Blake felt a faint breeze, and the plants swayed gently as it passed over them. The sky was an exquisite shade of blue, and only a few small, white clouds floated through it. Whatever this place was, it was beautiful.

Where am I? What's going on? How did I get here?

Blake let his eyes wander to the open area on his left. To his surprise, he noticed an enormous boulder standing there in the middle of the field. With its gray color and bumpy-looking texture, the thing seemed ordinary enough, but it was very strange to see a boulder out here with no other rocks nearby. There was something even stranger about it than that. The boulder was oblong in shape, but instead of lying on its side, it stood on one end, pointing up at the sky like some sort of giant, dull spearhead. The boulder seemed perfectly stable in this position, but how it could have come to rest like that was a complete mystery to Blake.

Blake heard a faint rustling in the grass to his right. He followed the sound and spotted a little rabbit emerging from the grass a short distance from his reclining chair. The rabbit remained partially concealed for a moment, but it soon hopped into a clearing where it was more visible.

That's cute. I wonder what it's doing here.

The tiny creature nibbled on a few blades of grass and unhurriedly downed them. It rubbed its snout with its forepaws and scratched its flank with a hind paw. The rabbit remained still for a while, but then it hopped away and disappeared in the grass on Blake's left.

Nothing happened for a few minutes, but Blake did not mind. He watched the swaying plants and drifting clouds and let them lull him into a calm, quiet, trancelike state.

Eventually, Blake noticed a deer emerge from the trees. He could see immediately that this was an adult and a doe, and as she came closer to his chair, he also realized that she was a whitetail. Like most deer, the doe seemed cautious enough, but she was not particularly skittish or frightened. She foraged on the plants as she walked along, but she was choosy, plucking a particularly lush blade of grass here or an especially tender leaf there. Blake watched the doe intently as she approached.

In time, she stood directly in front of Blake with her flank facing him and her body still pointing to the left. The doe ducked her head back into the foliage and came up with a big, green clump of grass. As she chewed on her food, her head pivoted on her long, graceful neck, allowing her to look directly at Blake. Her big, keen ears swiveled toward him, and her moist, black nose twitched as she took in his scent. Blake remained perfectly still and avoided looking the deer directly in the eye; he did not want to frighten her away. It had been years since he had come this close to a deer without frightening it, and he relished this opportunity to observe one now.

After a few minutes, the doe's ears rotated about her head again. They lingered in a position facing behind her, and the doe looked back at the grove of trees as though she had heard something. Then, with a lone blade of grass still sticking out of her mouth, she bounded away to the left. Blake watched her until she was gone. Then he looked back at the trees. At first, he saw nothing unusual, but then he saw what had frightened the doe away.

It was a wolf, and it was bigger than most. With its thick, gray fur and long, loping gait, Blake could tell that this one was healthy and powerful. The wolf jogged down the hill and easily closed the distance between the human and itself. Blake watched it closely. The wolf came to a stop only a few paces away from Blake's restrained, elevated feet. Holding its head up high, the wolf sniffed him.

Blake maintained eye contact, for he knew that predators pick off the sick and the weak, and he did not want to appear like either one. The wolf's eyes were a rich yellow color; they would have been beautiful to Blake had he not felt so afraid. In time, the wolf lost interest. It lowered its muzzle into the grass, picked up the deer's trail, and followed it again. Then it, too, was gone.

Blake let out a sigh of relief. He stretched as much as he could, confined as he was to the chair, and relaxed. This time, he felt less inclined to let the pretty scenery lull him into a tranquil state. He did not feel tense, but he was now alert and aware, and proficiently monitored his surroundings.

Several more minutes passed, but nothing changed. The plants still swayed in the breeze, the clouds still drifted by. Blake began to feel sleepy and his eyelids began to close. But they snapped open when he heard a rustling in the grass.

Another rabbit? No, this sounds bigger. Farther, but bigger.

Blake looked at the trees again. This time, the creature that emerged from the grove was a big, male lion.

No. No. No. Not again. Don't move. Don't move. Maybe he won't notice you. Don't move.

But the lion did notice Blake. Almost as easily as the wolf had done, the lion trotted down the hill and stopped just short of Blake's reclining chair. Blake's heart raced and his breathing became rapid and shallow, but he controlled himself and remained perfectly still.

If only I could run away. If only I weren't chained to this damn chair I could just run away.

The lion crouched low in the tall grass. It was strange how this massive creature could almost disappear in such little cover, and with such little difficultly. Blake tried to keep his eye on the carnivore, but it was difficult with those straps on his chest and hips, and with the lion being so close.

Then the lion stood tall and lifted himself above the grass. This action surprised Blake, for in all his years of watching and avoiding lions, he had never seen one betray its position like that. Then again, he had never seen a lion stalk a man in a chair before, so he put the thought out of his mind.

The lion took a few steps forward until he was almost within striking distance. From here, the creature was overwhelming. His full, shaggy mane made his head look as big as one whole man, and each of his paws could smother Blake's entire face.

The lion sniffed Blake like the other animals had done, but then opened his mighty jaws and let out a deafening roar. Blake winced. He wanted to close his eyes, but he forced them open and willed himself to watch. The lion's fangs were enormous, each one as long as Blake's fingers, and the tongue was broad, pink, and covered with sharp, prickly barbs. Blake dreaded the hot, fetid breath of the great beast, but to his surprise, it never came.

The lion crouched, obviously preparing to attack, and Blake began yelling in an attempt to scare him away.

"Go away!" cried Blake in a roar of his own. "Ho! Go away!" The tactic was failing, however, for the lion not only refused to leave, but remained crouched and snarled menacingly.

Then the lion launched himself at Blake. He flew up, high above the human, and described a huge arc in the air as he descended on his victim.

"No! No! No!" Blake yelled pathetically. He shut his eyes and braced himself for the end.

Then all was quiet and still. Blake cracked an eyelid open and saw that the field was gone, and so was the lion. Instead, Blake found himself back in the white room with the plain, white walls and the shiny, white floor. Blake felt faint.

The door swung open, and Dr. Lindberg and Verax entered the room. Dr. Lindberg tied another rubber tube around Blake's upper arm and wiped the crook of Blake's elbow with another moist pad. Blake was so dazed that he took no notice of the cool sensation on his skin, nor did he notice the slight pain of a needle entering his vein for another blood draw. When Dr. Lindberg filled another syringe with blood, he repeated the cleanup procedure and stowed the sample with the one he had taken earlier.

"Verax," said Dr. Lindberg. "Release him."

Verax removed all of the monitoring bands from Blake's body and unfastened all of the straps that had kept him bound to the chair.

"All right, Blake," said Dr. Lindberg flatly. "We're done here. You can get up now."

Blake staggered to his feet. He felt so dizzy that he almost collapsed, but Verax caught him and helped him right himself. Then the scientist and the robot escorted Blake out of the testing room and back into the main laboratory.

There, Blake saw Lana emerging from her room on the other side of the lab. He could see that his mate was just as dazed and frightened as he was. However, seeing each other again gave the couple renewed energy, and they somehow found the strength to run to one anther. They met in the middle of the room and embraced desperately and powerfully. Their arms were wrapped tightly around each other, their heads pressed firmly together, and their eyes shut tight. They did not speak, or kiss, or even caress; they only clung to one another out of fear, and worry, and relief.

Blake and Lana heard the scientists say something, but they paid no attention to what it was. They felt the robots prod them back toward the enclosure, and allowed themselves to be treated this way. Without fully letting go of one another, they clambered back up into their cell. The glass wall came down behind them, trapping them in that tiny space again, but they did not care. A hole opened in the wall and two servings of food and drink magically appeared, but Blake and Lana ignored them completely. They did not even open their eyes. All they did was crouch down in the middle of their cell and cling to each other for dear life.

Chapter 22

Weeks passed, but Blake, Lana, and Rita remained captive at the Earth Research Center. All of Dr. Lindberg's research subjects, including the two humans, had to have weekly physiological examinations, so the blood draws continued. The other animals were restrained during these periods to make handling them safer and easier, but blood could be drawn from the humans while they were still awake, as long as they promised to cooperate. Despite their initial fear, Blake and Lana soon grew accustomed to the needles and their associated minor pain and bleeding. Nevertheless, being inmates at the Earth Research Center was exasperating, and the two of them often commiserated about the cramped quarters, constant monitoring, and forced blood draws.

Dr. Lindberg treated Blake and Lana the way he treated Rita or any other animal in his lab — like possessions. These creatures were merely subjects in his experimental regime, and as such had lost their autonomy. Dr. Lindberg knew that he caused them considerable discomfort and distress, but he took pride in knowing that he did not harm them intentionally.

Despite his rigorous and dispassionate approach to research, Dr. Lindberg strived to remain as open-minded as possible, and was willing to interview and listen to his human subjects rather than merely observe them. In time, a kind of relationship developed between the scientist and the travelers, and an unspoken and unconscious kind of transaction had developed between them. In exchange for certain freedoms, such as extended time in the Sun Run or with their dog, Blake and Lana agreed to give Dr. Lindberg information.

At first, Dr. Lindberg was reluctant to interview the couple, thinking it too subjective a practice at this point in the study. Soon, however, he found himself asking them questions about how they lived, what they believed, and what they valued in life. He was even surprised to find himself revealing the same information about himself and his people to the couple.

At first, the three explored their differences, but it did not take long for Dr. Lindberg to realize that they had more in common. He found this disturbing, for he had always somehow considered the Lunari superior to the Earthlings, albeit on a subconscious level. However, being a true scientist, he consciously decided to proceed with his investigation and uncover the truth, whatever it may be.

Dr. Lindberg became quite attached to his little anthropological project, and to his subjects. It made him feel passionate again, which was the reason he had chosen a career in research to begin with. For the first time in a long time, Dr. Lindberg's professional life merged with his personal life. Not since his days at the university had he felt so involved in his work and so eager to do it. He found it rewarding to converse with Blake and Lana, and he felt confident that they were benefiting from their association with him, too. Every once in a while he permitted himself to fantasize about the glory and praise he would reap when he finally published his monograph on these Earthling humans. His mind was absolutely swimming with ideas. He even chose a name for this new study — Project Anthrop. He knew that this was professionally inadvisable, but he couldn't help it; he was inspired.

One morning, Dr. Lindberg ran a routine check on his menagerie, unaccompanied by Verax. He stopped in front of Blake and Lana's cage for a few observations, where he found them already awake.

"Good morning," said Dr. Lindberg.

"Morning," said Blake and Lana, simultaneously.

"How are you doing today?"

"Fine," said Blake and Lana. The bland expressions on their faces betrayed their boredom, but Dr. Lindberg was not surprised. They were in good condition, and they were not stir-crazy, so he was satisfied.

"Where's Verax?" asked Lana.

"Oh, he's off doing some work with a few other robots," said Dr. Lindberg casually, without looking up from his tablet. He did not notice the flicker of excitement that crossed both Lana's and Blake's faces, nor the way they made eye contact, nor the almost imperceptible nod they gave one another.

"What do you have planned for today?" A curious and innocent expression suddenly appeared on Lana's face.

That's a curious question, thought Dr. Lindberg. "Well," he began, "mostly routine things, really. After I finish here, I have to go back to my personal lab and run a couple of experiments. Then I have to write a report, and then I'll have to check on my experiments again. And I guess that's it."

"Nothing out of the ordinary, huh?" she said.

"No, not really ... oh wait. Actually, I do have something kind of exciting to do today. I am going to make my monthly aerial survey of the Research Center."

"An aerial survey?" asked Blake. "What's that?"

"Well, once a month I get into a Stingray, fly around over the Research Center, and make sure everything is all right."

"What's a Stingray?" asked Lana.

"A Stingray? Oh, that's a K-43 ... it's a flying machine, like the one that first collected you and brought you here." Blake and Lana's eyes immediately widened.

"The flying machine?" repeated Blake. "Really? You fly around in the flying machine!" Blake was amazed. He did not understand how the machine worked in the first place, or what it was used for, or what it was capable of. It frightened him, and he knew it. However, he also found it fascinating, and he wondered if he would ever see it again. Now here was Dr. Lindberg, speaking so casually about how regularly he flies over the Earth in the machine himself. "Isn't it scary?"

"No, not anymore," said the scientist. "At first, learning how to use it was a bit scary, but it was also quite fun, and very exciting. Now, it's fairly easy for me to use it, so I don't find it scary anymore." Blake and Lana stared at Dr. Lindberg in amazement. Then they looked to each other, as if to silently ask one another if they could believe what they were hearing. Dr. Lindberg watched them for a moment as they ignored him and grappled with the concept of a flying human being.

At first, Dr. Lindberg felt powerful and smug. Until now, he had never actually met tribal people. The only people he had ever known were other Lunari. It was only a year ago that he descended to Earth to take up this position as a biologist at the Earth Research Center in Houston. Since then, he had come into contact with several tribal Earthlings, but he had never met any of them before Blake and Lana. Earthlings had always been mere specimens to him, always something to be poked, prodded, or sampled, but never a real person worthy of acquaintance. Now, he actually knew two Earthlings. Impressing Blake and Lana in this way, he felt superior. *Look at how animal-like they are. It's hard to believe that they are of the same species as I am.* For a moment, Henry Lindberg felt like a god.

That thought was fleeting. As he studied Blake's and Lana's faces, Dr. Lindberg saw something he had not seen in a long, long time. He saw a spark of wonder in their eyes, and he instantly knew he had seen that spark before. It was the same spark he had as a child when he used to look up into the sky and see the Earth. It was the same spark he had seen in his classmates back at the university. It was the same spark he saw in the eyes of his colleagues when he conversed with them about their research. How he adored that spark.

It was humanity.

"Well," said Dr. Lindberg, suddenly flustered. "I must move on. I'll see you later." Then he spun on his heels and hurriedly walked away.

Chapter 23

Dr. Lindberg sat down at his desk several nights later. It was almost midnight, but he liked to work late sometimes, and tonight was one such night. He wore blue pajamas — a silken outfit with long sleeves and long pant legs — and soft, blue slippers. He was in the bedroom of his quarters, where he lived alone. His home here at the Center was modest but adequate. It was a small apartment with one bedroom, a complete bathroom, a living room, and a kitchen; the Lunari seldom needed more than this. Dr. Lindberg's bedroom doubled as his home office, and the furniture in it was minimal: a single bed, two tall bookcases, and a slight desk with a simple chair. The desk was usually free of clutter, but it was home to a container full of pens, a palm-sized computer, and a small, posable lamp.

Tonight, the desk lamp was the only light in Dr. Lindberg's bedroom. Its glow illuminated his desk well enough, but it did not reach far beyond that, allowing the corners of the room to hide in shadow.

Dr. Lindberg ran his fingers through his hair and blew through pursed lips. "All right," he said to himself. "Let's get started." He pushed a series of buttons on his computer to turn it on. The tiny screen lit up, and the message, "Ready to record" appeared. Dr. Lindberg pressed another key and the message changed to, "Now recording."

"This is Henry Lindberg, Director of Life Science at the Earth Research Center in Houston. The date is December 20, 5046 CE. The time is…" He paused to look at his watch. "23:47 hours. My study into Earthling human population and behavioral genetics is proceeding as planned and with only a few, minor problems, which I will discuss later. I continue to explore the following questions: How much have Lunari and Earthling humans diverged? When did this divergence take place? And to what extent have the Earthlings degenerated?

"The two Earthlings, Blake and Lana, remain in my custody. Their behavior appears normal and they have become compliant with procedures. However, the last resting blood sample taken from the male appears to have coagulated, which may interfere with analysis. This is very surprising, because it happens so rarely; perhaps the collecting syringe was defective or deficient in anticoagulant. Verax will attempt to break up the microclots tomorrow. If he fails, then we may be missing a day's worth of data for certain parameters, but certainly not all. In any case, it's only one day of sampling, so the study remains secure.

"Beyond the genetic aspects of the study, we continue to examine the Earthlings' artifacts, which were confiscated during their initial period of unconsciousness several weeks ago. I am in possession of their travel bags, and I am going to begin inspecting one of them right now."

While still seated in his chair, Dr. Lindberg bent down, reached below his desk, and retrieved from there a large, leather satchel. He shook it gently and listened to the items inside jostle and rub against each other. With a grunt, he upended the bag and emptied its contents onto the desk. To his surprise, a small leather pouch and four books wrapped in rags fell out.

"Hmmm ... let's see what we have here then." Dr. Lindberg began by giving the pouch a cursory examination. He found that it was full of little, stone arrowheads. "How interesting. Look at all these stone weapons. I'll have to add them to our collection. Petra will be very pleased." Dr. Lindberg put the pouch back into the leather satchel and turned his attention to the books. He removed the protective rags — animal hides — and took a closer look.

Two of the books were small, tattered hardbacks, while the other two were big, leather-bound tomes. Dr. Lindberg first looked at the hardbacks. They were both very old and very worn, but somehow still intact enough to be legible. One of the books was called, *A History of Warfare*, and the other, simply *Mammals*. Dr. Lindberg gingerly leafed through the two reference books, skimming a passage here and looking at a picture there.

"Amazing. How did those two get their hands on books like these?"

Dr. Lindberg decided to inquire about the hardbacks later. For now, the ornate, impressive-looking volumes sitting side by side on his desk were calling to him, so he returned the reference books to the satchel and stowed them under his desk once more. Then he leaned forward in his chair and huddled eagerly over the leather-bound tomes.

Dr. Lindberg immediately deduced that these books were two copies of the same text, but his jaw dropped when he read the titles on the covers and realized what he had found.

"Bebel," Dr. Lindberg muttered. "The Bebel. Sweet moon rocks … I cannot believe this!" He sat up straight in his chair, a childish grin on his face. "It's their holy book! I am the first Lunari to discover the holy book of the Earthlings! This finding is going to make me … obscenely famous. Oh, Petra is not going to believe this. She is just not going to believe this!"

After a moment of giddiness, Dr. Lindberg managed to settle down and concentrate on the books once more. He carefully compared the two tomes. Both were big, thick, and old, but one of them — the smaller one — appeared a bit younger. The leather covers were shabby, but their decorative imprints and flourishes were still visible. Each book's back cover was bare. One word alone appeared on the front — "Bebel." Dr. Lindberg first opened the big book, then the little one, and began to peruse them.

"Hmmm … I'll need to examine these more closely, but the text seems to be the same — or at least very similar — in both. But how can that be? These people don't have replication technology. Copying by hand couldn't be that accurate, could it?" He noticed that, despite the odd stained or wrinkled page, both books were in remarkably good condition. "These books couldn't possibly be very old — a century, at most. Who wrote all this down? How could they still be in such good condition?"

Dr. Lindberg closed the bigger, older book and gently shoved it to one side of his desk. Then he centered the smaller, newer Bebel and began to read more slowly. He was amazed when he realized what was actually inside.

"Why, these writings come from the ancient Jews and Christians! I can't believe this; I thought their influence was gone. Everyone thinks they're extinct, but…" Dr. Lindberg's specialty was life science, not archaeology. He did have some training in the social sciences, however, and his work on genetics had forced him to become more familiar with history as well. He ticked off the groupings of books as he turned the pages. "Law, Prophets, Writings, Gospels, Epistles; yes, they're all here."

Dr. Lindberg skimmed through the tome, stopping only here and there for a few passages, but his excitement soon gave way to boredom as he read the material. "Oh," he sighed. "I can't believe the Earthlings still read this stuff. What am I saying? I can't believe they can even read. But they couldn't possibly use these ancient texts. Or if they do, they don't really believe in them, do they?"

At length, Dr. Lindberg reached the end of the collection of millennia-old writings. To his surprise, there was still more to read. "What's this? I've gone through everything, but I'm not even close to the end." He turned the page. To his amazement, he found himself staring at something completely new.

"'The Books of the New Days,'" he read aloud from the top of the page. "The Books of the New Days? What New Days? What Books? Who wrote this? What does this mean?" Dr. Lindberg looked farther down the page and discovered the titles of three new books, written by three new authors. "'The Book of Causes by Jonathan; The Book of Means by Belgrath; The Book of Conduct by Ecolta.' What is this? Who are those people? Why haven't I heard of them before?" The scientist turned the page again and continued reading, first from the Book of Causes:

> I am Jonathan Stein. I was born on December 18, 537 years after the Great Crash, when the asteroid Apophis collided with the Earth on Sunday, April 13, 2036 CE. The time since the Great Crash has come to be known as the New Days. Our calendar is measured in years following the Great Crash, with the number of the year followed by the words 'New Days," or 'ND' for short. Thus, I was born on December 18, 537 ND, to my father, Michael Stein, and my mother, Rachel Stein, in the town of Cincinnati, which used to be part of the state of Ohio, in what was once a mighty nation called the United States of America...

Dr. Lindberg stared silently and intently at the page. His breath came slow and deep. His spine tingled. He read on:

> The times we live in are full of change. The world today is not like it was, but more like it used to be. People know new things, but they have forgotten the old. I have decided to teach the people of the New Days what the Old Timers new, but also to help them avoid making the same mistakes

> the Managers made, now and forevermore. This Book will teach anyone who wishes to learn, the history of the Ancient Days and the Old Days, the way of the world toward the end of the Age of Management, and the series of events surrounding the Great Crash...

Dr. Lindberg was shocked. "Can this be true? Do the Earthlings really have such a detailed account of the apocalypse?" Excitedly, he skipped to the Book of Means:

> I am Belgrath. I was born on June 23, 1648 ND, to my father, Greg, and my mother, Wanda of the Yorkishi tribe. My place of residence is a city once known as New York, in the state of New York, in a nation called the United States of America. Now, this territory is simply called Yorkis. There are no more national boundaries, countries, states, counties, or cities. Now all people live in territories. These are expanses of land occupied by tribes, each consisting of about two hundred people. Only tribe members may inhabit a tribal territory...

"History," said Dr. Lindberg. "They get their history from the Bebel. How fascinating! I imagined they had some sort of information, but I had no idea they knew this much about their past. What about this third book? What's that one about?" Dr. Lindberg leafed ahead to the Book of Conduct:

> My name is Ecolta. I was born on September 9, 2041 ND. I am the daughter of Rofu the Warrior and Toba the Teacher, and I was born and raised in the territory of Omaha. I have proudly served my people, the Omahashi, as a healer since I began my training at the age of 15. At the time of this writing, I have 47 years.
>
> Our world is beautiful, and we live in a joyful time. The Creator has blessed us with food, water, and loved ones. He has given us a homeland of our own, and he has made the creatures of the earth, water, and sky our friends and neighbors.

But alas, we are only human, and every now and then, we want more. This is the way of the world, for the Creator has also given us the freedom to choose. We may choose the right path of love, kindness, and generosity; or we may choose the wrong path of greed, hatred, and wickedness. Every one of us has the power to choose, and sooner or later, every one of us will. At times, we may even choose the wrong path. But as long as we are willing to learn and atone for our mistakes, then it is never too late to return to the right path again.

In recent times, the voices of greed have grown stronger, while the voices of love have grown weaker. But it is not too late for us to return to the right path. I have felt fear for my people, because I have heard them talk of returning to the Old Ways. But this talk is wrong, and my people must learn why. I have heard the call, and I have decided to answer it. I have written this Book of Conduct to help the people see the right path, and to help them follow it..."

"A path?" Dr. Lindberg asked himself. "What sort of path? What sort of nonsense is this?"

...The Managers were powerful in the Old Days. They had power over the elements, other creatures, and even themselves. And yet, despite their knowledge, they did not realize that they were destroying their own world...

The Old Timers made many discoveries and created many beautiful things, but their excesses were many, and their greed practically insatiable. Nothing was ever enough for them, and all they wanted was more, more, more...

For all their success, the Managers were not content with what they had, and in trying to expand and conquer, they lost the very things they loved...

"This is how the Earthlings view their ancestors?" said Dr. Lindberg. "Our ancestors? As ravenous exploiters of the world? This only shows how much these Earth-bound humans have degenerated. They have no concept whatsoever of education or enlightenment; of art, research, or civics. Their ignorance is even more profound than I thought." He read on.

> ...The Great Crash changed everything. Even the mighty Managers were not strong enough to stop it, and when Apophis struck the Earth, the Managers' reign was over. However, let us not forget that we owe the Old Timers a debt of gratitude. After all, had it not been for their technology, their rocket, or their bomb, no one would have survived. We must thank them for the service they performed for us — their last act before they disappeared — but we must also remember that they committed many misdeeds before the Great Crash ever took place. We must never become like them again...

Dr. Lindberg looked up from the book in astonishment. "They know. They know about the apocalypse, and the nuclear bomb that broke up the asteroid. It's in their goddamn written historical record! Then why? What happened to them? If they know all this, then why do they live like filthy animals? Why don't they lift themselves up? Why don't they work at regaining the glory of the civilization that came before them? What could have possibly damaged them so badly, that they became unable to live as anything more than primitive beasts?"

> ...Thus, all life on Earth could have been destroyed, but it was not. Apophis was small enough, and the Managers powerful enough, that life was spared. Death was everywhere, but there were those who survived, and the New Days arrived. The Creator took mercy on us, and instead of annihilation came Rakamahn...
>
> At first, the people thought about going back to the Old Ways. They thought about going back to raising crops, breeding livestock, developing machines, and erecting cities. They thought about rebuilding their civilization, regaining their power,

> and preserving their knowledge, but they chose against it...

"What? They chose against it? Why? What does that mean?"

> ...The people knew that the spoils of Management came at a terrible price, and they were no longer willing to pay it. And so, the people chose the New Way...

Dr. Lindberg shook his head. "They *chose* to live this way? No, no, that doesn't make any sense. Why would they do that? Why would they choose to live like wild animals?"

> No life is without sacrifice, and the life of one who follows the New Way is no exception. Life in the New Days can be difficult, and there are many dangers to be overcome...

> But those who follow the New Way gain so much more than they lose. They lose permanence, but they gain experience. They lose power, but they gain wisdom. They lose security, but they gain freedom. And they lose possessions, but they gain love. Those who follow the New Way face their own challenges, but they will earn their own rewards, and they will be blessed..."

> And so, do not give up on the New Way, do not return to the Old Ways, and do not be tempted by spoils and riches. Greed and impatience will lead you down the wrong path, and ultimately to the undoing of yourself and all you hold dear. Only love and compassion can lead you down the right path, where you will find the wisdom and contentment we all seek. The Creator has laid out a simple way of life for us, and we need to follow it. Live by the New Way, and you will be happy..."

"This is unbelievable," said Dr. Lindberg. "Ecolta preached simplicity a millennium ago, and these people *still* live by that code today. Amazing." He continued to the final section of the Book of Conduct, which concluded with Ecolta's advice for following the New Way.

We must be good to the Earth, not only for the sake of the landscape, or the creatures who share the Earth with us, but for our own sake…

Give of yourself, for it is noble to serve others. Provide for yourself, because loving and respecting oneself is virtuous. However, do not be overly selfish, for the path to evil begins with greed…

Being resourceful does not mean being ruthless…

Protect yourselves, your people, and your land against all intruders who pose a threat. However, strive to live peaceably with others, and do not seek to bring down your neighbors. If you find someone who is all alone, welcome that person to live among you…

Take care not to let your numbers grow too large, so that you do not become crowded…

There are always more individuals born than can be supported by the resources available. It has always been this way, and so it will always remain…

Seek balance in all you do. True balance may be hard to find, but striving to attain it is among our noblest of tasks…

For the Creator there is no good or evil; there is only existence. For us living beings, good and evil seem real because we cherish the fire of life and fear the void of death. Fear not, however. Remember that life is a wonder and a gift, and you will go on…

Learn from the past, enjoy the present, look to the future, and you will be happy…

> Do not rush through life as though only its completion were important. Rather, take time to cherish each day for the gift that it is...

Dr. Lindberg became engrossed in Ecolta's writings and lost all track of time. He read on for hours until at last, in the early hours of the morning, he reached the end of the Book of Conduct, and the end of the entire Bebel. He shut the tome and stared at the front cover for a moment, contemplating the ancient teachings that had just confronted him.

"These people did not degenerate. They *chose* to live like that. They value their connection with the Earth so much, that ... they'd rather accept nature than struggle against it. Amazing." He sat for a time, silent and motionless, lost in thought. Then he grunted with finality. "I wonder," he said.

Dr. Lindberg wrapped both Bebels in their rags, slipped them back into the leather satchel, and returned the satchel to its temporary storage place under his desk. He pushed away from the desk, walked out of his bedroom and home office, and left his apartment, still wearing his blue pajamas and slippers. Then he headed down the white, brightly lit hallway and made his way to a shiny metal door. He punched a code into the keypad on the wall, unlocking the door. Dr. Lindberg swung the door open. The cool, moist night air ruffled his short, brown hair, played with the fabric of his pajamas, and brushed against his pale face. He smiled slightly to himself and went outside, letting the thick door close and lock itself behind him. A bright overhead spotlight shone down onto the step, where numerous tiny insects, drawn to the light, silently churned and swarmed without end. Dr. Lindberg stepped away from the building, walked out of the patch of light, and disappeared into the darkness.

Chapter 24

Blake and Lana saw nothing of either Dr. Lindberg or Verax the next morning, or even at midday. Being accustomed to a routine, they found this development particularly strange, and even disturbing. No one even came to see them during mealtime; instead, they received their food from the automatic contraption in the wall.

Then, at about three o'clock in the afternoon, Dr. Lindberg came barging into the lab, swinging his tablet wildly as his arms swung back and forth. Like two curious kittens, Blake and Lana looked up and watched the scientist march right up to their cell. He struck a button on the wall and spoke.

"How would you two like to go for a field trip today?" he asked eagerly. The couple looked at each other questioningly. They were intrigued by the idea, of course, but they were also a bit startled by the usually somber scientist's behavior.

"That sounds great," said Blake, "but where do you want to go?"

"Up," said Dr. Lindberg.

"Up?" echoed Blake. "What do you mean?"

"I want to take you for a ride in the Stingray," Dr. Lindberg said. Upon hearing this, Blake and Lana became exceedingly agitated and began backing away from the glass.

"Oh, I don't know about that, Dr. Lindberg," said Blake. "That doesn't sound like such a good idea after all."

"I agree," said Lana. "How about if we just go for a walk outside?" Blake and Lana had still not abandoned the idea of escaping from the Station. They had been waiting for an opportunity when Dr. Lindberg would take them outside without taking Verax along. At first, that was what they thought was about to happen now. Suddenly, this lunatic Astronaut had turned their expectations upside-down with his demonic idea of kidnapping them and hurtling them into the sky.

"Not a bad idea," said Dr. Lindberg, "but I like my idea better. Come on." He pushed a button on the wall and the front glass opened. Ordinarily, Blake and Lana would have leaped to the floor as soon as possible. This time, they remained in their cell, anxiously watching Dr. Lindberg. "Come on, now. Let's not delay. It's already after three o'clock."

"We're not going," said Blake firmly.

"Of course you are," said Dr. Lindberg.

"No, we're not," repeated Blake, "and don't try to make us."

"I will try to make you. If you don't stop acting so silly right now, I'm going to get Verax in here to carry you forcibly to the Stingray and keep you there. Now, come on."

"Why?" asked Lana.

"Because, it will be fun. Trust me."

"Why should we trust you?" she asked. "Have you given us any reason to trust you?"

"No…" said Dr. Lindberg. "No, I haven't. I know that now. That's all about to change, though. From this moment on, you can trust me. Now quit stalling and come out from there." Reluctantly, Blake and Lana stepped down and stood beside the scientist. They waited expectantly for him to pull out some restraints and to fasten them to their wrists and ankles, but he did no such thing.

"You're not…" said Lana, "you're not going to put us in chains?"

"No, I'm not. Not anymore." Dr. Lindberg pushed a few buttons and the heavy glass panel began to close once more. "Follow me." The couple walked after the scientist until they all stood in front of Rita's cell. Dr. Lindberg pushed a sequence of buttons, releasing the dog from her enclosure. Eagerly, Rita jumped down and greeted Blake and Lana with licking, whining, and pawing. Dr. Lindberg smiled to himself at seeing this reunion. He then pushed the buttons again and closed the dog's cell once more. "Now then," he said, "let's get going."

"No leash?" asked Blake timidly, despite his efforts to be assertive.

"No, no leash. I trust you … and I trust the dog. Now, let's go. Follow me." Together, the group walked through the lab doors and turned to go down the hall. Blake noticed that they were going in the opposite direction of the Sun Run.

"Where are we going?" asked Blake.

"We're going to the hangar," said Dr. Lindberg. "That's where we keep most of the vehicles, including the Stingrays." They marched at a quick pace down a labyrinth of corridors and rooms. For some of them, the group had to pause while Dr. Lindberg looked into a beam of red light that shone from a machine on the wall, in order to open the obstructing doors.

"What are those things?" asked Lana.

"Oh, those are just retinal scanners. They are machines that examine my retina, or the back of my eyeball, to make sure that it is really me requesting access to these areas. It's a security precaution."

They left the restricted areas of the facility and walked past elegant lobbies furnished with beautiful area rugs and large potted plants. There were several sets of thick, metal double doors here, too. Their surfaces had a warm, golden glow, and they were so much more pleasant to behold than the cold, silvery doors seen elsewhere at the Earth Research Center. Blake and Lana were impressed. Past another series of security doors they went, until they finally emerged in the hangar. It was enormous, with an impossibly high ceiling and an impossibly wide area used solely for vehicle storage. Ironically, most of the space went unused, for only a few Stingray ships were parked here, along with some other flying machines and several powerful-looking ground vehicles.

"There she is," said Dr. Lindberg, pointing at one of the ships. "That's my Stingray K-43. Her serial number is K43111, but I call her Daisy." As they approached the machine, Blake and Lana couldn't help but feel intimidated. This was, after all, the very same device that had attacked, tranquilized, and kidnapped them. Reluctant to get any closer, they stood back, while Rita remained faithfully by their side. Dr. Lindberg noticed their anxiety. "Don't worry. It's perfectly safe. She's not going to hurt you this time. She's completely under my control."

"Is it female?" asked Lana.

"No, it's neither male nor female. It's not alive. We just call it a 'she' because it's the traditional thing to do. I think it has something to do with the big ships that people used to sail back during the Expansive Age, or in the Old Days, as you call it."

"Does it have any 'safety advisories'?" she asked again. Dr. Lindberg laughed out loud. It was the first time that either Blake or Lana had seen him laugh, and it made them feel more at ease.

"So, you've been doing your homework, I see!" he said. "Well, yes, as a matter of fact it does have several safety advisories, but don't worry — all machines have those. Everything is under control." Dr. Lindberg pushed a series of buttons on the control panel next to the shiny door. With a hiss, the door swung upwards to reveal the interior of the machine. This startled Blake, Lana, and Rita, but they leaned forward to inspect Daisy nonetheless.

Inside, they could see the small, but not cramped, passenger compartment. They saw a dizzying array of lights, buttons, and switches, all of which were completely alien to them. Dr. Lindberg stepped up into the ship, turned around, and extended his silver-gloved hand.

"Come on, hop on board!" he exclaimed. With his help, the two humans stepped up and boarded the ship. Rita was much more reluctant to do so, but with a great deal of coaxing, she finally acquiesced and boarded as well. Then, with a few commands to the control panel, Dr. Lindberg sealed the ship. "Please, have a seat," he said, gesturing to the two other shiny, black plastic chairs in the cabin. Blake and Lana gingerly sat down, while Rita curled up at their feet. They looked around in awe as Dr. Lindberg took a few moments to make his pre-flight check.

"Look, Lana," whispered Blake. "We can see outside, even though before, it was impossible to see inside."

"Everything seems a lot darker looking out, though," she said.

Soon, Dr. Lindberg completed his routine, and with a few commands, Daisy suddenly began to make a low, humming sound. This reminded Lana of that first day when she and the others had been captured and she became very tense. Then, Daisy began to rise. Lana felt her pulse quicken and her heart thumping in her chest. To her surprise, it was not an unpleasant sensation. The passengers could hear various clicking and thumping sounds as the ship continued to rise higher and higher.

"Don't be alarmed at any of those sounds," said Dr. Lindberg over his back. "That humming is the just the engine — the thing that gives Daisy the power to fly — and those knocks are just the legs being withdrawn into the body."

Dr. Lindberg took hold of a large stick-like device in the center of his control panel and moved it to one side. The ship moved slightly forward. Then it banked and turned. Now, the Stingray faced the hangar doors. With a push of a button, the doors slowly swung open, and bright sunlight poured in. Blake and Lana were absolutely spellbound. Slowly, the ship edged forward until it had left the hangar. Now, it hovered motionless, some thirty feet above the ground.

Dr. Lindberg turned around and faced his anxious passengers. "Are you ready?" he asked. Too frightened to speak, both Blake and

Lana slowly shook their heads. "Silly question. Don't worry!" He patted each of them on the knee encouragingly. "Everything is going to be just fine. Now just sit back and enjoy the ride." With that, he turned around until he faced forward again and took hold of the controls. "Don't forget to look around you," he said. "That's half the fun. Man, sometimes I sure love this job. Well, here we go!"

Then, with a nudge of the steering column, he ordered the ship onward and it accelerated rapidly. There was a slight sensation of nausea as the thrumming of the Stingray grew stronger, and the ship flew farther, higher, and faster. Blake and Lana carefully peered out the windows as they held onto each other for comfort. They watched the objects below them get smaller and smaller, and they watched the world change right before their eyes. The ship turned again and again as it continued to ascend. The Research Center below, which had appeared so enormous before, now became increasingly tiny. The trees became clumps of grass. The deer in the Sun Run became ants, and the rabbits vanished from sight. A lagoon that lay just beyond the borders of the Research Center came into in view, but from here it looked like a tiny rain puddle after a storm. Higher and higher they ascended at an incredible speed, yet it felt as though they were barely moving.

"Our ancestors — the Managers as you call them — used to fly ships, or airplanes, that were not unlike this one," said Dr. Lindberg. "They were not quite as fast or nearly as maneuverable, but they were impressive nonetheless. It was difficult for a lot of people to tolerate the way those planes made them feel, though. Most people felt sick or even lost consciousness, so only an elite few were qualified to pilot them, and even they were not immune to their effects. Today, ships like this one can accelerate and maneuver at incredible speeds and we hardly feel a thing. It's pretty amazing. Maybe I'll explain it to you someday."

Blake and Lana had hardly heard a word that Dr. Lindberg had said. They were too busy staring out the windows, which was what Dr. Lindberg had hoped for, anyway. Now, the Stingray began to pass through tufts of white in the otherwise blue sky.

"What is all of this white stuff?" asked Lana.

"Oh, those are clouds," said Dr. Lindberg.

"Clouds?" she asked rhetorically. "Clouds. Clouds! Blake, we're flying through clouds!"

"Amazing," said Blake, as though he were in a trance.

Off to one side, the vast savanna stretched out before them. There were large patches of dark green here and there — the groves of trees — and in between were the vast expanses of green and gold grass and sand. On the other side lay the Gulf of Mexico, its giant, white-capped waves barely visible now. Yet, looking down upon the Gulf in this way and seeing so much of it all at once, its vast size became apparent. While the objects down below seemed to shrink, change shape, and merge with each other into even larger shapes, the Gulf simply became larger and more overwhelming with each gain in altitude. Off in the distance in either direction lay the faithful horizon. Never before had the horizon seemed so incredibly far away. Blake and Lana thought that they could see forever.

"Ordinarily, or course," said Dr. Lindberg, "I don't go this high, but today I thought I'd make an exception."

Soon, the ship leveled off. It headed east over the Gulf, then turned around and headed west once more. Dr. Lindberg and his passengers cruised above the savanna for a while. They flew over lakes and rivers, which Dr. Lindberg pointed out for his guests. To Blake and Lana, they all looked remarkably like puddles and rivulets. They headed south, passing over a swamp, whose shimmering green left the Kamishi breathless. Then Dr. Lindberg began the ship's descent and headed north once more, flying below the level of the clouds and low enough to discern the objects below. Blake and Lana were astonished to see a herd of horses directly beneath them. Afraid of the ship that flew over their heads, the horses began to gallop in an attempt to escape.

"Look at them, Lana!" cried Blake as though he were a small boy. "Look at them!" They watched the horses veer off to one side while they continued flying north, leaving the spooked horses far behind. "That was incredible. Just incredible, wasn't it?" Lana grinned.

On and on they flew as they headed back toward the Research Center. They were only a few hundred feet above the ground now, and Blake and Lana delighted in watching things whiz by below.

"How fast are we going?" Lana asked.

"Fairly fast, about three hundred miles per hour," said Dr. Lindberg. "Don't worry: there are no other ships anywhere for thousands of miles. We're the only ones."

They watched the flocks of bountiful egrets — white shore birds that flew just above the treetops. It felt so strange and wonderful to be looking *down* at them now instead of watching them from below.

Eventually, the Earth Research Center in Houston came into view again up ahead. It was getting late, and dusk was approaching. As they neared the metal, chain-link fence along the periphery of the Outer Field, Dr. Lindberg brought Daisy to a stop and landed just outside the border.

"What are you stopping here for?" asked Blake.

Dr. Lindberg swiveled in his chair and faced his passengers. "The time has come for us to part ways," he said pensively. "I can no longer keep you at the Station. There is so much more we could teach each other, but I know that is not possible right now. Perhaps someday we will meet again, but for now, I must say goodbye."

The Stingray's hatch opened and everyone stepped out.

"I'd be lying if I said I wasn't looking forward to this day," said Blake.

"I know," said Dr. Lindberg. "I expect no gratitude from you, nor do I deserve it. I have been unfair to you, but I see that now, and I am sorry."

Blake nodded. "Thank you," he said.

"What about other Bebelishi?" asked Lana. "Are you still going to take others in the future? And what about the animals in your lab? Are you going to release them, too?"

"I don't know," said Dr. Lindberg. "Actually, I have been doing a lot of thinking lately…"

"It's obvious you can think," said Lana. "You're a very smart person."

"Well, I feel different now, too. I don't know what I'm going to do, but I can tell you this — there will be some changes around here. I'm not sure what yet, but there will be some."

"I'm glad to hear that," said Lana. "Thank you for taking us on that ride in the Stingray."

"Yes, thank you," said Blake. "I know neither one of us will ever forget it."

"It is I who should be thanking you," said Dr. Lindberg. "You have opened my eyes. I lost the spark of wonder that I once had. It's that spark that keeps me striving to learn and to help others. Thanks to you, that spark is alive again."

Dr. Lindberg stopped to think. "Now, I was going to give you something, but I forgot what it was. Oh, yes! I remember now. Wait right here." He went back into his ship. A moment later, he emerged carrying all of Lana and Blake's belongings: spears, bows, arrows, knives, and even their bags and books.

"Oh, thank goodness!" exclaimed Lana. "I was worried about what we'd do without our things."

"I know you are resourceful," said Dr. Lindberg, "but I thought you might need these things."

"It would've taken some time," Blake said, "but we could've replaced most of our tools and weapons. We could never replace our two Bebels, though."

"I know how much your holy book means to you," replied Dr. Lindberg.

The Kamishi collected their supplies and slung their bags over their shoulders. At last, they were ready to go.

"Well, goodbye, Blake. Goodbye, Lana, and good luck."

"Goodbye," they said together.

Dr. Lindberg boarded his Stingray, closed the hatch, and took off. Then he guided his ship over the fence, across the Field, and behind the Research Center, where it disappeared from view.

Blake and Lana turned their attention southward to a dense stand of trees nearby.

"That's where we need to go," said Blake.

"And then what?" asked Lana. "Houston is so far from the path we were following."

"That could be to our advantage. If I remember Brillum's instructions correctly, we're actually closer to Corpus now than we were when Dr. Lindberg picked us up."

"You mean Dr. Lindberg did us a favor?"

"Sort of," said Blake.

"So which way do we go?"

"Southwest. We head toward the coast, and then follow it until we reach the Rubbletown of Corpus." Blake looked thoughtfully at Lana. "Are you looking forward to that? I mean, going back to a Rubbletown again."

"A little, I guess," Lana admitted. "Actually, from what the Tulsashi and Dallashi told us, Corpus sounds quite different from what

I'm used to. It's not really a Rubbletown. The Corpushi are hunters, like the Kamishi. You'll fit right in, won't you?"

"I don't know," said Blake. "A built-up Rubbletown, occupied by Bebelishi, who both hunt the plains and fish the seas. It sounds strange to me."

"I guess it's different from what either one of us is used to." Lana hugged Blake and leaned her head against his chest. He hugged her in return and rested his cheek against the top of her head. "Let's get going," she said as she looked up at Blake once more. "The sooner we get out of here, the better."

"I'll bet there are mosquitoes in those woods. I hate mosquitoes."

"I do, too," said Lana, "but I much prefer them over the Research Center."

"So do I," said Blake contemplatively. The two of them let go their embrace, and Blake patted Rita on her side. The dog wagged her tail excitedly. "Come on, girl! Let's go." The travelers walked toward the woodland. Then, in the fading twilight of the evening, they disappeared among the trees.

Chapter 25

The Kamishi awoke the next morning, packed their belongings, and continued southwest toward Corpus. They walked on steadily for miles. Rita trotted ahead of Blake and Lana, her nose close to the ground, sniffing as she went. Restless and alert, she seemed to be searching for something. Blake and Lana assumed she was hungry.

Later that afternoon, the landscape changed from scrubby woodland to sandy dunes. The ground here consisted of pale, loose sand that was soft and yielding to the touch, but still warm from an entire day of sitting out under the sun. Now, however, the sun hovered low in the dimming sky and bathed this place in golden light. A soft, warm breeze followed the travelers, lovingly stroking their cheeks and hair, and playfully tossing the dry, loose sand they kicked up with each step. Patches of grass grew here. So did tall bushes with round, rubbery leaves, although they bore no fruits this time of year. When the group came to a large dune, they proceeded to climb it in a routine fashion.

However, as they neared the summit, Lana and Blake could hardly believe their eyes. Instead of more sand, a line of blue filled their vision. They continued climbing higher and higher up the gentle slope, until they stood at the top and gazed out at a welcoming blue horizon. This was the Gulf of Mexico. They were instantly enchanted. Water stretched out as far as they could see. Small, lively waves bounced up and down, while gulls glided high above. The sun had begun setting to their right — a glorious, scarlet ball preparing to touch down on the sand beneath it. The beach that lay below and ahead of them was bare and tranquil. Waves lapped up onto the dusky, wet shore with mysterious claps and trickles, and then receded to the Gulf once more. It was mesmerizing.

Blake and Lana watched Rita wander down the hill. She sniffed the dark, wet sand of the seashore, then turned to the right and wandered off into the distance. At length she paused and turned around to look at the humans, but then disappeared around another mound.

"What's she doing?" asked Lana.

"I don't know, but don't worry about her. She won't go far."

Lana and Blake descended the slope hand in hand. When they reached the beach, they put their supplies down in a pile and took off their moccasins. Now barefoot, their toes and soles delighted in the soft sand.

They stood there together, looking out at the water, and became engrossed in this peaceful moment. All the misfortune that had befallen them suddenly melted away. Both had lost loved ones. Both had survived bitter cold, hunger and thirst. They had fought off hungry animals and escaped the wrath of vengeful people. They had endured imprisonment as laboratory specimens, and traveled hundreds of miles. But all of these travails only served to sweeten this moment of joy.

The sun continued to shine its last rays, as though it were watching over them. Lana and Blake took in their surroundings. In their hearts, they thanked the Creator for letting them come here. They held each other as they watched the water sway and dance and splash. The Warmland was no longer just a dream to them. It was real, and they were now part of it. A feeling of calm came over them. Their mission was not complete, but they suddenly appreciated just how far they had already come.

Blake and Lana turned to one another, their hands intimately linked. As they looked into each other's eyes, they felt warmth growing between them. They pressed their lips together and embraced. When their lips parted, Blake and Lana continued to hold onto one another, and a feeling of contentment lingered. They had come all this way to find a place where they belonged, and now they were sure they had found it.

The couple sat down on the beach and watched the Gulf in the fading light. Stars appeared as the sun dipped below the horizon.

Blake turned to Lana. "Do you want to go for a swim?"

"Of course," she said with a smile.

They disrobed and ventured out together to the water's mercurial edge, walking through the surf and reveling in the sensation of the wet sand. Then they stepped into the shallows, which were cool and inviting. Lana and Blake kicked and jumped about gleefully, lightly splashing each other all the while.

"It's hard to believe," said Lana. "Just yesterday, we were flying over the Gulf of Mexico. Today, we're standing in it."

"And it's still huge," said Blake as low, foamy waves came crashing to the shore. He brought a finger to his mouth. "Salty," he said.

Lana copied the gesture and nodded, noting the pleasant but strong flavor.

At last, they waded out into deeper water and dove in. First they submerged themselves and wriggled under the surface. Then they erupted into the air like dolphins, their hair sending tiny droplets everywhere. They let the water wash away the clinging mud and dirt, and a powerful sensation of freshness came over them — they were clean.

Blake and Lana swam and frolicked in the twilight, splashing and laughing and having a wonderful time. It was their way of celebrating their arrival. When it finally got dark, they returned to the beach and dried each other off with their clothing. Then it was time to look for a place to spend the night. Soon, they found a sandy ledge with several bushes sticking out of it. They eased their tired bodies down underneath this impromptu shelter, cuddled up, and fell asleep.

Chapter 26

The Kamishi followed the shoreline for days, trekking through coastal dunes and sparse, scrubby vegetation, the vast Gulf of Mexico always to their left. At night, they camped with these mounds between themselves and the Gulf, and huddled together for warmth against the chilly sea breeze. When morning came, they were on their way again.

In time, they left the dunes behind and entered a dense mangrove swamp. The roots of the trees there spread out like crooked fingers and held the rest of the tree up above the muddy, brackish water. Blake, Lana, and Rita had no choice but to wade in and clamber about the ubiquitous tangle of leaves and wood. It was exhausting.

At last, they emerged from the swamp and found themselves on flat land once more. They walked through several Ruins, but they did not stop to look for food or supplies. Eventually, they arrived at the shore of a broad, slow-flowing, muddy river.

"It's going to be tricky getting across this one," said Blake. "We could swim, but it would be risky. We could weave a raft out of branches, but that would take some time. We could look for someone around here who we could barter with for a boat…"

"Or we could just cross that bridge over there," said Lana.

"What?" Blake spun around and followed Lana's line of sight. Indeed, about a quarter of a mile upstream was a giant bridge that spanned the width of the river and promised safe crossing. "Well what are we waiting for? Let's go!"

Together, the troupe ran toward the entry of the bridge, but as they approached, they slowed down to catch their breath. The place where they stood was strange to them. It resembled a Rubbletown, but it was not nearly as large, nor as complex. Instead, small piles of Rubble were simply spread about everywhere. There were ancient houses, demolished buildings, and wiped-out roads, but few of these structures were recognizable anymore. Rocks, concrete, asphalt, brick, metal, and even plastic could be seen here and there in clumps of various shapes and sizes. However, most of the Ruins had been uniformly eroded to indistinguishable debris, from which various types of plants grew.

Blake and Lana noticed the remnants of what was once the asphalt street that led up to the bridge. The bridge itself was immense and impressive. Its frame was steel, its pathway concrete, and its foundations built right into the earth, allowing it to survive the violence of the Great Crash and the erosive forces of the three millennia that had followed. Though rusted and grimy, it was nearly as solid as ever.

The company walked ever closer. Just as they reached the front of the bridge, they noticed an obstacle to their passing. A wooden fence blocked their access and a small shack stood to the side. In front of this shack, sitting on a stool, was a man with a dog asleep at his feet. The man was middle-aged, and his dog was past its prime. The relatively short, skinny man wore next to nothing; only a leather loincloth adorned his waist. His skin was dark and his hair was curly. He rested his elbows over his knees and looked off into the distance. A small stick used as a toothpick protruded from the corner of his mouth. His dog had a long snout and tall, erect ears — like Rita. However, unlike Rita, its fur was short and black. It was also bigger.

When the man detected the travelers out of the corner of his eye, he promptly sat up at attention and awaited their approach. The dog, suddenly aware of the man's change in attitude, stirred and watched the strangers as they came closer.

"Hello, sir," said Blake in the Common Tongue. "I am Blake of the Kamishi, and this is my mate, Lana."

"I am Paulo," said the man gruffly. Using the Common Tongue, he spoke clearly and fluently, but his accent seemed exotic to Blake's and Lana's ears.

"Would you be so kind as to tell us where we are?"

"You do not know?"

"No, sir, we do not," replied Blake.

"You must be Newcomers, then," said Paulo, eyeing the travelers suspiciously.

"Yes sir, we are," said Blake. "Could you please tell us what place we have reached?"

"This is a crossroads for travelers like you."

"Well then," pleaded Lana, "could you tell us what river this is?"

"This is the Nueces River," said Paulo. "It gives us water for drinking, playing, and traveling. It is the Gift of the Maker."

"Very well," replied Lana. "Then I am pleased to see the Nueces with my own eyes."

Paulo said nothing.

"Do you get many travelers coming through here?" asked Blake.

"Some."

"Do you get much traffic over your bridge?" asked Blake again.

"Some," said Paulo.

"What do travelers need to give you in exchange for passage over your bridge?" asked Blake.

"We usually require a small item of food, clothing, or a small tool or weapon. Now it is my turn to ask the questions. Where are you from and what brings you here?"

"We are travelers from the Plains and we wish to cross to the other side of the river."

"Hmmm ... I thought you looked strange. I've never seen anyone dressed like you before. Well, of course you want to cross to the other side. You wouldn't be here if you didn't. What do you want?"

Lana noticed that Blake was a bit perturbed by the guard's terseness, but she knew that the guard might not let them pass if he considered them at all a threat. So, remembering Tegg's and Brillum's warnings about how suspicious Warmlanders could be, she decided to try being diplomatic.

"Please sir," said Lana, "we are on private business."

"Well, it's my business now," replied Paulo.

Blake was losing his temper. He abruptly threw down his possessions, strode forward with his fists clenched, his lips puckered, and his brows furrowed.

"Listen here, you dirty little man!" exclaimed Blake. "You treat the lady with respect or you'll be sorry!"

Paulo rose to his feet, reached behind his stool, brought out a long spear, and held it at an angle in front of him. His dog rose to its feet, too. With hairs bristling, it bared its teeth and growled low. Rita, not willing to tolerate such aggression, barked and snarled at the guardians of the bridge.

"Dirty little man, am I?" quipped Paulo. "Well, you'll never get across now." Paulo jabbed his spear directly at Blake's abdomen.

Reflexively, Blake thwarted the attack by swerving to one side and delivering a punch to Paulo's face with an outstretched arm.

"No, Blake, don't!" cried Lana, but it was too late.

Reeling from the blow, Paulo staggered backward. When he recovered, a hardened look came over his face. Despite his small size and slight build, he was a trained fighter and knew just what to do. He jabbed his spear at Blake again, but Blake dodged the weapon, snatched it, and tossed it aside. Paulo now looked up at Blake with wide, fearful eyes while Blake glowered down at the man, protecting his face with his fists.

"Get him, Bobo!" exclaimed Paulo, releasing his angry dog on Blake. Instantly, the dog leaped at Blake, its mouth agape as saliva trailed behind. Suddenly, in mid-air, the dog's neck was struck by a blow from the side that sent it flying. It was Rita. She had anticipated Bobo's attack and was now on top of him. Bobo and Rita were a mass of fur and dust, now standing on their feet, now rolling on the ground. Their snarls were deafening as they bit at each other's throats and flung each other around.

Shifting his weight from side to side and holding his hands in front of him, the guard looked for a break in Blake's defenses. He took a desperate swing, but Blake sidestepped the attack and simultaneously delivered a swift blow to Paulo's jaw. Paulo was knocked to the ground, but then stood up once more, squinting and rubbing his jaw.

"You son of a bitch," muttered the guard. He took another swing, but Blake avoided it and countered with a punch to Paulo's eye, flattening him on the ground once more. Lana stepped back and winced at the gruesome sounds of the dogs and the men clashing. Rita and Bobo were locked in combat, constantly repositioning themselves and trying to throttle one another.

Slowly, Paulo rose, holding his head as he swayed. Then, regaining some of his coordination, he faced Blake again. The two men circled each other for a moment, feigning an attack now and then. Blake threw a jab to Paulo's nose, but Paulo stepped in toward Blake with a sucker punch to his belly. However, it was second nature for Blake to tense his abdominal muscles during an attack, and the blow glanced off impotently. Then Blake seized the opportunity to deliver an elbow to the nape of Paulo's neck. Paulo collapsed, fell to the ground, and remained motionless.

Rita and Bobo were still fighting furiously. Bobo had the advantage of being a larger, stronger male dog in his own territory. He clamped his jaws onto Rita's nape and held on tightly, making it difficult for her to maneuver or retaliate. However, the skin of her neck was loose and the mane of thick fur there provided some protection. Rita also had youth, speed, and stamina on her side.

Bobo tired and slowed down. He struggled less forcefully and shook his opponent less frequently. As soon as Rita felt she had the chance, she wriggled out of Bobo's grip and turned the tables; now his neck was locked between her jaws. Despite his short fur, the looseness of his skin protected him, just as Rita's had protected her. Nevertheless, Rita shook her head back and forth vigorously until Bobo became disoriented and weak. Soon, he rolled onto his back in submission, and Rita relented. Then, Bobo crept toward his fallen master and stood guard over him.

"Oh my," cried Lana as she ran to attend to Blake. "Are you all right? Did he hurt you?"

"I'm fine," said Blake. "Just a little bruised, I suppose. What about Rita?" They crouched to the ground and summoned Rita, who slowly walked toward Blake in a crouching posture. Blake stroked the dog while he looked her over. Rita's fur was tussled, and her head and neck were covered with foamy saliva. "I think she's all right," said Blake. "She just needs some time to rest."

"I'm glad you weren't hurt," said Lana, "but you shouldn't have started that fight, Blake."

"That bastard was being disrespectful to you!"

"There are other ways of dealing with that than starting a fight! What if you had killed him?"

"I couldn't have…" said Blake, although he was concerned about that himself. Together, Blake and Lana went to see if the guard was still alive. Ever protective of his master, the defeated dog growled at the intruders, so Blake and Lana kept a respectful distance. "Look, Lana, he's still breathing. I think he's going to be all right."

"I hope so, Blake, because now we are going to be in big trouble if his people ever find us. They might even send out a posse to hunt us down!"

"No, they wouldn't … would they?"

"I don't know," said Lana.

"Well, look at this way," said Blake. "Now we get to cross the bridge."

"At least we have that. Now come on. Let's just get our things and get the hell out of here." Lana opened the wooden gate and began running across the bridge, with Blake and Rita close behind. As they ran, they looked over the sides of the bridge at the vast river below. The shimmering water stretched out to the horizon in either direction. When they reached the other side of the bridge, they found that another barricade standing in their way. "Oh no! There's probably another guard on the other side of this gate, too! We're finished!"

"Now wait a minute. Don't panic just yet. We've got to think here." After a moment of silence, Blake spoke up again. "Well, first, let me just see if there's anyone even on the other side."

"Okay, but be quiet!" whispered Lana.

"Okay, I will," replied Blake. Then he carefully crept up to the gate and peeked through the cracks in the fence. Indeed, there was another guard there, situated much like the first had been, except without a dog. Blake then returned to Lana and told her what he had seen. "There's another guard there, too."

"Oh no!" cried Lana in a muffled voice. "That's it! They're going to kill us!"

"Wait! Just wait a second! I have an idea. Why don't we just knock on the gate, pretend like we're all squared away with the first guard, and then walk on through as though nothing had happened?"

"That just might work," said Lana. "All right, let's try it."

"Okay. Just remember — act natural."

"Got it. Act natural. Okay. Now let's just hurry up and get this over with."

"All right, all right," said Blake. "Just relax. Here we go." The travelers strode up to the wooden gate before them and gave it a light tap. They heard the man on the other side get up and open it. With a faint creaking sound, the gate swung open and there stood the other guard, brandishing a long, well crafted spear. He was much younger than the first guard, and apparently more energetic and alert. Blake tried not to let his anxiety show.

"What is the password?" asked the handsome young guard.

"What?" asked Blake. Lana held her breath.

"What is the password?" repeated the guard verbatim.

"Um..." said Blake. "What password?"

"The password the other guard gave you to let you cross the bridge. Tell me what it was."

"Um ... 'Please'?"

Without warning, the young guard slammed Blake against the gate, the shaft of his spear pressing on Blake's neck.

Blake groaned and struggled, but he was unable to fend off the fresh, well-trained guard. His vision began to blur and his consciousness began to fade. Suddenly, he felt the pressure on his neck lessen and his senses returning. Blake looked down to find Rita growling as she pulled the man away by the seat of his loincloth.

"Stop!" screamed the man. "Stop it! Get her off me!" But Blake and Lana did not interfere. They simply watched as the dog yanked him farther backward and then slam him down to the ground. With incredible adeptness, Rita then leaped on top of him and pinned him by his shoulders, growling softly all the while. The man — perfectly confident and capable only a moment before — was now breathless and wide-eyed with fear.

Blake seized this opportunity to gain the upper hand. He ran over to the supine man and pointed his spear directly at his temple.

"Do as we say or you're finished. Got it?" asked Blake tersely. The man nodded nervously. "All right. Rita, back off." The obedient dog hopped off of the guard's chest and stood quietly to one side. "Lana, get some twine out of your bag and come here with it." Lana complied as well. "Now, you. Get up slowly." The frightened guard cautiously got to his feet and rose. "Now go stand over there and put your nose against that tree."

"What?" asked the man incredulously.

"Do it!" barked Blake. The man walked over to a thick oak tree. "Now face the tree and get as close to it as you can — until your toes are touching the base and your nose is up against the trunk." The man was reluctant to comply. "Do it now or I'll stab you through the belly and pin you to that tree permanently!" Finally, cowed by Blake's threat, the guard did as he was told. "Good, now hug the tree like you're about to make love to it." The man complied. "All right, Lana, tie him up. Bind his hands first, and then wrap your twine all the way around his body. Make sure it's tight, but not too tight. And leave his legs alone. I want him immobilized, not gangrenous."

Lana immediately got to work and tethered the guard to the tree. Once he was secured, she backed away and joined Blake and Rita.

The bound man glared at Blake spitefully. "What did you do to the guard on the other side?"

"He'll be fine," said Blake flatly. "Don't worry about him."

The young guard shook his head and scoffed. "You don't know what you've just done. Somebody's going to come here soon to change guards, and when they do, they're going to release me."

"I'm counting on it," said Blake. "My intent was to get past you, not kill you."

"But then we're all going to come after you, and when we find you, we're going to kill you."

"We'll see about that. Come on," Blake said to Lana. "Let's go." Blake slapped his thigh as a signal for Rita to follow him. Then he marched past the guard with Lana at his side and Rita right behind him.

"You'll never get away with this!" the guard shouted after them as they walked away. "You'll pay for this!"

Blake and Lana ignored the man and continued walking. They noticed that there was a similar Ruin on this side of the Nueces River as on the previous side, and they quickly passed through it. Soon, they reached the high-pine woodland again. Blake and Lana wanted to stop and rest after the ordeal they had just been through, and they wanted to give Rita a chance to rest as well, but they knew they couldn't stop moving now. Someone would soon discover what had happened, so the travelers had to avoid detection at all costs.

Weary but determined, the group continued their trek until dusk. They soon found a nice, quiet spot under a cluster of palm trees and bedded down for the night.

Chapter 27

Blake woke up at dawn again and quietly rose to his feet. Lana was sleeping soundly, but Rita was missing again. *I'll find her*, he thought. *She must be around here somewhere.* At first, he simply went about his business, confident that he would come across his dog before long. However, after searching and calling for over an hour, he still could not find her. Exasperated, Blake returned to the campsite, where he found Lana rummaging through one of their bags.

"Have you seen Rita yet this morning?" he asked.

"No, actually I haven't," Lana replied. "Do you think she's okay?"

"I don't know. She's never stayed away this long. We should go look for her."

"Okay," agreed Lana. She got up, and the two of them went off to look for the dog. They called to her and whistled for her, but they got no response.

"Maybe she made a den last night," said Blake.

"Could be. We should look for signs of digging, or some kind of hole big enough for a dog to fit through."

Still calling the dog's name periodically, they began to look for burrows. They found several, but all of them were uninhabited. Eventually, they came upon a fairly large, but inconspicuous hole.

Lana brought her head near the opening. "Rita? Are you in there?" A loud growl came from inside. "Blake! Blake, I think I might have found her! Come over here!"

Blake came running and looked into the hole. It was not very deep, and in the shadows he could see that Rita was lying curled up, growling at him with her teeth bared. "That's her," he said, "but why is she acting so aggressive?" He reached in to pet the dog, but she snapped at him. Blake quickly retracted his hand. He was unharmed, but very confused. He scolded the dog, but it was no use. "I don't understand," he said. "She's never acted this way before. What's going on?"

"I'm not sure," said Lana, peeking into the den, "but I…" Her eyes widened. She gasped, covered her mouth, and pointed inside.

"What? What is it?"

"Look Blake!" cried Lana. Blake complied and, peering into the den, he noticed seven small, wriggling balls of fuzz. "Puppies! Those are Rita's puppies!" Blake and Lana danced about excitedly together and then returned to watching the pups. They were all equally tiny, but they sported subtle differences in their color despite the fact that they were nearly naked. Their eyes were sealed shut, but they wriggled vigorously as they suckled milk from their mother.

"Isn't that incredible?" said Lana. "Do you suppose their Saamu's puppies?"

"Must be," said Blake. "He was Rita's only mate. It's too bad he isn't here to see them."

"It's too bad he can't help her out, either. What are we going to do? Maybe we should bring her some food or something."

"Good idea. The only trouble is, I haven't found anything to eat all morning. Well, not anything I can catch with my bare hands, anyway."

"Hmmm, that is a problem. Blake, do you think she'll be okay here for a while?"

"Oh, sure. She'll be fine. Why? What do you have in mind?"

"What do you say we go exploring? Maybe we'll find something."

"All right. Actually, while I was looking for Rita earlier, I noticed some sort of big structure over that way," Blake said, pointing.

"What was it?" asked Lana.

"I'm not sure. Probably another Ruin of some kind. Let's go have a look around and see if we can't find some food there."

"Okay," said Lana. "With a little luck, we'll find enough for all three of us."

They headed in the direction Blake had indicated, all the while keeping an eye out for Ruins or other conspicuous landmarks. As they walked among the trees and shrubs, Lana suddenly noticed something in the distance.

"Look over there, Blake!" she gasped. "That's not just a Ruin. It looks like … a Rubbletown."

"Oh no," said Blake. "I wasn't expecting that. I thought there would be something smaller than that, something simpler. Do you still want to go there?"

"Sure," said Lana. "We'll just look for what we need and leave, all right?"

Blake was reluctant. "All right," he said.

As they came closer, they emerged from the woods and stepped out into the open. Surprisingly, they could see the coast and the Gulf of Mexico from where they stood.

Now the Rubbletown came into sharper view. It was indeed enormous, certainly larger than any of the other Ruins in the area. Strangely, it also appeared far less dilapidated. Several stone houses stood there. Made from worked Rubble and other materials, they were sturdy in design and beautifully crafted as well. Statues of animals of both land and sea, sculpted in dramatic poses, could be seen here and there. Even the debris on the ground seemed eroded, small, and difficult to distinguish as Rubble at all. Some of the original white and gray of rock could be seen, but almost everything was painted in muted shades of orange, yellow, and red.

There was another important distinction as well — one of the buildings was still standing. Majestic in its bearing, it stood near the beach, scarcely eroded at all and proudly overlooking the Gulf of Mexico. This was a peculiar sight for Blake and Lana, who knew that whole cities and towns had been devastated in the Great Crash by falling asteroid fragments and giant tsunami waves. Blake and Lana also knew that, after 3,000 years of weather and erosion, buildings from the Old Days simply could not stand anymore. A building on a beach such as this should have crumbled and fallen into the water, but this one showed almost no signs of decay whatsoever. This structure did not appear dilapidated like Rubbletown buildings at all. In fact, there was no trace of Rubble anywhere near it, giving it a fresh and youthful appearance. It would have been impossible for such a structure to survive intact for this long without someone renovating it.

The building stood five stories high and sported exquisite designs. It was tough and strong, having been reconstructed from big blocks of the most durable limestone around, but it was beautiful in its ornamentation as well. Contoured lines enriched its façades and detailed statues adorned its corners, taking the forms of fish, sharks, and dolphins. Everything was colored with earth tones, which suffused the place with a sense of cohesion and unity with the environment.

Blake and Lana strolled down the paths and peered at the structures of the artificial environment. They were especially fascinated by the tall building. Lana, having read about architecture in the ancient library of her old Rubbletown, pointed out a few things about the building to Blake, who listened eagerly.

"See how it's tall and rectangular?" Lana said. "It's like a building from just before the Great Crash, except for the overhangs, which are actually from an even older style. Look at the arches and the gargoyles statues sticking out."

"Impressive," said Blake.

"Well, it's interesting."

"Only interesting? I thought you liked this thing."

"Not really," said Lana. "It's just a monument to the power of the Managers."

"You envy the Old Timers?"

"No, I pity them."

"Why?" asked Blake, cocking his head.

"They were slaves to their own ambition," said Lana. "We have the same passion for life as our ancestors had. It's just that we have different priorities. We give life the space to grow, and we allow living things to do what they will. Why make impressive things when the natural world is more beautiful than anything we could ever design ourselves? Why bother trying to leave a legacy when all we have to do is let life be? Buildings and monuments may last a long time, but they will crumble sooner or later. They can't withstand the elements forever. Nothing can. Our legacy is the life that shares our world. Individually they may be fragile, but they carry with them the spark of life, and they have the potential to go on forever."

Blake slowly shook his head, but he smiled at Lana appreciatively. "Thank you," he said.

"For what?" she asked.

"For reminding me why I'm Bebelishi."

Blake and Lana had hoped to find some plants growing amid the Rubble, or even an old dilapidated food store, but they found none.

"This is so odd," said Blake. "Why can't we find any food around here? You'd think there'd be at least *something*. The Rubbletown you used to live in had plenty of snacks, remember?"

"Well, I wouldn't say it had 'plenty,' but there were some," said Lana. "Of course, I rarely saw anyone else around."

"There's no one here, either," said Blake.

"This place is no Rubbletown, though. Someone has rebuilt it. I would call it a city now. We're not going to find anything to eat here, Blake. I think we should look for *real* food — food that grows, not food that stays preserved in little plastic packages."

"That might be tough," said Blake. He thought for a moment. "I guess there's no real winter down here, but this doesn't seem like the growing season, either."

"Well, there must be something," said Lana. "Let's keep looking."

Blake agreed. Then he and Lana walked beyond the edge of the city and toward the coastal woodland once more. They were relieved when they found a citrus grove.

Lana ran up to one of the trees and plucked a firm, pendulous fruit from it. It had an orange-green color, and its surface was shiny and dimpled. Lana quickly peeled off the skin, removed a section of the fruit, and popped it into her mouth. She hummed contentedly. "This is delicious, Blake! Here, try one." She tossed him another. Blake quickly peeled it and began enjoying it as well.

"Very good," said Blake, his mouth full.

"Do you think Rita will eat them?"

"They might not be her first choice, but I think she will. They're good enough for now, anyway." He and Lana plucked as many of the fruits as they could carry and began heading back toward Rita's den.

Suddenly, someone poked his head up from behind the wreckage of a small building, and then quickly dove back down.

"Blake! Did you see that?"

"See what?"

"There's someone watching us from behind that Rubble!"

"Really?" Blake scanned the area as well. "Hmmm ... I wonder who it was. Maybe someone lives here after all."

Blake and Lana then saw four heads emerge from behind the Rubble. They could even make out the eyes staring at them. The heads sank back down.

"Did you see it that time?" asked Lana, starting to panic.

"Yeah, I saw it. This doesn't look good. Come on, let's get out of here."

They turned around and began swiftly walking back in the direction from which they had come. Just then, they heard some loud slamming and clattering sounds coming from the Ruins behind them. Looking over their shoulders, they saw four men charging down a pile of Rubble, brandishing spears and shields.

Excitedly, the men banged their implements together, making intimidating clanging and knocking sounds. With a spirited battle cry, they reached the ground and ran toward Blake and Lana.

"This is not good, Lana," cried Blake. "Run!"

Lana and Blake ran as fast they could, but the warriors were approaching rapidly. A moment later, they were right behind the Kamishi.

"Go, Lana, go! I'll stay back and fight them off."

"No, Blake! They'll kill you! Let me stay with you!"

"No, Lana! Then they'll kill us both. At least this way you have a chance."

"Blake..."

"No!" barked Blake. "Now run!"

Lana looked into Blake's eyes and saw the determination in them. For a split-second she was appalled at his anger, but she quickly realized that he was only trying to preserve her life. She held his gaze to acknowledge his demand, and then looked ahead once more.

Blake turned and faced the men while Lana ran on, kicking up sand as she went.

Two of the men collided with Blake; one punched him in the mouth, and the other in the gut. Overwhelmed, Blake collapsed on the ground as the prickly sand bit into his skin. His attackers picked up his struggling body up by the armpits. Then two more assailants came forward. Taking turns, they punched Blake in the gut repeatedly until he spat up blood and vomited. After a few more hits, Blake lost consciousness and went limp. The two men holding him released their grip and let him plummet to the sand face first.

Meanwhile, farther inland, Lana was still running. Her toes dug into the sand with each step, and weeds snapped at her shins as she sped by. Tears streamed from her eyes as she thought about what evils Blake was enduring now. *If I just stay safe, I'll be able to come back for him,* she thought. Still fearing for her life, she ran on.

On the beach, the four victorious men dragged Blake back into the city. They clambered over a pile of Rubble and ducked into a dark, secluded cave in the Ruins of a building. When they reached a large, crude wooden door, one of them untied the bindings and let the others in. The warriors filtered past a small chamber where various tools were stored: weapons made of wood and metal, and bindings of leather and rope. Two of the men collected their compatriot's arms and deposited them neatly in this room, while the other two carried Blake into a second chamber and plunked him down in a corner. Then they left him alone, closing and securing the thick, wooden door behind them.

დ ൪

Lana waited nervously in the surrounding woods all afternoon, pacing and biting her fingernails. She tried desperately to come up with an ingenious plan for rescuing Blake, but she was so worried that she could barely think.

That evening, however, Lana came back to the Ruins. The sun was going down and the moist, salty scent of the sea wafted through the air. Lana crept over the dunes, the grass hissing as she walked through it. She paused at the dune's crest and peered out at the city ahead. *What am I going to do? I have no idea how to get him back. I don't even have Rita to help me. I have to think of something soon, or I'll regret it for the rest of my life.*

Lana paced for a moment, gazing at the city every once in a while as she tried to think of a plan. The air was getting chillier and the wind was getting stronger. Lana looked far out to sea. In the fading light, she could see dark clouds forming and large, white-capped waves bobbing and drifting ashore. *A storm is brewing. I have to get in there and find him, but how? I don't know where he could be. And what will I do once I get there? I don't even know how I could get him out. I'd better think of something soon.*

Lana continued to pace. A tremendous bolt of lightning flashed above, and a mighty clap of thunder shook Lana's body. Then, as if a heavenly bucket had been overturned, rain came pouring down. Each drop was large enough to drink, and whatever they struck was met with a forceful splash. Within seconds, everything was wet. This rain was bitterly cold, and so was the wind that came careening off the waves of the Gulf.

Anxiously, Lana sprinted down the gradual slope of the dune and headed for the city. Frantically running among the piles of Rubble, she retraced her steps from earlier that day until she found the very same pile where she and Blake had first been attacked. Lana was thoroughly soaked, as much as if she had just emerged from the Gulf itself. She clambered over the Rubble and slid down the other side.

Lana stood at the bottom of the hill and looked around. Dripping like a washcloth, she strained to peer through the storm and the darkness, but she could barely see anything at all, and she could hardly hear anything above of the raucous rainfall. Nevertheless, despite the cacophonous squall, she heard laughter. It was the harsh, brazen laughter of unruly men, a sound which sent chills through her already frozen body. With little difficulty, she identified the direction from which the sound was coming and followed it. The laughter became louder and louder, so she knew she was nearing her target. Standing outside of a large but remarkably cryptic entrance to a cave, Lana noticed a faint, flickering light inside. *So this is it. This is the place. I have to go in.*

Lana marched right into the cave and came to a thick wooden door. She banged on it loudly. It opened only slightly, and a pair of eyes peeked out at her.

"What do you want?" asked the pair of eyes, speaking the Common Tongue with a strange, foreign accent.

"I want my man back," replied Lana, enunciating her words.

The door closed. A moment later it swung wide open. Four tall men stood before Lana, their arms crossed, glaring at her.

Lana glared back at them all and repeated, "I want my man back."

One of the men grabbed Lana by the upper arm, yanked her inside, and slammed the door.

Chapter 28

The fortress no longer received any appreciable light from the setting sun, and now relied on the wavering, orange glow of torches on its walls and candles on its tables. Lana slowly looked around the room where she sat and took in her surroundings. She tried to calm herself, but her heart beat wildly inside her chest.

"Who are you?" asked one of the men. His hair was short, black, and messy, and he had an abundance of energy.

"I am Lana of the Kamishi," she said.

"Who is he?" asked the young man, jerking his head.

"He is Blake of the Kamishi, and he is my mate."

Another man stepped forward, slightly older than the first. He towered over Lana, and she had to crane her neck back to look up into his eyes. This man was powerfully built, and his curly, light brown hair stood up all around his head like a mane, making him seem even bigger than he already was. "What do you want?" asked the big man.

"We seek passage to Corpus to request an audience with Zaaru."

"Passage denied!" roared the big man. There was silence.

"Why?" asked Lana.

"Why?" repeated the man. "Because you are Outlanders, that's why! Look, who the hell are you? Who are the Kamishi, anyway? We've never even heard of that name before."

"We are from the northern Great Plains," said Lana, stoically.

"The northern Great Plains? That's a thousand miles away! What the hell are you doing here?"

"We seek safe passage to the Warmland."

"Passage denied!" repeated the man.

"You see, Murdoch?" said a third man. He was young as well, and shorter than the other two, but his firm muscles were well-defined on his athletic frame. Lana noted the name he had just spoken. *Murdoch*, she told herself. "I told you. They're no different from any other Outlander. All they want is to come to the Warmland, just like everyone else."

"Ah, but they're different, Aries," said Murdoch. *Aries.* "They're different because, not only are they trespassers, but they're aggressors, too. They deserve to be not only removed from our territory, but punished as well."

"Aggressors?" asked Lana indignantly. "Blake and I have done nothing to you!"

"You are trespassers!" exclaimed Murdoch.

"I realize that," Lana admitted, "but we did nothing but run when we saw you come out and attack us. You're the aggressors!"

"No," said Murdoch as he came nose to nose with Lana. "We are Corpushi."

Lana's eyes widened. "You mean this is … Corpus?"

"Yes," hissed the first man, "and we always avenge any wrongdoing to a fellow tribesman. Perhaps you've already met our cousins: the bridge guards at the Nueces River!"

Lana gasped and her face grew pale.

"Ah-ha!" exclaimed the man. "You see? She knows exactly what I'm talking about. That proves they did it!"

Lana was speechless.

"Yes, Peter," said Murdoch. "That proves it all right, as though we needed any further proof." *Peter.*

Peter turned to Lana. "You are wanted for assaulting Brent and Paulo."

"Brent?" asked Lana. "I remember Paulo, but who's Brent?"

"Oh, don't play dumb," said Murdoch. "You know who he is. He was the other guard at the bridge."

"But we did not hurt him!" pleaded Lana.

"Oh no? Then why did we find him tied to a tree?"

"He attacked us! We had to do that to defend ourselves … and to avoid hurting him, too."

"You assaulted two guards," persisted Murdoch. "That's reason enough."

More silence.

"How…" began Lana, "how did you know it was us?"

"A call was issued for your capture," Peter said. "When we saw you, we knew you had to be the ones. Who else but stupid Outlanders would dare trespass on Corpus?"

Lana scowled at the man. "What are you going to do with us?" she asked.

"Among our people, it is customary for a criminal to receive in punishment the same treatment he gave to his victim," said Murdoch. "In your case, since you tied up Brent and severely beat Paulo, then you will be restrained and beaten as well."

"Murdoch," said the fourth man, "this woman is not to blame. It is obviously the man who must be punished." This last member of the company was nearly as tall as Murdoch, but wiry and lean. Although still young, he was more mature and composed than the others, moving and speaking slowly and deliberately. A kind of quiet confidence emanated from him as he made his presence known.

"She is his accomplice, Spartan," Murdoch replied. "She may not get the full sentence, but she still deserves some kind of punishment."

"Like what?" barked Lana. Now she had the fourth man's name. *Spartan. He seems reasonable enough. If I could just get him to believe me, then we might have a chance after all.*

"Like a few lashes across your back, that's what," said Murdoch.

Lana bristled. She was frightened, but she also knew that, if trespassers had attacked her own kind, she would be just as furious as these people, and rightly so.

"How is Paulo?" she asked.

"What do you care?" asked Murdoch rhetorically.

"I just do. How is he?"

"He is alive, but he is badly bruised and in much pain."

"Was anything broken?" asked Lana.

"No, but his eye is swollen, and so is his jaw."

"I am sorry to hear that."

"You should be," said Murdoch. "Paulo is not a young man anymore. He cannot take that kind of abuse from a warrior."

"Then he should not be a bridge guard," said Lana matter-of-factly.

"Shut up!" shouted Murdoch. "Nobody's asking for your opinion."

"Well then, just hear us out."

"What?" asked Murdoch incredulously.

"Let us tell you our side of the story before you cast judgment against us."

"You will lie!"

"No, we will not," said Lana.

"How do I know that?"

"Because we are honorable people."

"How could you possibly be honorable? You are wanted for assaulting two bridge guards!"

"Even honorable people fight," said Lana. Silence again.

"All right," said Murdoch. "Go get the man and bring him out here."

Aries and Peter immediately went back into the prisoners' quarters. They came out with Blake between them. He was walking under his own power, but his head was slumped, his posture was droopy, and he had dried blood and dirt all over him.

"Blake!" cried Lana. She ran to attend to him and wrapped her arms around him for support.

Blake looked up at her weakly. "Lana," he said softly, "what are you doing here? I told you to get away."

"I did," she said. "I did, but I came back for you."

Blake smiled despite himself. "You shouldn't have," he said. "You should've just run away."

"We'll see about that," she said confidently. "These men want to ask us questions about the incident with Paulo and the other bridge guard at the Nueces River. Are you up to talking about it?"

"Is that what this is all about?" asked Blake rhetorically. "Sure, I can talk about it. Just let me sit down somewhere." They guided him to a table and pulled out a chair for him, where he promptly seated himself. Murdoch sat down across from him.

"I am Murdoch of the Corpushi," he said, "and leader of this band of warriors. I want to ask you about what happened at the bridge."

"Ask," said Blake.

Murdoch became flustered. "Well?"

"Lana, my mate here, and I wanted to cross the bridge so that we could continue our journey. We had come from the Plains and we were headed for Corpus."

"Why did you leave the Plains?" asked Murdoch. "Were you wanted for a crime there, too?"

"No, no, nothing like that," said Blake, still looking down at the ground. "Our territory, Kamis, was invaded by a neighboring tribe, the Ravashi. Everyone in my tribe was killed except for me; my best friend, Manosh; and my two dogs."

"Where is your friend? Where are the dogs? And what about this woman? I thought she was Kamishi, too!"

"Just wait, Murdoch," interceded Spartan. "Give him a chance to talk."

Murdoch frowned but, conceding to Spartan, leaned back in his chair, folded his arms, and waited quietly for Blake to speak.

"Thank you, sir," said Blake. He took a moment to collect his thoughts. "Manosh and I, along with my dogs were the only survivors. So, we ran away from Kamis — which would now become part of Ravas — and decided to emigrate to some other place."

"So you chose the Warmland, right?" sneered Murdoch.

"That's right. That was what we chose, so we began traveling south. About halfway, we came across a huge Rubbletown and went in. That was where we met Lana. We stayed there for some time, and after a while we decided to induct Lana into our tribe."

"Or what was left of it," said Murdoch.

"Yeah," replied Blake, reluctantly. "Then we left the Rubbletown and headed south again. Along the way, we were attacked by the Podeshi, and they killed one of my dogs. Then near Tulsa, my friend, Manosh was killed by lions. That left just Lana and me, and one dog, but we kept going, and now here we are."

"Where is your other dog?" Murdoch asked.

Blake had no intention of revealing Rita's location, especially now that she was nursing a new litter of puppies, so he feigned ignorance. "You mean she's not here?"

"Just answer the damn question," snapped Murdoch.

"Well, if she's not here, then she must be out there somewhere."

"What's your dog's name?"

Blake said nothing.

Murdoch slapped Blake across the face with the back of his hand. "What's your dog's name, Outlander?"

I suppose no harm could come from their knowing her name. "Rita."

"Ah, a female. Aries, Peter," said Murdoch, "remind me tomorrow to find that dog. Rita."

"You'll never find her," said Blake.

"You'd be surprised."

"What would you do with her if you did?" asked Blake.

"Never mind that, Outlander." Murdoch rubbed his chin thoughtfully. "So. What made you come all the way down here to Corpus? There are plenty of other territories in the Warmland you could've infested, you know?"

"Do you know Tegg, Chief of the Tulsashi?" Blake asked.

"I know of him, but I've never met him myself."

"Well, he advised us to seek out Zaaru, Chief of the Corpushi, and ask to join his tribe."

"Well, wise Tegg couldn't have picked a more difficult tribe for you to join," said Murdoch sarcastically. "Didn't he tell you how we would perceive you? Didn't he tell you that you are invaders to us? Didn't he tell you that we are no kinder to Outlanders than any other tribe in the Warmland?"

"He told us that much," said Blake, "but he also said that Zaaru was a personal friend of his, and that he would consider accepting us if we had Tegg's blessing, which we have."

Murdoch exchanged concerned glances with Brent and Spartan. He turned his attention back to Blake. "All right, now tell us about the incident at the bridge. Tell us your version of what happened."

"Lana and I asked permission to cross the bridge," began Blake. "We were willing to trade goods in exchange for crossing, but Paulo was rude to us. When he was disrespectful of Lana, I became angry."

"My father was disrespectful of the woman?" asked Spartan.

Blake balked at hearing this. "He's your father?"

"Yes."

"Well, I'm sorry to have caused you trouble, but yes, he was."

"How?" asked Spartan.

"When Lana wished to keep the nature of our business a secret, he pried and demanded that she tell him why we wished to cross the bridge."

"I see," said Spartan. "Then what happened?"

"I asked him to be more polite," said Blake, "but he refused. Then he tried to stab me with his spear, so I dodged it and hit him. We struggled for a while, I hit him several more times, and then he collapsed on the ground."

"Wait a moment," said Murdoch. "Did you say he came at you first?"

"That's right."

"And when it was over," said Spartan, "you just left him there?"

"Yes," admitted Blake, "we did."

"This does not bode well for you, Outlander," said Murdoch. "I admit that you had reason to be angry if your mate was insulted or if Paulo attacked you first, but your conflict could have been resolved without coming to blows. You should have just left when you were told to leave. On top of that, abandoning him was very unkind and unwise of you. You are lucky that Paulo is still alive."

"He is all right, then?" asked Blake.

"He is recovering," said Murdoch.

Blake nodded. "If it is of any relevance, you should know that Lana tried to stop us from fighting. She is not to be blamed for any of this."

"I see," said Murdoch. "We will take that into consideration. If you were traders this might be easier for you, but you are just Outlander invaders, so don't expect any mercy from us."

"We are traders, too," said Lana.

"What do you mean?" asked Murdoch.

"We have goods to trade and knowledge and skills to teach. We have not come to the Warmland empty-handed!"

"If that is true, then this could turn out differently for you," said Murdoch. "What do you have to offer us?"

"Please let me show you. Turn out the lights," said Lana.

Blake and Lana exchanged glances, and the weakened Blake smiled at his mate, for he knew what she was about to do.

"Are you mad?" Murdoch said. "It's already night, and a storm is blowing outside. We need our flames lit. Do you have any idea how long it takes us to start a fire?"

"I think she lacks goods to trade, as well as brains to think!" shouted Aries. The other men chuckled.

Lana frowned and did her best to ignore the insult. "I realize you need fire tonight," she said, "but if you will just trust me, then I promise you won't be disappointed."

Murdoch conferred with the others and then turned to Lana. "Very well. Proceed."

"Thank you," said Lana. "Again, I ask that you turn out the lights."

Murdoch directed Aries and Peter to the task. One by one, the candles were blown out and the torches extinguished. Gradually, the room grew darker and darker until it was pitch black.

Lana was accustomed to conditions such as these. Back in the Rubbletown where she grew up, she would often have to feel around in the dark for things she needed. The situation here was not very different. Lana carefully walked over to the table where Blake and Murdoch were sitting and felt around for the candle. She reached into her cloak, pulled out a matchbook, and tore out a match. She struck it against the rough strip on the back of the book, but nothing happened. She struck it again, and still nothing happened. *What could be wrong? Why can't I light this fire stick?* Lana tried several more times before she realized that the fire stick and the matchbook were still wet from the storm outside.

"Well?" said Murdoch. "We're waiting."

"I know," pleaded Lana. "Just a moment."

Frantically, she felt around her cloak for a dry patch, but found none. Then she had an idea. She reached for Blake, whose tunic was still as dry as ever. She rested her hand on his shoulder in the dark and felt his hand reassuringly touch hers. Using Blake's tunic, she quickly dried the fire stick and the entire matchbook as much as possible. It worked, and although the matches were still somewhat damp, Lana hoped that they had been adequately dried off.

Once again, she struck a fire stick against the matchbook. Still nothing happened. Feverishly, she struck it again and again, making it grow steadily hotter. Then suddenly, the match ignited and a tiny, orange flame erupted from its head.

Anxious not to lose what she had started, she cautiously brought the match to the candle. The flame flickered for an instant. Then the wick caught fire and released a pleasant, warm glow. There was a murmur among the men. Lana placed the matchbook on the table. She patiently walked around the room with the candle until all of the other candles and torches were ablaze once more.

"How did you do that?" asked Murdoch.

"Is this magic?" asked Peter.

"If by magic, you mean something strange and mysterious, then yes, this is magic," said Lana, "but magic becomes mundane and commonplace once it is understood and no longer feared. Look," she said, "I did it with this." Lana held up the spent match between her fingers. "We call it a fire stick. Each stick can be used only once, which is why we must carry around several at a time." She held up the matchbook for all to see. "We use fire sticks to start fires whenever we want to."

"It works so fast!" said Peter.

"It would have worked even faster if it had not been so wet from the rain," said Lana. "It took the fire stick longer to ignite because I had to dry it off. Only then was I able to light it. A dry fire stick can be ignited in seconds."

"Very impressive," said Murdoch. "Where can we get some?"

"We found a whole collection of them in the Rubbletown where I'm from. Unfortunately, we don't have many left, but I give this set to you as a token of our good faith. I'm sure we'll be able to find more if we just search for them."

"Maybe we can even figure out how the Old Timers made them so we can make them ourselves," said Spartan.

"I don't know," said Peter. "I don't like it. It sounds like Management to me."

"Management," said Lana, "is a way of thinking that guides your way of doing. We are all Bebelishi here. None of us wishes to be Managers, but here is a piece of technology that we can use. If it comes from the Managers, then so be it. It would not be the first time that we Bebelishi have learned something from the Old Timers."

"Well," said Murdoch, "maybe we can do some trading after all. However, there is still the matter of the wrong that you have done, and we must resolve it. Even if you are not punished with the same treatment that you gave Brent and Paulo, you will still need to compensate them for their losses."

"I understand," said Blake.

"Good. Tomorrow, we will take you to meet the others, that is, the tribal Elders and Chief Zaaru."

"Zaaru?" repeated Lana. "We will meet Zaaru tomorrow?"

"Yes," replied Murdoch flatly, "but it is late, and time to turn in. Come. Let me show you where you will be sleeping tonight."

Blake and Lana followed Murdoch down a passage, passing compartments where the other men stayed. Everything about this cave was gloomy. The stone walls and gravelly floor were hard, gray, and cold. The orange glow of the torches cast long, trembling shadows all around. Echoing footsteps and voices of people could be heard throughout the place. The pounding rain and the howling wind outside were easily audible through the porous walls. Yet somehow, there was a sense of calm and safety here.

When they reached the chamber at the end of the passage, Murdoch opened the thick wooden door and let Blake and Lana in. "Here you are," he said. "This is your room. There will be at least one guard up at all times, so don't try anything funny. See you in the morning." Murdoch left and locked the door behind him.

The chamber was small, but there was enough room for the two burning torches on the wall, and for the straw mattress in the corner. Lana gave Blake a gentle push from behind to direct him to bed. She knew he was weary after his ordeal and she wanted him to lie down. Blake sat on the mattress and Lana kneeled in front of him.

"Lie down," she said. "You need your rest."

"All right," said Blake, and he lowered himself onto the bed.

Lana lay beside him and rested her body against his. "How are you feeling? What do they do to you?"

"Oh, they kicked me and punched me. I've got a fat lip and a soar belly, and some cuts and scrapes, too."

"You poor thing," Lana said, fussing over her mate.

Blake was a proud man, and for a moment he resisted this attention. However, when he realized he enjoyed receiving it, and that Lana enjoyed giving it, he relaxed and allowed her to continue. She stroked his hair, petted his arms, and kissed him repeatedly.

Blake wrapped his arm around her and held her close. "Oh, Lana. You have no idea how relieved I am."

"Relieved? You look as though you were gored by a bull!"

"I know, but for a while there I thought we were going to become prisoners again. After what we went through in Houston, I don't think I could take that."

"But we *are* prisoners, Blake," said Lana.

"I know, but it's not the same. Thanks to you, they think of us as traders. I will have to make up for what I did to their tribesmen, but at least they respect us now."

"I suppose."

"We're lucky they liked your fire sticks so much," said Blake.

"We're lucky the fire sticks lit at all, they were so wet! Once they did, I knew they would do the trick. Still, it's not over yet. We'll see how things go tomorrow when we meet Zaaru and the Elders."

Blake frowned and shook his head. "Don't remind me. I can't believe things turned out this way. This is not how I wanted to meet Zaaru and the Corpushi, believe me!"

"I know, but we can't change that now. All we can do is try to make as good an impression on him as we can. It wouldn't hurt to make a good impression on the Elders, either." Lana tilted her head and looked at Blake. "Thank you for all you did today, Blake. You saved my life. Again."

"Please. You saved *my* life today. Besides, we wouldn't even be in this mess in the first place if I'd just stayed out of trouble."

"Maybe. And maybe next time you'll listen to me, hmm?"

"I will … but why didn't you listen to *me*? I told you run away."

"I did," said Lana, "but I came back. For you."

"You shouldn't have."

"Why not?" said Lana, feigning irritation. "Don't you want me here?"

"You know what I mean. I'd never forgive myself if anything bad happened to you."

"But I couldn't just leave you, Blake. I'd never forgive myself, either!"

"You should be someplace safe," said Blake. "Someplace far away from here."

"But what about our plan to join the Corpushi?"

"It's over," said Blake, his eyes downcast.

"Not yet," said Lana solemnly.

Blake softened and reached out to Lana. Drained of his energy, he smiled weakly. "Thank you for coming back for me."

Lana lovingly ran her hands across Blake's knees and shoulders. "I'm just glad you're safe," she said as she cried onto his shoulder. They hugged and kissed one another.

"I'm glad you're safe, too, Lana." Tears welled up in his eyes and he felt a catch in his throat. "When I think about what could've happened to you, I just…"

Lana shushed him gently. "It's okay. We're here now, and we're going to be fine."

"What about Rita and her pups?" asked Blake fretfully. "She's out there fending for them all by herself, with no help from anyone. What are we going to do?"

"Don't worry about them. They're all right. We'll go out and check on them as soon as we can."

"But what about Murdoch? You heard what he said. He's going to go look for Rita tomorrow. What if he finds them?"

"He won't find them," said Lana reassuringly. "They're hidden away in that burrow of hers. She and the pups will be fine. Now, just get some rest, all right?"

Blake sighed. "All right," he said.

Lana stroked his hair to soothe him, and he soon drifted off to sleep. She stayed awake for a while, watching over him, until fatigue overcame her and she fell asleep, too.

Chapter 29

A loud pounding on the door roused Lana and Blake from their slumber.

"Time to go!" cried Murdoch.

Lana buried her head in Blake's shoulder and moaned. Blake stroked her hair and kissed her warmly. They reluctantly rose, groaned, stretched, and got dressed. They straightened out their mattress, groomed themselves and each other, and left their chambers.

"Morning," said Murdoch. "Have some breakfast. Then we'll return to our village." He motioned toward a large table where the others were already seated and eating. Lana and Blake greeted them and sat down. They soon realized that most of the foods were strange and new to them. There were rounded slices of a soft, brown food; a mushy, yellowish-white puree; and numerous fruits and vegetables they had never seen before. A flask of water was also passed around the table, and everyone poured some into a cup and drank.

"What is all this stuff?" asked Blake. "I'm afraid we are not familiar with it."

"This is bread," said Murdoch, holding up a sample. "These here are mashed potatoes. Over there we have some oranges, bananas, and carrots."

Blake and Lana knew it would be rude to refuse, so they sampled the new fair. They were not disappointed.

After breakfast, the Corpushi men cleaned up, gathered their belongings, and prepared to leave. Blake and Lana were allowed to keep their leather satchels, which contained their books and supplies. However, all their weapons — knives, spears, bows, and arrows — were confiscated and added to the Corpushi men's own collection. They carried these things with them now, along with their other tools and weapons.

"All right," said Murdoch, "Let's go."

Everyone exited the dwelling, and Peter was the last to come out. He closed the door behind him and fastened it shut with a thick sturdy rope from the door handle to a peg on the doorjamb.

The crew marched through the city, heading for the tall building in the distance. They passed several smaller, less developed structures. These varied in their level of complexity, from shabby, barely livable piles of Rubble to clean, charming houses made of wood, rock, or even metal.

Gravel and sand crunched beneath their moccasin-covered feet as they walked along. They soon came to a fence made of widely spaced wooden posts. Blake noticed a small herd of horses standing behind it.

"Look, Lana, horses!" he cried. "Strange to see them near a beach, though. I wonder why they're here."

"Because," said Murdoch, "they are ours."

Blake was confused. He stared at the troop leader. "Oh, you mean you haven't eaten them yet."

"Eat them?" asked Murdoch. "Why would we eat our own horses?"

"What do you mean 'your' horses?"

"The same way your dogs belonged to you, these are our horses."

"What?" exclaimed Blake. "What do you feed them?"

"Grass, mostly — both wet and dry — but also grains and fruit from time to time."

"How do you get enough?" asked Blake.

"We grow it. We have crops for ourselves and the horses."

A horrified look came over Blake's face "But that's ... that's Management!" he cried.

"I suppose, but it does no harm," said Murdoch.

"The Managers used their power to bring pain and suffering to the world. It's forbidden to be like them, at least among Bebelishi. You are Bebelishi, aren't you?"

"We are," said Murdoch, "but things are not as simple as all that."

"What do you mean?" asked Blake.

"Isn't everyone both alike and different at the same time? Doesn't each tribe have its own customs, traditions, and beliefs?"

"Of course, but..."

"Then listen and I will explain the ways of my people to you."

The group approached the horses, but they did not try to flee. They were calm and undisturbed, and Blake knew then that they were tame. Even if they had wanted to bolt, however, they would not have been able to, for the wooden fence formed a large, spacious enclosure around them. They stopped in front of the enclosure. Aries and Peter extended their hands, and the horses came closer, allowing the men to pet and scratch them.

Murdoch turned to Lana and Blake once more. "You see? We care for these creatures. We are not their lords, nor are they our servants. Rather, we are their protectors. The plants, the dogs, and the horses. We care for all of them, and they give us services in return. Is that not the way you feel toward your dog?"

"No," said Blake. "To my people, the Human and the Dog are partners. As children of the Creator, we are brothers who have walked the earth together and cared for each other for thousands of years, and we gladly continue to do so. We lead and the dogs follow, but we know that we rely on each other."

"Then this is not very different from our own way," said Murdoch.

"You grow these plants and these animals so that you can use them. Was this not the downfall of the Managers? Was that not their undoing? The Managers became so good at controlling all of the creatures around them that they became obsessed and forgot about the sanctity of all living things. The evil of Management is that it is selfish and greedy. It makes you hoard things instead of sharing them."

"You are right, but we do not take advantage of these creatures. We do not selectively breed them. We do not exclude other animals from our fields just so we can harvest more food. We do not use chemicals to get more food the way the Managers used to. Our plants and animals gain protection from us. They are safe here. We give them food, water, and shelter and in exchange they provide us with what we need, too. It is true that we manage these plants and animals, but we also give them the respect they deserve. We do not abuse them or take advantage of them, and that is why our Management is fair and just."

"Interesting," said Blake.

Lana listened attentively. She was intrigued by the worldview of the Corpushi. It was quite different from hers and Blake's, but it did not seem evil. In fact, it seemed quite reasonable, at least so far. *Perhaps the ways of the Corpushi are merely different. Then again, perhaps they have already begun to backslide into the Old Ways. We must be careful.*

"So," began Lana, "what exactly do you get from this arrangement?"

"Well," said Murdoch, "we get food and medicine from the plants, defense and companionship from the dogs, and transportation from the horses."

"Transportation?" asked Blake. "What do you mean?"

"I mean we ride them!"

"You ride…" Blake murmured.

Lana, who had read about many things in her ancient library, took this news in stride. "Just like they used to in the Old Days," she said.

"More or less, yes," replied Murdoch. "Come, we have business to attend to. It's time to meet Chief Zaaru and the Elder Council."

Blake and Lana pretended to be calm, but they were trembling inside. They had come a long way to find Corpus, and now their future hung in the balance. They might be convicted as criminals or welcomed as traders. Given the circumstances and tension surrounding their arrival, however, it could be difficult to find favor with the leaders and members of the Corpushi tribe. Blake and Lana knew they had to proceed carefully if they were to have any chance at making a good impression or gaining acceptance among these people.

Murdoch and the other Corpushi warriors escorted Blake and Lana toward the tall building overlooking the Gulf of Mexico. It seemed large from a distance, but it now it seemed positively enormous. It was totally alien to Blake. Even Lana, who had grown up in a Rubbletown, had never seen a structure like this still standing. The pale, craggy rocks of the walls gleamed in the morning light, and its many statues and precipices brought the stoic structure to life.

"This place is amazing," said Lana. "It's beautiful."

"Thank you," said Murdoch. "We are very proud of the Rookery."

"The Rookery? Is that what you call it?"

"Yes. It's not only our home, but also our lookout to the sea, and our protection against outsiders. It's the envy of the Warmland."

"I can see why," said Lana. "How … how did you build it?"

"Oh, we didn't build it," said Murdoch. "We only restored it."

"You restored it?"

"According to legend, this was the only building left standing in Corpus after the Great Crash; all the others were razed to the ground. For the next two millennia, the only things to live here were thugs and animals. Then a thousand years ago, our ancestors came here from the north. They kicked out — or assimilated — the thugs, removed the animals, and claimed this building as their own. Of course, it was in very bad shape, so they used stones and Rubble to build it back up."

"How did it get the name of the 'Rookery'?"

"It is said that about two hundred years ago, there was a great battle here. The Corpushi had to fight off a fleet of ships coming in from the sea, and used the height of this building to their advantage."

"How?" asked Lana.

"Fire. They launched burning arrows and catapulted fireballs from the top of the building. That destroyed most of the ships, but some got through and made it to the beach. Again, the archers were ready and shot down the advancing foot soldiers. By the time the stragglers made it to the building, the Corpushi warriors faced them in combat and defeated them. This place has been called the Rookery ever since."

As the group approached the Rookery, other people suddenly came into view. Standing around the base of the giant building, these men, women, and children seemed absurdly small by comparison. Reticently, they watched as their tribesmen returned with two strangers in their midst. Blake and Lana were shocked to see them; the city had seemed deserted only a day before.

"Where did all these people come from?" asked Lana. "There was no one here yesterday."

"It only seemed that way," said Aries. "In fact, we were watching you the whole time."

Lana stifled a shudder.

The people wore very little — perhaps a loin cloth, a cloak, or a dress, for the weather was mild here in Corpus, even on a winter morning like this one. The men's clothes were black, brown, or red. Some of the women were dressed in more colorful garbs of green, blue, and orange, as well as fabrics with floral or geometric patterns. All of the people had dark skin. They wore their dark hair in subtly different lengths and styles. Their eyes were green or brown, but showed no hint of warmth toward the Outlanders. A few of these Corpushi looked on in curiosity, but most simply glowered at Blake and Lana.

Some of the children wanted to run out to greet the warriors and have a closer look at the two Newcomers, but their somber parents restrained them. There would be no lighthearted introductions here. Lana and Blake bristled at this chilly reception.

Murdoch and the others led Blake and Lana right past the crowd and into the first floor of the Rookery, where it was shady and cool. They walked down a corridor lined with doors, all of which led to separate apartments. Murdoch opened a door on the right and motioned for everyone to enter. Inside, Blake and Lana found themselves in a sparsely decorated but pleasant room.

"Sit down," said Murdoch, gesturing to a long wooden bench with fabric draped on the seat to make it more comfortable. Lana and Blake complied. Murdoch turned to Aries and Peter. "Spartan and I are going upstairs. You stay here and guard the captives until we get back. We won't be long."

"Yes, Murdoch," said Aries and Peter almost simultaneously. Murdoch and Spartan left, taking most of the weapons with them, while Aries and Peter carried only their own. Aries pulled up a chair beside the table and sat down, while Peter stayed beside the entrance. They took their orders seriously.

"Don't try to escape or anything," said Aries, looking Blake and Lana directly in the eye. "If you do, Peter and I will finish you off real quick. You understand?"

"Of course," said Blake as calmly as he could.

"Good."

"So, where did your friends go?" asked Lana.

"They went to talk to Chief Zaaru and the Elders," said Peter.

"Oh," said Lana. "What's going to happen now?"

"We're going to wait right here until they call us, that's what."

"Oh," she said again. Then she folded her hands, placed them in her lap, and stared at the floor.

Chapter 30

Murdoch opened the apartment's front door and stuck his head inside. "Let's go," he said.

Blake and Lana stood up and, with Aries and Peter behind them, followed Murdoch. They walked to the end of a quiet corridor and passed through a doorway. There, they encountered a flight of stairs and proceeded to climb it. Higher and higher they went, passing floor after floor, until they reached the fifth story. Except for the roof, this was the highest floor.

Once again, Murdoch led the group down another corridor. At last, they stopped in front of a wooden door that sported numerous symbols and decorations in pure white, brick red, and sky blue paint. Murdoch knocked.

"Who is it?" asked a mature man's voice from inside.

"It's Murdoch with the two Kamishi."

"Come in," said the voice.

Aries and Peter remained in the corridor to stand guard, but Murdoch opened the door and went inside with Blake and Lana. They entered a large meeting room, dimly lit by the morning light that crept in through a glassless window. There was a colorful, woven elliptical rug at the center of the room, surrounded by a ring of a dozen firm pillows that served as seats. Two women and seven men sat on these pillows. One woman and three men were old, but the others were middle-aged, except for two young men who sat on one end of the Council. Blake and Lana immediately recognized one of them as Spartan. The other looked familiar, but it took them a moment to realize that this was the other guard from the bridge. This was Brent, and he was scowling conspicuously.

The group had been in the middle of a discussion.

"I apologize for disturbing you," said Murdoch.

"Not at all," said the middle-aged man at one end of the group. "We've been expecting you. Please, sit down," he said, gesturing to the pillows. The three visitors promptly complied.

"Honored Council Members," said Murdoch, "These people are Blake and Lana of the Kamishi. Blake and Lana, may I present the leaders of Corpus." Then, Murdoch began to introduce each one in turn, beginning with the kindly old man on the left.

"This is Morty," he said. Morty bowed his head in greeting. "He is the most senior Member of the Council." Murdoch gestured to the old woman seated next to Morty. "This is Morty's wife, Marge, who is an advisor to the Council. Next is Uchara. She is an Elder and a healer." The middle-aged Uchara smiled pleasantly. Then Murdoch gestured to a middle-aged man. "This is Hector, who is an Elder and a sage. This is Lobo," continued Murdoch as he motioned to the old man, "who is our Bebel teacher. Finally, this is Bufo, who is a former warrior and craftsman." This last man, also aged, gave a short nod.

"It is an honor," said Blake.

"You already know Spartan," said Murdoch, "and this is Brent."

Brent made eye contact with the Kamishi, but he said nothing and only continued to scowl. Blake and Lana felt the distinct urge to fidget or squirm, but they resisted it.

"Finally," said Murdoch, "may I present Chief Zaaru."

Blake and Lana looked across the room at the Chief of the Corpushi. Although seated, it was clear that this mature yet youthful man was tall and in good physical condition. He sat cross-legged, his back straight, his eyes fixed on the Newcomers. It was difficult to meet his gaze. Confronted with this austere personage, Blake and Lana were at a loss for words. With all the muted tension in the room, they felt quite uncomfortable.

Morty addressed the visitors. "It is my understanding that you have come a long way to reach Corpus. Is this true?"

Blake recognized Morty's voice as the one he had heard while standing in the corridor. "Yes," he began. "As Murdoch may have already told you, I am a fugitive from the northern Great Plains. Another tribe attacked my tribe, and the only survivors were me, my friend, and my two dogs. Along the way, both my friend and one of my dogs were killed. Before they died, we were fortunate to meet Lana in a Rubbletown. She became a member of our small tribe, and she has been with me ever since. She is my mate now."

"Are you married?" asked Morty.

"No, but we are a pair. In fact, we hope to get married soon."

"I see," said Morty. "Well, you are certainly two of the most interesting people to pass through Corpus. We've encountered Outlanders before, but never someone from the northern Great Plains or a Rubbletown. I'm sure you have many stories to tell, but first we must attend to this matter between you and the bridge guards. We have already heard from Paulo, Brent, Spartan, and Murdoch about the situation at the Nueces River, and about what has happened since then. Now, please tell us your version of the story."

Blake explained the altercation at the Nueces Bridge with Brent, Paulo, and Paulo's dog, Bobo. Then he explained what happened when Murdoch and the others captured him, and when Lana came to rescue him. Then Lana related her account as well, including what had transpired with the Corpushi warriors the previous night in the cave.

"Is it true that you can make fire in seconds?" asked Morty once Lana had finished speaking.

"Yes," said Lana. "Blake and I found a set of small sticks from the Old Days. If used properly, they can make fire very quickly. That's why we call them fire sticks."

"Fascinating," remarked Morty.

"Indeed," said Bufo edgily. "We will have plenty of time to talk about these fire sticks later. For now, let us finish with this business of assaulting the bridge guards first."

"Of course," replied Morty. "We must asses the guilt or innocence of these two Newcomers, and we must determine what kind of reparations Brent and Paulo are entitled to. Let's begin with you, Brent. What do you have to say?"

"Well," began Brent, clearing his throat. "As I said, I was not injured like Paulo was, but I was still attacked. I think the Council should punish this man for his violence, and the woman for being his accomplice."

"Thank you, Brent," said Morty. "The Council will take your recommendation into consideration. Spartan, you represent your father here. What kind of compensation does he require?"

"He is the head of a family and the provider for a household," said Spartan. "Now that he is injured, he will not be able to provide until he has healed. Therefore, he requires the equivalent of two weeks' worth of food in meats and vegetables. As for my father's dog, there was no permanent damage done. However, my father agrees with Brent that these Outlanders should be punished for their assault, in addition to any payment they may owe."

"That sounds reasonable," said Morty. "Are the other members of this Council agreed that this approach is fitting?" The other Elders, Marge, and Zaaru nodded quietly in accord. "Good. Then I propose to the Council that we grant Paulo's request for two weeks of provisions. For attacking Paulo and his dog, the Outlanders must also give Paulo enough food to last an additional week. Lastly, for attacking Brent, I propose they provide a week's worth of meat or vegetables to Brent as well. May we vote on this?"

The other Council members nodded once more.

"Very well," said Morty. "All those in favor of this proposal, raise your hand." Chief Zaaru and all the Elders raised their hands. "And all those opposed?" asked Morty ceremoniously. No one responded. "Then the decision is unanimous. Blake and Lana, between the two of you, you must provide Brent with one week's worth of food, and Paulo and his family three weeks' worth of food. Thus, your penalty amounts to four weeks' worth of rations. When can you provide this compensation?"

Blake's jaw dropped. "Forgive me," he said, "but that will be a difficult amount to pay at present. Lana and I are poor, and all we own are our clothes and tools we have with us right now. Of course, we could go out and obtain the food for Brent and Paulo, but because Murdoch and the others attacked me yesterday, I am in a weakened state and cannot hunt."

"I see," said Morty. "In that case, we must give this man time to recuperate so he can fulfill his obligation. The Outlanders can live in the lodge where they stayed last night. Blake will begin paying off his debt as soon as he is able; Lana will begin paying it off today. When they have finished, they will leave Corpus."

"What?" cried Lana. Everyone turned to stare at her, surprised at this outburst.

This time, Zaaru answered. "You should consider yourselves lucky," he said, speaking up for the first time. His voice was deep and low. He was calm and cool, but there was an air of agitation about him. "Instead of having to pay back your victims, you could have been given lashings or even killed. We have been merciful enough with you. What happens to you once you leave here is no concern of ours."

"But where will we go?" Lana pleaded.

"You should have thought of that before traveling one thousand miles just to assault two members of the Corpushi tribe!" Zaaru boomed, his irritation rising.

"Peace, Zaaru," said Morty, raising his hand soothingly.

"No, Morty!" exclaimed Zaaru. "I am tired of dealing with Outlander dregs like these! Let's just finish this sentencing and get on with things."

"Precisely," replied Morty, "but as you know, we must proceed in an orderly fashion. Patience, Chief Zaaru."

"By Apophis," muttered Zaaru. He pursed his lips and exhaled through his nostrils. Then he shifted in his seat and looked away, but held his tongue.

Morty turned to the other members of the Council. "Now then, let us rule on their sentencing, shall we?"

"Wait!" exclaimed Lana once more.

"What is it now, girl?" asked Morty. Blake eyed his mate warily. He tried to think of something polite to say in case Lana aroused the ire of the entire Council.

"Blake and I have not come all this way to assault your people. We have come so we could ask to join your tribe." Lana's statement was met with stifled chuckles among the Elders, and with outright laughter from Zaaru, Spartan, and Brent.

"Oh, that is good," bellowed Zaaru. "Lana, I thought you had ruined my morning, but I think you have more than made up for it now. What an absurd notion! Why would we even consider initiating you into our tribe?"

"Well, for one thing, we know Chief Tegg of Tulsa. He directed us to you with his good wishes and with his approval."

"Chief Tegg is a brave and wise man, and a valued friend, but his opinion does not change our position on Outlanders. We don't even like Outlanders who deal kindly with us, let alone criminals like you."

"I think you misjudge us, Chief Zaaru," said Lana.

"I don't see how," retorted Zaaru.

"Well, for one thing, you treat us like criminals when we come before you as traders."

"Ah yes," said Morty. "You are referring to your special fire sticks?"

"Not only that. Blake and I also have foods, fabrics, and tools to trade."

"So what?" remarked Zaaru. "We have plenty of materials. More than you know, I'm sure."

"We also have books we can offer you," said Lana. The Council members were visibly intrigued by this suggestion.

"Really?" said Lobo. "What sort of books?"

Blake tugged on Lana's arm. "Excuse us for a moment," said Blake to the Council. Then he leaned in to Lana's ear. "What are you doing? What are you offering them?"

"They like our fire sticks, but that might not be enough," she said in a hushed tone. "When they weren't impressed by our supplies, I thought maybe our books would do the trick."

"Are you sure about this?" Blake asked nervously.

"No, but it's better than getting punished and kicked out. We have to get them to like us Blake, and the sooner the better."

"Fine. Then what books?"

"We have two books from the old library. There's *Mammals: Past and Present*, which you brought, and there's *A History of Warfare*, which Manosh picked out. And of course, there's the Bebel…"

"You want to give away our Bebel?" Blake asked in alarm.

"No, Blake, to trade it for our future!" Lana exclaimed, allowing her voice to rise above a whisper before lowering it again. "Anyway, what are you so worried about? We have two of them, remember? One from me and one from you."

Blake groaned. "Fine. Just make sure we keep the one that's in better condition."

"You mean the newer one?"

"They're both old."

"The one that's less old then," Lana said.

"All right, yes," said Blake.

"That would be the one from me."

"But the Bebel I brought is from Kamis. It's been in our tribe for a hundred years. It's too precious."

"Mine comes from my deceased parents, so it's precious, too," said Lana. "Besides, if the Corpushi accept us, it's the same as keeping it."

Morty cleared his throat. "Blake, Lana, we cannot wait any longer," he said.

Blake hesitated. "All right, fine. Go ahead and offer it to them. Just remember what I did here."

"Of course," said Lana. She gave Blake a wry smile. Then she addressed the Council once more. "We have two books from a Rubbletown library — one on history, the other on nature. We also have a Bebel that's more than a hundred years old. We are willing to trade these things, but only if we receive a suitable offer."

Lobo was visibly intrigued, and made little effort to conceal it. "Well now, that is interesting," he said. "We have one Bebel, of course, but no other books. It seems these Newcomers do have some valuable items. Perhaps we should consider trading with them after all."

"Perhaps," said Bufo. "What of those fire sticks?"

"Ah, yes," said Morty as he turned to Lana. "I suppose now would be a good time to show them to us."

Lana reached into her cloak, brought out a matchbook, and held it out for all to see.

"Would you be so kind as to give us a demonstration?" asked Uchara.

"Of course," said Lana. She pulled out a match and struck it on the back of the book, instantly lighting it. The Council looked on in awe. They were quite impressed.

"Very interesting, Lana," said Lobo. "How did you do that?"

"To be honest," she said, "I am not certain how it works. These fire sticks are a creation of the Old Timers. Blake and I found many of these little packets back in my old Rubbletown. We do not have many left, but we are willing to trade them. We can also help you look for more in the Ruins around here. There must be some old stores there where we could find some."

"I doubt it," snapped Bufo. "Our people have lived here for centuries. If there were such a thing to be found, we would have found it by now."

"Maybe so," said Lana, "but sooner or later, Blake and I will run out of these. With your permission, we'd like to search through the Ruins in your territory for more. We'd be happy to include you in that search."

"Thank you," replied Morty. "I think your finding is most interesting."

"It may be interesting," said Bufo, "but it is also worrisome. It has long been said that one should be wary of the inventions of the Old Timers. Who knows what kinds of strange evils lurk among them?"

Lana bristled at hearing this comment, for she was leery of the widespread fear of the Old Days. Nevertheless, Bufo was an Elder, and Lana felt obliged to give him her respect. She also realized that the Elder's concerns were not unfounded. The fire sticks were new to the Bebelishi, and they hailed from an ancient time when many mysterious and evil things influenced the world. Perhaps it was unwise to reawaken these slumbering demons. Perhaps it would be better to leave the past behind and focus solely on the present and future. In an instant, Lana considered these notions, but she quickly rejected them and came to a different conclusion.

"You speak wisely, sir, of course," said Lana, "but I have a different perspective. I agree that the Managers were ruled by evil in most ways. Nevertheless, they, like we, were human beings who were capable of choosing the good over the bad. Although one can speak of good or bad things that control people, ultimately it is up to the individual person whether he will do good or evil. Creations from the Old Days, such as these fire sticks, may have been created for an evil purpose in the name of Management or in the spirit of domination over the Earth. But that does not necessarily mean that we must use them for that same purpose. We can use technology such as this to improve our lives without upsetting the balance of the New Days."

"That is a gamble that I am reluctant to take," replied Bufo.

"Do you see the risk involved in associating with Outlanders, Morty?" said Hector. "Of course, I mean no disrespect to our guests, but if we are not careful, we may find ourselves following the path of Management once more. Then the whole world — ourselves included — will weep."

"I admire your caution, Bufo and Hector," said Morty, "but let us not reject wisdom in the name of prudence. It is true that we must protect the New Ways and not relapse into the Old ones. However, is it not the spirit of the New Way to embrace change and to move forward, come what may?"

"Yes," said Hector, "which is precisely the reason I reject the notion that raiding the Ruins could be productive. It is a step backward, not forward."

"It could be," said Uchara, "but I believe I understand the direction in which Morty's mind is flowing. On the one hand, reaching into the past, into the time of the Old Days, could lead to ruin, just as it did for the Managers. On the other hand, their legacy is part of reality after all. Perhaps we could benefit from learning from them. We could learn about what they did right, and we could learn about what they did wrong. Currently, the only means we have for knowing anything about the Old Days are the legends handed down from generation to generation, and the Bebel…"

"That is all we need," said Bufo hoarsely.

"Perhaps not," said Uchara, "Perhaps we would do well to learn still more by looking in the Ruins for ourselves."

"Some tribes believe that they are cursed," said Bufo. "Of course, many of us Warmlanders do not view them quite so harshly. After all, our own Corpus is rebuilt from Rubble." A fit of coughing seized Bufo, and everyone waited in silence for it to subside. When he could breathe normally again, Bufo continued. "Still, most of us agree that rummaging around in feral Ruins is dangerous."

"As well we should," said Uchara. "Like Morty said, a healthy dose of caution is welcome. But look at the wondrous thing that Blake and Lana discovered in an untamed Rubbletown! They discovered the ability to make fire in an instant! Do you not see how useful such a thing is? If Lana is right, then we could find many more of these fire sticks if we would only look for them. Who knows? Perhaps we will find other useful things, or other interesting facts about the Old Days. We have so much to learn from the world around us, from the past as well as the present."

"Thank you, Uchara," said Morty. "You expressed my ideas better than I could have myself. It seems to me that we should vote on whether or not we should acquire these fire sticks." He turned to Murdoch, Blake, and Lana. "Go wait in the corridor. We will call you to give you our decision shortly."

"As you wish, Elder," said Murdoch. Then he escorted Blake and Lana outside, where they waited for the Council to finish deliberating amongst themselves inside. Soon, Morty called the trio back in and addressed the Kamishi once more.

"You are indeed a unique pair, Blake and Lana. Your punishment to compensate your victims still stands, but the Council has decided to let you stay in Corpus as guests for the time being. While you are here, you will pay off your debt to Brent and Paulo. You will also trade with us, but exactly what will be traded remains to be seen. You will live in the lodge for the time being."

"This does not necessarily mean they will join us!" Chief Zaaru hastened to add.

"That's correct," agreed Morty. "They are our guests." Zaaru stiffened. "When the time comes, we will decide what kind of relations the Corpushi and the … Kamishi … are to have with one another. Is that clear?"

Blake and Lana nodded. They were both relieved, but Lana found it hard to contain her excitement. "Yes!" she exclaimed. "We understand."

"Good," said Morty. Then he turned to his tribesmen once more. "Are there any further comments to be made or issues to be raised?" All of the Corpushi present shook their heads. "Very well. The ruling of this Council is complete and final. Meeting adjourned."

The assembly dispersed. Zaaru and the Elders stayed behind to converse. Murdoch, Spartan, and Brent walked off as a group, chatting all the while. Blake and Lana simply stood in the corridor and hugged each other.

"Thank the Creator," said Blake, "and thank you, Lana. You were great! You gave us a second chance."

"We got lucky," said Lana. "We're lucky that the penalty they gave us is only several weeks' rations, and that they took an interest in what we have. But you're right: that was enough to give us a second chance. Now we have one month to prove ourselves."

"How will we do that?"

"Hard work. A little charm wouldn't hurt, either." Together, Blake and Lana returned to their lodge on the outskirts of Corpus.

Chapter 31

Lana was busy. She was trying to turn the dreary lodge where she and Blake now dwelled into a home of sorts. Only a few rays from the midday sun entered through bare portals in the walls, obstructed by piles of debris outside. *I'll have to clear away some of that Rubble and find coverings for those windows later.* Lana swept the floors, straightened up the sparse furniture, and dusted the surfaces. The place was beginning to look a bit more welcoming. Blake was napping in one of the rooms. Lana knew he needed to recover from the beating he had received. *Could that really have been just two days ago?* He needed his strength, so she was content to let him be.

There was a loud knock on the wooden front door, and Lana went to answer it. It was Murdoch and Spartan.

"How are you?" asked Murdoch, rather sheepishly.

"Fine," said Lana.

"Spartan and I would like to invite you up to our homes this evening. We'd like you to meet our families."

"Really?" asked Lana, surprised. "Well, Blake is sleeping right now…"

"Oh, it doesn't have to be right now," said Murdoch. "In fact, we were thinking it could be this evening. For supper."

"All right," said Lana. "I'll tell Blake when he wakes up. When should we come?"

"How about at sundown?"

"That's fine. Where do you live?"

"Spartan and I are next-door neighbors. We live on the second story of the Rookery. Do you think you will be able to find us?"

"Yes," said Lana hesitantly.

"Good. See you then," said Murdoch. Then he and Spartan spun about and left just as abruptly as they had arrived.

That evening, Lana and Blake returned to the Rookery and made their way to the stairs. With a timid smile or wave, they greeted the few people loitering about, but these Corpushi simply ignored them or scowled in return. Lana and Blake couldn't help but lower their heads in embarrassment. They were relieved when they began to ascend the stairs.

On the second floor, Blake and Lana saw a series of doors on either side of the hallway. Most had some kind of decorations on them, although a few were bare.

"Which one is Murdoch's or Spartan's?" asked Blake.

"I don't know," said Lana. "These doors seem to have some kind of inscription on them, but it's not Bebelishi writing, so I can't read it. Can you?"

"No, of course not. At least, not yet."

"Wait a second…" Lana approached one of the doors. It was ajar. "Maybe it's this one." The door sported a few symbols and designs, painted simply in red and blue. Lana rapped softly on it with the middle knuckle of her inverted, loosely clenched hand. The door swung open and Murdoch stood in the entrance.

"Hello!" he said with surprising warmth. "Come in."

Blake and Lana followed the sweep of his arm into the apartment and into the living room. The hard floor was covered with a gigantic, elliptical, woven rug. Dyed directly into the fabric were numerous geometrical star shapes, as well as several zigzag lines of red, black, blue, green, and yellow. The walls were beautifully decorated with colorfully patterned blankets that hung all around the room. On the right side of the room was an area for recreation and relaxation. There were a couple of wash basins, one of which was half full of water, the other of which contained ceramic dishes and wooden eating utensils. There were a few comfortable looking pillows for reclining, and a couple of blankets folded neatly beside them. Along the back wall, resting safely on thin-framed wooden racks, were the family's weapons. There were five long, handsome spears with fine points made of metal, and three wooden shields that were nearly as tall as a man, each decorated with a different animal. One bore the stylized image of a snake, arranged in a zigzag pattern so as to suggest simultaneously a bolt of lightning. Another bore a rendering of a black bear, while the third was decorated with the image of a male lion's head.

"Serena!" Murdoch called. "Come and meet our guests." A woman rounded a corner and came into view. She was attractive and slender, with the usual dark skin and brown eyes. Her raven hair was long, straight, and course. She wore an off-white dress made of a cotton-like fabric, a pair of leather moccasins on her feet, and beaded jewelry on her neck and wrists. "Serena, I'd like to introduce you to our guests, Blake and Lana of the Kamishi. Blake and Lana, this is my wife, Serena." The three people smiled, greeted one another, and shook hands.

"Can I get you anything to eat or drink?" asked Serena.

"Something to drink would be wonderful," said Lana.

"All right. I'll be right back." Serena went into another room and returned with a flask of clear, fresh water and cups for everyone. "Please, come sit down." The four people were seated on a set of large, comfortable cushions. "So what brings you to Corpus?"

"Well," said Blake, "that's sort of a long story."

"I've got time," said Serena.

Blake and Lana shared the story of their journey with Murdoch and Serena. Blake told them about the Ravashi attack on Kamis, and how he and his best friend, Manosh, had left in search of the Warmland. Lana told of how Blake and Manosh had found her in the Rubbletown. Together, they related the inauspicious series of events that had brought them there that night.

"So you see," said Blake, "we never meant to cause anyone pain. Quite the opposite — we had hoped to meet you, the Corpushi, under much more favorable circumstances. Unfortunately, it didn't work out that way, and I'm to blame for that. I really am sorry."

"You have endured much," Serena said. "It would be a shame if you had to leave. I hope that everything gets resolved between you and the others."

"Thank you," said Lana with a sigh of relief. "It's nice of you to say that. We've been having a hard time making friends around here."

"I know," said Serena. "The past several days have been difficult. Hopefully, things will start to turn around soon. How about you, Blake? How are you feeling? Any better?"

"A little better. Still kind of sore. I should be able to hunt by tomorrow or the day after that, though."

"Oh, good," said Serena. There was a knock on the front door.

"That's probably Spartan and his wife now," said Murdoch, standing up. Blake's stomach was aflutter as he anticipated the worst from this encounter. He was, after all, about to become acquainted with the family of the man he had battered. Murdoch went to the entrance and opened the door. As he had predicted, his neighbors were there waiting for him. Murdoch welcomed the couple inside. "Blake, Lana, you already know Spartan. This is his wife, Becca."

Becca was somewhat plump and quite a bit shorter than her husband. Her long, black hair hung in braids past her shoulders, and lay flat against them in the front. She wore a dress made of soft, supple, tanned leather. Her disposition was cheerful and endearing. She smiled broadly as she shook hands with Blake and Lana, immediately putting them at ease.

"It's good to meet you," said Becca. "I look forward to getting to know you better."

Spartan and Becca sat down with Blake and Lana in the living area and made themselves comfortable. Murdoch and Serena expediently brought out some hot tea, flat baked bread, and dried texin beef for their guests before joining them. The group engaged in small talk for a while, but soon the conversation turned to the Kamishi's travels. Blake and Lana retold some of their experiences — including those of which Murdoch and Serena had not yet heard. They talked about how the Podeshi had killed their dog, Saamu, with a spear through the chest, and how a pride of lions had recently killed and devoured their dear friend, Manosh. They also told of the places they had seen, the people they had met, and the creatures they had encountered. The Corpushi were fascinated.

The six youths were enjoying their evening together, but eventually the subject of Paulo surfaced again.

"Listen," said Spartan. "We have some plans." Blake and Lana looked at him attentively. "Tomorrow, you are going to meet the rest of my family, including my father." Blake sighed heavily. "It will probably be a difficult meeting, but we have to have it."

"The sooner the better, I suppose," said Blake.

"I suppose," replied Spartan. Then he rose to his feet and helped his wife up, who was comfortably embedded in the soft cushion on the floor. "Thank you, Serena and Murdoch. This was wonderful. The next time, we will be at our place. Blake, Lana, until tomorrow." The couple left and retired to their home in the adjacent apartment.

"We should go, too," said Blake to Murdoch and Serena. "Thank you so much for tonight."

"You're welcome," said Murdoch, extending his hand. Blake stared at the hand for a moment. It was big, strong, and rough. This was the same hand that, only a day earlier, had punched him in the face and the belly, and had brought him to his knees. Now, it was being extended in friendship. Blake clasped the outstretched hand in his own and gave it a firm shake. "We'll see you tomorrow."

"See you then," said Blake. He and Lana said their goodbyes and left as well. They walked down the corridor to the staircase, descended to the ground floor, and began walking across the town of Corpus. It was late, but a few lights could still be seen. There were torches perched high atop wooden posts, and back in the Rookery, candlelight flickered from a few windows, even at this hour. The waxing moon shone brightly, and countless stars filled the night sky. Blake and Lana looked out at the Gulf. Its silver, dimpled waves scintillated. Shifting constantly and roaring softly, they rolled in to shore. The wind that came off the water was chilly, and it reminded the couple that they should hurry home.

There was no one else around, except for a few sentinels. Unlike the bridge guards, all of these men were necessarily young and fit, and they wielded sturdy, reliable spears and small forearm shields for defense. One of them stood in Blake and Lana's path, leaning against his spear and doing his best to remain alert. He detected them from a considerable distance away and turned to face them. He studied them for a moment in the faint light. Then he acknowledged them with an approving nod. Lana held onto Blake's arm and leaned into him instinctively as they passed by. The soft sand beneath their feet hissed as they walked along, heading inland toward the dark edge of town.

At last, they reached their cryptic lodge in the Ruins. Blake untied the rope and pushed on the door, which swung open on its decrepit hinges. Then Blake and Lana stepped inside and, with a muffled thud, shut the door behind them.

Chapter 32

Blake answered the knock at the front door and found Spartan standing there. It was a bright and sunny morning, but Blake was in no mood to appreciate it.

"It's time," said Spartan.

"All right," said Blake. "Come in." Spartan entered and seated himself at an old wooden table while Blake went back to the bedroom. He found Lana lying in bed, still dozing. The blanket covered only part of her body, but it was hot and that was all she needed. Blake kissed her forehead and gave her a gentle nudge. "Wake up, my love."

Lana budged. Her eyes fluttered open. She squinted reflexively and stretched. Then she looked up at Blake. "Mmmm," she groaned.

"It's time."

"Time for what?"

"Spartan is here. We have to go see Paulo."

Lana covered her eyes with her forearm melodramatically. "Oh, no," she said. "Give me a minute to get ready."

"Sure," Blake said, and returned to the main room to entertain Spartan. After a few moments, Lana came out as well, looking a bit more awake and feeling more presentable. Then the trio headed back to the Rookery.

"Where does your father live?" asked Blake as they ascended the stairs.

"He lives on the third floor," replied Spartan.

"Oh. Why does he live way up there? Wouldn't it be easier just to live on the ground floor?"

"Actually, most people prefer to live as high up as possible."

"Why?" asked Blake.

"Safety."

"How do you mean?"

"I mean the higher you go, the safer you are," said Spartan. "Do you remember the story Murdoch told you, about how the Corpushi fought off a fleet of attacking ships? Well, it seems that when the enemy soldiers were advancing, they managed to reach the lower levels of the Rookery and kill many people. People in higher levels were only injured or even completely unharmed. Ever since then, most people have preferred to live on the higher floors."

"Do you get attacked often?" Blake asked.

"No, not anymore," said Spartan. "Not in my lifetime, actually. It's said that in the past, Corpus had to defend against enemies from all sides: the sea, the hinterland, and both sides. Those days are gone, though. Today, Corpus is prosperous and safe."

"Is that because you are the biggest tribe?"

"No, not really. We have about as many members as most other tribes — about two hundred people."

"Then what's changed?" asked Blake.

"We have good relations with most of our neighbors now."

"Why?"

"Trade. We hunt the hinterland for big game, but we also catch fish from the Gulf, so we have plenty to trade. The only tribe we go to war with anymore are the Laredoshi, to the south and west, but there are plenty of other tribes to the north who want things from the sea that only we can get for them. We get along fine with the Santonishi, Ostenishi, Wacoshi, and Dallashi tribes of the Warmland. We even trade with the Tulsashi now and then."

"With Tegg?" asked Blake, recalling the name of the Tulsashi chief who had kindly advised him and Lana weeks before.

"Yeah," said Spartan sourly, "with Tegg. Anyway, besides the threat of war, there are also animals that come around every once in a while."

"What kinds of animals?" asked Lana.

"Oh, all kinds: insects, rodents, foxes, pumas. We've even had lions. If you live on the ground floor, you're more likely to have to deal with animals invading your home."

"Hmmm," said Blake thoughtfully, "still, I would think it's convenient to live on the ground floor."

"It is," replied Spartan, "and some people do choose to live on there for that reason. It's tradition, though, to try to live as high up as you can. In fact, the higher your rank, the higher up you tend to live."

"Really?" asked Lana.

"Sure. I mean, people can choose where they want to live, but they don't have unlimited choices. If you want to live high up, you have to earn it."

"So," said Lana as she furrowed her eyebrows, "who lives where then?"

"Well, generally the people on the ground floor are low-ranking adults, young people just starting out, or crippled or old people who have trouble with the stairs. People on the second floor are usually a bit older, but still young or not tribal leaders. That's why Becca and I, and Murdoch and Serena, live on the second floor."

"Do you hope to move up?" Lana asked.

"Someday. All in good time. People on the third and fourth floors are senior members of the tribe, but again, they are not necessarily the leaders. That's why my father and his family live on the third floor. Now, most of the leaders live on the fourth and fifth floors. The Elders and their families live on the fifth floor, and so do Chief Zaaru and his family."

"And is every single one of these apartments occupied?" asked Lana again.

"They are all used for something, yes," Spartan said. "That is, most of them are homes, but a few apartments on the first and fifth floors are reserved for certain occasions."

"Such as?" Blake asked.

"Well, for example, the conference room on the fifth floor where we all met yesterday. Nobody lives there; it's only used for Council meetings. On the first floor, the Elders Hector and Uchara each have their domains where they help people. Hector is a sage, so that's where he gives people advice. And Uchara is a healer, so that's where she helps people when they are sick. Other people have their domains on the first floor, too."

When the trio reached Paulo's home, Spartan opened the door, entered with Blake and Lana, and announced his presence. "Mother, we're here!" Two children — a boy and a younger girl — were playing on the floor with figurines of people and animals. "Hi, kids," said Spartan.

"Hi, Spartan," the two children said at the same time.

"These are two of my siblings, Jed and Kayla," said Spartan.

"Hello," said Lana with a warm smile and curt wave. Jed only frowned, but Kayla smiled shyly in return. A dowdy, middle-aged woman came into the main room and approached her son. She hugged him and gave him a kiss. Then she turned to Blake and Lana.

"So, these are the Outlanders, eh?" she said.

"Blake, Lana," began Spartan in as calm a tone as he could muster, "this is my mother, Wendy. Mother, this is Blake and Lana."

"Hmmph," said Wendy. "Well, I know you're here to see Paulo. This way." She led the others to a secluded room in the back of the apartment. Curtains partly covered the window, providing only dim lighting. Paulo lay on the straw mattress in the corner of the room, his head propped up with cushions as he stared glumly forward at nothing.

"Hello, Father," said Spartan. "I have brought the Kamishi to speak with you, just as you asked."

Paulo slowly turned his head toward the door and glared at Blake and Lana. "Come forward," he said. Blake and Lana complied. Blake was horrified by what he saw. Paulo's entire face was puffy and bruised. In each place where Blake had punched him, there was a swollen lump surrounded with purple, blue, and yellow blotches. Paulo could scarcely talk. "So, you are Blake, the brave Kamishi warrior who bested two Corpushi bridge guards. Well, how do you like what you see now?"

Blake kneeled on the floor beside Paulo's bed and humbly lowered his head. "I am truly sorry," he said. "It was not my intention to bring harm to you or your people."

"My people are unharmed, Outlander," quipped Paulo. "My people are brave and strong. They have overcome far worse threats than you, and they always will. It is I who was harmed here, not them."

"Again, I am sorry," repeated Blake. "The Council made their judgment against Lana and me, and we have every intention of complying—"

"I know, I know, I'm sure you will," said Paulo irritably. Then he stared straight ahead at the wall once more.

"I was angry," said Blake. "I should not have lashed out the way I did."

Paulo only shook his head dejectedly and sighed. "I know. At first, I was furious at you, but now that I've had some time to think ... I don't know." Paulo turned to Blake once more and looked directly at Blake with his big, brown, sad eyes. "I gave you little choice, didn't I, Blake? It was I who acted out of anger. I brought this upon myself."

"But, sir," said Blake, softly, "you are a guard. You were just doing your job—"

"Brent was doing his job!" Paulo yelled, slurring his words. Spittle flew from his mouth. His eyes blazed fiercely and his face turned red. "And I was acting like a damn fool!" Paulo slumped. His eyes moistened. His lips turned down and trembled. "I've been too reckless for too long, and I've made life miserable for anyone who said so. I'm too old…"

"No, Father," said Spartan tenderly.

"It's true!" yelled Paulo again. "I'm getting too old for these games. There was a time when people feared me. Now, everyone thinks of me as a joke."

Spartan kneeled by his father and held his hand. "No, Father. You're not a joke. You're respected and feared."

Paulo patted the back of his son's hand. "That's kind of you to say, Son, but even if I'm still lucky enough to be respected, I'm certainly no longer feared. Anyway, neither one of those things are as important as being loved."

"But we love you, Father. Mother, and the kids, and I, we all love you."

"I know, and I'm grateful for that. But what about everyone else? They don't even like me. And why should they? I never gave them reason to."

"You did your job faithfully all these years," said Spartan.

"That's all I did, though. I never helped anyone, I never spent time with anyone. I have many regrets, Son, and now I'm too old to make up for them."

Lana looked on as she leaned against the wall near the entrance. She had barely moved since stepping into the room, and she could hardly believe the spectacle she was watching now. She had dreaded this meeting, but she had not expected anything like this.

"No you're not," Spartan said. "This is madness. You are not old, and you are not dying. You have only been beaten in battle."

"That's enough. I'm ashamed," said Paulo.

"Sir," said Lana as she stepped forward, "you have nothing to be ashamed of. I was there, remember?"

"Ah, yes, I remember you. Lana, right?"

"I saw the whole thing. You fought well."

"No, I didn't. I fought like an old fool, and I failed."

"You make it sound as though you've never failed at anything before," said Lana.

"I'm not used it, no," said Paulo. "I thought I was the perfect warrior. Indeed, I was a good warrior, but now, when I look back, and I think of how I treated people, I see just how wrong I was. All those stupid mistakes — I have failed in so many ways."

"Then consider this a valuable lesson," said Lana. "You have lost a battle as a warrior, but you have been given a second chance as a man."

Paulo looked up at Lana for a moment. "We will see. We will see." Then he sat up in bed and looked at Blake. "Thank you for coming. You did not have to come."

"I will repay my debt to you, Paulo," said Blake. "I give you my word."

"I know. Go now. I must rest."

Blake and Lana headed for the door. Spartan hugged his father and then got up to leave as well. In the main room, they encountered Wendy once again.

"Are you finished in there?" she asked impatiently.

"Yes," said Spartan.

"Good," she said. She went to the small kitchen and retrieved a tray with a pitcher of water, a cup, and a dish of dried meat with mashed tubers and fruits. "Well, I'll see you later, Son. I have to tend to your father."

"See you later," said Spartan. Then Wendy took the tray back to Paulo. "Bye, kids." Jed and Kayla waved to their big brother. Then Spartan left with Lana and Blake.

Chapter 33

"Lana!" cried Blake as he stood in the corridor of the lodge.

"What?" came Lana's reply from another room.

"I'm going to go check on Rita. Are you coming?"

Lana popped her head into the corridor. "Just a minute." When they were ready, the couple left their lodge and headed further away from town toward Rita's secret den. Toting a canteen of clean water and a sack full of dried meat, their plan was to give her some more provisions without anyone else knowing about it.

"Blake, how long are we going to need to keep this up?"

"As long as it takes." Lana raised her eyebrows to invite a more detailed response. "She'll probably start weaning the puppies off milk at around three to four weeks, but they might not be totally off it until six to eight weeks."

"Eight weeks?"

"Of course, dogs are social beings. After the pups are weaned, we'll still need to help Rita raise them, or else some predator might get them."

"How long would that take?" asked Lana.

"Oh, probably about another six months…"

"This is ridiculous. That's too long."

"So what are you saying?" asked Blake indignantly. "Are you saying that we should just give up on them? Is that what you're saying?"

"No!" Lana retorted. "Of course not. Don't get all excited, Blake. I just meant that we can't keep sneaking around like this, especially if we want to make a good impression on the Corpushi. Either we shorten the process, or we tell someone."

"I don't want to tell anyone."

"Why not?"

"I don't trust these people — at least, not yet," said Blake. "You heard Murdoch. He said he was going to look for Rita."

"So?"

"When I asked him what he would do when he found her, he refused to tell me. What if he harms her, Lana? What if he harms the puppies? We can't let that happen."

"I think you're worried about nothing. The Corpushi obviously keep dogs. Hell, they even keep horses! I don't think they're going to do anything to hurt Rita or her puppies. Actually, these people seem very orderly to me. I don't see any reason why they wouldn't let us keep them, and if they didn't, then I think they would take good care of them."

"I don't know. Maybe, but I don't want to take that chance. I say we keep bringing Rita food and drink at least once a day until the puppies are weaned. When they're bigger and have a better chance, then we can tell someone."

Lana sighed. "All right, Blake. We'll try this your way, but I still don't think it's necessary."

"Well, we'll see," said Blake.

They sneaked off into the woods to look for the den. When they finally found it, they looked inside. Rita was visible, but none of the pups were.

"Where are they?" asked Lana.

"I bet their sleeping," said Blake. "They're probably behind her. Come on, let's she if she'll come out." Blake called to the dog. This time, instead of growling, he heard whining. A moment later, Rita slowly crept out of the large hole. She crouched low, with her ears flatted against her head and her tail between her legs. She licked her lips and whined continuously. Blake offered her the dried meat, and she bolted it down hungrily. Then he offered her a bowl of water, which she also quickly finished off.

"Oh, look at her," said Lana. "The poor dog is starving."

"It's all that milk she's making. She can't go out to hunt as she normally would. She'll be all right, as long as she gets what she needs. I'm glad we came out here today. We just have to keep doing it, that's all."

"I still think we should tell someone."

"No!"

Lana was taken aback, but she said, "Don't you see? It would be good for the dog. The more of us there are to bring her food and drink, the better."

Blake only stroked Rita's fur affectionately, which seemed to relax her. She was clearly feeling sociable again, and she knew that

Blake and Lana were there to help. She welcomed their presence, but she still felt quite anxious, so she soon disappeared into the den once more.

"Blake, did you hear what I said?" asked Lana. "I think Rita could use more—"

"No!" cried Blake.

Lana sighed and shook her head.

"Did you see any of the puppies?" Blake asked.

"No, I didn't," replied Lana sullenly.

"Me neither, but she seems so protective, she must still have at least a few. Come on, let's leave her in peace. We'll come back again as soon as we can — tomorrow at the latest." Then Blake and Lana hurried back to their lodge.

Chapter 34

"Wake up, Blake! Wake up!"

Blake opened his eyes to see the lovely face of his beloved Lana leaning over him. She smiled at him as she shook him gently.

"Wake up!" she repeated, nudging him once more.

"I'm up. I'm up," croaked Blake as he took a moment to orient himself. Struggling, he raised himself to a seated position. "It's barely light out."

Blake and Lana had been living in Corpus for over a week. Blake was almost fully recovered. He and Lana had already decorated and cleaned up their lodge and renovate it using various building materials from the area. Now, it felt almost like home. They had even amassed a small collection of fruits and vegetables for themselves, and each day, they cared for Rita without anyone knowing about it. People had seen them come and go, but Blake and Lana managed to appear so nonchalant that no one really knew or cared why or where they went. The couple had also begun working to pay off their debt to Brent and Paulo, providing them with fruits and vegetables as well. However, Blake had not resumed hunting yet.

"They're already up. A bunch of people are," said Lana.

"Why? What's going on?"

"We're going on a fishing trip," she said enthusiastically.

"A what?"

"A fishing trip. We're going out on boats so we can catch some fish."

"Really?" exclaimed Blake. Suddenly, he felt infused with excitement as well. "That sounds great. Can I come?"

"Of course, you fool," giggled Lana. "Why else would I wake you up just before dawn?"

"Oh, right," said Blake. Lana tugged on his lax arm, and he slowly rose to his feet. Blake rubbed his face and got dressed. Soon, they were ready to leave.

Blake followed Lana outside and walked with her toward the Rookery. There, they joined seven other youths who had already gathered around the base of the Rookery. The group consisted of people whom Lana and Blake already knew. Serena and Becca were there, as were Murdoch, Spartan, Aries, and Peter. Brent was there as well.

"Well," said Murdoch, "I think everyone's here. Let's get our things and go!" They enthusiastically ran to the shore and set their belongings down on the sand. The sun was just starting to rise over the vast, blue horizon of the Gulf. All of the youths remarked at what a lovely a sight it was, but none were more impressed than Lana and Blake, for whom this entire experience was new and exciting. Soon, the sun hovered above the water, bathing Corpus in a glorious, ruddy light.

The group wandered into a small inlet. There, a large canoe with an attached outrigger rested steadily on the beach. It was also securely anchored to shore with a rope tied to a post in the sand. The canoe had been dug out in one piece from a single tree, and was large enough to seat the entire crew of nine. Stowed inside were fishing and boating supplies, such as woven nets, wooden poles, some twine, and spears.

Blake admired the canoe for a moment, noting its simple, skillful craftsmanship and the variety of implements within it. Then he turned his attention to his comrades, who reached into their bags and brought out small leather masks, each with circles of glass embedded in the eyeholes.

Lana noticed this, too. She turned to Becca and Spartan. "What are you doing?" she asked.

"Oh, we're getting our diving masks out," said Becca.

"Your what?"

"Our diving masks," Becca repeated.

Blake and Lana were puzzled. They had not realized that swimming would be involved. To them, fishing meant standing on the shore, watching for fish, and thrusting one's spear into them as they passed by. They noticed that none of the group had taken up their spears yet.

"I don't understand," said Lana.

"Oh dear," exclaimed Becca. "I suppose we should've explained this to you first! Here's what we do." Blake and Lana listened carefully. "We take our canoe out and put on these masks, which allow us to see underwater. Then we go in with our spears and look around for fish and other marine animals. When we find them, we spear them, bring them back to the boat, and come home."

"What do you mean, you 'go in'?" asked Blake.

"Why, swimming," she said.

"Swimming?"

"Sure."

"And how far from shore do you take your canoe?" he asked.

"Oh, not very far, usually," said Becca. "Most of the good things to eat are inshore anyway. Most of the pretty things to decorate with are inshore, too. Now, come on, you two. We brought some extra diving masks for you. Here you go." Becca handed each of her guests a mask. Blake and Lana turned them over in their hands. The masks were made of leather and glass. The leather was a single piece, consisting of a single strap that wrapped around the head and a pair of circles that went around the eyes. Sewn into these leather circles was a pair of glass plates to block the water. Blake and Lana put them on, cinching them in the back with a sturdy knot.

"Not bad," said Lana, looking through the lenses. "I can still see pretty clearly, actually."

"You'll see even better underwater," said Becca.

"You can see underwater with these?" echoed Lana.

"Better than without, anyway," said Spartan.

"How do you make them?" asked Lana, astonished at this piece of technology.

"Well," began Spartan, "we get the leather from the cattle we hunt, and just cut it to size. We find the glass just by looking around the savanna, or the beach, or even the Ruins. A while back, somebody figured out how to heat the glass, which is how we shaped it into these lenses. Then we just sew the lenses into the leather, and that's it."

"Ah ha!" exclaimed Lana. "So your people plunder the Ruins for relics, too!"

"Well…"

"Then our discovery of fire sticks must not have seemed so strange to you after all."

"I suppose not," admitted Spartan. "Maybe that's why the Elders decided to allow them into the tribe."

"I should've known," Lana muttered to herself under her breath. "So this diving mask really allows you to see underwater then?"

"And pretty well, too," said Spartan.

"That's amazing," said Lana. "Just amazing."

Now the entire group was standing around on the beach with their big, bulky diving masks tied to their faces. Blake and Lana couldn't help but chuckle at the ridiculous sight.

"Laugh if you like," said Spartan, "but they work!"

"I hope so," said Blake, still chuckling to himself.

The band of young divers disrobed in preparation for entering the water, stripping down to only their loin cloths. They stood on the beach, their lithe, bronze bodies shimmering in the ever-growing sunlight. A cold breeze came off the sea, but they intended to swim anyway. They adjusted their diving masks one last time.

"Come on," said Spartan to Lana and Blake. "We'll take the canoe out later. For now, let's just dive in!"

All of the Corpushi took their spears in hand and headed for the water. Not wanting to be left behind, Blake and Lana ran after them. Consequently, they were the last to enter. Wading in at first, they felt the brisk coolness of the winter water envelop their toes and creep up their ankles until it lapped at their calves. Timidly wading in farther, the two Newcomers relished the feeling of the frothy brine encircling their knees. They hesitated when they felt the shockingly cold water cling to their thighs and groins. Their distress faded quickly, however, so they waded out even farther until the chilly water reached their bellies.

"This water is cold!" exclaimed Blake.

"Oh, quit being such a baby," teased Lana.

"Oh, I'm a baby, am I?" quipped Blake. "Well, why don't you just dive right in then?"

"No, I'm taking it slow. Bit by bit."

"Well, my bits are getting cold. Come on, it's best to just jump in and get it over with all at once anyway. Look, the others are out there swimming already."

"Oh ... I don't know ... I just want to take it slow," said Lana.

"Come on..." said Blake with a mischievous look in his eye, "do it, or I'll make you do it!"

"You wouldn't dare!"

"Oh, wouldn't I?"

"No! You wouldn't ... ah!"

Blake grabbed Lana around the waist and hoisted her upwards. Then he dunked her down into the water. Lana immediately burst forth from the water, pushing her long, wet hair back and squealing all the while.

"You beast!" she cried, her mouth open wide as she gasped for breath, but she couldn't help but laugh. "I'll show you!" She took hold of Blake's shoulders and pushed down firmly. Blake scarcely resisted and the two of them submerged together. Once they had gone underwater, their horseplay ceased as they took notice of the world around them. Though both were new to diving, they had enough coordination to hold their breath and control their movements at the same time. Letting go of one another, they spread their limbs out and maintained their position in the water with slight adjustments of their hands and feet as the surf tirelessly rushed toward them. As long as they stayed at the surface, the waves repeatedly caused them to bob up and down. However, they soon realized that if they dove deeper, then they could avoid the reach of the energetic surface until they had to rise for a breath again.

Blake and Lana looked around through their new set of underwater eyes. The water was clear and inviting, and the light was a bright, playful mixture of blue and white. Smothering the sandy floor of the Gulf were marine shells that swayed in the current and enchanted the Newcomers with musical cracking and rattling sounds. Golden webs of light danced across these shells as the sun shone its rays into the sea. The alluring whisper of flowing water filled the Newcomers' ears.

Everywhere they looked they saw life. Tiny silvery fish danced in the wave-swept shallows. Deep-bodied fish hovered over the sandy bottom, gracefully opposing the current as they probed the sand for food with their protrusible mouths. Near the surface, small anchovies darted about in large schools as they searched for floating plankton on which to feed. They were hard to see, since their translucent, shiny bodies allowed them to nearly disappear in the scattered light. When Lana noticed them, she tapped Blake on the shoulder to get his attention, and the two of them watched as the school of fish swam by. Lana tried to get near them, but this proved impossible. The anchovies maintained a constant distance between themselves and the humans. They were too timid to allow the Newcomers to get very close, but brave enough not to flee.

The water gradually became deeper as Lana and Blake swam out farther still. Their comrades were just ahead of them, already actively seeking out fish, but Lana and Blake were still learning. Now larger, more numerous fish swam beneath them as well. Blake and Lana were fascinated by these mysterious new creatures. A school of yellow-and-silver fish swam by in mid-water, suspiciously eyeing the intimidating humans. Down below, an abundance of pointy-snouted fish — some gray overall, others with yellow and blue horizontal stripes — foraged over the bottom. They huddled together in giant schools so dense, that at times they obscured the substrate below.

Soon Blake and Lana came upon a small series of rocky patch reefs. The large rocks were carpeted with bulbous sponges, ablaze in red and orange. On some of the smaller rock formations, tufts of green algae swayed back and forth. It was here, near all of this structure, that the marine life was truly abundant. Numerous elongated, multicolored fish swarmed around the reef and chased each other, while small, plump, iridescent green fish darted about, lunging at the miniscule plankton drifting by. Large green fish with powerful beaks and a dignified bearing pecked at the reefs themselves. They diligently and meticulously scrutinized the calcareous rocks and algae. When they found a suitable area, they applied their mighty jaws to bite large chunks out of it.

Blake and Lana were reeling from this lavish display of color and form. They dove down to inspect the reefs themselves and saw tiny shrimp and crabs crawling in and out of the crevices. Dressed in bold spots and stripes, the shrimp waved their antennae about as they simultaneously looked for prey and predators. Some of the crabs were quite large, however, and did not hesitate to flaunt their mighty claws in front of the humans, as if to prove that it would be a mistake to molest them. At this distance, Blake and Lana could also see the baby fish that peeked out of their secluded shelters, ever watchful and ever quick to respond.

Blake and Lana returned to the surface for a breath of air, and then continued to float and peer down at the reef. With spears in hand, they hovered in place and watched the animals below, letting the waves rock them gently. However, the water felt too cold unless they kept moving, so they resumed swimming once again.

They passed through a cloud of little bell-shaped jellyfish. The palm-sized creatures were a ghostly translucent, bluish-white color. They undulated slightly as they floated along, but they were at the mercy of the Gulf's currents. These creatures frightened Lana and Blake, who did not know whether they were dangerous or not. However, they proved to be merely a nuisance, sticking to the humans' skin when they tried to brush them aside.

An enormous fish, patterned with black and white blotches all over its body, emerged from behind one of the reefs. As big as a human being, the imposing fish had a cavernous, down-turned mouth that made it look rather serious or contemplative. The fish seemed calm and aloof as it paused under a rocky outcrop, and then nonchalantly swam to another reef nearby.

Blake and Lana swam out into the deeper waters beyond the reefs. Although the substrate surrounding the reefs had been white with the bleached shells of invertebrates, the substrate here was nearly invisible by virtue of the lush bed of seagrass that covered it.

Lana noticed an even larger animal out of the corner of her eye. Turning, she spotted a huge sea turtle swimming toward them from open water, and alerted Blake. The turtle came closer, flapping its huge forelimbs like wings to propel itself. Curious about the humans, it inspected them from afar, but it dared not approach them. Then it dove down to the bottom and began munching on the seagrass contentedly. Blake and Lana followed the tranquil turtle for a few minutes, but the turtle soon became sated, abandoned its slow plodding along the bottom, and moved up into the water column once more. Then, with scarcely a parting glance, it quickly swam off parallel to the shore. Lana and Blake watched it go until it disappeared in the distance.

Just then, Murdoch approached the couple and pointed up, signaling them to rise to the surface. Blake and Lana complied. With their heads above water, the trio inhaled deeply as the salty water dripped into their mouths.

"So," began Murdoch, "what do you think?"

"It's incredible!" cried Lana. "It's beautiful! I've never seen anything like it!"

"Me neither," said Blake. "I'm amazed."

"That's how I felt when I first went diving," said Murdoch, "and I still do whenever I find something new. Actually, today is a particularly good day for diving. The tide is in, so all the fish are inshore. The weather is good, which is probably why they're staying here, and the moon is almost full, which means they are getting ready to spawn. Some of them have even begun to spawn already. So how's the fishing going?"

"Oh, we haven't caught anything," said Lana. "We've just been watching."

"I figured," said Murdoch with a smirk.

"How about you?" asked Blake. "Catch anything?" Murdoch held his spear tip out of the water to reveal six bleeding, struggling fish impaled on it. "Wow! Look at that!" Blake touched the fish gently to make sure they were real.

"Not bad, eh?" said Murdoch. "The others are doing just as well. That's why they're swimming back to shore."

"I don't understand," said Blake.

"Now that we've caught all these small fish, we're all going to get in the boat."

"Why?" asked Blake. "Don't you want to keep fishing?"

"Sure, but it's too dangerous with all this blood floating around now. We'll be safer in the boat. Besides, that way we can catch the really big fish."

"Really big fish?" asked Lana. "What do you call the really big fish?"

"Sharks," said Murdoch. "Come on."

Chapter 35

Murdoch, Blake, and Lana swam back to shore and joined the others on the beach. Their wet, thinly clad bodies shivered in the cold morning wind and goose bumps grew on their skin. They dried off under their clothes, which formed a welcome barrier against the elements, and soon warmed up again. Spartan led everyone in a short prayer. They all bowed their heads and thanked the Creator for the fish they had already caught, and finished by asking for a safe and successful hunt as well.

Everyone, except for Blake and Lana, had speared at least a few fish. The fish were still alive, and were now doomed to be used as bait for the real quarry of the day — sharks. To prepare their bait, the youths removed the fish from their spears. The spearheads were barbed, so the people removed their fish by sliding them down the shaft and pulling them off the back end. Twine stored in the boat was used as a tether for the bait. The fishermen cut the twine with their knives, threaded it through the fish's gills, and tied it back into a loop again. Still alive, the fish flapped and floundered, but in vain; they were trapped. At last, the loops were tied together to create several strings of bloody baitfish: a tempting prospect for any shark in the area.

"All right," said Murdoch, "let's take the canoe out."

Peter bent down and untied the knot at the boat's bow. Then he motioned for help in carrying the canoe to water. Everyone obliged him and together, they carried the canoe out to sea and threw it in with a loud splash. Brent and Peter tied the strings of baitfish to the two beams that connected the outrigger to the canoe. Then everyone clambered aboard and began paddling away from shore.

As they paddled, they let their baitfish dangle and trail behind. The weak, dying fish bobbed and shimmied, both under their own fading power and by virtue of the canoe's wake. Once the fishers reached a respectable distance from the beach, they turned the canoe about and more or less held their position against the waves.

The sun was well above the horizon now, and the light had gone from red to gold to yellow. The tethered baitfish were plainly visible between the canoe and outrigger, lurching and convulsing in the clear water below. Thin, faint clouds of blood could be seen trailing from their gills and flanks where they had been wounded. The fishers watched the water attentively, expecting the sharks to arrive at any moment. They sat poised at the edge of the dugout canoe, spear in hand, and waited. Eventually, the baitfish's movement became less and less vigorous, and the trails of blood emanating from their bodies became less and less visible. Still, there was no sign of sharks.

"So, how big are these sharks?" asked Blake.

"They're big," said Murdoch.

"How big?"

"Very big."

"As big as a person?"

"Sometimes even bigger."

"Wow," said Blake to himself. Until this day, the largest fish he had ever seen was a four-foot-long trout back in Kamis. Now, he was already impressed by the giant fish he had seen earlier on the reef, and he found the prospect of seeing an even bigger one — let alone catching it — both exciting and frightening at the same time. "So, what do sharks look like?"

"They're unmistakable," said Murdoch. "They don't look very much like regular fish. Groupers get big, too — over six feet long — but they still look like these other fish."

"I think we saw one over by the rocks."

"We see those quite a bit," said Murdoch. "We catch them, too, but sharks are different. Their bodies have only one or two colors on them, usually white underneath and gray, blue, or brown on top. Some kinds have brown spots or stripes on them. They have a long, pointy tail and a sharp, pointy nose. Their fins are all stiff and pointy, too, and they don't have scales like regular fish, either. You might think they have no scales at all, but if you touch them, they feel rough. Their mouths are probably the most unique thing about them, though. They're just loaded with sharp teeth, just crammed in next to each other. Everything about them looks dangerous."

"Sounds like it. So how do we catch them?"

"When they come near the boat to eat the fish, we stab them with our spears."

"Sounds simple enough," said Blake.

"It sounds simple, but it can be very hard," said Murdoch. "The spears are barbed so that they will stay in their flesh. When you stab them, the sharks will get startled and try to swim away. So the trick is to try and stay in the boat while holding onto the struggling shark."

"Wow ... that does sound hard."

The group sat in the boat for a while longer, still watching the water for the arrival of the sharks, or any large fish for that matter. They waited and waited, but there was no sign of sharks anywhere. Eventually, they did see some large animals, but they were not fish. They were dolphins breaching several feet away. The gray animals arched their backs at the water's surface, allowing their dorsal fins to come entirely out of the water. When they took a breath, they opened their blowholes wide, exhaling and inhaling in quick succession, and sending a misty jet of moisture up into the air as they did so. In time, the pod of dolphins moved on, leaving the humans to wait for the sharks once more.

Blake saw a disturbance at the surface several feet from the canoe, but the sunlight reflecting from the water made it hard for him to see what had caused it. "Did you see that?" asked Blake as he turned to Spartan.

"No, but I heard it," said Spartan. "By the sound of it, it was big, whatever it was." The others peered into the water all around the boat, but they saw nothing.

Suddenly, Lana gasped and pointed. "Look!" she whispered hoarsely. "Look at that! What's that?" Everyone turned to look.

"Those," said Peter, "are the sharks."

First just one shark was visible, but another quickly joined and then another until eight could be seen circling around the baitfish. The smallest one seemed about six feet long, the largest about twelve feet. They were whitish on their bellies and a grayish brown color on their backs, giving them a bronze appearance. With broad fins and thick, fusiform bodies, the sharks were robust and intimidating.

"They're ... they're huge!" exclaimed Blake.

Peter smiled. "Bull sharks," he said. "Very dangerous. We must be careful today. Come on, we don't have much time until they either eat all the bait or lose interest. We must act quickly." Peter stood up in the canoe. With his knees bent, he balanced himself and aimed at the nearest bull shark, which was intermediate in size and a fine specimen.

Peter cocked his arm back in preparation to strike, but before he had the chance to throw the spear, the shark had already eaten one of the baitfish and circled away from the boat. "Damn. That's all right. We're not through yet. Here, Blake, you give it a try." Peter gestured for Blake to rise and try spearing a shark himself.

Anxiously, Blake stood up and adjusted the spear in his hand. A wave rocked the canoe, and Blake suddenly lost his balance, falling back down into a seated position.

"Happens all the time," said Peter. "Think nothing of it. Just give it another try."

Once more, Blake stood up. This time he kept his knees bent the way he had seen Peter do a moment before, and found that it helped a great deal. From this standing height, Blake suddenly found that he could peer into the water even more effectively than when he was seated. Gazing down, he could see only see five or six of the eight sharks at any given time because they swam constantly and continually alternated their position. The sharks made repeated passes at the baitfish, occasionally taking a bite when they got close enough. Waving their round, protruding noses over the fish, they could smell their prey and the blood that oozed from them.

Blake felt a mixture of fascination and horror as he watched the bull sharks circling below. They were majestic in their sleek design, their graceful power, and their silent predatory efficiency, but they were also terrifying. The beasts filled Blake's field of vision. He was awestruck by their magnificent size, and he marveled at their speed and agility. Blake sensed the rising nervousness within him. His heart pounded, his pulse quickened, his breath grew shallow and rapid, and his knees grew weak. His spear hand trembled slightly as he tried to single out just one of the sharks — whichever was most accessible — for his target. Despite his apprehension, Blake was also aware of the excitement he felt. This experience was so incredibly new, and so incredibly fascinating, that it took his breath away. But this was no time for reflection. It was time for action, and Blake forced himself to concentrate on the task at hand. This was simply a marine version, he realized, of a hunt on the plains, and he reminded himself that it was now up to him to bring down a beast for the others.

Narrowing his eyes, Blake's vision penetrated the glare of the surface of the water. He soon located the bull shark that was nearest the canoe as it bit at a dangling baitfish. He quickly realized that this shark also happened to be the largest one, the individual that measured over twelve feet long. Blake swallowed and focused his attention.

As the shark fed, it repeatedly applied its massive jaws to its prey. With each bite, the mouth protruded from the head to clamp down on the fish, and then retracted back into the head again. The shark's teeth gouged out massive chunks of flesh from the jumbled mass of bait. Some bits of muscle and guts floated about in the water, but most of the meal was instantly ingested with a series of exaggerated gulps. The giant predator left only vestiges of dead, mutilated fish on the tether.

Blake was momentarily mesmerized by this display of brutality and skill. Remaining nearly stationary in the water, the shark appeared completely absorbed in the act of feeding, and seemed oblivious to the other creatures around it.

This was the moment to strike. Blake drew his arm back. Then with all his might, he thrust his spear down into the monstrous bull shark's flank, still holding on near the spear's back end. Instantly, the shark abandoned its food and bolted away.

Blake held fast onto the spear, but before he had the opportunity to sit down or brace himself, the shark yanked him clear of the boat, and he fell into the water with a splash. Blake refused to let go. The mighty shark was now towing him along as it sped off, circling about as it tried to dislodge the offending spear and cargo.

"He got the biggest one!" exclaimed Peter at the top of his lungs. "He got the biggest one!" Everyone in the boat looked around for Blake and the shark, but they had lost sight of them.

"Oh my!" said Lana. "It's going to kill him! We have to do something right now!"

Murdoch clasped Lana about her arms. "Now hold on there, Lana. It's going to be all right. Blake's going to be fine. We just have to locate him again and bring him back on board."

"Especially before he lets go of the spear and the other sharks find him," said Peter.

"No!" cried Lana.

"Will you shut up, Peter?" said Murdoch. "Just for once! Can't you see Lana is upset?" Then he turned to Lana once more. "Now, don't worry. Blake's going to be fine." Murdoch looked into the water again to see if he could locate Blake, but he could not. "All right, everyone! We have to find Blake. Serena and Becca, you paddle. The rest of us will keep our eyes peeled. Let's go."

Underwater, Blake was trying desperately not to let go of his spear; he could see nothing without his diving mask. The bull shark refused to come to the surface, and Blake could not breathe. All he knew was that the bull shark was traveling incredibly fast. It alternated between racing straight ahead and darting back and forth as it frantically tried to rid itself of its burden. The shark surfaced briefly, and Blake managed to take a gulp of air before it dove back down again.

"Look!" cried Brent, pointing. "Over there!" The fishers saw a massive dorsal fin break through the water, and then Blake's flailing limbs and gasping head. The shark and man remained in view for a few seconds, but then disappeared once more.

"Go after them!" said Murdoch with a sweep of his arm. The crew paddled in the direction where they had seen Blake struggling, but by the time they arrived, neither Blake nor the shark could be seen. "Damn!"

Suddenly, several of the other sharks came into view, followed by the largest shark with Blake still holding on.

"There he is! Stab the shark!" said Murdoch.

The party of fishers rose to their feet like lightning and aimed their spears. One after another, the spears flew from their hands and met their marks in the flanks of Blake's monstrous shark. With four spears protruding from its body, including the one Blake still held, the shark swam in wide arcs as large, red plumes trailed behind it.

Smelling this carnage, the other sharks instantly became aroused and began following the largest one ... as well as Blake. The bleeding shark circled near the canoe again, and everyone on board watched in horror as the other sharks followed just behind Blake.

"No!" cried Lana. "They're going to eat him!"

"No," said Murdoch. "They're going to try to attack the biggest one because she's wounded."

"What if Blake gets in their way?"

"I don't know," said Murdoch. "I ... I don't know."

"Stop them!"

"I'm afraid if we shed anymore blood, then they'll go into a feeding frenzy."

"A what?"

"A feeding frenzy," repeated Murdoch. "They might start biting at everything in sight, and then Blake would really be in trouble. I ... I'm not sure what to do."

Just then, Blake popped his head out of the water near the canoe's outrigger. The giant shark thrashed about at the surface, but it was beginning to weaken from the loss of blood.

"Hey!" cried Blake amid the loud splashes. "Hey! I've got it! I've got the shark!"

"No, Blake!" Lana yelled. "That shark has you! Just let go and climb back in here!"

"No, I've got it! I've got it!"

"He's completely insane," said Murdoch. "Damn it, Blake! Let go!"

"No!" said Blake. "Stab it! Just stab…" Then he fell silent again as he disappeared underwater.

"What should we do?" asked Peter. "If we stab it, we might make things worse."

"I know," said Murdoch, "but the damn fool won't listen to reason. We have to do as he says."

The giant shark soon wandered back within range, and four more spears slammed into its flank all at once. Exhausted, the wounded shark barely reacted this time; blood poured profusely from its body.

A feeding frenzy broke out, just as Murdoch had foreseen. The healthy sharks bit the wounded one and snapped at anything that got in their way. Two of them removed massive chunks of flesh from their victim's body. Then one shark attacked a smaller member of the group as well. The people in the boat could only watch as the predators continued to pile in on top of each other.

In the water, Blake could feel their sandpaper-like skin brushing up against him. One shark after another approached him. Blake felt their weight pressing down upon him, but continued to hold onto the spear lodged in his prey. For a brief moment, Blake broke through the surface again.

"Stab more! Stab more!" he cried, coughing and sputtering, before vanishing amid the writhing mass of sharks once more.

"Does he want us to stab more sharks?" asked Peter.

"I guess so," said Brent, "but we're running out of spears."

"Doesn't matter," said Murdoch. "Let's do it! Throw them all in!" Everyone hurled the last of their spears at the sharks. First one shark fell victim to the weapons, then a second, then a third.

Blake emerged from the fray and latched onto the rear outrigger beam. He tried frantically to climb out of the water, but it was hard to gain leverage. Blake was afraid that if he struggled too much, he might attract the attention of the frenzied sharks, and then he'd be finished. The firm muscles of Blake's arms, abdomen, and legs bulged as he hauled himself toward the canoe, but the going was slow.

Then Blake noticed someone leaning over him at the stern of the canoe. It was Brent. Time stopped as the two made eye contact, and Blake's mind raced. He considered what sort of action his crewmate might take, but Brent seemed frozen, making it difficult to discern his intentions. *Why isn't he doing anything? Maybe he's just trying to think of the best way to pull me up. Then again, what if he's carrying a grudge against me for what happened at the bridge? He wouldn't push me back into the water ... would he?*

Brent reached down and offered his hand. The two men reached past each other's hands and clasped each other by the forearm for a more secure hold. Brent braced himself against the hull of the canoe. Then, straining and groaning, he began dragging Blake back in.

Murdoch and Peter, who had been standing right behind Brent, took notice of what was happening. Lana stood directly behind them. Although she was unable to physically make contact with Blake, she called out for the others to help him.

"Look down there! There he is! Help him!" she pleaded anxiously.

"We see him," said Murdoch, grunting as he and Peter pressed against Brent in the narrow canoe. They reached down, grabbed Blake by his arms and shoulders, and hoisted him upward. Within seconds, they brought him back to safety. Remarkably, his only injuries appeared to be the cuts and bruises he had sustained from the rough denticles of the sharks' skin.

Blake sat down on the floor of the boat to catch his breath. He looked up at the others. They had stopped trying to catch sharks, and were watching him instead to see if he was all right.

Lana reached past Peter and Murdoch, and clasped her mate by the hand. "Thank the Creator you're all right," she said with a sigh.

Blake clutched Lana's hand tightly. "Yes," he said, "and thank you." With gratitude in his eyes, he looked at each one of his crewmates in turn, finishing with Brent. "Thank you for saving me."

Brent smiled in return.

"Now come on!" said Blake. "I've got one of the sharks. See if the rest of you can grab another one. Let's get them back to shore!"

The others looked at Blake as though he were mad, but soon realized the opportunity he had given them. After only a moment's hesitation, they returned to watching the frenzy below. There were three wounded sharks with spears in their flanks: Blake's giant and two smaller ones. The other sharks continued to bite chunks out of all three, leaving big patches of white, ragged tissue behind.

The people took hold of the spears that protruded like handles from these sharks and gingerly brought their prey closer to the boat.

"Row!" cried Murdoch. "To the beach! Row!" Then everyone not towing a shark paddled back to shore.

Chapter 36

The feeding frenzy followed the canoe, with the healthy sharks continuously taking bites out of their three fallen brethren. This diminished the prize, but it proved more helpful than harmful, for it further weakened the captured sharks and made their transport easier. When the fishing party reached shallow water, they hopped out of their canoe and began towing both the canoe and their catch to the beach. At this time, it became quite clear that the captured sharks were still very much alive. They struggled and thrashed about, and repeatedly attempted to swim away.

Several people dragged the canoe out of the water and back onto the beach. Then everyone joined the effort to land the sharks. These animals could not completely submerge themselves here, but they continued to resist just the same. The contest seemed endless. Everyone developed blisters and bled from their hands, feet, and legs, but the sharks refused to give up.

Suddenly, a bull shark from the frenzy appeared in the shallows. Its dorsal fin protruded conspicuously out of the water as it raced toward the struggling sharks.

"Look out!" cried Brent. "Free shark!" Everyone was tempted to run ashore to safety, but no one was willing to abandon his comrades or come home empty-handed, especially after working so hard and coming so close to success. So, the crew continued to hang on.

The free shark, which was over six feet long, rushed into the mass of wounded ones and began gouging out massive pieces for itself. The humans were helpless to do anything about this, so they continued to drag their quarry ashore and allowed the invader to eat its fill. At last, when it became sated, this shark swam sluggishly back out to sea.

The three wounded sharks continued to struggle and managed to drag their pursuers back into deeper water, but the tenacious humans held on. Weakened by their huge wounds, the sharks eventually became lethargic, and this allowed the people to gain ground once more. They hauled the sharks into ever-shallower water, where swimming became increasingly difficult. After nearly an hour, the fishing party dragged their dying catch onto the beach and collapsed.

Everyone was exhausted. Some sat, others lay down; all caught their breath. They inspected themselves and each other for serious injuries, and were happy to discover that there were none. The people sat down together and stared at the beached sharks, which were still alive despite the damage they had sustained, and continued to flap their fins or beat their tails reflexively in a vain attempt to escape. The sharks' mouths moved slightly, and their gills still functioned, but they were quickly becoming deprived of oxygen and moisture, and their movements became ever more imperceptible. Numerous spears were lodged in their bodies, and several bit bites had been taken out of them. Nevertheless, there was still plenty of meat left for the taking. Blake's twelve-foot-long giant still looked intimidating, even as it lay stranded on the beach. The two other sharks were of respectable size — about six and nine feet long — but looked small by comparison.

While the party lay there resting on the sand, Lana embraced Blake tightly and kissed him powerfully on the lips.

"Good job," she whispered. "Now don't you ever do that again!"

Blake grinned broadly. He became the focus of tremendous attention, warm handshakes, and friendly pats on the back.

"That was incredible!" exclaimed Peter. "How did you do that? Why did you do that? What's the matter with you?"

"I don't know," said Blake. "I just realized we had a great opportunity there, so I thought we should take it."

"Well," said Brent, "you're right about that being a good opportunity. I don't think we've ever had a daytrip as successful as this. I don't think you realize just how lucky you are. You could've been crippled for life, or even killed, but you came out with just a few cuts and scrapes. I'm amazed."

"I certainly fared better than those sharks," said Blake in jest. The others chuckled. "Can we start carving them up yet?"

"No," said Murdoch. "Give it just a little more time. They may already be dead, but their reflexes could still be active. They could still do us some serious damage if they bite." While they waited, they returned the canoe to its proper storage place on the beach and tied it to its post once more. In time, the party went over to the sharks to inspect them. Indeed, they were not only dead but also inactive, so it was safe to work on them.

Becca went back to the Rookery to enlist the help of others, while the rest of the fishing party started cutting up the bull sharks into smaller pieces. Becca soon returned with many more people, who immediately joined in dividing up the carcasses and transporting the goods back up the beach.

Leaving the skin in place, the Corpushi used their knives to separate the muscle from the organs and the soft skeleton. Then they painstaking separated the thick skin from the muscle so that it could be dried and later turned into leather and abrasives. The people harvested oil from the liver, and even cooked parts of the liver and most of the meat on the spot while they were still relatively fresh. The rest of the liver and muscle, along with parts of the soft skeleton, were dried and cured. This turned them into a kind of tasty, seasoned jerky for later consumption. Other portions of the skeleton were kept moist in tubs of treated water, to be consumed later with the meal. However, the majority of the skeleton would be cleaned and turned into household tools. Lastly, the huge, sharp teeth from the jaws were eagerly removed and distributed to anyone who wanted them for spear tips, jewelry, or collectors' items.

The people washed everything in the Gulf, taking care to rinse the blood from the parts they needed. They gave everything a light squeeze to rid it of the juices that would foul it if not removed. When they finished, they returned to the seashore to wash themselves clean of shark blood and slime. The parts were taken to an area next to the Rookery. There, they would be dried to avoid spoiling and prepared for long term storage. The process would not be completed today, but it could be started.

"There must be enough meat here to feed the entire tribe for days!" exclaimed Spartan. "Blake, I'd say you've come a long way to paying off your debt today."

"You really think so?" asked Blake.

"You did well, Blake. You did very well." Spartan patted Blake on the shoulder and walked off. Blake was delighted. Then a pang of sorrow overcame him.

Lana noticed this subtle change in her mate. "What's wrong, Blake?" she asked.

"Manosh," said Blake as he stared blankly forward. "I was just thinking about Manosh. He would've loved this. I wish he could've been here today."

Lana held Blake's hand. "I know. So do I." She could see the distress in his eyes. She wished there were something she could say to make it go away, but she knew that there was not. All she could do was stand by Blake's side and be there for him. At length, she spoke once more. "Come on, let's go." Together, Blake and Lana headed back up the beach to rejoin the others.

Chapter 37

The fishing expedition was a success, and Blake and Lana received praise and thanks for their roles in capturing the enormous sharks. However, the Corpushi distributed the meat from this catch among everyone in the entire tribe. Therefore, Brent's and Paulo's shares, although enough to last for several days, would still not eliminate Blake and Lana's debt.

By now, the cuts and bruises that Paulo had received in the fight were nearly all healed. His pride was still hurt, and he was still depressed, but at least his physical health and strength had returned. One morning, however, Spartan came to Blake and Lana's and gave them the news that Paulo was ailing again.

"Why?" asked Blake, alarmed. "What happened?"

"It's nothing you did. He injured his foot," said Spartan.

"When? How?" asked Lana.

"Just yesterday. He was walking in the shallows and stepped on a stingray."

"A st— ...did ... did you say, 'stingray'?" echoed Blake.

"It's a kind of fish. They're big and flat and round, like a saucer, and they swim along the bottom by flapping their fins like wings."

"How could such a fish injure Paulo?" asked Lana.

"They have a long tail with a long, sharp, barbed spine on it. When Paulo stepped on the stingray, it stabbed him in the sole of his right foot."

"So that's why he called it a 'stingray,'" Blake muttered to himself.

"What? Who?" asked Spartan.

"Never mind," said Lana. "That's awful about Paulo. How is he feeling now?"

"Not very well, I'm afraid. The sting itself is very painful. We tried to treat him yesterday, but the spine made a pretty big gash. It doesn't seem to be healing, and we're all very worried about him."

"What about your healer, Uchara? Has she seen him yet?"

"She's with him now, but nobody's really sure what to do."

"Will you let us see him?" asked Lana.

"Sure, but ... why?" said Spartan.

"Maybe we can help. Besides, as long as Paulo doesn't mind, there's no harm in it."

"All right. Come, I'll take you to see him right now."

Lana and Blake followed Spartan to the first floor of the Rookery, where Spartan led them to Uchara's domain. Like many other tribe members, Uchara lived on a higher floor, but worked on the ground floor. Several stools were lined up against the wall in the corridor, where people would sometimes wait until they could enter. Today, however, the trio breezed passed the empty stools and went directly into the healer's domain.

Inside, they found Paulo lying on a small but comfortable bed. He was covered in several warm blankets, and he sat propped up in place with several cushions. His right foot was propped up and dressed with bandages. Paulo quietly sipped a hot, steaming herbal tea that Uchara had prepared for him. Paulo's wife and younger children sat around him, along with Uchara and the other Elders, as well as Becca, Murdoch, and Serena. Spartan, Blake, and Lana exchanged subdued greetings with the others and joined them at Paulo's bedside.

"Thank you, everyone, for coming to visit me today," said Paulo. "It warms my heart to feel such affection from everyone, and to see how loving the coming generation is." Paulo looked tired and frail. His normally dark complexion had become pallid and, although Paulo said he felt cold, his skin was warm and sweaty.

"We are glad we could see you," said Spartan, "but we are sad to know that you are suffering. How do you feel?"

"I'll tell you what I tell everyone. I'm feeling as well as can be hoped for, but my foot still hurts, and I think I have the chills."

Spartan looked to the healer for her expert opinion. "Uchara?"

"Paulo is brave," she said, "but he is not getting any better. In fact, I hate to say it, but his wound has gotten worse. It's festering, and the disease is spreading. Paulo has become feverish, too. I'm trying to stop it with wraps soaked in herbal extracts, but it is not helping very much."

"I know that my illness has worsened," croaked Paulo. "I may not have much time left, but I'm thankful that I still have enough strength to spend that time with the people I love."

"Oh, Paulo," said Murdoch, "that's a nice thought, but you don't have to be so grim."

"I have little choice but to be content with what I have."

"I wish there was something we could do," said Spartan.

"We have done all we can," said Paulo. "Uchara has treated me well. She has helped ease my pain and alleviate the suffering of others, but there's only so much she can do."

"Perhaps I can help," said Lana.

"Please, my child," said Paulo. "There's no need for false hope. I must accept my fate."

"You have found peace, Paulo," said Lana. "No one can take that away from you, but I may be able to help you heal after all."

"What can you do, my dear?" asked Uchara. "I have tried all that I know, and have succeeded only in prolonging the inevitable. Where have you learned what needs to be done for this man?"

"I was raised in a Rubbletown that lies far away in the central Great Plains. There are many secrets locked away in the Ruins of the Managers, and I had the opportunity to learn some of them. It was in this Rubbletown that Blake and I discovered the secret of making instant fire. Even before that, I used to constantly visit the library, where the Managers stored their knowledge in books. I read the information written in them, and I remember most of what I learned. I think I may know how to help Paulo."

"If what you say is true, then speak and enlighten us," said Uchara.

"I read about these substances the Old Timers discovered. They were called 'antibiotics,' and they were used to kill the tiny creatures that invade the body and cause disease. Some of the chemicals were very complicated, but others were quite simple and easy to produce."

"What are you suggesting?"

"Well, Corpus might still have some old ruined stores where we might be able to find some ancient antibiotics. However, 3,000 years have passed since they were made, so they would've decomposed by now."

"Then there's no hope after all," said Uchara.

"Don't be so sure. We still have one other option. We could produce our own."

"Ha!" exclaimed Uchara. "Impossible! We do not have the technology that the Old Timers had, nor would we want it. Your idea will not work."

"It might," said Lana. "The Old Timers didn't have the technology needed to produce antibiotics at first, either. That came later. In the beginning, they relied on other creatures to produce them, and they harvested them from those other creatures. Actually, that's the way they usually operated. Their success depended on their ability to copy the natural world; their downfall was because they thought they could replace it."

"What does all this mean?"

"It means that we can learn from their mistakes, and we can be wise in our actions. You already harness the power that is innate in other creatures. Like us, you use dogs to protect you and help you hunt. You use the strength and speed of horses to help you transport things and travel quickly from one place to another, and you use the life force of plants to produce food for your animals and yourselves."

Uchara sighed and shook her head. "Even if you're right, we have no creatures to produce these antibiotics for us."

"Not yet, no," agreed Lana.

"But there's no time…"

"It won't take long."

"Very well," said Uchara in exasperation, "then what sort of creature should we look to?"

"Mold." Lana's reply caused a stir among the gathered people.

"Mold?" said Uchara in disbelief. "That's ridiculous! What are you talking about? Molds make things rot and decay. How could they possibly help wounds to heal?"

"The Old Timers discovered antibiotics when they realized that molds can resist attacks from other germs. They do this by secreting toxic juices that protect them. It was from these juices that the Managers harvested an antibiotic called penicillin, and I'll bet we can do the same. We must act quickly, though. We need to find a place where mold grows and collect penicillin from it."

"Hmmm," said Uchara thoughtfully. "That is interesting. Well, I don't think it could do any harm, anyway. All right … it's certainly worth a try. But please, let me to help you."

"Of course," said Lana. "Blake, Murdoch, Spartan … I want you to come, too. We have to find a place where mold is most likely to grow — someplace moist, warm, and dark. Do you know of any place like that in Corpus?"

"Sure," said Murdoch. "In fact, there's a cave not too far from the lodge where you and Blake are staying."

"Great," said Lana. "Let's go."

Chapter 38

Lana and her party returned to Paulo's bedside with a bowl full of a thick, whitish liquid.

"Did you find what you needed?" asked Paulo, weakly.

"Yes," said Lana, handing the bowl over to Uchara. "Murdoch and Spartan led us right to the cave. Sure enough, it was dark and wet inside — the perfect place for mold to grow. We brought several handfuls of the stuff back in our pouches. Then we went up to Uchara's home and pressed it to extract the antibiotic. It was a sort of yellowish fluid with a strong smell, so Uchara diluted it with water and added some herbs to make it taste better and soothe the stomach."

Uchara presented the liquid to Paulo.

"Here," she said.

"What is it?" asked Paulo reluctantly.

"It's the medicine."

"What am I supposed to do with it?"

"I'm going to apply some of it directly to your foot, but I want you to drink it, too."

"When?" asked Paulo.

"Right now," said Uchara.

"But it stinks."

"I know," said Uchara, "but you have to start taking it today. The treatment will probably need to continue for some time; I'll monitor you to see for how long. If it works, that is. But we need to start today and see how you are feeling tomorrow first."

"Oh, all right," said Paulo. He reached out his hands and took hold of the bowl. Paulo's wife helped him bring the bowl to his lips. He took a sip. The solution was bitter, and Paulo's face took on a look of disgust. The taste was not unbearable, however, so he quaffed the drink, and let his wife return the bowl to Uchara.

"What did you think?" asked Uchara.

"The taste is awful, but it would be worth it if it cures me," said Paulo.

"That's right," said Uchara, "it would. Well, I think we should let him rest now. I'll be back later to see how are doing, Paulo. Until then, good night."

"Good night," said Paulo, "and thank you for what you have done today. No matter what happens, know that you have helped ease my pain." The others departed and walked together before going their separate ways.

"Let's hope it works," said Lana. "Thank you for being willing to try something new, Uchara ... or, something old."

Uchara chuckled. "Very old indeed! We'll soon see how much we were able to do. I'm glad you gave us that suggestion, Lana. I'll keep you all informed on how Paulo is doing. Until then, good night."

Chapter 39

Another week passed, and Sabat — the day of rest — had arrived. That morning, Blake and Lana were enjoying breakfast with Murdoch, Serena, Spartan, and Becca in front of their lodge on the outskirts of Corpus. As they sat conversing, they were soon approached by Uchara.

"Good morning!" said the healer. "How are you today?"

"Just fine, thank you," said Spartan, "and you?"

"Very well, very well. Actually, I'm glad that you are all here. I have good news."

"Is it about Paulo?" asked Lana.

"As a matter of fact, it is. I thought you should all know how he was doing."

"Of course!" exclaimed Becca. "Let's hear it!"

"Paulo's condition is actually improving! He appears to be on the mend!"

"That's wonderful!" said Lana.

"Clearly, it's due to the medicine you gave us, Lana. I have been applying it to his foot and giving it to him as a drink every morning and night. With each passing day, he has grown a little stronger and a little healthier."

"Is he still in pain? Is he still feverish?" asked Lana.

"A little, but he has more energy, and his spirits are up, too. I expect him to make a full recovery in the next few weeks. We have you to thank for this, Lana. Paulo is not yet cured, but if it hadn't been for you and your medicine, he would not have had this second chance at life."

"I'm glad I could help," said Lana, beaming. "I'm so glad."

"So am I. Well, I must be off," said Uchara. "I have other people to visit. Until next time, then." Uchara waved as she walked away, and the youths waved back. Blake hugged Lana tightly.

"I'm so proud of you," he said.

"Thank you, I…" she stammered, "thank you." The six youths continued with their simple breakfast, chatting about the goings-on of the village. Blake and Lana were enjoying the company of their new friends. Nevertheless, they were eager to repay their debt as soon as possible.

"Don't despair," said Spartan cheerfully. "At the rate you're going, you'll be done in no time!"

"Well, thank you for that encouragement," said Blake. "I guess I just had my hopes up because I thought that the shark meat would've been enough. I forgot that people like to share their catch, though. We used to do the same thing back in Kamis."

"I understand," said Spartan. "Like I say, don't worry about it. You'll be done soon enough."

"I just wish I knew when the next big hunt was coming up," said Blake.

"Tomorrow."

"What?"

"Tomorrow," repeated Spartan, his face nearly deadpan save for the faint upturned corners of his mouth.

"Really? When? Where? How?"

"The young warriors and the tribe's men are heading out to the savanna tomorrow. We're leaving just before dusk on horseback. Do you want to come?"

"Do you even have to ask? Of course I want to come! Although … I don't know how to ride your horses."

"That's all right," said Spartan. "I can teach you later today, if you like. You may not master it in one day, but at least you'll be able to keep up."

"That would be great. I can hardly wait." Blake turned to his mate. "What about you, Lana?"

"We women have our own little gathering planned for tomorrow, right here in the village," said Lana.

"Really? What are you going to do?"

Serena spoke up. "We expect you'll come back with a fine prize in the evening, so we're taking care of the preparations for the feast."

"That's awfully nice of you," said Blake.

"You do your part," said Serena, "and we'll do ours. That's the way of it, and it can be quite fun if people work together and make the occasion festive."

"What if we fail to bring down any big game? What then?"

"Somehow," said Serena, "I doubt if that will be a problem, particularly since you, Blake the Shark Killer, will be along." Blake blushed and smiled modestly. "Even if you don't come back with a big catch, we'll still have other dishes to serve for the evening."

"Well, I'm glad of that," said Blake. The group continued to eat their breakfast.

"You know, Blake," said Murdoch, "it's a shame you lost that dog of yours."

Blake slowly looked up from his dish. "Why is that?"

"Because we could use another dog."

"Don't you already have dogs?"

"We need all the help we can get," said Murdoch.

Blake played dumb. "I thought you went looking for her one day. You mean you didn't find her?"

"No. Aries, Peter, and I looked for hours, but we didn't find anything."

"Oh well."

"Eh, it's just as well," said Murdoch. "I'd have no use for a runaway."

"She's not a runaway!" shouted Blake. Everyone was taken aback by this outburst, except for Lana, who rolled her eyes and sighed.

"What are you talking about? When we found you a couple of weeks ago, you told us that you had lost track of her. Sounds like a runaway to me."

"Well, she's not."

"What do you mean?" asked Murdoch, losing his patience. "Where is she then?"

Blake refused to reveal the location of his dog's den. Lana intervened. "Tell him, Blake," she said.

"Tell me what?"

"We know where Rita is," said Lana.

"Lana!" exclaimed Blake.

"Forget it, Blake!" said Lana. "It's over. We have to tell them."

"You mean, you've known where your dog has been all this time, and you didn't tell anyone?" said Murdoch. "Why would you do that?"

"Why do you think?" asked Blake, rhetorically. "You made it sound like you were going to hunt her down and kill her."

"We would if we had to, but that was not our intention. I'd rather bring in new a dog than destroy it, as long as it's healthy. Is there something wrong with that dog, Blake?"

"No! There's nothing wrong with her at all."

"Then why all the secrecy?" asked Murdoch.

"If I tell you, then you must swear not to do anything to harm her."

Murdoch stiffened. "I give you my word."

Blake hesitated. "She has puppies."

"Puppies? Well, that's wonderful! Why did you lie to us, Blake?"

"I didn't lie. You asked me if she had bred before, but this is her first litter."

Murdoch scoffed. "You didn't have to keep that a secret."

"Then you're not going to take them away from her?" asked Blake.

"No, of course not. You should know that by now."

"Well, I didn't."

"All right," said Murdoch. "Well, there's no sense in arguing about it now. So, where are they?"

"They're in a den, not far from here."

"Will you take us there?" Becca asked eagerly.

"Only on one condition," said Blake. "You have to do as I say. If Rita's ready to let you see her puppies, that's fine. If she's not ready, then we leave her alone. Understood?" The others agreed. "All right, let's go." They cleaned up the area and followed Blake toward Rita's den.

"You see?" said Lana smartly to Blake. "I told you we had nothing to worry about."

"Not now," said Blake. "I don't want to hear it."

Chapter 40

Rita's den was surrounded by weeds and obscured by shadows, allowing it to remain inconspicuous despite its rather large entrance. However, Blake and Lana had already visited it many times, and they now led their comrades there with relative ease. Blake crouched in front of the den and called for Rita. A moment later, the big, wolfish dog crawled out and crept toward her master with her ears low. She repeatedly licked her lips and tried to lick his as well, but Blake gently thwarted her attempts. Lana bent down to stroke Rita's fur. The dog was clearly enjoying the company. Murdoch, Serena, Spartan, and Becca were immediately taken with her.

"She's beautiful," said Serena. "I can see why you kept her a secret."

"Look how long her fur is," said Spartan. "The dogs around here have much shorter coats."

"She's a northern dog," said Murdoch. "She'll probably shed much of it, but it will always be longer than the other dogs'." Murdoch extended his hand and allowed Rita to smell it. She sensed the relaxed atmosphere, so she let her guard down and allowed the man pet her as well.

"What about the puppies?" asked Becca. "When can we see the puppies?"

"To be honest," said Blake, "we haven't seen the puppies in a long time ourselves."

"Are you sure they're still in there?"

"Well, judging by Rita's behavior, they must be. Here, let me take a look again." Blake approached the hole in the ground and peered inside. "I can see them! They're moving around! Come, have a look." Becca kneeled on the opposite side of the hole and looked through it as well. Her eyes grew wide with excitement when she finally saw the puppies.

"Oh!" she exclaimed. "They're adorable! How many are there?"

"There are supposed to be seven," said Blake. He quickly performed another head count. "I can only see six, though."

"Do you think one of them died, Blake?" asked Lana.

"Could be; it's not unusual. Still, the six remaining ones look great!"

Everyone took turns looking in and admiring the puppies. Rita did not seem to object, especially because Blake and Lana kept her occupied by giving her food and water, which she desperately needed.

"Listen," said Murdoch, "there's no need to keep Rita and her pups out here anymore. Why don't you bring them back to the village? We have that big kennel next to the Rookery — near the stables — with plenty of room for them. What do you say?"

Blake considered the offer for a moment. "What do you think, Lana?"

"I think it's a great idea. In fact, I think it's long overdue."

"All right, let's do it. Murdoch, Spartan, do you have a big, soft sack we could carry the pups in?"

"Sure," said Spartan. "Let me go get it. I'll be right back."

"Good. Thank you," said Blake. Then Spartan jogged back home. "All right, now let me see if Rita will let me get her puppies." He reached into the den. Rita watched him, but she did not protest. Blake brought out a beautiful black-and-brown puppy and set it on the ground in front of its mother, who sniffed it and licked it lovingly. The rotund little animal was covered in soft fur. Its ears were still flimsy, and it could scarcely crawl, but its eyes were open. Then Blake retrieved the others. He set the next one down beside the first, but handed the subsequent pups to Lana and the others. Becca and Serena fussed and cooed over the tiny creatures, while Blake continued to search the den for stragglers. He found none. "I can't find anymore," he said. "I guess it's just these six."

"Not even a body?" asked Lana.

"No. Rita must have disposed of it after it died."

"Still," said Murdoch, "six pups is a fine litter. The rest of them look quite healthy. You have nothing to worry about."

When Spartan returned with the sack, Blake carefully placed each of the puppies inside and cradled the bundle in his arms.

"All right," said Blake. "If everyone's ready, let's go."

The crew headed back to the Rookery, careful not to walk too fast for the delicate puppies in the sack. Rita walked alongside Blake, anxiously looking up and sniffing at his precious cargo. Soon, they reached the kennel. Murdoch opened the gate and let everyone in. They walked passed several dogs in their pens, some of whom tried to meet Rita through the wooden bars of their enclosures. Others, however, barked at her aggressively, for they considered her an intruder. Rita would have liked to confront these dogs, but more important concerns weighed on her mind, so she stuck close to Blake and her sack full of puppies.

When they reached an empty pen, Blake entered and released the puppies near one of the corners. Rita lay down on her side. Her puppies instantly crawled toward her and began suckling.

"Oh," said Becca tenderly, "that's the sweetest thing I've ever seen."

"It is pretty amazing," said Spartan.

"I'll be right back," said Murdoch. He soon returned with several blankets and set them down beside the nursing mother. Rita paid little attention to them, choosing instead to remain lying on the earthen floor. "If she doesn't find a use for those blankets, I'm sure the puppies will. Come on. Let's leave them alone." Then everyone walked out of the pen, and Murdoch shut the gate behind him.

Chapter 41

Blake awoke early the next morning. It was still dark out, and he did his best to stay quiet so as not to disturb Lana. She looked so soft and dainty laying there on her side, the blanket covering her up to her chest. Her arms were curled in front of her and her hands rested before her face with the fingers slightly flexed. Her long, black hair flowed all over her pillow and shoulders, and a few stray strands lay across her cheek. Lana was a light sleeper, however, and when she heard Blake stirring, she awoke, too.

"Mmm…" she muttered softly, "wait, Blake."

"Go back to sleep, my love," he whispered, "I'll see you when I get back."

"Wait…" she said, keeping her eyes shut. "I want to see you off."

"You don't have to do that…"

"No, I want to," said Lana.

"You're so sweet," said Blake with a smile. "All right."

Lana smiled, too, her eyes still closed. Then she sat up, stretched, and got out of bed. She did not bother changing out of her sleeping clothes — an off-white dress made of soft fabric — and threw on her thick, black robe instead. Then she slipped into her moccasins and was ready.

Blake and Lana quietly made their way to the horse stables in the dark. The weather was humid and chilly that morning, and there was a heavy fog adrift in the air. When they reached the stables, they found about thirty men gathered there. There were no women among them, for women rarely hunted with men, just as men rarely collected the fruits of the field with women; everyone knew that Lana had come only to bid Blake farewell. Blake would be the only Outlander on this excursion, but he would ride alongside the Corpushi as a member of their team, as an equal.

Everyone was still groggy, except for those rare few who lived for early mornings such as these. Blake, like the other hunters, was decked out in his woven riding outfit. Lana hugged herself against the cold. She squinted slightly and rubbed her eyes as she yawned and tried to wake up, but she did not mind the inconvenience if it meant seeing off Blake on an exciting day like this.

Blake and Lana walked over to where the horses stood and joined those already gathered there. These men were busy preparing for the long journey into the savanna. They tended to their horses and fitted them with leather reins and simple, woven saddles. They packed supplies for themselves, such as canteens full of water, packets of dried meat and nuts for energy, extra clothing, and even bandages and herbal medicines in case someone was injured. The men also had their spears, their bows, and their quivers full of arrows; it was as though they were preparing for battle, except without the shields. Many had also brought foot snares, which were made from strong rope with rocks tied to both ends. The hunters would twirl these over their heads and hurl them at their prey's ankles to trip them up. Other men arrived with atlatls — short spears to be loaded into a wooden sheath and ejected with a quick flick of the arm. A powerful weapon, the atlatl functionally increased a hunter's reach, allowing him to throw his spear faster, harder, and farther.

Spartan stepped up to Blake and clapped him on the shoulder. "You ready?" he asked.

"Not exactly," admitted Blake.

"Well, don't worry. You will be. Once we get out there, I'm sure your instincts will kick in."

"I hope so. So, what are we hunting today, anyway?"

"Elephant," said Spartan.

Blake was alarmed. "Really? Are you sure?"

"Of course. The bigger the prey, the more meat. We've got the entire Corpushi tribe to feed here. Come on, you should be excited."

"I know," said Blake, "and I am, but this is all so new. Do you have any advice for me?"

"Yeah ... don't get too close to them," said Spartan.

"Thanks," said Blake sarcastically.

"And one more thing: elephants may be big, and their hide may be thick, but they still have the same target areas as any other animal."

"All right," Blake said, smiling appreciatively, "I'll remember that."

Soon, everyone was nearly ready to leave, but they all looked to one man for guidance — Chief Zaaru. He was well respected both at home and in the field, and it was only natural that he should lead this hunting expedition. Slowly, confidently, and ceremoniously, he raised his hand and held it above his compatriots' heads. He took a moment to look each man in the eyes and to acknowledge him for the role that he would play this day.

"Friends," said Zaaru in his resonating baritone, "today we hunt for those we love. We have come together in the name of friendship and camaraderie, and we are as one. As we prepare to partake of the savanna's bounty, let us remember the Source of this great bounty. Please join me in praising the Creator for all He has provided us, now and always."

"Telpah," everyone said, in unison.

"We request, oh Creator, that You grant us this wish," said Zaaru. "We ask for a successful hunt and a safe return home. For the sake of this brotherhood assembled here today, and all those for whom we hunt, and all the creatures with which we share this world, we offer our praise."

"Telpah," they all uttered once again. There was a moment of silence as the men paused to think of the people who depended on them. Then they envisioned a safe, successful hunt before the end of the day. Blake, his head lowered and his eyes shut, marveled at how similar this tradition was to his own Kamishi tradition. There was, it seemed to him, a grand unity among the Bebelishi, and he felt proud to be part of it. One by one, the men raised their heads and looked to each other, giving encouraging nods and murmurs in anticipation of the dangerous hunt before them. The men mounted their horses and prepared to depart.

"You be careful out there today," said Lana. "Don't do anything crazy, all right?"

"All right," said Blake. They embraced and kissed each other warmly. Then Blake gave his mate one final hug and hopped onto his horse. "I'll see you soon!" he said as he maneuvered his mount into position. Lana blew him a kiss and waved goodbye.

"Now, my friends, we ride," said Zaaru solemnly, but there was a trace of excitement in his voice. It was the same excitement that they all felt. It was the thrill of the hunt mixed with the anxiety of knowing that one or more of them might not come home that day. Still, without this risk, there would be no glory, nor would there be such enthusiasm. As the men looked at each other, they knew that they all shared this feeling, and they were united. Then they headed out of the village.

Blake was the last to leave. Being a novice horseback rider, he inadvertently left a large gap between himself and the rest of the group. He turned around and waved to Lana one last time. Lana blew him another kiss and waved once more while she still hugged her belly with her other hand. She watched him gallop away as he held the horse's reins firmly in his hands, his hair and his shirt fluttering in the breeze. Then he veered to one side and commanded his horse to gallop and catch up with the rest of the hunting party. Lana watched him rise and fall with his horse as he rode ever farther away, the fog obscuring him more and more until he disappeared. Lana smiled to herself and sighed. Then she turned around and went home.

Chapter 42

The light of that early morning was growing, but still faint. It was a bluish purple, and it had a dreamlike quality that served to preserve the drowsiness of the hunters rather than awaken them. There was a chill in the air, and a wind blew in from the Gulf. It was only moderately strong, but it blew steadily. It flattened the grass, pushed against tree branches, and tossed the hair of man and horse alike. The wind roared monotonously in the men's ears and numbed their senses, but they rode on.

The hunters entered the surrounding woodland. Dense with trees of oak, pine, and palm, it was the only thing separating Corpus from the savanna. The horses made their way, single file, through a well-worn trail until they emerged on the other side. When they reached the savanna they broke ranks and took on a more clumped, amorphous formation. The sun had still not risen, and the men were pleased, for if they could reach the hunting grounds before full morning light, their chances of bringing down some big game would be all the better. However, there were no set hunting grounds, so it was impossible to know just where the herds of ungulates, or hoof beasts, would be on any given day. Instead, the hunters used their knowledge of these herbivorous animals' behavior to track them down. They knew the general range that they tended to occupy; whether they preferred flat or sloping land, open or wooded areas; and whether they could stray far from water. The Corpushi studied the grasses and shrubs, and took notice of which areas were lush, withered, or depleted, to help them find their prey.

Even Blake, although he was new to the Warmland, already knew some of the signs to look for: hoof prints, dung piles, bent blades of grass, or bare patches on trees where bark had been scraped away. The skills he had gained in Kamis served him well in Corpus, and he was able to contribute his fair share to the hunting effort. Like the other men, he could tell if a game trail was fresh or old. He knew whether or not a field was lush enough to support a large herd of herbivores.

He knew what grass looked like if it had been recently grazed, and he was improving in his ability to determine what leaves looked like if they had been recently browsed. Blake was struck by how similar this savanna was to his own plains back in Kamis, the main differences being that this region was warmer, wetter, and supported more trees. Many of the hoof beasts here also left behind signs similar to those of the northern Great Plains. However, Blake was beginning to realize that there was still much for him to learn.

The light was still dim and the air still brisk, and the men paused to examine the seemingly featureless expanse of grass that lay before them. They conferred with each other and came to the consensus that the grass to the northwest appeared full but recently trampled. The Corpushi also knew that a large lake lay in that direction, which provided water for both the animals and much of the vegetation upon which the animals relied. Therefore, the men concluded that the animals had gone to graze and drink, and decided to head northwest for the lake. They rode into the savanna in their new, tighter formation.

The group followed what appeared to be the trail of a large ungulate herd. The horses walked patiently, causing their riders to sway with each step. Their hooves made soft clopping sounds, and their legs swished as they brushed past the vegetation. Blake watched the grass below as his horse marched on. Their countless blades looked blue at this hour, and the sight of their going by mesmerized him. In this world of dim light and blowing wind, Blake felt as though he were not himself, but rather somehow part of the scenery. He forced himself to pay attention to the other riders and the horses, and to look for subtle clues in his surroundings.

The light grew stronger, and the world took on a pink and orange hue. Now the game trail became more evident than before. There appeared to be a large swath of disturbed grass, about a quarter of a mile wide. Bent and broken blades were common, and they were still more green than yellow. This trail was fresh. It suddenly dawned on Blake how large the herd they were tracking was, and how large its members must have been. He dared not speak or ask for anyone else's interpretation of the trail, for it was important to remain as silent as possible.

The hunters continued riding for more than an hour. The low sun cast long, thin shadows on the bronze earth, but there was still no big game. Then one of the young men suddenly held up his hand and pointed into the distance.

"Look!" he exclaimed in a subdued, hoarse-sounding whisper. Everyone else followed his finger until they, too, saw what he saw. At first, it was indistinct and cryptic, but as the men approached, an enormous herd of not only one, but many different kinds of ungulates came into view. Blake, consumed with excitement, felt his heart rise within his chest. He relished this sensation, but, being an experienced hunter, maintained his composure. He narrowed his gaze, straightened his back, set his jaw, and focused.

Blake could see the lake clearly. It was large and round, and the wind agitated its surface. Some animals drank at its shore, while others grazed from the surrounding fields or browsed the sparse trees. The hunters now realized exactly what they had been tracking, and they watched carefully to single out their prey. Blake marveled at this immense mixed herd. Observing it closely, he compared it to those he had known in the North. He had seen assemblages of this size before, but none so diverse; he recognized only a handful of the beasts he saw here.

Texins were plentiful here. They numbered in the hundreds, and were similar to the ones Blake had seen in Tulsa. There were horses, too. They resembled their northern counterparts but were smaller. Blake could see camels browsing on the shrubs, just like in Dallas. Deer and wild boars stayed close to the bushes as well. Turkeys and emus roamed freely among the ungulates and searched the ground for fruits and seeds. Blake saw wild macaques — those small, gray monkeys familiar to him from the Earth Research Center. How different they looked here, living free instead of clinging to one another in a cage.

However, Blake also saw a dizzying variety of antelope. They reminded him of deer or pronghorn, but there were many different kinds, and they were all new to him. Some were large and some were small. Some had sandy-colored coats, while others were a dark brown. Most had long, swept-back horns with prominent ridges. They flicked their tails as they wandered through the field, grazing contentedly.

The hunters rode toward the lake, where a multitude of hoof beasts, monkeys, and birds crowded on the shore to drink. The animals were eager to quench their thirst, but were always on the lookout for danger. When they detected the hunters, they immediately stopped what they were doing and looked up. However, they noticed only the horses, and not the humans riding on their backs. Sensing no real danger, they lowered their heads and drank once more.

Suddenly, a loud thrashing sound erupted from the water. A host of antelope scattered in panic, but one remained, struggling and splashing in the shallows, apparently unable to return to shore. Blake could not determine what was wrong with it until he caught a glimpse of something holding on to its hind leg. It was a giant, black, lizard-like animal, with long, powerful jaws and innumerable, sharp teeth.
That must be a gator.
The antelope hopped and scrambled, but the gator only dragged it out to deeper water. The gator performed a death roll, turning itself over and over, its jaws still clamped vice-like onto its prey. Then it disappeared with the antelope beneath the surface. There were a few more splashes, a few bubbles, and the water became still once more. A moment later, the gator returned to the surface with the lifeless carcass of the antelope in its long, broad jaws, and proceeded to devour it. Soon, six other monstrous gators arrived on the scene, eager to eat any scraps the killer might leave behind, or better yet, to steal the carcass altogether.

This spectacle enthralled Blake, but the hunting party was still on the move. They rode along the edge of the lake, where the sandy shore met the dense grass of the savanna.

"Aren't we in danger from those gators?" Blake whispered.

"Nah," said Spartan, "horses are too big for them. Don't worry about it."

In the distance, Blake noticed some creatures unlike any he had ever seen before. They were huge — easily the largest animals on all the savanna. Their gray bodies were naked, except for the tuft of long, course hair on their tails, and their massive, banner-like ears flapped intermittently. *These must be the creatures the Dallashi warned me about. These must be elephants!*

There was an entire herd of them, feasting on trees high above the other animals. They plucked leaves or even whole boughs with their powerful, dexterous trunks, and then gently pushed them into their mouths. They used their long, conspicuous ivory tusks to tear into trees, or simply as something on which to rest their trunks. Several infant and juvenile elephants stood among the adults, well protected against almost any threat.

These elephants fascinated Blake. He had expected them to be large, but he never imagined them to be quite so massive and intimidating. Spartan rode up next to Blake and gave him a gentle tap to bring him out of his trance. Somewhat startled, Blake turned to see that his companion grinning at him. Spartan made a sweeping motion with his hand and silently pointed forward, signaling to Blake that the hunting party would be moving toward the lake. Blake nodded and drove his horse on by lightly kicking his heels into its ribs. Blake caught up with Spartan and maintained his position.

"Are these the elephants we're going after?" asked Blake.

"No," said Spartan. "These are just cows and their young. We're going to leave them alone."

Just then, a trumpeting sound resonated from about a hundred feet away, and the men swerved to follow it. It was a gigantic bull elephant. He was nearly twice the size of the cows, and many times more aggressive. He charged toward the men at maximum velocity with his ears fully extended, making him appear even more enormous than he already was. His trunk was twisted and contorted over his forehead, and he roared and screamed in fury, instantly striking terror into the men and their horses. Like the flying shards of a clay pot smashing on the ground, the mounted hunters and other animals in the area scattered in every direction to escape the elephant's wrath.

Once they had put some distance between themselves and the giant bull, the men spun around to see whether they were being pursued. They discovered that the elephant was not targeting any one rider, but was charging around aimlessly instead. Not yet ready to give up, the hunters circled the big male at a distance too close for his liking, but still out of his immediate reach. Irritable and impatient, he continued his attacks, first running after one elusive rider and then the next. The riders, however, always managed to outrun him. The elephant became furious and began kicking up dirt and shaking his head.

"Why is he attacking us?" hollered Blake.

"Look at his forehead," said Spartan. Blake noticed the large stains there for the first time. It was as though the elephant were sweating or had somehow gotten his temples wet.

"What does it mean?" asked Blake.

"He's in musth," replied Spartan as he adeptly maneuvered his horse. "It's his time to breed, so he's very aggressive. All these bulls get like that. It helps them mate. Look over there." Spartan pointed at the other elephants. One of the cows was standing conspicuously away from the herd, sniffing the air, and watching the commotion. "Do you see that female standing apart from the others?" asked Spartan. Blake nodded. "She's probably in heat. That bull wants her, and as long as he does, he'll stop at nothing to keep every potential threat away, including us."

The swarm of riders continued to buzz around the giant bull, pestering him like mosquitoes.

"What's going on?" asked Blake.

Spartan held up his hand as a signal to wait. Through a cloud of dust he watched Zaaru and Murdoch, who commanded their horses to stay on one side of the enraged bull. The duo looked serious as they kept their eyes on the elephant and shouted to each other.

"We're moving on," said Spartan at last. "We're going to look for another elephant."

"Another one?" cried Blake. "Why? What about this one?"

"We can't attack him," yelled Spartan over the horses' pounding hooves and the elephant's menacing roars. "He and that cow make a pair. It wouldn't be right. We have to find another one, preferably an old one."

"Really?" asked Blake. He was impressed that the Corpushi chose not to interfere with a courting pair of animals, and to hunt an old or lame one instead. Now that he knew what was afoot, Blake looked forward to bringing down an old bull elephant. It would be a real challenge and a glorious catch, and what's more, it might release him from his debt. "All right!" he said.

Then Spartan, Blake, and the other men fled from the enraged bull and joined Zaaru and Murdoch. The group rounded the lake and headed for a distant clump of trees in the middle of the savanna. Blake and a few others looked back at the elephants as they rode away. The big bull swaggered in victory at having run off the pesky horse-human hybrids. Then he approached the cow and took up courting her again.

Chapter 43

As the riders approached the copse, they spotted another herd of elephants, this one more loosely organized. Its members were young bachelors too young to mate and old bulls past their breeding age, and they stayed several body lengths apart as they browsed the trees. One of the old males stood deep in the shade of the trees. He was a giant among giants, but his worn teeth made feeding difficult, which left him hungry and weak.

Zaaru gave the signal, and the hunting party gradually advanced.

The old bull became visibly agitated and stopped feeding. He flapped his massive ears, nervously shook his trunk, and pawed the ground. Trying to put more distance between himself and the humans, he backed away and ventured deeper into the grove.

The humans followed and, allowing their horses to walk normally, slowly drew closer. Zaaru made another sign and directed about ten men to the other side of the grove. He motioned for another ten to dismount and proceed on foot. The last group of ten, which included Murdoch, Spartan, Brent, and Blake, remained beside Zaaru on horseback.

As the threat from the humans appeared to subside, the elephant began to settle down; he did not notice that the humans were actually positioning themselves for a kill. Still uncomfortable but less frightened, the elephant slowed his retreat to a near halt and continued to shuffle back and forth nervously.

Soon, the hunters were in place. Zaaru led his group slowly forward again. This time, the elephant knew he was in danger and panicked. With a mighty trumpet from his trunk and a seismic, guttural roar, the bull wheeled about and fled through the trees, heading for the field on the other side.

"Charge!" cried Zaaru. His men let out a resounding war cry and attacked.

The horsemen on the other side of the grove held their position as they watched their target advance, while the footmen ran forward, their spears and arrows drawn. Zaaru and his horsemen drew their weapons as well and galloped into the grove after the frenzied elephant, which dodged trees as he ran.

The horsemen were gaining on him. Zaaru, who was closest to the bull, let fly a spear that stuck into the bull's rump. Feeling the pain, the elephant trumpeted loudly. Murdoch's spear was the next to find its mark, this time in the elephant's thigh. The beast cried out again, but neither of these attacks mortally wounded him or even slowed him down. In fact, they served only to frighten him more and spur him on. He broke into a full, straight run, ignoring trees and smashing them apart.

As the footmen approached from one angle, Zaaru's horsemen negotiated their way through the woods, which slowed them considerably. However, the footmen were gaining on their prey and proceeded to launch their arrows in the thickest part of the grove. The projectiles struck the elephant in the legs, flank, and face. Wild with fear and pain, the creature finally wheeled around again to face his attackers. He forcefully collided with more trees and splintered them, sending branches and pieces of their boles flying everywhere.

The footmen stood directly before the bull, waving their weapons to intimidate him and keep him in place. The tactic was working, for despite the fact that he dwarfed the humans, he was mad with fear. He dared not leave his position, for at least he knew where he was and what to do to defend himself.

The horsemen were catching up to him from both sides of the grove, and his other flank was bombarded with spears and arrows. Faced with no way out, the elephant's fear matured to anger, and he began to lash out. He slashed at the footmen with his massive tusks and struck two in one blow, sending them crashing into a tree and knocking them both unconscious. The bull then initiated a charge of his own and ran toward the remaining footmen, who dove to either side to escape his trampling feet.

Wheeling about once more, the elephant watched the horseback riders gallop toward him. He felt a sudden sting in his forehead as an arrow struck him between the eyes. The arrow could not penetrate his thick skull, so the blow was not lethal, but it did become lodged in the base of his trunk, which made breathing more difficult.

Just prior to reaching the giant bull, the riders leaped off their horses and encircled him. Free of their masters' wills, the horses kept their distance while the men surrounded the elephant. Those who had atlatls quickly brought them out and assembled them, placing the short spears into their wooden holders. With their elbows cocked and knees bent, the hunters edged toward their prey.

The elephant thrashed about. He swung his powerful trunk at the men and lashed out with his forelimbs. A blow from his trunk sent one man flying, and then another. A third man collapsed on the spot when he received an explosive kick to his gut. Still the men kept coming.

"Now!" cried Zaaru.

Atlatls sent spears flying into the elephant's ribcage. Five made their mark forcefully — three on one side and two on the other. The elephant straightened himself to his full height and towered over the men. Then he raised his head and let out a deafening roar, accompanied by the sickening sound of gurgling, frothing fluid. Blood oozed out of every wound in the ailing elephant's body. The dark, rich liquid spewed forth from two spear wounds on one side and one on the other, garnished with foam and bubbles. Both of the beast's lungs had been punctured; he was suffocating.

Yelling passionately and holding his spear high, Blake ran up to the elephant and paused directly in front of him. He looked up into the elephant's enormous, black eyes, which glared down at him in return. With another guttural roar, the elephant reared up and lifted one of his forelimbs high off the ground to crush Blake. But Blake thrust his spear forward and jammed it into the center of the elephant's throat.

The elephant stopped screaming and brought his weight back down to all four feet. Blake backed away, still eyeing the elephant keenly. Shuffling slightly, the giant bull swayed from side to side in complete silence. He was spotty from the dripping of his own blood, and spears and arrows protruded from wounds all over his body. The men fell silent, too, and the only sound came from the stirring of their feet in the leaf litter. Slowly, they stepped back and watched as the great beast's movements became less and less frequent. His great ears flapped several times, but then lay flat against his body. His eyes blinked with increasing drowsiness. His chest heaved deeply as he tried to breathe, but his wounds continued to gurgle and hiss. Soon, even his respiration slowed down, and he staggered.

"Stand back!" hollered Zaaru, and everyone complied.

The elephant began to lose his footing. He stumbled into a tree and snapped it in half before regaining his balance once more. The recovery was short-lived, however, and the elephant's feet soon gave way again, tripping over each other in turn. At last, he stood with all four feet spread far apart to help maintain his position, his chest still heaving slowly. In an instant, both legs on one side buckled. The elephant leaned toward that side and fell. He crashed into the ground with a reverberating thud, sending leaves, dust, and debris flying everywhere. His chest rose and fell for a moment until, at last, he lay perfectly still and dead.

The men did not cheer at their achievement, but turned to caring for their wounded instead. The bull had injured five men, and they were attended to now. Luckily for the men, no one had been maimed or killed; they had sustained injuries, but they would recover. When the group was certain that everyone was safe, they gathered around the elephant carcass and prayed. They thanked the Creator for granting them this victory, and wished the spirit of the elephant a safe journey in the next world. Then, once they had finished, they commenced the long, laborious process of butchering their kill.

Zaaru sent two hunters back to Corpus for more help. Eventually, a multitude of excited men, women, and children arrived. With such a grand trophy and no one hurt, everyone was excited and in high spirits. Lana was among the team of new arrivals.

"Blake!" she cried as she waved to her mate. "Blake! Are you all right?" She hugged him. He smelled of grass and blood and sweat. Lana took a step back and gawked at the downed elephant and the shattered trees all around it. She approached the enormous carcass, her mouth agape. "I can hardly believe it," she said. Lana slowly reached out to touch the elephant's dusty, gray-brown hide. It was rough, deeply creased, and covered in sparse, course hairs. And it was still warm. Lana was dazed. "Incredible," she said. Then she snapped her head in Blake's direction, stepped toward him, and scrutinized him as she looked into his eyes. "You sure you're all right?"

"Yeah," he said with an exhausted tone in his voice. "I'm fine."

"He's more than fine," said Murdoch. "He's great. You should be very proud of him."

Lana gave Murdoch a puzzled look.

"He's the one who delivered the final deathblow. He's the one who brought it down."

"Murdoch," began Blake, "you know as well as I do that we all brought it down. We all sent our spears and arrows into it, and some of us even got knocked over. In the end, this elephant couldn't breathe, and we all helped bring that about. I only delivered my blow when it was so weak that it couldn't move anymore."

"But your blow hastened the kill. You did your part, Blake. That much is clear. I have no doubt that after what you did today, your debt to Paulo will be more than repaid."

"Well…" Blake let out a sigh in spite of himself. "I hope you're right." He clasped hands with Murdoch and smiled. Then the two of them and Lana joined the others in dividing up the carcass into usable parts.

The people cut the meat into steaks, gathered the organs for use at home, and even collected most of the skin to make leather. They removed the ivory tusks and stored them with the large bones as material for making tools, weapons, trinkets, and jewelry.

While the people worked, a host of scavengers gathered nearby. Vultures circled overhead and coyotes sat at a distance, licking their lips hungrily, but none dared come too close to the fearsome humans.

Eventually, a pack of wolves arrived and scared off the coyotes. However, they were not bold enough to take on this large gathering of humans, who were not only well-armed, but also reinforced with dogs of their own. With some shouting, barking, and bluffing, the Corpushi succeeded in keeping the wolves at bay.

Sunset was near, and the Corpushi were nearly ready to bring their bounty home. Suddenly, the wolves abandoned their posts and left. They looked over their shoulders periodically, but they did not stop to turn around again until they were far away.

An adolescent sentinel boy discovered what the wolves had seen and sounded the alert. "Lions!" he cried. "Lions are coming!"

Everyone looked up. A large pride approached. It consisted of two big males, a dozen lionesses, and a litter of cubs. The people knew that a pride this strong would be difficult to oppose. Besides, it was not worth putting up a fight when most of the meat and materials from the kill had already been collected anyway.

Blake became apprehensive. "Let's get the hell out of here," he said.

"We will, but what's your hurry?" asked Murdoch. "We still have a few minutes before they get too close."

"Lions killed my best friend, Manosh, remember? Don't underestimate them!"

Murdoch stared at Blake for a moment. "You're right. Come on, let's not waste anymore time." The group left what little remained of the elephant carcass for the lions and the other scavengers. Then they hurriedly packed their things, marched into the woods, and headed back home.

Chapter 44

The whole Corpushi tribe held a bonfire feast on the beach the following night and everyone ate well. The elephant steaks were delicious and so were the many other foods that people had brought: fruits, vegetables, and seasoned meat from smaller game. There was dancing and singing, and the sounds of human glee filled the woods around Corpus. Tonight was a particularly joyful occasion, for the Corpushi were celebrating something else besides the successful hunt.

Blake stood inside a large, ceremonial tent that had been erected that afternoon for just this occasion. Despite the Rookery's great size, it had no single space big enough to accommodate every member of the tribe at once. Tents allowed people to come together outdoors in one place, while still maintaining a secluded area for those who needed it. A tent like this one had a symbolic function, too; it served to remind the Corpushi that their ancestors had been nomads of the field, and it helped them honor those ancestors.

Blake could hear the festivities outside and it gladdened him to know that the people were rejoicing around the campfire. This tradition was familiar to Blake, and a welcome event. *I wonder if all people keep the tradition of the bonfire feast alive. I suppose they do.* Blake was not ready to join the others yet. He was still preparing himself. In a few moments, however, he would leave this tent and head toward the fire, where everyone would be expecting him.

Blake was dressed smartly in a full-length, leather tunic, which was decorated with numerous small, attractive stones of various shapes and colors. His long, wavy hair had been neatly arranged and combed. He wore one silver bracelet on each wrist and two identical necklaces with a single golden ring hanging from each one. Murdoch and Spartan stood on either side of him, and helped groom him so he could look his best.

"This is your big day," said Spartan. "How do you feel?"

"I'm so excited," Blake said. "I mean, I'm kind of nervous, but I feel so giddy and happy at the same time."

"I know what you mean," said Spartan. "That's how I felt, too."

"Don't worry about a thing," said Murdoch. "You'll do fine, just fine."

Outside by the bonfire, the Corpushi were concluding their dancing and feasting. After everyone had completed most of their meal, the leading Elder of the tribe, Morty, stood up on a pedestal and raised his arms. Tonight he was dressed in his formal garb — a long, flowing white robe. Out of respect, everyone fell silent and turned their attention to him.

"My friends, tonight is a very special night indeed. We honor our brave hunters and give thanks to the Creator for our good fortune. We have also gathered here to celebrate the union of two young people in love, Blake and Lana. Let me now present to you, the groom, Blake."

"That's your cue!" whispered Murdoch hoarsely from inside the tent.

Blake swept the entrance flap aside and stepped out. Now all eyes were on him as he strode nobly toward the bonfire. Murdoch and Spartan escorted him, walking behind him and on either side. Three musicians sat some distance behind the audience. One held a drum made of leather stretched taut over a wooden frame. Another held two wooden rattlers that had been filled with dry beans, and a third had a beautifully carved wooden flute in his hands. Blake and his men marched down an aisle that parted the audience into two halves. They made their way toward the bonfire, where Morty stood waiting for them. At last, they reached the Elder, who motioned for them to stand to his left. Murdoch and Spartan lined up next to Blake.

"Now," said Morty, "I present to you, the bride, Lana."

Once again, everyone in the audience turned their heads. This time they focused their attention on another tent nearby. The Corpushi had raised this one earlier that day, too, and positioned it so that the two tents' entrances faced each other. The front flap flew open. Serena and Becca came out and stepped to either side of the doorway. Then another figure emerged, ducking her head slightly as she passed through. It was Lana.

When Blake saw her, his eyes grew wide and his heart began to race. The way she looked took his breath away, and Blake thanked the Creator that he had lived to see this day.

Lana wore a white woven dress. It was sleeveless to display her lovely shoulders, but its hem reached her ankles. Lana's graceful neck was clearly visible above the low neckline, but bare and devoid of ornamentation. However, beautiful silver hoop earrings dangled from her earlobes, and numerous metal bangles and seashell bracelets adorned her forearms. She wore white, leather moccasins with beads on her feet, and a wreath of fresh flowers and leaves atop her head.

The musical trio began to play and Lana began her procession down the aisle, followed by Serena and Becca. The sounds of the drum, the rattlers, and the flute danced in the air, casting a mystical, otherworldly mood over the entire ceremony.

As Lana approached the bonfire, she made eye contact with Blake. They held each other's gaze for a moment and smiled to one another. Soon Lana stood before Morty. He instructed her to stand to his right, and for Serena and Becca to line up beside her — an arrangement that mirrored the men. Blake noticed Lana's sweet, flowery fragrance, which he found incredibly alluring and sensuous. With everyone in position, Morty addressed the audience once more.

"Friends," he said, "we have come together today to witness the union of Blake and Lana as husband and wife. Blake and Lana came to us only a few weeks ago, but since then, they have already endeared themselves to us so much. Although we met them under difficult circumstances, they have become our friends since then, and our lives are brighter for knowing them. They have helped us bring down the shark and the elephant. They have shown us a new way to make fire. They have even shown us how to treat stab wounds and cure blood poisoning. What's more, they always did this with joy in their hearts, and with a sincere desire to help others. They are fine people and a fine young couple, and for that reason, it is my privilege and pleasure to conduct their wedding ceremony today. Blake and Lana, are you ready to begin?"

They both nodded.

"Good, then let's begin. Blake, do you choose this woman, Lana, to be your wife, and to keep her as your only wife as long as she lives? Do you welcome her into your heart as your own? Do you agree to provide for her and be her companion in this world? Do you accept her for all of her qualities and all of her shortcomings, and for all that she is? And do you take these vows in complete openness, in love and in good faith, and with all your heart?"

"Yes," said Blake.

"And do you, Lana, choose this man, Blake, to be your husband, and to keep him as your only husband as long as he lives? Do you welcome him into your heart as your own? Do you agree to provide for him and be his companion in this world? Do you accept him for all of his qualities and all of his shortcomings, and for all that he is? And do you take these vows in complete openness, in love and in good faith, and with all your heart?"

"Yes," said Lana, her voice cracking as tears welled up in her eyes.

Now Morty turned to Blake once more. "Blake," he said, "are you ready to give Lana one of your wedding necklaces?" Blake nodded. "Very well. Then Lana, please remove one of the necklaces from his neck." Lana did as Morty asked. She reached around Blake's neck and unfastened the clasp on one of the two identical necklaces. "Now, give it to Blake so that he can place it around your neck." The necklace changed hands and Blake reached around Lana's neck to fasten it around her neck.

"Blake and Lana have exchanged their vows, and the necklaces they wear are tokens of their love and devotion for each other. As Chief Tribal Elder of Corpus, and in the name of the Corpushi people, I proclaim you, Blake and Lana, as husband and wife. You may now embrace."

Blake and Lana looked deeply into each other's eyes. Lana was on the verge of openly crying. Even Blake felt a catch in his throat as his eyes became moist. It had been done. They were now publicly declared as soulmates and united for life, and they were the happiest they had ever been. As they gazed into each other's eyes, they felt a change come over them. Although they were still cognizant of the rest of the world, all they could really sense was each other. Despite not physically moving, Blake and Lana felt drawn to one another. They were melding, and the attraction was irresistible. Feeling as though they were spinning and reeling, they had been set in motion. It was a welcome sensation, and the only thing left to do was allow their bodies to follow their spirits. They pulled each other close, embraced, and kissed warmly and firmly. Only a small voice in the backs of their minds reminded them that they stood before other people, and that they must have restraint. At last, they parted and, with hands clasped, turned to face all those assembled before them.

"Friends," said Morty, "I present you Blake and Lana, mated pair."

Cheering and applause erupted from the audience, as well as from Morty, the band, and the whole wedding party standing beside the couple. Everything about the ceremony had been exquisite, and everyone gathered at the event was inspired.

"Since this is Blake and Lana's night," said Morty, "they will have the rest of it to spend without interruption in a tent of their own. We will continue with the festivities shortly, but first let us give the newlyweds a few moments alone." Morty turned to the wedding party. "Please escort the bride and groom to their quarters." Murdoch and Serena led Blake and Lana, who walked hand in hand, back to Blake's tent. They opened the front flap, let the newlyweds in, and then sealed the tent back up again.

Once inside, Blake and Lana were alone together at last. They sat down on the big fur rug in the middle of the tent. Lana nestled herself snugly into Blake's arms. Blake kissed his new wife tenderly on the cheek.

"Well, we made it," he said.

"Finally," said Lana, closing her eyes blissfully. Then she turned to her new husband, kissed him, and leaned on him.

"Lana, now that we're together, I feel like we should say something. Something that expresses our love for each other, and that clears a path for a long, happy life together."

"What would you like to say?"

"Well, I guess nothing really needs to be said. After all, we are married now. We are soulmates, and we have declared to each other and the whole community how much we love each other and how dedicated we are to each other. Still, I feel like I need to say something."

"What is it, my love?" asked Lana.

"I was going to tell you how much I love you. I was going to tell you that my love for you is undying, and that I would do anything for you. And I do, and it is, and I would. I was going to tell how much you mean to me, and that I would give my life for you, because that's how much I love you. But I feel guilty for being selfish."

"Selfish? What do you mean?"

"I need you, Lana. Without you, I'm just an aimless wanderer, looking for a better tomorrow that will never come. Before I met you, I had no purpose in life and no real direction, nothing to live for. You give me that purpose; you give me that direction. You give me life, and you give my life meaning. You have rescued me from the emptiness inside myself, and for that I will always be grateful to you. I would be lying if I told you that I married you just to care for you. The truth is that I married you not only to care for you, but also because I need you for me. Can you forgive me?"

Lana laughed out loud and hugged her husband.

"Why are you laughing at me?" asked Blake.

"I'm not laughing at you," she said. "I'm laughing because I'm happy. You are such an honest man, Blake, just like my father was. I wish that every woman in this world could be as lucky as my mother was, and as lucky as I am now. There's nothing to forgive you for, Blake. You understand exactly what our marriage is about. You just weren't listening. Remember the vows we took? We promised to care for each other. It's a mutual agreement. We give and we receive, we provide for the other but we also provide for ourselves. You have done nothing wrong, Blake. In fact, you have done only right by me."

Blake sighed. "I'm relieved. Is there anything you want to tell me?"

"Actually, there is. I understand how you feel about me, Blake, and about the love we have. Now what I want to tell you is how I feel about us, and what we are to each other."

"All right," said Blake.

"As I said, you have always been good to me, and I adore you for it. The only thing that you are guilty of is being too serious all the time!" Lana smirked and pretended to slap her husband on the shoulder. "Just listen to yourself, Blake. You're so worried about doing harm that you almost forgot to enjoy yourself today, and it's your day every bit as much as mine. That's why we're here, Blake — to complement each other. I bring you the carefree outlook on life that you lack. I bring you sunlight when you are drowning in the rain. I free you from the shackles that you've put on yourself."

"You're right, that's exactly what you do."

"Now let me tell you what you do for me. When you found me, I was miserable. I was half-alive. I was barely surviving in a cold world all by myself. Everyday was the same. There were good days, but most days were just dreary and lifeless. When you came, all that literally changed overnight. When you came, I had friends again. And now…" Lana paused and took Blake's hand in her own. "Now, I have family again. You saved me just as I saved you. You gave me life, and you gave my life meaning, just as I did for you. Now I'm the happiest I've ever been. What you do for me, Blake, is give me strength. If I'm the breeze that sends your spirit flying, then you are the anchor that steadies mine. I part the clouds that loom over you, and you are the cave that shelters me from the storm. So you see, Blake, we really are perfect for each other. We really are soulmates."

"Yes, we are," said Blake, caressing Lana's arm. "We're partners. Our paths were separate before, but now we travel together, you and I."

"Always," said Lana.

"Always," said Blake. "I love you."

"I love you, too."

They embraced one another tightly, allowing the passion that had been welling up inside them that entire evening to spill forth. They pressed their lips together, animatedly mouthing one another and lavishing each other with kisses. Clinging to one another, they kissed and swayed from side to side.

In time, their fervor subsided. Blake and Lana knew that they should rejoin the festivities outside once again, and indeed, they looked forward to laughing and dancing with their new friends. However, they found joy and comfort in the realization that, after the party was over, they would retire to their humble lodge together as husband and wife and celebrate their marriage throughout the night.

Chapter 45

About a week later, the bright sunshine gave way to an overcast sky, thick with gray clouds. The wind blew, and there was every indication that, sooner or later, there would be rain. Drizzle fell and matured to a proper downpour. Huge drops fell, each almost finger-sized. The wind grew stronger, and by evening the rain came down nearly sideways. The storm continued to grow all night and into the next morning.

By about midday, the storm had worsened even further. Murdoch and Blake stood beneath an overhang near the entrance to the Rookery and watched the entire phenomenon unfold. The air was laden with humidity.

"I don't like this," said Murdoch. "I don't like this at all."

"Why not?" asked Blake. "I mean, it's only a storm, right?"

"I'm not so sure about that. I think this could be the beginning of a hurricane."

"Are you sure?"

"It's late in the season, but it's not impossible," said Murdoch as the storm grew steadily all around them. "I want to check something. Come with me." Murdoch led Blake to the horse stables and dog kennels. The animals were clearly agitated. The horses tossed their heads and nickered, racing back and forth in what little space they had, while the dogs paced inside their pens and whined nervously. Blake looked in on Rita. She was curled up in a ball with her six pups nestled snuggly beside her, but with her head high and alert. "These animals sense something. It could be serious."

"What should we do then?"

"Let's go tell the Elders."

Murdoch and Blake ran up the stairs to the fifth floor. There, they ran around, knocking on every door to alert the tribe's leaders. Zaaru was the first to answer.

"What is it?" asked Zaaru, leaning through the entrance.

"Chief Zaaru!" said Murdoch, backtracking to the Chief's doorway, nearly out of breath. "There's a storm coming, sir!"

"Coming? I'd say it's already here, young man!" said Zaaru.

"Yes sir," replied Murdoch, "but I think it's going to get worse. I think it might even be a hurricane."

"Unlikely," said Zaaru. "It's already January. The chances of a hurricane coming now are very small."

"Is there no record of a hurricane in January at all?"

"Well, there is one, but…"

"Then maybe we should take this seriously!" said Murdoch. "Please, come outside with us, just for a moment. Then you can decide."

"All right. Just a moment." Zaaru stepped back into his home and threw on a thick robe. As he joined Murdoch and Blake in the hallway, three Elders — Bufo, Hector, and Uchara — finally opened their doors.

"What's going on?" asked Uchara, bewildered, cinching her cloak around her waist.

"These two seem to think there's a hurricane on the way. I'm going down to take a look for myself. I'll be right back." Zaaru accompanied Murdoch and Blake downstairs. When they reached the ground floor, they went back to the overhang so that Zaaru have a look around.

"So what do you think?" asked Murdoch, nearly shouting above the din of the storm.

"Well, I have to admit," said Zaaru, "I haven't seen a storm this bad in years. You could be right, Murdoch. We could be seeing the first January hurricane in over a century." Sheets of water blew in diagonally from the sky. Not a dry spot remained, and within seconds, the trio was drenched. The sound of raindrops striking the earth was deafening. Zaaru watched the dark, ominous clouds that stretched from horizon to horizon, and the churning, foaming waves that crashed onto the beach. Murdoch and Blake waited impatiently for a decision. "All right, let's get everyone to the bunker. I'll go upstairs and tell the Elders and Advisors; Lobo will need to transport our Bebel safely. You two tell the rest of the village that we're evacuating. Tell them you speak for me, or they might not listen to you. Appoint aides to help you spread the word and to start moving people and animals to safety right away, is that clear?"

"Yes, sir," said Murdoch and Blake simultaneously.

"Murdoch, you're my deputy. After me and the Elders, you're in charge of this operation. Outlander," said Zaaru, looking Blake in the eye, "you're his second-in-command. You answer to him, but otherwise, both of you are acting under my authority. You two did the right thing by alerting us; now go help the others. And Outlander: don't let me down!"

"No, sir, I won't," said Blake.

"Good. Now, let's move!" Then Zaaru ran back upstairs to alert the Elders.

Murdoch turned to Blake. "All right, here's the plan. Let's split up. Is there anyone out at your place?"

"Just Lana."

"Then you go out there and bring her back here. I'm going door-to-door and telling people to head straight for the bunker."

"What is this 'bunker'?" asked Blake.

"It's an underground shelter in the Rubble," said Murdoch. "It's inland, due north of here, about a mile or so. That's where we go during emergencies like this. Don't worry, you and Lana will find it; you'll be with us Corpushi the whole time." Blake nodded tersely. "I have to get Spartan, Peter, and Aries to give us a hand."

"What should Lana and I do when we get back?"

"Lana's going straight to the bunker along with everyone else. You'll rejoin me and the boys and help us get everyone to safety. As long as the people are all right, we can move the dogs, including Rita and the puppies."

"What about the horses?" Blake asked.

"We have no choice but to release them," said Murdoch. "Hopefully, when this thing is all over, they'll come back. All right, now let's go. We have to finish this before nightfall. Got it?"

"Got it."

Murdoch set upon banging on the doors of all the ground floor homes, while Blake sprinted back to his lodge. Rain splashed off his body as he dashed through the puddles and the mud. He was driven to find Lana as soon as possible. When he reached the lodge, he threw open the front door and hurried inside.

"Lana! Lana!" he cried desperately. "Lana, are you here?" There was no reply. *Oh no! Of all the times to disappear on me, she had to pick today!* "Lana! Lana, where are you?" Blake ran from room to room, but his wife was nowhere in sight. "Damn it! Where is she?"

Suddenly, he remembered the books. He went to the main room and picked up a leather satchel off the floor. It still contained his and

Lana's Bebels and their two other books. Blake tied the satchel, and then wrapped it in three layers of treated, water-resistant deer skins. *Forgive me. This is the best I can do.* He swung the reinforced satchel over his shoulder and ran outside.

Blake circled the lodge twice, calling Lana's name all the while, but he could not find her. Blake stood still in the rain, trying to peer through the downpour, but all he could see was water. Blake's mind was flooded with visions of Lana drowning or freezing to death all alone somewhere. After searching so frantically, his heart raced and he gasped for breath. Blake was now thoroughly soaked. Exasperated, he shivered.

Then he heard Lana call his name. She came running from the surrounding woods, carrying a basket in her hand. She, too, was drenched. She ran up to Blake and embraced him.

"Where were you?" asked Blake, yelling over the roar of falling water.

"I thought I could collect a few fruits, but the storm got worse!" replied Lana.

"All right, all right, never mind that," said Blake with a dismissive wave. "Listen, we have to go now!"

"What? Go where?"

"Back to the Rookery!" exclaimed Blake.

"Why can't we just go inside?"

"There's a hurricane coming! Everyone is evacuating to a special shelter underground! We have to go with them right now!"

"You mean we have to go all the way…"

"Quit arguing and just come with me!" Blake seized Lana's hand and pulled her along back to the Rookery. They ran nearly side by side, with Blake only slightly ahead.

When they reached the Rookery, people were pouring out of the building and filing north through the woods. Everyone was drenched. Families stayed together, the children in between the adults, and the dogs toward the outside. Blake and Lana soon located their friends and briefly conferred with them. They decided that Lana would join Serena and Becca.

Blake faced Lana and held her shoulders between his hands. "You go with the others," he told her. "I'll be along soon."

"What about Rita and the puppies?" asked Lana.

"I'll get them before we leave. Here, take this." Blake foisted his satchel onto Lana.

"What is it?"

"The books," said Blake.

"What if they get damaged?" she asked, worried.

"Just do the best you can. Whatever you do, it will be better than losing them. Now go."

"Be careful!" pleaded Lana.

"Don't worry. I'll be with Murdoch and the others. We'll be fine. Go." Blake kissed his wife flush on the lips and squeezed her arm reassuringly. Then Lana hurried off to catch up with Becca and Serena. She turned around, waved goodbye to her husband, and joined the procession of evacuees.

Blake met up with Murdoch and Spartan, who stood at the bottom of the stairs, directing people to the evacuation line.

"Aries is over at the stables letting the horses out," said Murdoch. "Peter is still upstairs knocking on doors. I want you to go help him."

"Of course," Blake said. He charged up the stairs, brushing against the crowd coming down in the opposite direction. Squeezing between people, he finally found Peter on the third floor.

"Blake!" called Peter. "I'm glad you're here. We have just one more floor to evacuate — the fourth floor. Can you go up there and take care of that?"

"Right away," said Blake. When he reached the next floor up, he pounded on the first door on the right. An impatient, middle-aged man answered.

"What the hell do you want?" the man demanded.

"A hurricane is coming. We're evacuating to the bunker in the woods to the north. Please get your family and come downstairs."

"Why should I listen to you, Outlander? For all I know, this is some sort of trick."

"It's no trick. Murdoch and I speak for Zaaru himself. There really is a hurricane coming, and it's very important that you take your family and leave now!"

"And how do I know you speak for Zaaru?" the man asked suspiciously.

Blake was impassioned. "Haven't you noticed what's going on around you? Don't you know the storm is getting worse? Can't you hear your neighbors stirring in the floors below you?"

"Actually, I did hear —"

"Good. Then don't trust me. Trust your senses instead and do something! Now, please, I can't waste anymore time. Get your family and leave!" Blake ran down the corridor to alert the next household. The residents there were far more receptive to Blake's warning and left immediately. When the man in the first apartment saw this, he quickly followed suit. Soon, the entire floor was empty at last.

Peter arrived at the top of the stairs. "Blake! What's the situation up here?"

"This floor's clear."

"Good, then we've cleared the entire building. Well done. Let's go find Aries and see if he needs any help."

The two men rushed back down the stairs and went to the stables and kennels, where they found Aries prodding the horses out through the main gate. The horses cautiously emerged from the corral, somewhat confused and disoriented. However, being anxious and eager to flee, they soon galloped off into the woods. Peter and Blake approached their friend.

"What can we do?" asked Peter.

"Peter, you go stand by the evacuation line and keep the horses from getting too close. They're spooked, and I don't know what they might do. If they try to get through the line, just scare them in the other direction. They should figure out that they have to go inland soon enough, but until they do, keep an eye out, all right?"

"Understood," said Peter, and he was gone.

"Blake, you take care of the dogs. Most of them are actually gone already; most of the masters came and got them a while ago. You bring the rest."

Blake nodded and hurried to the kennels. Inside it was dry and safe, but Blake knew that it might not be for much longer. The scent of dogs and their accoutrements filled the cold air. Blake looked in each pen to see which dogs were still there. Indeed, most of the pens were empty by now, but a few still remained. When Blake let them out of their pens, the frightened dogs licked him appreciatively. They had known him for only a short time, but they sensed that he was there to help. Rather than bolting, they stayed close to him as he went from pen to pen.

Lastly, Blake went to Rita's pen. Preventing the other dogs from entering, he stepped inside. Laying on her side, Rita wagged her tail enthusiastically, her tiny pups clambering all over her. Blake smiled as he pet the fuzzy little balls of brown fluff, and they wriggled under his touch. However, aware of the urgency of the situation, he did not dote on them for long. Having grown and developed, the puppies had already become more active and difficult to manage. Blake knew they would not all fit in the same sack. So, he picked up two sacks and placed three of the pups in one, and three in the other.

"Come on, Rita," said Blake. "Let's go." The tired but motivated dog rose to her feet and followed her master out of her pen. In the main walkway, she was met by the other dogs. Rita had been kept in isolation, so she had not met any of them until now. These other dogs were extremely curious about her. They crowded around her, sniffing and poking at her all at once. As a new mother, Rita was in no mood to socialize, particularly under these circumstances and at this stressful time. She bared her teeth and growled low, but the other dogs persisted. Then Blake intervened. "Come on, dogs, let's go," he said, holding one sack of puppies in each hand. "Come, come," he repeated and headed for the exit. The Corpushi dogs were still curious about Rita, but they followed Blake.

Outside, the tribe proceeded toward the bunker. The line of more than two hundred Corpushi streamed through the woods, while chaperones stood by for support. Zaaru was on the other side of the line, confidently waving people forward, while Murdoch served a similar function on the near side. Bringing the dogs with him, Blake fell in line.

Chapter 46

The wind whipped harder and roared louder, and the rain's pounding became even more brutal. Blake knew what it meant to survive the freezing, biting blasts of the northern Great Plains, but he had never experienced a gale as fast or as strong as this. It tugged on his face, hair, and eyes, which would have dried out had it not been for the deluge. Its howl was deafening, and Blake could not understand what anyone else was saying, for he could neither hear nor see well enough to read lips. The only form of communication that remained was the most primitive one — the comforting sense of touch.

Trees and smaller plants rocked and swayed with each gust. Massive drops pelted their leaves and drove them downward. The wind yanked at them in every other direction, causing them to bob and dance manically, as though controlled by some demonic force.

Suddenly, things began to fly. Weeds leaped into the air. Driftwood and rotting logs flew overhead, while old trees collapsed like rag dolls. The people cowered in the wake of the hurricane, crouching as low to the ground as possible, clutching each other in fear. Airborne leaves, twigs, and soil pelted their drenched backs. However, they dared not look up even for a moment, lest they be clobbered by some ordinary object accelerated to a lethal velocity.

The palm trees seemed to be the only plants really suited to coping with the hurricane. Instead of trying to stand up to it, they submitted. The wind passed right through their tattered fronds. It bent and twisted their thin, fibrous trunks, but it did not break them.

Blake followed the Corpushi through the woods to a mound of Rubble protruding from the ground. Its entrance was a small opening on one side, halfway up the mound. Blake gingerly toted the sacks of puppies up the mound with Rita and the other dogs right behind him. Despite their wet fur and the glum expressions on their faces, the dogs stoically endured the storm. However, when Blake ducked through the opening and entered the bunker, the dogs were quick to follow.

Once inside, Blake was amazed at the shelter's complexity. Light from the surface could scarcely penetrate here, but the walls sported numerous brightly burning torches. The shelter was a labyrinth of rooms and hallways. The passages and doorways were narrow, but the ceilings were high, creating the illusion of spaciousness. Blake wondered if he might get lost. He imagined that, when empty, this shelter must have seemed quite roomy. Now, however, with the entire tribe down here, the place was busy, crowded, and confusing. Nevertheless, everyone made due.

Blake located Spartan and approached him. "Where's Lana?" he asked.

"She's with Becca and Serena. We house several families in a single chamber together down here, otherwise we'd run out of room. The two of you will be staying with us. I can show you where."

"Later. Where can I take the dogs?"

"There's a room down the hall, on the left," said Spartan, pointing. "That's where we usually keep them."

"Great. Listen, would you do something for me? Tell Lana to meet me there."

"Right away," replied Spartan. Then he and Blake separated once more. Blake took the dogs in his care to the designated room. He let them arrange themselves as they pleased, but he made sure that Rita had a corner to herself. Still, he was unsure of what to do with the puppies. Just then, Lana arrived.

"Thank the Creator," she said, hugging her husband tightly. "Are you all right?"

"I'm fine. You?"

"I'm fine. What's happening?"

"We're almost done with the evacuation, but I need you to do something for me."

"Anything," said Lana.

"I have to go back and check on Zaaru and Murdoch," Blake said. "Take over watching the dogs for me, especially the puppies. I don't think there'll be any trouble, but make sure none of the other dogs try to hurt them, and that no fights break out. Can you do that?"

"Sure," said Lana.

Then Blake was off again. He found Zaaru and Murdoch as they stepped through the entrance to the bunker. "What news?" he asked.

"That should be everyone," said Zaaru. "Murdoch and I did a search for stragglers, but we found none. It's time to seal the entrance and ride out the storm." With that, Zaaru took hold of a massive, wooden door. Straining, he pulled on the door and slammed it shut. The shelter now became virtually impermeable not only to daylight and fresh air, but also water.

Zaaru, Murdoch, and Blake returned to the depths of the bunker and prepared for the long wait. Suddenly, they heard a woman's terrified scream. The trio followed the sound to its source — the chamber where Paulo's family was staying. They quickly realized that the scream had come from Wendy, Paulo's wife. Wendy and Paulo were beside themselves with anxiety. Even their old dog, Bobo, seemed uneasy. The other family sharing the room with them was horribly distraught as well.

"What is it?" asked Zaaru. "What has happened?"

"My children!" cried Wendy. "Jed and Kayla! They're gone!"

"Gone? What do you mean 'gone'?"

"I left them in the care of this family so that I could help my husband, because of his limp. But I just learned that these people have lost track of our children and don't know where they are!" Wendy was weeping openly. "Zaaru, is there anyone still out there who can look for them?"

"I'm afraid not, Wendy. In fact, I have just sealed the entrance to the bunker."

Wendy howled pitiably. "Please, Zaaru! Please send one of your men out to find them!"

"It's not so simple. We are now in the midst of a true hurricane. The sea will be rising soon, and it's not safe to leave the hatch open."

"No!" cried Wendy. "We have to save my children!"

"I'm so sorry, but it's my duty to protect the whole tribe. I can't jeopardize the well-being of the whole tribe by waiting for two of its members."

"I'm the one who's sorry," said Paulo. "I'm a burden on my family and my tribe. Now, my selfishness has killed my own children."

"Not necessarily," said Blake. "There's still a chance to save them."

"What do you mean?" asked Zaaru.

"Let me go back out there, Chief," said Blake. "I'll find them."

"You don't know that."

"But I have to try."

"It's brutal out there!" Zaaru said. "All three of you could die. Besides, even if you do make it back, I can't guarantee that I'll be able to let you in. Leaving a doorway open during a hurricane is worse than standing in the middle of one; it could be deadly for everyone."

"Well, if we're too late, then you don't have to let us in. All I'm asking is that you open the door for five seconds right now to let me out. That's all."

Zaaru stared at Blake for a moment. "All right, let's hurry up and get this over with." The two men rushed back to the exit. "Are you ready?" asked Zaaru.

"Ready," said Blake.

"Good luck, Outlander."

Zaaru threw open the door. Blake leaped outside and was immediately drenched in the downpour. Behind him, the massive door creaked on its ancient hinges. Then it slammed shut with a loud, reverberating thud.

Chapter 47

"He did what?" demanded Lana as the puppies crawled around in her lap.

"He went to look for Jed and Kayla," replied Murdoch softly.

"Oh, no," Lana mumbled. "Oh, no, I don't believe this." Maintaining her composure, Lana gently put the pups back down on the floor next to their mother. Then she slowly rose to her feet and paced the room. She stared at the floor and chewed on her fingernails, her eyes darting back and forth wildly. Her pacing grew more and more frenetic until she brought her hands to her head and nervously mussed up her hair. Then Lana threw her hands up in the air screamed out loud. "Why did you let him go? How could you let him go out there? This is a wild goose chase! He's finished! He's going to die out there, don't you understand?"

"Please, Lana, keep your voice down."

"You idiot!" Lana launched herself at Murdoch, pounding on his chest with the flesh of her closed fists. "You lunatic! You killed my husband!" Murdoch stood up straight and kept his head out of harm's way. He towered over the woman, and her attack did little to injure him. He wrapped his arms around Lana and pressed her toward him. Gradually, her fury subsided and she collapsed against him, sobbing convulsively. "I'm sorry," she said as tears streamed down her cheeks. "I didn't mean it. It's just..."

"No need to apologize," Murdoch said as he held her and stroked her back. "I know."

ಸಂ ೧೩

Outside, Blake staggered against the pounding wind and rain. He held his forearm up in front of his face, but still could see almost nothing.

"Jed! Kayla!" he cried. *How could they possibly hear me? I can't even hear myself.* Blake fought against the surging water and sloshed through the swirling mud, but there was still no sign of the children. *I can't keep wandering around like this. This is pointless. Think, Blake. Where would two small, frightened children hide in the middle of a hurricane?* Blake leaned against a tree for support. *What am I saying? There's nowhere to hide. Practically nothing is safe right now. Hell, if I were a child, I'd probably just want to go ... home.*

Inspired by this insight, Blake ran back to the Rookery. The closer he came to the Corpushi stronghold, the deeper the gushing water became. He soon found himself knee-deep in seawater. *It's the surge from the Gulf. This place is already flooding.*

Blake emerged from the trees. *Not much farther now. I can't see the Rookery, but it should be right over there.* Bracing himself, he took a deep breath and sprinted forward. He squinted against the driving rain and struggled against the ever rising storm surge, lifting his knees high with each step. Then he lost his footing and fell face first with a splash into the brine. Submerged rocks dug into his palms and his shins, and saltwater stung his eyes. Blake picked himself back up and looked himself over. *It's all right. Just a few scrapes. Got to keep moving.*

Blake continued to trudge through the water until he reached the Rookery. There, he found the stairs and quickly ascended to the third story — the children's home. Once inside the stairwell, Blake was protected from the wind and rain for the time being. The sound of rainfall echoed against the walls, but at least this place was dry.

When Blake reached the third story, he looked down the corridor toward Paulo and Wendy's apartment. To his relief, he saw Jed and Kayla sitting on the floor in the middle of the doorway, facing each other.

"Jed! Kayla!" he called. The children looked up excitedly. "Are you all right?"

"Yes," replied Jed, the elder of the two.

Blake walked up to the children and sat down next to them. "Is your sister all right?"

"Yeah. She just doesn't feel like talking right now."

Blake smiled. "All right, that's fine. Jed, can you tell me what happened?"

"We got lost," said Jed, beginning to cry. "We tried to keep up, but we couldn't. We're sorry. Are we going to be in trouble?"

"No, not at all," said Blake. "You did the right thing by coming back home. And it looks like you're taking good care of your little sister, too. But why are you sitting in the doorway?"

"Mama and Papa always told us this is the safest place — after the bunker."

"Well, in that case, good thinking. Come on, I'm going to take you to the bunker now."

"But we don't want to go," said Jed, still whimpering. "It's scary out there."

"It is a little scary, yes, but it'll be worth it when you get to see Mama, Papa, Spartan, Becca, and everyone else. And it'll be warm and dry inside in the bunker, too. Doesn't that sound nice?"

"Yes," admitted Jed, drying his eyes.

"Then let's go into your home and get you some nice warm hides to keep you dry on the way there." Blake and the children got up, and went into their apartment. Blake picked out three deer hides of various sizes — one for each of them — and covered up the children and then himself. They went downstairs, with Jed holding onto Blake's hand, and little Kayla holding onto Jed's. When they reached the ground floor, Blake surveyed the area once more. "Jed, is the water too deep, or do you think you can run alongside me?"

Jed was apprehensive, but he furrowed his eyebrows and spoke in a serious tone. "I think I can run alongside you."

"Great. Kayla, will you get up on my shoulders?" The little girl only brought her thumb and index finger to her mouth and stared back at Blake. "Jed, what's wrong with her?"

"She's all right. She's scared, but she'll do it."

"Good." Blake hoisted Kayla up onto his shoulders and took Jed by the hand. "Are you ready?" Jed nodded succinctly. "All right, let's go." With that, they charged into the open and headed inland.

Blake pressed through the rain. He held onto Kayla's leg with his right hand as she clung to his hair and steadied herself. In his left hand, Blake tightly clutched Jake's right, but the little boy was having trouble keeping up. The water was getting deeper by the second, and slogging through it was even harder now than before. Everything was in motion, and Blake and the children could hardly see anything. The rain pounded on their backs, the trees swayed violently, and the water all around them pushed against the backs of their legs as it flowed passed them.

Blake could hear Kayla crying from her perch on his shoulders. He squeezed her leg reassuringly, but this did nothing to calm her. *All I can do is hurry. The sooner we get there, the less these kids have to suffer ... and the less danger I'll be in, too. But the problem is, Jed can't run nearly as fast as I can, and certainly not as long. I'll just have to give him as much prodding as he can handle.* Blake held onto Jed's hand and quickened his pace. Jed hastened, too, but his acceleration was negligible, and Blake could feel the boy's weight on his arm. Had Blake gone any faster, he would have been dragging Jed along instead of leading him.

The pelts that Blake and the children wore offered little defense against the cold of the driving rain, surging seawater, and ruthless wind, which robbed the people of their precious body heat and tried to knock them down. First the children began to shiver, and then Blake's muscles became stiff and tense in an effort to keep him warm. Simply moving his arms, legs, or torso felt like monumental tasks for Blake, and he became impatient and angry with his own body for betraying him. He tried to stay limber by flexing his knees and elbows a bit, but the thought that he and the children might succumb to hypothermia weighed heavily on his mind.

"Wait, Blake!" cried Jed. "Wait for me!" The water was past Blake's knees now, but it was halfway up Jed's thighs. Blake glanced backward, straining to see through the torrential rain, his face overcome with worry. Jed could barely walk in this mess, let alone run in it. Nevertheless, the boy was determined to persevere. Blake admired him for his courage, but courage alone would not get them through this ordeal. They needed speed. Blake stopped and turned to face Jed.

"Jed!" he called out. "The water's rising, so we really have to move. I'm going to pick you up, okay?"

"But what about my sister?" Jed had trouble getting the words out because he was shivering so badly.

"It's all right. She's going to stay on my back. I'm going to pick you up in my arms. Come on." Blake bent down. "Kayla, you have to hold on tight with both hands, all right?" He heard nothing from the little girl. "Does she understand, Jed?"

Jed nodded his head repeatedly, now unable to speak due to his trembling jaw and chattering teeth.

Blake scooped up the boy and pressed him up to his chest. Then he pushed on through the water as fast as he could. He felt Kayla bouncing up and down on his shoulders and her tiny hands pulling on his hair and neck. Jed remained fairly steady in his arms, although his little legs flailed uncontrollably to one side with each stride.

Blake hurried through the deep, flowing water. He knew he wasn't going nearly fast enough, but he also knew that if he rushed too much, he could lose his footing and doom himself and both children. Blake could see nothing beneath the murky surface, but he could feel the ground perfectly with his feet. Always mindful of where he stepped, Blake was relieved to find himself treading over sand, grass, and weeds. Every now and then, he would step on a rock or a sunken log, but on the whole, the way seemed free and clear.

The surface of the water roiled and churned, developing white, foamy formations atop the thick, brown liquid below. Many objects floated past Blake, swept along by the powerful inward movement of the storm surge. Most of these objects were driftwood of various sizes, but others were odd Corpushi textiles, uprooted plants, and even the corpses of small, drowned wild animals.

Jed and Kayla continued to hold onto Blake, as though he were an island in the middle of a stormy sea.

The wind grew even stronger, pushing on Blake and the children from behind and either side. Blake felt Jed huddling at his chest in fear. Kayla released her grip on Blake's hair, but only for a moment, then wrapped her arms around his neck and interlaced her fingers over his Adam's apple. She pulled backward and unwittingly began to choke him.

"Kayla," he whispered hoarsely, "Kayla, let go."

The frightened little girl remained silent and refused to adjust her constricting hold on Blake's windpipe.

"Please," croaked Blake again. "Please, just a little." Blake wanted to reposition Kayla, but his arms were full, and putting Jed down was simply not possible. Not only was time running out, but setting the boy down could mean losing him to the current. Blake had no choice but to keep moving forward, although he was starting to feel lightheaded.

Debris flew through the air wildly. The storm sprayed Blake, Jed, and Kayla with leaves and silt, and whole branches whizzed past them. Suddenly, a giant palm frond landed directly on top of Blake. The force of the blow disoriented him and he staggered to keep his balance. A submerged root caught him by the foot and he stumbled.

He fell down into the water with a loud splash. Jed and Kayla held fast and fell with him.

Blake, fearful of crushing Jed and drowning Kayla, swerved at the last second so that he came down on his back instead of his belly. The combined momentum was so great that the three of them sank below the surface.

Blake felt the frigid water cover his face and torso, and instinctively held his breath and closed his eyes. Then a current swept over his body, and before he could react, it tore Jed from his hands.

With a violent wrench and a kick, Blake exploded from the surface to keep Kayla above water, and looked around feverishly for Jed.

"Are you okay?" Blake asked desperately of Kayla. The girl gave no reply, but Blake judged that she was all right because she still clung to him vigorously. The fall had forced Kayla to shift her hold on Blake from his throat back to his head, and Blake was grateful to be able to breathe normally again.

"Jed!" cried Blake. Blake tried to penetrate the pouring rain, but he could scarcely see more than an arm's length ahead. *It's no good. Where is he? I can't see a thing!* Then Blake got an idea. He looked down at the water itself. Foamy swirls still surrounded him, but in one particular direction, he thought he could see wake. *Jed.*

"Blake!" came a faint, barely audible cry in the distance; the wake seemed to point to the position of the voice.

"Jed!" The water was too deep to wade through now. Blake quickly lowered himself and began to swim in the direction of the voice. He kept his head above water, and therefore, Kayla's head, too. Blake propelled himself with froglike kicks of his arms and legs, and the swift current pushed him along.

"Blake!" The voice came louder now.

"I'm coming, Jed!" A second later, Blake saw him.

He was bobbing in the water, his chin submerged, his mouth barely clearing the surface. The boy fought the current with his feet and one hand, but he had enough sense to wave his other hand high in the air to be more visible. Jed could see nothing, for his eyes were shut tight against the rain and brine, but Blake knew he was there and made directly for him.

When Blake reached Jed, he instantly seized him and clutched him tightly to his body.

"Kayla!" said Blake. "Kayla, you have to let go!"

"No!" cried the terrified girl for the first time.

"I can't hold onto both you and Jed like this. Let go and I'll carry you a different way!"

"No!"

"It's all right! Trust me! I promise, I won't let either one of you go. I promise!"

Kayla ignored Blake, but then without warning, she let go and began to drift away. Blake reacted quickly this time. Like a viper striking at its prey, Blake shot out his hand and grabbed Kayla tightly by the upper arm. He wrapped his calloused fingers around the child's slender limb and immediately pulled her toward him.

Blake struggled to maintain his position with his legs as he held both children against his body. Walking had become impossible, and he knew he could not swim like this. Then he remembered.

It's just like the lake back home. Only saltier.

"Come on, kids," said Blake. He rolled over onto his back and brought the children to his front. He pressed their backs to his chest, with Jed on the right and Kayla on the left. Blake wrapped his arms around them so that their necks were nestled in the crooks of his elbows. Then, pressing down on them with his forearms and loose fists, he kicked forcefully.

Kayla squirmed and fought, but Blake tightened his hold on her and reined her in. She soon settled down. Then with Jed and Kayla in tow, Blake swam backwards, following the current of the surge, and heading inland once more.

ઈ ଔ

Chief Zaaru sat just inside the entrance to the bunker. Several people had wanted to join him, but the passage was just too small and he turned them all away. He stayed there, alone, and waited for Blake to knock on the door. Despite his calm, stoic exterior, he was inwardly anxious to see Jed and Kayla again. So far, though, there was no sign of them at all.

Zaaru had waited there for hours, listening to the rain pound on the shelter, and the wind throw sand, rocks, and countless branches against the sturdy bunker door. He had felt the temperature drop over an hour earlier, and he knew that night had arrived.

But the wind isn't that strong yet, and it's still not flooding. If they arrive right now, I could still open the door. It's not too late for them. They can still make it. It's not too late.

Zaaru listened to the sounds on the other side of the door, and even pressed his ear against it from time to time to get an idea of what the storm was doing. He had heard several squalls come through, but even they were not enough to squelch his hope.

Then he heard a fierce howling outside. There was moaning and screaming, and Zaaru could hear the limbs of trees snapping everywhere. The door to the bunker itself creaked and rattled, but even that did not compare to the chilling, melancholy wailing of the hurricane's awesome winds.

It's started. It's here. I couldn't open the door now, could I? No, I'd be jeopardizing the whole tribe. I'd be sacrificing two hundred and fifty people for the sake of only three. And even then, there's no guarantee I could save them. No, Jed, Kayla ... Outlander. I'm sorry. Well, maybe. Maybe if they arrive right now, I mean right now. Maybe then I could do it. Maybe then.

But that was when Zaaru heard a sound that seized his chest and knotted his stomach. It was the sound of sloshing water. The surge had reached the sealed, bunker door. The flood had arrived. It was too late.

Chapter 48

The hurricane arrived that night in full force. Few people could sleep, kept awake by the awful howling outside the shelter, the sound of debris smashing against the walls, and the knowledge that Blake, Jed, and Kayla were out there somewhere in the midst of it all. In the middle of the night, everything fell silent, as though the storm had suddenly ceased to exist. The noise soon resumed, however, just as strong as before. This ordeal went on for hours, and the Corpushi had no choice but to endure it and wait for it to end.

Morning came, but nothing changed. Fortunately for the Corpushi, they had stocked their shelter for emergencies like this one, and faced no shortage of food or drink. They remained safely concealed in their refuge for a while longer.

It was not until the following day that they noticed some improvement. Things became quieter; both the wind and the rain had passed. Eventually, the time to go outside finally arrived.

When the Corpushi emerged from hiding, they immediately began to look for Jed, Kayla, and Blake. They called out to them as they searched, determined not to rest until they had found their loved ones — or their bodies.

As soon as they left their bunker, the people were shocked by how much their world had changed. The majestic-looking foliage of their woodland, which had once stood out against the vast, flat savanna, had been transformed into wreckage. Felled trees lay haphazardly on the ground, littering the savanna with the mosses and vines that had once lived on them. Wood and leaves were everywhere, and disembodied palm fronds lay draped over it all. Everything was wet and shiny, and all of this destruction had overtaken Corpus in only one day.

"Let's split up," said Zaaru sensibly. "Form small groups and stay alert. They could be anywhere, but there's enough of us that we should be able to find them soon."

"Not if they got washed out to sea," Aries said, carelessly.

Murdoch cuffed him over the head. "Will you shut up? I don't wanna hear…"

"Enough!" bellowed Zaaru. "Now get to work!"

With that, the tribe did as the chief commanded and spread out to conduct their search.

"Jed! Kayla!" cried Paulo and Wendy plaintively. "Kids!" Spartan and Becca were with them, as were Murdoch, Serena, and Lana. Zaaru was with them, too. The group wandered aimlessly through the mess of mud and soggy plants. They constantly turned over the debris and looked underneath, but found nothing.

In time, they came to a stand of oak trees. A few still bore leaves, but most had lost a large portion of their foliage and branches. Again, the group rummaged through the debris to no avail.

However, something caught Zaaru's attention, and he alerted the others.

"Hey," he said tersely. "Over there. What's that?" He pointed to the base of one of the oak trees, a few hundred paces away.

Murdoch hesitated. "Nothing. It's just a bunch of leaves."

"Exactly. That's a lot of leaves isn't it? I mean, look around you. There's garbage everywhere. Why is there a pile of the stuff in that particular spot?"

"I don't know, Zaaru," replied Murdoch.

"Well, let's take a look. Come on." Zaaru led the others to the pile of leaves. Indeed, it was an odd looking pile. In fact, it was almost pyramidal in shape and, even more strangely, most of the pyramid was made of palm fronds, even though it was at the base of an oak tree.

Zaaru crept toward the mound with the others close behind him. When he stood directly in front of it, he crouched and quickly whisked off a couple of the biggest palm fronds he could find. To his surprise, he found another layer of fronds underneath.

"This is no coincidence," said Zaaru.

Then something stirred within the mound. Zaaru held out his arms, palms facing backward, and signaled his group to stay away. A hand emerged from the mound and swept clear the leaves. After a moment, the entire arm came out, then the shoulder, then the neck. When the head surfaced, it became clear that this was Blake.

"Blake!" cried Lana, and she rushed over to his side and helped him dig his way out of the mound. The rest of the group joined in, and they soon discovered that Jed and Kayla were in there with him, too.

"Jed! Kayla!" said Paulo and Wendy, practically weeping with relief and joy. They extricated the children and looked them over for injuries; besides a few scratches, they were fine. Paulo, Wendy, Spartan, and Becca all hugged the children tightly, grateful to have them alive.

Lana examined Blake and found that his hands and legs were covered with cuts and bruises. "Oh my God," said Lana unselfconsciously. "You're all torn up! Are you all right?"

Blake nodded. "Yeah, it's nothing serious. I'll be okay."

"But look at you! You're injured. Can you walk? Let me dress those wounds."

"I'm all right," Blake said calmly. "I can walk, just give me a moment."

"Here, let me help you," said Lana. Blake draped his arm over Lana's shoulder and let her help him up. He gingerly rose to his feet and stepped out of the mound, still leaning on Lana for support. The others watched him with concern and admiration in their eyes.

"Did you three stay under that pile of leaves through the whole thing?" asked Spartan.

"No. The water was too deep. Actually, we were up in this tree here for most of the time," he pointed up at the oak, "about a day and a half. Then we came down, built this shelter, and spent the night in it."

Zaaru approached Blake. "Where did you find the kids?"

"They were pretty smart. They went home."

"You mean you went all the way to the Rookery and halfway back in this hellish weather?" asked Zaaru incredulously. Blake nodded with his eyes closed.

Then Paulo and Wendy stepped forward.

"Blake," said Paulo. "We just want to thank you for what you did."

"Thank you," echoed Wendy. "Thank you for saving our children. We'll never forget this. Now we're in *your* debt."

"Please," said Blake, holding up a hand. "That's enough talk of debt. I'm just glad everyone's safe. Let's all just go home ... if we still have one."

The group turned around and headed back toward the Rookery, all the while looking for their fellows to tell them the search was over. As Blake and Lana walked together, arm in arm, Zaaru came up next to them and spoke.

"Hey," said Zaaru. The Kamishi turned and looked at him. "Nice work ... Blake."

Chapter 49

Soon, everyone heard the news that Blake and the children had been found and were all right. Happily, the search was called off, and the Corpushi made their way to the Rookery again. A motley caravan, they carried only a few supplies, but were far less organized than when they had first left. They were anxious about what awaited them, but they were also far less frightened than before. Lobo carried the Corpushi Bebel, while Blake toted his satchel of books; both were grateful that the hurricane had spared their precious documents.

Men and women sloshed through the residual shallow water, their dogs close by. Rita trailed behind Blake and Lana, each of whom held one sack with her pups inside. The children, however, seemed to be enjoying their short jaunt through the woods, chasing each other and splashing in every puddle they could find.

Blake turned to Spartan, who hiked alongside him. "What about the horses? Will they come back?"

"We'll see," said Spartan. "Hopefully, at least a few of them will in the next few days. Some of them, though, we may never see again."

The Corpushi were shocked when they reached their village. It was hardly recognizable. The sandy soil was saturated, and dark, sudsy water seeped to the surface with each footstep. Most of the familiar structures were gone. Mounds of Rubble were either rearranged or completely absent, although they were not really missed. However, there was no more stable or kennel, and even a few of the small, stone houses had been destroyed. Only the Rookery remained, but even it was not left unscathed. The hurricane had blown away many of its tiles and statues, and ransacked the apartments, scattering their contents all over the ground. Nevertheless, the Rookery was still standing.

When Lana and Blake returned to the outskirts of town, they discovered that their old lodge had been flattened. It had already been a ruin anyway, but now it was completely uninhabitable. The doorway was gone, and its feeble walls and roof had caved in. It was nothing but Rubble now. So, having nowhere else to go, Blake and Lana went back to the Rookery, where they found other people wandering about aimlessly as well.

Serena was relieved when she saw them coming, for she wanted someone to talk to. "Hello, Lana. Hello, Blake," she said, visibly exhausted.

"Hello, Serena," said Lana. "What news?"

"Oh, it doesn't look good," breathed Serena. "We've lost so much. It will take us months, maybe even years, to rebuild."

"I'm sorry," said Lana.

"So am I," said Blake. "I hate to see you suffer like this."

"Thank you," Serena said, her eyes downcast. "What about you? How does your lodge look?"

"It's totally destroyed," said Lana simply.

"You seem to be taking it rather well."

"I'm just glad that no one was hurt and we're all still here," Lana said.

"Thank the Creator for that. That's what really matters. But don't you find this whole thing a bit … unnerving?" asked Serena.

"Well, remember, both Blake and I come from a very different world. I grew up in a Rubbletown — I mean a real Rubbletown, not a village like this one. I never knew luxury until I came here, so seeing Rubble everywhere doesn't really bother me."

"And my people were nomads," said Blake. "We used to pick up and move all the time, so we never had much, either. I guess I'm not really upset because, in the back of my mind, I didn't really expect my things to last very long anyway. The Bebel is the only really irreplaceable possession we have." Blake patted the sack that hung from his shoulder. "As long as we have that, we can always start over."

"I guess you two are lucky that way."

"That is lucky," said Lana, "but we're not blind to what has happened here. We can see what you're going through. Tell us how we can help."

"Thank you," said Serena, touching Lana's arm. "Really, thank you. For now, I think Murdoch and I just have to look for some supplies."

"We want to help. What can we do?"

"There will be plenty to do soon enough, but I think people first need to figure out what that will be. I have to return to Murdoch now. We'll talk later, all right?"

"Of course," said Lana. As Serena walked back to the Rookery, Lana turned to Blake. "It's hard to believe one event can be this devastating."

"I know," said Blake, "but the Corpushi will recover from this. It may take time, but they will recover."

"Do you think we'll be among them when they do?" asked Lana.

"I wish I knew."

Lana looked up at Blake. "Well, do you *want* us to be among them when they do?"

"Yeah, I do," he said, plainly.

Lana smiled weakly. "So do I."

The couple wandered down to the beach. They sat down on the sand and looked out over the water. The Gulf was blue and calm and beautiful. It was hard to believe that only a day ago, standing on this very spot would have been deadly.

Blake turned to Lana. "You know, it's strange."

"What's strange?"

"Do you remember when we first left for the Warmland? I had such high hopes for the future. I was so confident that we would find good things."

"We both felt that way. We have found good things, haven't we?"

"Look at all we've been through, though," said Blake. "We were naïve to think that coming here would make everything all right. It's time we realized that, no matter where we go, there will always be difficulties to overcome."

"So what are you saying?" asked Lana petulantly. "After all we've been through, don't you want to become Corpushi anymore?"

"No, I do. All I'm saying is, if these people do accept us, we have to realize that their problems will become our problems, and their struggles will become our struggles."

"Of course, but the reverse is true, too. Our problems will become their problems, and we'll work to solve them together. We'll share burdens, and then we'll share in the success."

"I just didn't know what we were getting into," said Blake.

"You regret coming here," said Lana morosely.

"No!"

"You're disappointed then."

"A little, but there are more things that are even better than I'd hoped for. It's all just so different from what I'm used to."

"I thought that was what you wanted," Lana said.

Blake chuckled. "I suppose it was."

"Then what's the problem?"

"I'm going to have to get used to this place."

"You will." Lana leaned over and kissed Blake softly on the cheek. "Perfection is only an illusion, my love. The sooner you appreciate that, the better off you'll be."

Blake smiled. "You're right, but when will that be?"

"I don't know, but you will." Lana inhaled deeply and grinned with satisfaction. "I never knew I'd love the smell of the sea so much! This place *is* beautiful, isn't it?"

"Oh, yes," said Blake. "Very beautiful."

Just then, Zaaru came walking along the beach. "There you are," he said. "Serena told me I'd find you down here."

"How are you, Zaaru?" asked Lana, sincerity in her voice.

"I am well, thank you." Indeed, except for some signs of fatigue, Zaaru looked as powerful and imposing as he always did. However, there was a certain softness to him now, and it was not because of the storm or the damage it had caused; it was something else. "Blake, may I speak with you?"

"Of course," said Blake.

"I'll see you soon," said Lana as she turned to go.

"You don't have to leave," said Zaaru. "In fact, I'd rather you stay."

"All right," said Lana. The couple faced Zaaru. Expecting their eviction notice, they subtly braced themselves.

"I want to thank you, Blake," said Zaaru.

"Thank me? For what?"

"For all the ways you helped during this disaster. You directed people, transported animals, and helped keep us safe. You did all these things for people in a tribe that wasn't your own, who you hardly knew, and who had even treated you badly. It's hard to understand. Most of all, what you did for Jed and Kayla…" Zaaru shook his head in disbelief. "We would have lost them if it hadn't been for you. Thank you."

Blake bowed his head.

"But it's not only that," said Zaaru. "The fire sticks, the books, the stories of your travels. We've seen traders, but you're different. I heard what happened on that fishing trip, what you did to land those sharks. And I saw with my own eyes, Blake, what you did to bring down that elephant. I thank you both, not only for myself but also on behalf of the Corpushi tribe, for all the things you've shown us and all the things you've done."

"We are humbled by your praise, Zaaru," said Blake, "and we are grateful."

"I met with the Council this morning. We talked for a long time — as long as we could, given the circumstances. Long enough, anyway. It's hard to believe that you two are the same dregs we found trespassing just a few weeks ago."

"Like I said — you misjudged us," asserted Lana.

"Well, apparently we did. Fortunately, we finally found out who you really are. I want you to know that your debt has been eliminated."

"Really?" asked Blake.

"Completely. You've paid it back and more. Your debt is gone, and your good name is restored. Now, let's talk about the future."

Oh no, thought Blake. Here it comes. *They're going to kick us out now.*

"On behalf of the Corpushi," said Zaaru, "I'm asking you to stay."

Blake and Lana looked on in disbelief.

"Do you mean it?" asked Lana.

"Don't be surprised. After all, it's partly for practical reasons. With the disaster we've just been through, there's much work to be done. You've already been of great help to us, but we could still use a couple of extra hands like yours."

"Oh," said Lana, trying to conceal her disappointment. "So, you mean, you just want us as workers then."

"No, I mean I want you to join us. Don't you understand what I've been trying to tell you? You two are fine people, and you'd be an asset to any tribe. We're lucky you've chosen ours. That is, if after all this, you still want to join us."

Lana and Blake first looked to each other, but they could hardly contain their enthusiasm. It was clear that nothing more needed to be said.

"Yes!" said Lana eagerly. "Yes, we will join you!"

"Wonderful," said Zaaru. "I'm glad."

"But when will that be?" asked Blake.

"Soon. There are things to do and arrangements to make, but it will happen soon enough. I'm so pleased you've agreed to join us. Congratulations, Blake and Lana of the Kamishi, and welcome to the Corpushi tribe."

"This is so exciting!" exclaimed Lana. "It's finally happening! Blake, aren't you excited?"

"Very excited, but I just realized something," said Blake. "Once we join the Corpushi, the Kamishi will be no more."

"I can't say I know how you feel," said Zaaru, laying a comforting hand on Blake's shoulder, "because Corpus is the only home I've every known. The same goes for most of the Corpushi, too— but not all. Talk to the others and you'll see. They'll show you the way."

"I'll do that," said Blake, a wry smile on his lips for the first time in a long time. "Thanks."

"You're welcome. Now come on, you two. Back to the Rookery. There's work to be done!" Zaaru trudged up the beach and Lana bounded after him, energetic and childlike. When she realized that Blake was not with her, she turned around and called to him.

"Blake!" cried Lana in her sweet voice.

Blake looked at her, a deep admiration welling up inside him. This moment captivated him, and he knew that he would remember it always. All he could think was how much he loved Lana, and how this place was where he wanted to be.

"I'm coming!" he shouted back, and ran up the gentle, sandy slope. When he reached Lana, he put his arm around her waist and walked along beside her. He gave her a squeeze, and she squeezed him back. They walked toward the Rookery, which stood proud and tall up ahead. Blake looked back to admire the beach once more; he knew that he would return to it many, many times.

CR

Glossary of Terms

Setting – The story of *The Feral World* begins in North America in the year 5046 CE, or 3010 ND — 3,010 years after the Great Crash.

People

Corpushi Tribe

Aries: Corpushi man & young warrior.
Becca: Corpushi woman & Spartan's wife.
Bobo: Paulo's male dog.
Brent: Corpushi man, young warrior, & bridge guard.
Bufo: Corpushi man, former warrior & craftsman, tribal Elder, & member of Elder Council.
Hector: Corpushi man, sage, tribal Elder, and member of Elder Council.
Jed: Corpushi boy & Paulo and Wendy's son.
Kayla: Corpushi girl & Paulo and Wendy's daughter.
Lobo: Corpushi man, Bebel teacher, tribal Elder, & member of Elder Council.
Marge: Corpushi woman, advisor to the Elder Council, & Morty's wife.
Morty: Corpushi man, tribal Elder, & most senior member of Elder Council.
Murdoch: Corpushi man, young warrior, leader of band of warriors, & Serena's husband.
Paulo: Corpushi man, mature warrior, bridge guard, & Wendy's husband.
Peter: Corpushi man & young warrior.
Serena: Corpushi woman & Murdoch's wife.
Spartan: Corpushi man, young warrior, & Becca's husband.
Uchara: Corpushi woman, healer, tribal Elder, & member of Elder Council.
Wendy: Corpushi woman & Paulo's wife.
Zaaru: Corpushi man, mature warrior, & Chief of Corpus.

Dallashi Tribe

Beldek: Dallashi man & young warrior.
Brillum: Dallashi man, young warrior, & leader of band of warriors.
Thomas — Dallashi man & young warrior.

Kamishi Tribe

Blake: Kamishi man, age 22. Leader of the small band of remaining Kamishi who migrate south toward the Warmland. Lana's mate.

Lana: Kamishi woman, age 19. Formerly of the Topekashi tribe, she lived alone in the Rubbletown of Wichita, Kansas until Blake and Manosh discover her and induct her as a full member of the Kamishi tribe. Blake's mate.

Manosh: Kamishi man & Blake's best friend.

Rita: Blake's female dog & Saamu's mate.

Saamu: Blake's male dog & Rita's mate.

Lunari Nation

Lindberg, Henry: Lunari man & scientist at the Earth Research Center in Houston.

Verax: Lunari robot, research assistant, & guard at the Earth Research Center.

Tulsashi Tribe

Dendin: Tulsashi man & young warrior.

Frenn: Tulsashi man & young warrior.

Plott: Tulsashi man & young warrior.

Raoul: Tulsashi man & young warrior.

Tegg: Tulsashi man, mature warrior, & Chief of Tulsa.

Cultural Features

Advisor: Respected adults whom the tribe's Chief and Elders consult on important issues.

Apophis: Asteroid that struck the Earth on Sunday, April 13, 2036, in an event known as the Great Crash. Brought about Rakamahn & destroyed advanced civilization on Earth.

Bebel: Holy book of many nomadic tribes on Earth. Includes the Old & New Testaments of the Bible, as well as the three New Books written after the Great Crash. These books are the Book of Causes by Jonathan, the Book of Means by Belgrath, & the Book of Conduct by Ecolta.

Bebelishi: People who revere the Bebel as holy & follow its teachings.

Camp: Location where nomadic tribes erect their tents & form a temporary village. Camp is relocated as needed, based on resource availability & interactions with neighboring tribes.

Council: Group of Elders who meet to discuss important issues facing the tribe. The Chief & advisors participate in certain Council meetings. During meetings, participants make decisions pertaining to tribal

Glossary of Terms

activities, relations among tribe members, & Bebelishi doctrine.
Chief: Military and political leader of a tribe.
Elder: Religious and spiritual leaders of a tribe.
Managers: Pejorative term used by people in the New Days. Refers to people who lived during the Old Days & who used technology to manipulate nature for their own goals. It is assumed that Managers had been excessively biased toward human life, and were therefore knowledgeable & sophisticated, but unwise & immoral.
Newcomer: Descriptive term for someone who has come to the Warmland from somewhere else.
Old Timers: Descriptive term used by people in the New Days to refer to people who lived during the Old Days.
Outlander: Pejorative term for someone who has come to the Warmland from somewhere else.
Warrior: A man who is respected as a defender of his tribe.

Fauna

In the Ancient Days, most regions of the world had fauna that were very diverse and part of complex ecosystems. Toward the end of the Ancient Days and during the Old Days, many ecosystems were disrupted, and many animals were extirpated or extinguished, resulting in much lower biodiversity. With the end of Management in the New Days, many wild animals regained their former ranges and numbers. Many captive animals also escaped from sanctuaries, zoos, and circuses and became established in the wild. In addition, many domestic animals escaped from urban and agricultural areas and became feral. Thus, New Days fauna and ecosystems are rich and diverse, much as they had been in the Ancient Days, but often in novel or unique ways.

Aquatic Animals

Dolphin, Bottlenose: Bottlenose dolphins are social and travel in pods of ten to twelve members. These animals hunt fish and squid, and are considered intelligent.
Gator: New Days name for Alligator. Although a small fraction of their diet consists of vegetation, these animals are efficient predators throughout their lives. When young, they must feed on snails, worms, spiders, insects, and fish. As they grow, their diet expands to include larger fish, frogs, turtles, and small mammals. As adults, they continue to prey on aquatic animals, but also on large terrestrial ungulates and carnivores that come near the water. Gators can even

prey on people, but they do so only rarely.

Shark, Bull: Although not the largest of sharks, bull sharks are among the most aggressive. Females can measure over eleven feet in length and up to seven hundred pounds in weight. Males are much smaller, reaching less than seven feet and less than two hundred pounds. Bull sharks frequent inshore waters, where they feed on a variety of prey animals. Their diet includes mollusks, crustaceans, fish, other sharks, turtles, birds, marine mammals, and even terrestrial mammals that venture into the water.

Birds

Emu: After the Great Crash, emus escaped from ranches to live on the savanna, where they feed on fruit, seeds, and insects. They are solitary in their habitats, but they can aggregate in favorable areas. They mingle freely with ungulates, contributing to and benefiting from the shared vigilance of a mixed herbivore assemblage.

Pelican, White: The white pelican's diet consists mostly of fish. Working together, these birds force their prey into shallow water. Small fish are scooped up with the throat pouch, while larger fish are snapped up with the bill.

Small mammals

Coypu: Coypus are large, aquatic rodents that weigh up to twenty pounds. As in most mammals, their fur has two layers: the coarse, dark guard hair layer and the soft, whitish undercoat. The fur on the end of the snout is whitish, too. Coypus have large, conspicuous incisor teeth that protrude from the front of the mouth. These teeth are long, sharp, and orange-brown in color. Coypus build their burrows near water. They spend most of their time in the water, and their webbed hind feet help make them capable swimmers. However, they occasionally venture onto land as well. Their diet consists mostly of aquatic and terrestrial grasses.

Macaque: Macaques are a kind of monkey. Their fur is brown-gray in color, but their faces are bare and have pink skin. Male macaques can weigh up to fifteen pounds, and females up to about twelve pounds. Macaques are social and live in troops of about twenty individuals or more.

Cats

Lion: The lion was a common North American carnivore during the Ancient Days, but was extirpated just prior to the Old Days. This event may have been due to climate change, the spread of disease, the loss of prey, competition with people, or a combination of these factors. After the Great Crash, some lions escaped from captivity and established themselves in their preferred habitat – open grassland and thinly wooded savanna. In the New Days, lions are common once more, and are among the largest of North American carnivores.

Puma: Pumas are large, versatile cats found over much of North America. Most pumas live in wooded areas, but they can inhabit either warm, moist lowlands or cool, dry uplands. Pumas are also found in Rubbletowns and they may occasionally venture into open country as well. In the southern part of the continent, the puma's range overlaps with that of the jaguar, which is larger and more powerful.

Dogs

Coyote: Coyotes are very adaptable and are capable of surviving in a variety of habitats and subsisting on a variety of prey.

Dog: Descended from wolves, dogs have lived with people since the Ancient Days, throughout the Old Days, and into the New Days. Many of the varieties of dogs found in the Old Days went extinct after the Great Crash. Those dogs that were particularly small and suited to life in Rubbletowns became poodles (see *Poodles*).

Wolf: Wolves are found all over North America in woodland, grassland, and even desert areas. However, because they hunt by wearing down their prey over long distances, they must avoid mountainous country.

Ungulates (hoofed mammals) and their relatives

Antelope: Antelope were popular game animals for Managers during the Old Days. After the Great Crash, they escaped from reserves and spread throughout the Warmland. Today, antelope are abundant on the savanna, but there are in fact many different kinds, including the following.

Addax, Blackbuck, Bontebok, Gazelle, Impala, Oryx, Sable, Springbok, Waterbuck, Wildebeest (despite their robust appearance, wildebeest are a kind of antelope).

Deer, Mule: Mule deer are a common ungulate in western North America.

Deer, Whitetail: Whitetail deer often occupy lower-altitude, lower-latitude, warmer, or moister areas.

Elephant: During the Great Crash and Rakamahn, many elephants escaped from captivity and became established in the Warmland, where they became common in the New Days. Elephants have few natural enemies; the only serious predator of adult elephants is the human.

Goat: Goats live in herds on the rocky hills of Rubbletowns, as well as in the Rocky Mountains, where they feed on various grasses, forbs (flowering plants), and shrubs.

Horse: The horse was a common North American ungulate during the Ancient Days, but was extirpated shortly before the Old Days began. This event may have been due to climate change, the spread of disease, overhunting by people, or a combination of these factors. In the Old Days, people brought horses to North America again, and feral populations of these animals became known as mustangs in the West or Chincoteague ponies in the East. After the Great Crash, horses became feral all over North America and came to form mixed herds with bison, pronghorn, and llama on the Great Plains.

Texin: Texins are descended from cattle that became feral after the Great Crash. They are related to bison, which live in the colder, northern parts of the Great Plains. Texins, however, live in the Warmland and surrounding areas, and are more suited to the hotter, more humid conditions found there. As with many other savanna animals, their fur is dense but short, and straw-yellow in color to help cool them in the heat of the day, as well as conceal them in the tall grass. Bulls can weigh more than a ton, and their horns are enormous. Thicker than a man's arm at their base, they stick straight out on either side of the head for about two feet before turning abruptly forward and upward, the blackened tips then curving backward somewhat. Cows are somewhat smaller than bulls, and their horns are slightly shorter and thinner.

Other large mammals

Crater Beast: Large beasts live in an impact crater on the Great Plains. Apparently a kind of giant sloth, these mysterious animals were thought to be extinct since the Ancient Days, or for over ten thousand years at the time of their discovery. However, with at least two individuals of this species still in existence, a breeding population may still survive. These animals are about twenty feet long, stand more than fifteen feet tall when erect, and weigh approximately five tons. They have long, dark brown fur and a strong, peculiar odor, perhaps due to an oil secreted from glands in their skin. These creatures have a long tongue for browsing from the trees, and very long claws on their fingers and toes to help them manipulate branches and split bark.

Places

Badlands: Harsh, dry region in the northern Great Plains. Contains sparse plant life, few animals, and remains unoccupied by people. Forms the western border of the Kamis territory.

Black Hills: Isolated mountain range in the Badlands region that harbors more vegetation than the surrounding, low-lying areas.

Corpus: Territory of the Corpushi tribe. Located in the southern part of the Warmland on the shore of the Gulf of Mexico, and extending far inland. It is bordered by the Nueces River to the north and by the Laredoshi territory to the south.

Dallas: Territory of the Dallashi tribe. Located in the northern part of the Warmland, Dallas consists mostly of woodland and contains many forest animals.

Houston: This town is avoided by all the tribes of the Warmland. Houston houses the Earth Research Center, where the Lunari conduct scientific experiments on earthly animals, including humans.

Impact Crater: Sites where fragments of the asteroid Apophis collided with the Earth.

Great Plains: Region in North America east of the Rocky Mountains with relatively arid climate and moderate rainfall, supporting only prairie grassland or savanna with sparse trees.

Kamis: Territory of the Kamishi people in the northern Great Plains. Known for having rich grasslands that support large herds of big game, which the nomadic Kamishi follow and hunt. Bordered by the Badlands to the west, the Missouri River to the east, the White River to the north, and the Niobrara River to the south.

Laredo: Territory of the Laredoshi tribe. Laredo extends from the eastern shores of the Grand River to hot, dry grasslands with few trees to the north and east. This territory is relatively harsh and poor in natural resources. It abuts Corpus.

Maris: Territory of the Marishi tribe. Located in the northern Great Plains of North America, Maris consists of open savannas with moderate resources.

Osten: Territory of the Ostenishi tribe. Located in the central part of the Warmland, Osten is dominated by open savanna country, but also contains upland hill country. This territory is bordered by the Colorado River to the west and the Brazos River to the east. Osten is rich in big game animals.

Podess: Territory of the Podeshi tribe. Located in the central Great Plains of North America, Podess is a heavily wooded area that conceals a Rubbletown.

Ravas: Territory of the Ravashi tribe. Ravas is located in the northern Great Plains of North America. It is relatively dry and resource-poor, and supports fewer animals than other territories to the south and east.

River, Nueces: Mid-sized river that flows southeasterly through the Corpus territory and empties into the Gulf of Mexico.

Rookery: The only building from the Old Days still standing in Corpus. Centuries ago, the Corpushi restored this building in a new style using different materials and made it habitable again. At five stories in height, it is shorter than it once was. It is now the home of the Corpushi.

Rubbletown: Remnant of any metropolis destroyed in the Great Crash, and which has undergone extensive erosion in the past 3,000 years. Constitute a new type of ecosystem that supports unique creatures adapted to this novel landscape. The Rubbletown of Wichita, Kansas, is where Lana was raised.

Ruin: Remnant of any small city or town destroyed in the Great Crash, and which has undergone extensive erosion in the past 3,000 years. Similar to a Rubbletown, but smaller and possibly less eroded. Does not necessarily constitute a new type of ecosystem, nor does it necessarily support unique, specially adapted organisms.

Santoni: Territory of the Santonishi tribe. Santoni is located in the southern part of the Warmland and supports substantial populations of big game animals. This territory is bordered by the Nueces River to the south and the Plateau to the north.

Topeka: Territory of the Topekashi tribe. Located in the central Great Plains of North America. Encompasses the Rubbletown of Topeka, Kansas. Birthplace of Lana.

Tulsa: Territory of the Tulsashi tribe. Tulsa is located in the central Great Plains of North America, just north of the Warmland. This territory encompasses both grassland and woodland areas.

Waco: Territory of the Wacoshi tribe. Located in the central part of the

Glossary of Terms

Warmland, this territory consists predominantly of open savanna and is home to many migrating herds of big game. Waco is bordered by the Brazos River to the west and the Dallashi woodlands to the north.

Warmland: Region in southern North America near the Gulf of Mexico. Characterized by high humidity; high, consistent temperatures; and high biodiversity. It is the focus of widespread legends that idealize its abundant resources and high standard of living.

Times

Days, Ancient: Prehistory. All time before systematic agriculture began approximately 10,000 BCE. Equivalent to the time prior to the Holocene geological epoch.

Days, New: All time from the Great Crash of the asteroid Apophis on April 13, 2036 CE, up through the time when *The Feral World* takes place. Characterized by humanity's abandonment of civilization and a return to living in hunter-gather societies all over the Earth. The Great Crash marks time Zero ND in the New Days calendar system.

Days, Old: History. All time between the Ancient Days and the New Days, or between approximately 10,000 BCE and April 13, 2036 CE, or Zero ND.

Great Crash: Collision of the asteroid Apophis with the Earth on Sunday, April 13, 2036. Human technology mitigated this collision, circumventing a much more deadly outcome. However, collision caused the immediate death of millions of people and other living beings, and the delayed death of millions more. Marks the start of the New Days, or the time Zero ND.

Rakamahn: Literally "The time when God has mercy on the Earth and transforms it but does not destroy it." Event brought about by the Great Crash, in which the Earth's climate was disrupted for years, causing the extinction of countless organisms. After Rakamahn, the Earth's climate became favorable for life once more.

Sabat: The seventh day of the week; a time for rest, contemplation, or prayer. Based on the concept of Sabbath from the preceding Judeo-Christian religions.

Tribes

Corpushi: Settled, Bebelishi tribe of the Corpus territory in the southern part of the Warmland. Corpus includes a large swath of land extending far inland to the north and west. However, the heart of Corpus is a village on the shore of the Gulf of Mexico. This village is derived from a Rubbletown, and contains a large building called the Rookery, where the Corpushi live. The Corpushi obtain their nourishment and supplies from both the land and sea. Famous throughout the Warmland for their unique innovations, the Corpushi ride on the backs of tame horses when hunting on the savanna, and use sturdy boats and ships on fishing expeditions in the Gulf.

Dallashi: Nomadic, Bebelishi tribe of the Dallas territory in the northern part of the Warmland. The Dallashi are hunters of woodland animals and peaceful traders, having friendly relations with other tribes in the Warmland.

Kamishi: Nomadic, Bebelishi tribe of the Kamis territory in the northern Great Plains of North America. Neighboring tribes covet their territory, which is rich in grass and supports large herds of hoof beasts. Renowned for being skillful hunters of big game. Have friendly relations with most neighbors, but hostile with the Marishi and Ravashi.

Laredoshi: Nomadic, Bebelishi tribe of the Laredo territory in the southern part of the Warmland. Laredo abuts the territories of the Corpushi and Santonishi, and the Laredoshi have hostile relations with both of these neighbors. The grasslands in the north and east of Laredo are relatively harsh and poor in natural resources. They are hot and dry, and have few trees. Thus, the Laredoshi are adept fishermen, taking advantage of the Grand River in the west of their territory. The Laredoshi are tough and practical, but often coarse and unfriendly.

Lunari: The Lunari are not really a tribe, but rather a race of people who live on the Moon. They diverged from the people of the Earth and took up full residence on the Moon after the Great Crash to continue leading and developing a technologically advanced way of life, while those who remained on the Earth returned to a more ancestral and natural way of life.

Marishi: Nomadic, Bebelishi tribe of the Maris territory in the northern Great Plains of North America. They are known for being intolerant of trespassers.

Ostenishi: Nomadic, Bebelishi tribe of the Osten territory in the central part of the Warmland. The Ostenishi are skilled hunters of big game, which are plentiful in this resource-rich territory.

Glossary of Terms

Podeshi: Settled, non-Bebelishi tribe of the Podess territory in the central Great Plains of North America. They are unusual in occupying a Rubbletown continually.

Ravashi: Nomadic, Bebelishi tribe of the Ravas territory in the northern Great Plains of North America. The Ravashi are notoriously intolerant of neighboring tribes, and enemies of the Kamishi.

Santonishi: Nomadic, Bebelishi tribe of the Santoni territory in the southern part of the Warmland. The Santonishi trade with most of their neighbors, although they are antagonistic with the Laredoshi to the south.

Topekashi: Nomadic, Bebelishi tribe of the Topeka territory in the central Great Plains of North America. Large, powerful tribe with strong allegiances to neighboring tribes but only an average share of resources.

Tulsashi: Nomadic, Bebelishi tribe of the Tulsa territory in the central Great Plains of North America. The Tulsashi are hunters of forest animals. They trade frequently with tribes further south in the Warmland.

Wacoshi: Nomadic, Bebelishi tribe of the Waco territory in the central part of the Warmland. The Wacoshi have peaceful relations with most of their neighboring tribes.

About the Author

Gaddy Bergmann was born in Petah-Tikva, Israel on August 15, 1975. At the age four, he moved to Denver, Colorado, the lovely city where he grew up and now resides. Gaddy has a bachelor's degree in Environmental, Population, and Organismic Biology from the University of Colorado at Boulder, and a master's degree in Zoology from the University of South Florida in Tampa. Gaddy has performed research in both ecology and microbiology. While in Florida, he worked on fish biology in several regions of the state, including the Everglades. Gaddy has also worked in education, teaching elementary, secondary, and university students in the subjects of math, science, and composition. An admirer of animals and wildlife since childhood, he was inspired to write The Feral World books by the beauty of the natural wonders he saw all around him.

Excerpt from *Riders of the Mapinguari,*
the third book in *The Feral World* series

by Gaddy Bergmann

Available from Flying Pen Press, September 2008

    The sun was rising. The blackness of night had passed its peak, and now the dim, blue light of dawn was emerging. Although this time was the coldest of the day, on this summer's night, there was only a faint chill, prompting only a slight bundling of one's clothes and limbs. As one of the sentinels on guard that night, Felix was perched high above the ground. His post was in the wooden watch tower, located on the Western Edge of his large village, Laredo. It was a respected and necessary role, and Felix was proud to serve his beloved home in any way he could, but he hated sentinel duty. He absolutely hated it. Like all the other young men, he assumed it about once each month, but he dreaded it. Although a sprightly young man, he was decidedly diurnal. Whenever his turn came up in the rotation to stand guard for his tribe, the Laredoshi, Felix always felt as though his heart were being slowly crushed by boulders. Of course, he always managed to serve his duty. Then he could relax. However, his next turn was always only a month away. Felix longed for the day when he would become senior enough to be exempt from this tedious and miserable chore.
    That night, however, he was absolutely exhausted. He and his young wife had just had their first baby, and although they adored their new son, caring for him was absolutely enervating. So staying awake to watch over an endless savanna seemed impossible. Standing guard didn't really frighten Felix, as it did some of the other young guards, but that was simply because nothing ever really happened.
    Laredo was located in the hot, dry fields of the southern Warmland. Situated just east of the Grand River and not far west of the Gulf of Mexico, the climate here was hot and the land harsh. Laredo was not the most prosperous territory in the Warmland, but it was large and stable enough to discourage serious attacks; there had been none in the past four decades. Occasionally, there were skirmishes at the borders with the neighboring tribes, such as the Corpushi to the east or the Santonishi to the north, but these were more formalities than real threats. There was also the occasional interloper or band of thieving

trespassers, but even that was a rarity and easily rectified besides. There was nothing really to look forward to except the hourly, silent, torch signaling with the other sentinels, and the last one had just recently been completed. No, nothing ever happened, and to Felix, boredom combined with darkness and fatigue could only mean slumber. He grew tired of straining his eyes with nothing but his torch to aid them. The chirping field crickets and the occasional hooting owls seemed to be lulling him to sleep. With nothing but the sparse trees, wild emu birds, pronghorn antelope, and texins — the wild cattle of the Warmland — to keep him company, Felix drifted off to sleep.

Suddenly, a powerful jolt rocked Felix's watchtower, and like a tiny hatchling from its nest, he tumbled out and plummeted to the ground. Felix reflexively tried to break his fall, but he landed on his right wrist, first brushing past the short, wiry grass and then crashing onto the hard earth. Felix heard a sickening snapping sound as a jolt of pain shot up from his arm; he knew it was broken. Clutching his injured arm to his torso with his good one, he sat up quickly and frantically looked around to figure out what had happened. Just then a massive blow landed on the side of his head, which threw him back several feet and smashed him into the ground once more. Felix was dazed but still conscious, now both his arm and his head throbbing, and although he remained supine, his eyes darted about wildly as he tried to see what was happening in the growing morning light. He heard the soft crunching of grass off to one side, a kind of slow plodding of someone approaching him. Then, he saw it. Felix became wild with terror when he finally realized what was happening.

"Mapinguari!" he screamed as he looked directly at his assailant. "Mapinguari!"

Felix's assailant was not human. A giant beast with shaggy, brown fur was now slowly approaching him. Its odor was overpowering: a kind of musky, musty stench that filled Felix's nostrils and rattled his brain. The creature weighed some four tons and measured over twenty feet in length from the tip of its broad muzzle to the tip of its thick tail. It maintained a hunched-over posture and lumbered on its hind legs toward Felix, holding its forelimbs high off the ground and close to its body. Three of the four fingers on each hand bore massive, sharp claws, as did each of its inside toes. This caused it to walk peculiarly on the outsides of its feet, yet its footsteps fell lightly and gracefully onto the earth.

When the beast reached Felix's side, it reared up to its full height of over eighteen feet and gave out a deep, resonant bellow. As a thousand thoughts and emotions raced through Felix's mind, the most salient one was confusion. Then, beneath the shaggy fur, Felix saw that the beast wore a red, leather collar about its neck, and suddenly it began making sense. Laredo was under attack.

Felix's fear turned to horror when the beast, still standing tall, flexed its thick, long neck to an impossible degree and looked down directly at him. Then it bent over and, with one mighty swipe of its claw, tore his belly wide open. His body rocked slightly from the assault, but it didn't respond immediately. Within seconds, though, the blood began to flow and the ruptured organs began to protrude. Now in shock, Felix felt almost no pain, but in his terror he managed to let out one final sound.

"Mapinguari!" he cried one last time, but this time hoarse, faint, and gurgling. Then the beast inserted its muzzle into Felix's opened abdomen and began to feed, periodically causing the body to sway like a large, floppy rag. The beast grunted contentedly as it consumed more and more substance from Felix's body. Within moments, the life force left Felix, while that of the beast grew.

Available from

"Giving Flight to Great Books"

Watch for more of

The Feral World
by Gaddy Bergmann

Migration of the Kamishi

The first book in *The Feral World* series. Three thousand years after an asteroid has sent civilization reeling back to a new stone age, humanity survives. Blake and Monosh of the Kamishi tribe must journey through the wilds of the Great Plains and face the dangerous ruins of "Rubbletowns" in their migration to the Warmland. Gaddy Bergmann brings the majesty of American landscapes back to life with an incredible interplay between man and nature, in this, his first novel.

Migration of the Kamishi by Gaddy Bergmann
ISBN: 978-0-9795889-1-4, trade paperback, $16.95

Riders of the Mapinguari

In the Fifty-First Century, North America has once again become a majestic land, populated by tribes who have learned to live in harmony with nature, However, once again, North America is invaded by marauders. The enemy brings a mighty beast that seems unstoppable — the *mapinguari*. Blake must organize the scattered tribes into an army, or the Bebelishi tribes lose their North American homelands.

Riders of the Mapinguari by Gaddy Bergmann
on sale September 2008
ISBN: 978-0-9795889-5-2, trade paperback, $16.95

Be the first to know about The Feral World releases. Subscribe to the Flying Pen Press Publisher's Newsletter at the website **www.FlyingPenPress.com**. And be certain to visit Gaddy Bergmann's website: **www.GaddyBergmann.com**.

Look for these other titles from

"Giving Flight to Great Books"

Looking Glass by James R. Strickland
A serial killer is loose in cyperspace, in a dystopian future where the international network controls everything. A debut cyberpunk mystery thriller from the mind of James R. Strickland.
ISBN 978-0-9795889-0-7, trade paperback, $14.95
Now on sale

Seventh Daughter by Ronnie Seagren
The seventh daughter of a seventh daughter must reach her goal high atop the Peruvian Andes before the 1937 solar eclipse, in order to save the world. Seagren's long-awaited first novel.
ISBN 978-0-9795889-7-6, trade paperback, $16.95
On sale April 2008

Dragon Ring by Lettie Prell
Nadine's father is dead, and her search for answers uncovers alarming truths about his company's discovery of a new energy source, including the truths about magic. An intriguing mixture of fantasy and science fiction.
ISBN 979-0-9795889-6-9, trade paperback, $15.95
On sale May 2008

She Murdered Me with Science by David Boop
Noel Glass is a disgraced scientist in 1953 who has turned to the new field of forensic science to scratch out a living, but now a strange murder uncovers a conspiracy to take over the United States. A science fiction story in the style of 1950's pulp novels.
ISBN 978-0-9795889-9-0, trade paperback, $15.95
On sale August 2008

Flying Pen Press titles are available wherever great books are sold. They can also be ordered at www.FlyingPenPress.com, or by sending a check or money order to the following address. (U.S. mail orders only. Please add $5 for shipping and handling, Colorado residents please add sales tax.)

Flying Pen Press, Book Sales, 18601 Green Valley Ranch Blvd., Suite 112 No. 4, Denver, CO 80249

Printed in the United States
144050LV00002B/30/P